The Kopje Garrison A Story Of The Boer War

By

George Manville Fenn

The Kopje Garrison
A Story Of The Boer War
by George Manville Fenn

Copyright © 2023

All Rights reserved.

ISBN: 978-93-59954-46-2
Published by

DOUBLE 9 BOOKS

2/13-B, Ansari Road
Daryaganj, New Delhi – 110002
info@double9books.com
www.double9books.com
Tel. 011-40042856

ABOUT THE AUTHOR

George Manville Fenn was a very productive author of novels, a writer, an editor, and an educator from England. He was born on January 3, 1831, in Pimlico, London. He mostly learned on his own; he taught himself Italian, French, and German. During the years 1851–1854, he went to Battersea Training College for Teachers and then became the head of a state school in Alford, Lincolnshire. In the early 1850s, Fenn started to write short stories and pieces for newspapers and magazines. The Old Forest Ranger, his first book, came out in 1856. Afterward, he wrote more than 100 books, many of them for teenagers and young adults. He was one of the most famous writers of his time, and his books were well-liked and read by many people. He also worked as a reporter and writer for Fenn. Among the newspapers and magazines, he worked for was The Boy's Own Paper, which he ran from 1866 to 1874. He worked hard to make children's books better and was a strong supporter of education and reading. The Englishman Fenn passed away on August 26, 1909, in Isleworth.

CONTENTS

Chapter One
How Drew Lennox and Bob Dickenson went a-Fishing

They did not look like fishermen, those two young men in khaki, for people do not generally go fishing with magazine-rifles instead of fishing-rods—certainly not in England. But this was in South Africa, and that makes all the difference. In addition, they were fishing in a South African river, where both of them were in profound ignorance as to what might take their bait first; and they were talking about this when they first reached the bank and saw the swift river flowing onward—a lovely river whose banks were like cliffs, consequent upon ages of the swift stream cutting its way downward through the soft earth, while here and there clumps of trees grew luxuriantly green, and refreshed the eyes of the lookers-on after a couple of months spent in riding over the drab and dreary veldt.

"Tackle isn't half strong enough," said the younger of the two, who was nearly good-looking; in fact, he would have been handsome if he had not always worn so stupid an aspect. "Think there are any crocodiles here?"

"Likely enough, Bobby."

"S'pose one of them takes the bait?"

"Well, suppose he does!" said the other, who resembled his companion, minus the stupid look; for if the keen, dark-grey eyes were truth-tellers of what was behind them, he was, as the men in his company said, sharp as a needle.

"S'pose he does!" said the young man addressed as Bobby—otherwise Robert Dickenson, second lieutenant in Her Majesty's —th Mounted Infantry. "Well, that's a cool way of talking. Suppose he does! Why, suppose one of the great magnified efts swallows the bait?"

"Suppose he does. What then?"

"Why, he'll be more likely to pull me in than let me pull him out."

"No doubt about it, if the line doesn't break."

"What should I do then, Drew, old man?"

"I don't know what you'd do, my little man. I know what I should do."

"Yes. What?"

"Let go."

"Ah, I didn't think of that," said the young officer quite calmly. "I say, though, if it turned out to be a hippopotamus?"

"I wish it would, Bobby—that is, so long as it was a nice fat calf. I'm so ragingly hungry that I should look upon a steak off one of those india-rubber gentlemen as the greatest delicacy under the sun."

"Oh, don't talk nonsense. One of those things wouldn't be likely to bite. But I say, Drew, old chap, do you think there are any fish to be caught?"

"I haven't the slightest idea, Bobby. But here's a river; it looks likely. Fishes live in rivers; why shouldn't they be here?"

"To be sure; why not?" said the other, brightening up and looking better. "Who knows? There may be carp and tench, eels and pike."

"Not likely, Bobby, my lad; but most probably there are fish of some kind, such as live on this side of the equator."

"Mahseer, perhaps—eh?"

"Bah! This is Africa, not northern India. Let's get down and make a beginning. We had better get down through that woody rift."

"I wish I'd got my six-jointed rod, old fellow."

"But as you haven't, we must try what we can do with a line."

"I say, it was lucky you thought to bring some hooks."

"They were meant to try in the sea, old fellow, but I never had a chance. Come softly, and be on the lookout."

"Eh?" cried the young man addressed, bringing the rifle he carried to the ready. "Boers?"

"Oh no; our fellows are not likely to let any of those gentlemen approach. I thought we might perhaps put up a deer, antelope, buck, or something."

"Venison roast, hot, juicy! Oh Drew, old man, don't; pray don't! You gave me such an awful pang. Oh dear! oh dear!"

"Pst! Quiet! Don't build your hopes on anything, because I dare say we shall be disappointed; but still we might."

"Ah, might!" said the young officer. "Oh dear! I thought we might get wounded, or have a touch of fever, but I never expected that we should run the risk of being starved to death."

"Then give us a chance of escaping that fate by keeping your tongue quiet. If we don't get a shot at something down there, we may still hit upon a bag of fish."

"Forward!" whispered the young officer, and together the pair approached the wooded gully and cautiously began to descend it to reach the river; but all proved to be silent, and in spite of their caution not a bush rustled, and their patient movements were in vain.

"I did expect a shot at something," said the elder officer in a disappointed tone.

"Venison was too much," said Bobby. "I expected it would be a sneaking leopard, or one of those doggy-looking monkeys."

"The baboons? Oh no; they'd be among the rocky hills. But you need not be surprised, for this is the land of disappointments."

"Oh, I say, don't talk like that, Drew, old chap," said the younger officer. "Fishermen have bad luck enough always, without your prophesying ill before we begin."

"One can't help it out here. Hang it all! we've had nothing but misfortunes ever since we came. Now then, you sit down on that rock, and I'll sit on this."

"Why not keep close together?"

"Because if we do we shall be getting our lines tangled."

"Of course; I forgot that. Here, you'll want some bait."

The speaker took a small tin canister from his pocket, unscrewed the lid, and made by the help of his pocket-knife a fair division of some nasty, sticky-looking paste, which looked as if it would soon wash off the hook upon which it was placed; and then the two fishermen separated and took up their stations about fifty yards apart, the two stones standing well out in the rapid current which washed around them and proved advantageous, from the fact that they had only to drop the baited hook into the water at their feet, when the swift stream bore it outward and away, the fishers merely having to let out line and wait, watchful and patient, for a bite.

It was very calm and beautiful in the bend of the river that they had chosen. There was a faint breeze, apparently caused by the rush of the stream, whose rippling amongst the stones with which the shore beneath the cliff-like bank was strewed made pleasant music; and as soon as the whole of the line was paid out the two young men sat silent and watchful, waiting for the tug which should tell that there was a fish at work. But a good ten minutes elapsed, and there was no sign.

"Humph!" grunted Dickenson, after his patience was exhausted. "No mistake about there being fish here."

"How do you know?"

"One of them has taken my bait."

It was on Drew's lips to say, "Washed off by the stream;" but he remained silent as he softly pulled in his own line, to find nothing but the bare hook.

"There! do you see?" he said softly, the sound of his voice passing over the water so that it was like a whisper at his friend's ear, as he dangled the bare hook.

"Oh yes, I see: fish nibbled it off."

"Hope you are right," said Drew softly, as he rebaited, dropped in the white marble of paste, and watched it glide down the stream, drawing out one by one the rings of line which he had carefully coiled up on the rock when he drew it out.

Then stooping and picking a long, heavy, stream-washed, slaty fragment from out of the water by his side, he made the end of his line fast to it and laid it at his feet, so as to have his hands at liberty. With these he drew out a cigarette-case and opened it, but his brow puckered up as he looked disconsolately at its contents.

"The last two," he said softly. "Better keep 'em. Be more hungry perhaps by-and-by."

Closing the case, he replaced it in his breast-pocket.

"The hardest job I know of," he muttered, "practising self-denial." Then aloud, "Well, Bob, do they bite?"

"No: only suck. Lost two more baits; but I shall have a big one directly."

"Glad of it. How will you cook it—roast or boil?"

"Don't chaff. Mind your own line."

Drew Lennox smiled, glanced down at his line, which the stream had now drawn out tight, and, satisfied that the stone to which it was tied would give him fair warning if he were fortunate enough to get a bite, he stepped back, picked up his rifle, and taking out his handkerchief, began to give it a rub here and a rub there, to add polish to the well-cleaned barrel, trigger-guard, and lock.

He took some time over this, but at last all was to his satisfaction; and laying down the piece on the rock by his side, he once more drew up his line, glancing up-stream, to see that his companion was similarly occupied, both finding the bait gone.

"I say, isn't it aggravating?" said Dickenson. "I know what they are—sort of mullet-like fish with small mouths. Put on a smaller bait."

"All right; good plan," said Lennox.

"Wish to goodness I'd a few well-scoured English worms. I'd soon let the fish know!"

"Ah, I suppose they would be useful," said Lennox, moulding up a piece of paste and trying to make it as hard as he could. "I say, Bob."

"Hullo!"

"I've read that you can dig up great fat worms here in South Africa, eighteen inches long."

"Dig one up, then, and I'll cut it into eighteen inch-long baits."

"I didn't bring a spade with me, old fellow," said Drew, smiling.

"Humph! Why didn't you?"

"Same reason that you didn't bring out some worms in your kit. I say, are you loaded?"

"Of course. You asked me before."

Drew Lennox said no more, but glanced up-stream and down-stream, after starting his bait once again upon its swim. Then, after watching the rings uncoil till the line was tight, he swept the edge of the opposite bank some fifty yards away, carefully searching the clumps of trees and bushes, partly in search of a lurking enemy or spying Kaffir, taught now by experience always to be on the alert, and partly in the faint hope of catching a glimpse of something in the shape of game such as would prove welcome in the famine that he and his comrades were experiencing.

But, as he might have known in connection with game, their coming would have been quite sufficient to scare off the keen eared and eyed wild creatures; and he glanced down at his line again, thinking in a rather hopeless way that he and his friend might just as well have stayed in camp at the laager they had fortified with so much care.

His next act was to open the flap of his belt holster and carefully withdraw the revolver which now rarely left his side. After a short examination of the mechanism, this came in for a good rub and polish from the handkerchief before it was replaced.

"Nearly had one," cried his companion, after a snatch at the line he held.

"Didn't get a bite, did you?"

"Bite? A regular pull; but I was a bit too late. Why don't you attend to your fishing instead of fiddle-faddling with that revolver? Pull up your line."

Drew Lennox smiled doubtingly as he drew the leather cover of the holster over the stud before stooping to take hold of the line at his feet.

"I believe that was all fancy, Master Bobby," he said. "If there have been any fish here, the crocodiles have cleared them out, or the Boers have netted them. It will be dry biscuit for us again to-night, or—My word!"

"Got one?" cried Dickenson, excited in turn, for his brother officer's manner had suddenly changed from resigned indifference to eager action, as he felt the violent jerk given to his line by something or other that he had hooked.

"Got one? Yes; a monster. Look how he pulls."

"Oh, be careful; be careful old chap!" cried Dickenson wildly, and he left the stone upon which he was standing to hurry to his friend's side. "That's a fifteen or twenty pound fish, and it means dinner for the mess."

"I believe it's a young crocodile," said Lennox. "My word, how it tugs!"

"Play it—play it, man! Don't pull, or you'll drag the hook out of its jaws. Give it line."

"Can't; he has it all out."

"Then you'll have to follow it down-stream."

"What! go into the water? No, thanks."

"What! shrink from wading when you've got on a fish like that at the end of your line? Here, let me come."

"No; I'll play the brute and land him myself. But, I say, it's a fine one of some kind; pulls like an eel. Look how it's wagging its head from side to side."

"Better let me come," said Dickenson, whose face was scarlet from excitement.

"Get out!"

"I'll never forgive you if you lose that fish, Lennox, old man."

"Not going to lose him. Look; he has turned, and is coming up-stream;" for the line, which a few moments before was being violently jerked, suddenly grew slack.

"Gone! gone! gone!" cried Dickenson, with something of a sob in his throat.

"You be quiet!" said Drew. "I thought, it was only a bit of wood a few minutes ago."

"Fish, of course, and the hook's broken away."

"Think so?" was the cool reply, as foot after foot of the line was drawn in. "I was beginning to be of the opinion that he had given it up as a bad job and was swimming right in to surrender."

"No; I told you so. You've dragged the hook right out the fish's jaws, and—Oh, I'm blessed!"

"With a good opinion of yourself, Bobby," said Drew, laughing; for after softly hauling in about eight or ten yards of the stout water-cord he felt the fish again, when it gave one smart tug at the line and dashed up past the stone, running out all that had been recovered in a very few seconds.

Directly after there was a check and a jerk at the officer's hand, while a cry escaped his lips as he let the line go and stooped to pick up his rifle.

"That's no good," began Dickenson.

"Quick, man! Down with you!—Ah! you've left your rifle. Cover!"

"Oh!" ejaculated Dickenson; and his jaw dropped, and he stood motionless, staring across the river at the sight before him on the other bank.

"Hands up! Surrender! You're surrounded!" shouted a rough voice. "Drop that rifle, or we fire."

Drew Lennox was bent nearly double in the act of raising it as these words were uttered, and he saw before him some twenty or thirty barrels, whose holders had covered him, and apparently only awaited another movement on the young officer's part to shoot him down as they would have done a springbok.

"Oh dear!" groaned Dickenson; "to come to this!" And he was in the act of raising his hands in token of surrender when his comrade's head caught him full in the chest and drove him back among the bushes which grew densely at the mouth of the gully.

Crack! crack! crack! crack! rang out half-a-dozen rifles, and Lennox, who as the consequence of his spring was lying right across his comrade, rolled off him.

"Hurt?" panted the latter in agonised tones.

"No. Now then, crawl after me."

"What are you going to do?"

"Creep up level with your rifle, and cover you while you get it."

"Is it any use, old fellow? There's about fifty of them over yonder."

"I don't care if there are five hundred," growled Lennox through his teeth. "Come along; we must keep it up till help comes from the laager."

"Then you mean to fight?" panted Dickenson as he crawled after his leader; while the Boers from the other side kept up a dropping fire right into and up the gully, evidently under the impression that the two officers were making that their line of retreat instead of creeping under cover of the bushes at the foot of the cliff-like bank, till Drew stopped opposite where the abandoned rifle lay upon the stone Dickenson had left, so far unseen.

Where they stopped the bushes were shorter and thinner, and they had a good view of the enemy, who had taken cover close to the edge of their bank and were keeping up a steady fire, sending their bullets searching the dense growth of the ravine, while about a dozen mounted men now appeared, cantering along towards where there was a ford about a mile lower down.

"That's to surround us, old man," said Dickenson. "The miserable liars! There isn't a man this side. But oh, my chest! You've knocked in some of my ribs."

"Hang your ribs! We must get that rifle."

"Wait till I get my wind back," panted Dickenson.—"Oh, what a fool I was to lay it down!"

"You were, Bobby; you were," said Drew quietly. "Here, hold mine, and I'll dash out and bring it back."

"No, you don't!" cried the young officer; and as he crouched there on all fours he bounded out like a bear, seized the rifle from where it lay, and rushed back, followed by the shouts and bullets of four or five Boers, who saw him, but not quickly enough to get an effective aim.

"Now call me a fool again," panted Dickenson, shuffling himself behind a stone.

It was Drew Lennox's rifle that spoke, not he, as in reply to the fire they had brought upon them he took careful aim and drew trigger, when one of the Boers sprang up fully into sight, turned half-round, threw up his rifle, and fell back over the edge of the cliff among the bushes similar to those which sheltered the young Englishmen.

"Good shot, lad!"

"Yes. On his own head be it," said Lennox. "A cowardly ambush. Fire as soon as you can steady yourself. Where are you? I can't see you."

"Ahint this stone, laddie," replied Dickenson coolly enough now. "And you?"

"Behind this one here."

"That's right; I was afraid you were only bushed. Ah! my turn," — *crack!* — "now. Bull's-eye, old man."

As the words left his lips Lennox fired again, and another Boer who was badly hidden sprang up and dropped back.

"Two less," said Drew in a husky whisper, while *crack! crack!* went the Boer rifles, and a peculiar shattering echo arose from the far side of the river as the bullets flattened upon the rocks or cut the bushes like knives; while from being few in number they rapidly became more, those of the enemy who had been searching the gully down which the young men had come now concentrating their fire upon the little cluster of rocks and trees behind which they were hidden.

"Don't waste a cartridge, Bob lad," said Lennox, whose voice sounded strange to his companion, "and hold your magazine in case they try a rush."

"Or for those fellows who'll come round by the ford," replied Dickenson.

"Never mind them. The firing will bring our lads out, and they'll tackle those gentlemen."

"All right. — Ah! I've been waiting for you, my friend," whispered Dickenson, and he fired quickly at one of the enemy who was creeping along towards a spot from which he probably thought he would be able to command the spot where the young Englishmen lay. But he never reached it. He just exposed himself once for a few moments, crawling like a short, thick snake. Then his rifle was jerked upwards to the full extent of the poor wretch's arm and fell back. He made no other movement, but lay quite still, while the rifles around him cracked and the bullets pattered faster and faster about where the two young men were hidden.

"I say, how queer your voice is!" said Dickenson. "Not hurt, are you?"

"No, and yes. This hurts me, Bob lad. I almost wish I wasn't such a good shot."

"I don't," muttered the other. "I want to live." Then aloud, "Don't talk like that, man! It's their lives or ours. Hit every one you can.—Phew! that was near my skull. I say, I don't call this coming fishing."

He turned towards his comrade with a comical look of dismay upon his countenance after a very narrow escape from death, a bullet having passed through his cap, when *whizz! whizz! whirr!* half-a-dozen more bullets passed dangerously near.

"Mind, for goodness' sake!" shouted Lennox, in a voice full of the agony he felt. "Don't you see that you are exposing yourself?"

"What am I to do?" cried the young officer angrily. "If I lean an inch that way they fire at me, and if I turn this way it's the same."

"Creep closer to the stone."

"Then I can't take aim."

"Then don't try. We've got to shelter till their firing brings help."

"Oh, it's all very fine to talk, Drew, old chap, but I'm not going to lie here like a target for them to practise at without giving the beggars tit for tat.—Go it, you ugly Dutch ruffians! There, how do you like that?"

He fired as he spoke, after taking careful aim at another, who, from a post of vantage, kept on sending his bullets dangerously near.

"Did you hit?" asked Lennox.

"I think so," was the reply. "He has backed away."

"We must keep on firing at them," said Lennox; "but keep your shots for those who are highest up there among the trees."

He set the example as he spoke, firing, after taking a long and careful aim, at a big-bearded fellow who had crawled some distance to his right so as to try and take the pair in the flank. The Boer had reached his fresh position by making a rush, and his first shot struck the stones close to Drew's face, sending one up to inflict a stinging blow on the cheek, while in the ricochet it went whizzing by Dickenson's shoulder, making him start and utter an angry ejaculation, for he had again exposed himself.

"Wish I could break myself off bad habits," he muttered, as a little shower of bullets came whizzing about them, but too late to harm.

There was a certain amount of annoyance in his tones, for he noted that, while he had started up a little, his companion, in spite of the stinging blow he had received on the cheek, lay perfectly motionless upon his chest, waiting his time, finger on trigger, and ready to give it a gentle pressure when he had ceased to aim at one particular spot where he had seen the Boer's head for a moment.

He did not have long to wait; for the moment the Boer had fired he slightly raised his head to try and mark the effect of his shot.

That was sufficient. Lennox squeezed rather than pulled the trigger, and as the smoke rose the bush which had sheltered the Boer moved violently for a few moments, and all was still there; while the young officer quickly reloaded and waited to see if another man took his enemy's place.

Chapter Two
What they caught

"Serve him right!" Dickenson growled more than spoke. "There's another chap creeping away yonder so as to enfilade us from the left."

"Well, you know what to do," said Lennox grimly.

Dickenson uttered a grunt, and, paying no further heed to the bullets that kept on spattering about the rocks, every now and then striking up a shower of loose stones, waited, patiently watching a spot that he had marked down a couple of hundred yards away up the river to his left. For he had seen one of the most pertinacious of their aggressors draw back, apparently without reason.

"He couldn't have known that I meant to pick him out for my next shot," the young officer said to himself, "and he couldn't have been hurt, so he's up to the same sort of game as that fellow old Lennox brought down."

He turned his head sharply, not on account of a bullet coming too close, but to learn the effect of another shot from his companion.

"Hit or miss?" he said gruffly.

"Hit," was the laconic reply.

Dickenson had only glanced round, and then fixed his eyes once more upon the little clump of bushes he had before noted.

"That's the place he'll show at for certain," he muttered, and getting the sight of his rifle well upon one particular spot where a big grey stone reared itself up level with the tops of the bushes, he waited for quite five minutes, which were well dotted with leaden points.

"Ha! I was right," said Dickenson to himself, for all at once he caught a glimpse of the barrel of a rifle reared up and then lowered down over the top of the stone in his direction.

The distance was great, and the rifle-barrel looked no larger than a metal ramrod, but the clearness of the South African air showed it plainly enough; and hugging himself closer together, the young officer laid his cheek close to the stock of his piece, closed his left eye, and glanced along the barrel, waiting for the opportunity he felt sure must come.

The excitement of the moment made his heart beat fast, and his eyes glittered as he gazed; but there was nothing to see now save a beautiful green clump of thorn bush, with the great grey granite block in its midst.

"I make it two hundred and fifty yards good," he said to himself, and he raised the sight of his rifle. "I ought to be able to hit a steady mark at that distance when cool, and I feel as cool now as a cucumber. They're grand shots these chaps, and if he can make out my face he'll bring me down as sure as a gun; and if he does there's new mourning to be got at home, and a lot of crying, and the old lady and the girls breaking their hearts about stupid old me, so I must have first shot if I can get it. Very stupid of them at home. They don't know what a fool every one thinks me out here. Nice, though, all the same, and I like 'em—well, love 'em, say—love 'em all too well to let them go breaking their hearts about me; so here goes, Mr Boer. But he doesn't go. He must be waiting up there, because I saw his gun. What a while he is! Or is it I'm impatient and think the time long? Couldn't have been mistaken. I'd speak to old Lennox, but if I do it's a chance if the enemy don't show and get first shot."

Dickenson seemed to cease thinking for a few moments, and lay listening to the rattle of the Boers' guns across the river and the spattering echo-like sounds of the bullets striking around. Then he began to think again, with his eyes fixed upon the top of the grey stone in the distance, and noting now that a clearly-cut shadow from a long strand was cast right across the top of the stone.

"That's just in front of where his face ought to be when he takes aim," thought the young officer.—"Aim at me, to put them at home in mourning and make them go to church the next Sunday and hear our old vicar say a kind word for our gallant young friend who died out in the Transvaal. But he sha'n't if I can help it. Nasty, sneaking, cowardly beggar! I never did him any harm, and I don't want to do him any harm; but as he means to shoot me dead, why, common-sense seems to say, 'Have first shot at him, Bobby, old chap, if you can, for you're only twenty, and as the days of man are seventy years all told, he's going to do you out of fifty, which would be a dead robbery, of course; and in this case a dead robbery means murder into the bargain.'"

Bob Dickenson's musings stopped short for a few moments while he looked in vain for some sign of his enemy. Then he went on again in a desultory way, paying no heed to the bullets flying over and around him, and for the time being forgetting all about his comrade, who kept on firing whenever he had an opportunity.

"What a pity it seems!" he mused. "Birds flitting about, bees and butterflies sipping the honey out of the flowers, which are very beautiful; so is this gully, with the sparkling water and ferns and things all a-growing and a-blowing, as they say. Why, I should like nothing better than loafing round here enjoying myself by looking about and doing no harm to anything. I wouldn't even catch the fish if I wasn't so hungry; and yet, here I am with a magazine-rifle trying to shoot a Boer dead.

"Humph! yes," he continued after a short pause; "but only so that he sha'n't shoot me dead. This is being a soldier, this is. Why was I such a fool as to be one? The uniform and the band and the idea of being brave and all that sort of thing, I suppose. Rather different out here. No band; no uniform but this dirt-coloured khaki; no bed to sleep on; no cover but the tent; roasting by day, freezing by night: hardly a chance to wash one's self, and nothing to eat; and no one to look at you but the Boers, and when they come to see what the soldiers of the Queen are like they send word they are there with bullets, bless 'em! Well, I suppose it's all right. We must have soldiers, and I wanted to be one, and now I am one there does seem to be something more than the show in doing one's duty bravely, as they call it.

"Well," he muttered at last, "this is getting monotonous, and I'm growing tired of it. If they do shoot us both, they'll have had to pay for it. Why, they must have used a couple of hundred cartridges. Not very good work for such crack shots as they are said to be. If they spend a hundred cartridges to shoot one buck, it would come cheaper to buy their meat.

"All fancy," he muttered directly after; "that fellow couldn't have been going where I thought, and yet it seemed so likely. There's the clump of trees, and the very stone a fellow would make for to rest his rifle on when he took aim from his snug hiding-place. But there's no one there. The sun shines right upon it, so that I could see in a moment if a Boer was there. His face would be just beyond that shadow cast so clearly by what must be a dead bough. Yes, all a fancy of mine."

"Bob!" cried Lennox.

"Hullo!"

"I shall want some of your cartridges if help doesn't come soon."

Bob Dickenson made no further reply, but lay gazing with one eye along the barrel of his rifle; for as his comrade spoke it suddenly occurred to him that the top of the grey block of granite looked a little different, but in what way he could not have explained. He noted, too, that there was a tiny flash of light such as might have been thrown off a bright crystal of feldspar, and without pause now he held his rifle more firmly, laid the sight upon the flashing light, and the next moment he would have pulled the trigger. But ere he could tighten his finger upon the little curved piece of steel within the guard of his piece, there was a flash, a puff of smoke, and a sensation as if a wasp had whizzed by his ear. He did not move, only waited while one might have counted ten, and then tightened his grasp.

"Bah!" he ejaculated as the little puff of smoke rose slowly, "how this rifle kicks! Humph!" as the smoke cleared rapidly as soon as it rose enough for the wind to catch it, "I was right after all."

"Hit?" asked Lennox.

"Yes; and just in time, for we should have been in an awkward place directly."

"Yes; and I'm afraid we shall be all the same," said Lennox. "Try if you can do any good at a couple of fellows across yonder. I can't touch them from where I lie, and if I move I shall shoot no more."

Dickenson turned from where he was gazing hard at the top of the granite block, the appearance of which was now completely changed; for the Boer who, in accordance with what the young officer had anticipated, had sent so dangerous a bullet whizzing by his ear, had suddenly sprung up, fallen forward, and now lay there with outstretched hands still clutching his rifle, which rested upon the ground in front.

"Mind me firing over you?" said the young officer.

"No; but give me a hint first."

"All right. I shall have to—Stop a moment," he growled softly as a puff of smoke spurted up and another bullet came dangerously near. "That's the worst fellow, isn't he?"

"One's as bad as the other. Lie close."

"Can't lie any closer, old man. Skin seems to be growing to the rock as it is."

Crack!

There was another shot, the puff of smoke rising from close alongside the former one which Dickenson had seen.

"I say," he cried, "which of us are they firing at?"

"Both, I expect," said Lennox. "They're sheltered by the same rock; one fires from one side, the other from the second. I can't touch them. Try at once."

"Don't you hurry me, or I shall muff it, old man," said Dickenson coolly. "I want a better chance. There's nothing but a bit of wideawake to fire at now.—Ha! Lie still. He's reaching out to fire at me, I think."

Dickenson's rifle spurted, and their enemy's was like an echo; but the muzzle of the Boer's piece was suddenly jerked upward, and the bullet had an opportunity of proving how far a Mauser rifle would carry with a high trajectory.

"Thanks, old fellow," said Lennox. "That has halved the risk. Perhaps the other fellow will think it too dangerous to stay."

"Doesn't seem like it," said Dickenson, drawing in his breath sharply and clapping his left hand to his ear.

"Don't say you're hit, Bob!" cried Lennox in an agonised tone.

"All right; I won't if you don't want me to."

"But are you?"

"I suppose so. There's a bit taken out of my left ear, and I can feel something trickling down inside my collar."

"Oh Bob, old fellow!" cried Lennox.

"Lie still, man! What are you going to do?"

"Bind up the place."

"You won't if you stir."

There was pretty good proof of this, for another shot whizzed between them. But he who sent it had been too venturesome in taking aim to revenge his comrade's fall, and the result of Dickenson's return shot was fatal, for he too sprang up into a kneeling posture, and they saw him for a few moments trying to rise to his feet, but only to fall over to the left, right in view of the two officers.

Drew uttered a sigh of relief.

"If we are to escape," he said, "we must stop any one from getting into that position again."

"Look sharp, then," said Dickenson, whose keen eyes detected a movement on the other side of the river. "There's a chap creeping among the bushes on all fours."

"I see him," cried Drew; and as he followed the enemy's movements and took aim, Dickenson, who was in the better position for commanding them, followed his example.

"Missed!" cried Drew angrily as he fired and the Boer raised a hand and waved it derisively.

"Hit!" exclaimed Dickenson the next instant. For he too had fired, and with better aim, the Boer drawing himself together, springing up, and turning to run, but only to stagger the next minute and fall heavily among the bushes, which hid him from sight.

"Now for the next." continued Dickenson, coolly reloading. "Look out; I'm going to watch the other end."

He turned sharply as a fresh shower of bullets came scattering around them, and looked keenly at the granite rock and its burden, half-expecting to see a fresh occupant taking aim. But apparently no one seemed disposed to expose himself anew to the rifles of such deadly shots, and the terrible peril to which the two fishermen had been exposed ceased for the time being, though the pair waited in momentary expectation of its recurrence.

But the enemy did not slacken their efforts to finish their task by easier means, and the firing from the front went on more briskly than ever, the young officers contenting themselves with holding theirs and displaying no excitement now, their shelter, so long as they lay close, being sufficient, the worst befalling them now being a sharp rap from a scrap of stone struck from the rocks, or the fall of a half-flattened bullet.

"That's right; don't fire until we are in an emergency," said Drew at the end of a few minutes.

"In a what?" cried Dickenson.

"In regular peril."

"Why, what do you call this?" cried Dickerson, with a laugh. "I made my will half-an-hour ago—in fancy, of course."

"Well, it is a hot corner," said Drew, joining in his companion's grim mirth; "but we haven't got to the worst of it yet."

"What!" yelled Dickenson. "Oh Drew, old man, you are about the coolest fish in the regiment. It can't be worse than it has been."

"Can't it? Wait a few minutes, and the party who made for the ford will be at us."

"But they can't get their horses down the way we came."

"No; but they can leave them with a fourth of their fellows to hold while they get somewhere within shot, and then we're done. What do you say to tying a handkerchief to a rifle-barrel and holding it up? We've held out well."

"Nothing! What do you say?"

"Same as you do; but I thought I'd give you the option if you did not feel as obstinate as I do."

"Obstinate? I don't call it obstinate to hold out now. I've seen too many of our poor lads carried to the rear. Here," continued the speaker, after feeling, "I haven't used half my cartridges yet. Ask me again when they're all gone, and then I'll tell you the idea I've got."

"What is it? Tell me now."

"Very well. We'll fire the last cartridge at the cowardly brutes—fifty at least to two—and then give them a surprise."

"What! walk out and hold up your hands?"

"No; that would be a surprise, of course; but I've got a better."

"Let's have it."

"Walk in."

"What do you mean?"

"Well, crawl, then, into the river. Get quietly in from behind some of the overhanging bushes, and float down with the stream."

"Wouldn't do, Bobby; they wouldn't trust us. They'd see us floating."

"They'd think we were dead."

"Not they. The Boers are too slim, as they call it, and would pump a few bullets into us. Besides, I have no fancy for being dragged down by a crocodile or grabbed by a hippo."

"Think there are any crocs?"

"Plenty in some of the rivers."

"But the hippos, wouldn't touch us, would they?"

"Very likely. They don't hesitate about seizing a canoe and crunching it in two. No, your plan won't do, lad. I'd rather die ashore here."

"Dry?" said Dickenson quietly. "Well, I dare say it would be nicer. But there, we're not quite cornered yet."

Crack went a bullet overhead, and a report came from a fresh direction almost simultaneously.

"Wrong!" said Drew coolly. "We are cornered now. That's the first shot from the men who have crossed to our side."

"All right; I'm ready for them. Let's finish our cartridges."

"We will, Bob," said Drew quite calmly, in spite of their extremity.

"What do you want?" said Dickenson. "You haven't used all your cartridges?"

"No; only about half."

"Then why did you hold out your hand?"

"Shake! In case," said Drew laconically.

"Sha'n't! I'm not going to look upon the business as having come to that pitch yet. Look out; we ought to see some of them soon."

For shots were beginning to come about them to supplement those sent from across the river, but so ill directed that it was evident that their fresh assailants were guessing at their position below the perpendicular cliff-like bank.

"This won't hurt us," said Dickenson coolly.

"No; but some of them will be having their heads over the edge up there directly."

"They can't while their friends are firing from the other side as they are. But when they do look down it will be rather awkward for the first two."

"Here, quick, look out, Bob!" cried Lennox, for the firing from the farther bank suddenly ceased, and the rustling and cracking of twigs somewhere overhead told that the fresh danger was very near.

Dickenson's reply to his companion's order was to place himself quickly with his back to the rocks that had sheltered him, sitting with his rifle pointing upward.

Drew took the same position, and none too soon; for, following closely upon the rustling sound, the makers of which were still invisible, a couple of shots were fired down at them, the bullets striking the stones just over their heads.

No reply was made, for the enemy were quite hidden, and with beating hearts the two young Englishmen waited in horrible suspense for their chance—one which never came; for directly after quite a volley was fired, apparently from some distance back from the edge, and, to Drew's horror, a big burly Boer seemed to leap down from the top of the cliff to seize them for prisoners.

That was his first surmise. The next moment he knew the truth, for with a heavy thud the man struck the stones, falling sidewise, and then turned over upon his face, to lie with his limbs quivering slightly for a few moments before he lay perfectly still.

"Hurrah!" shouted Dickenson, springing to his feet.

"Down! down!" roared Drew, snatching at his brother officer's arm.

But the need for caution was at an end, for volley after volley came rolling down into the river-bed, and proof of help being at hand was given by the rapid firing of the Boers on the other side of the river, a duel on a large scale being kept up for some ten minutes before the firing on the far side ceased.

"Whopped!" shouted Dickenson excitedly. "Look! look!" he cried, pointing down the river and across at an open spot where some dozens of the enemy were streaming away, galloping as hard as their little Bechuana ponies could go, but not escaping scatheless, four saddles being emptied by the fire from the cliff above the watchers' heads.

"I wonder whether the other men who crossed have escaped," said Drew thoughtfully, as he took his whistle from his cross-belt and held it ready to blow.

"Take it for granted they have, my son," said Dickenson. "They really are clever at that sort of thing. I say, I'm glad I didn't go through that performance."

"What performance?" said Drew wonderingly.

"Hand-shaking in that sentimental way."

"It wouldn't have done you any harm."

"Perhaps not; but, I say, don't stand fiddling about with that whistle. Blow, man, blow, and let the lads know where we are. I don't want to be shot now by our own men: too degrading, that."

Drew placed the whistle to his lips, and the shrill, penetrating, chirruping call rang out, while Dickenson stood looking upward towards the top of the bank.

> Then Robin he put him his horn to his mouth
> And a blast he did loudly blow,
> While quick at the call his merry men all
> Came tripping along in a row!

He half-hummed, half-sang the old lines in a pleasant baritone voice, and then listened.

"Don't see many *merry men* tripping—poor, hungry beggars! Blow again, Drew, old man. Why don't they stop firing?"

Drew blew again, and, to the intense satisfaction of both, the whistle was answered from among the trees above.

"Ahoy there! Where are you?"

"Here! here!" shouted the young officers together.

"Cease firing!" came now in a familiar voice, and the shots died out.

"It's Roby," said Drew eagerly.

"Never liked him so well before," said Dickenson, laughing. "Ahoy! We're coming up."

"Oh, there you are!" came from above, and a good, manly, sun-tanned face was thrust over the edge of the cliff. "All right?"

"Yes! Yes!" was the reply.

"That's better than I expected, lads," cried the officer. "Does one good. I thought we were avenging your death. Well,"—the speaker's face expanded into a broad grin—"it's getting on towards dinner-time. What have you caught?"

"Tartars!" growled Drew shortly.

"Yes," said Dickenson; "a regular mess."

Chapter Three
On the Qui Vive

"So it seems," said the officer above. "But hullo, you! You're wounded."

"Pooh! stuff!" said Dickenson shortly; "bit picked out of my ear."

"But,"—began the head of the rescue party.

"Let it be," said Dickenson snappishly as he pressed his hand to the injured place. "If I don't howl about it, I'm sure you needn't."

"Very well, old fellow, I will not. Ugh! what's that down there—that fellow dead?"

The officer leaned out as far as he could so as to get a good look at the motionless figure at the foot of the cliff.

Drew glanced at the figure too, and nodded his head.

"Who shot him—you or Dickenson?"

"Neither of us," said Drew gravely. "It was the work of one of your fellows; he fell from up there. But what about the party who crossed by the ford?"

"Oh, we've accounted for them. Cut them off from the ford and surrounded them. Fifteen, and bagged the lot, horses and all."

"You were a precious long time coming, though, Roby," grumbled Dickenson. "We seem to have been firing here all day."

"That's gratitude!" said the officer. "We came as quickly as we could. Nice job, too, to advance on a gang well under cover and double covered by the strong body across the river. There must have been sixty or seventy of them; but," added the captain meaningly, "sixty or seventy have not gone back. How many do you think are down? We've accounted for a dozen, I should say, *hors de combat*."

"I don't know," said Drew shortly, "and don't want to."

"What do you say, Dickenson?" asked the captain.

"The same as Lennox here."

"Come, come, speak out and don't be so thin-skinned. We've got to report to Lindley."

"Six haven't moved since," said Dickenson, looking uneasy now that the excitement of the fight was at an end; "and I should say twice as many more wounded."

"Serve 'em right. Their own fault," said the captain.

It was decided to be too risky a proceeding to cross the river, for the Boers were certain to be only a short distance away, sheltered in some advantageous position, waiting to try and retrieve their dead and wounded; so a small party was posted by the ford to guard against any crossing of the river, and then the prisoners were marched off towards the village a couple of miles distant, where the detachment of infantry and mounted men had been holding the Boers across the river in check for some weeks past.

A few shots followed them from a distance at first; but the enemy had received quite as much punishment as they desired upon that occasion, and soon ceased the aggressive, being eager for a truce to communicate with the little rear-guard posted in the scrub by the river so as to recover their wounded and dead.

On the way back to the village the two young officer's had to relate in full their experience, which was given in a plain, unvarnished way; and then as a sharp descent was reached, and the rescued officers caught sight of the well-guarded prisoners marching on foot, their Bechuana ponies having been appropriated by their captors, Dickenson began to grow sarcastic.

"Glad you've made such a nice lot of prisoners, Roby," he said.

"Thanks," said the officer addressed, smiling contentedly. "Not so bad—eh? The colonel will be delighted. Nice useful lot of ponies—eh?"

"Ye-es. The old man must be delighted. We're all about starving, and you're taking him about a score more mouths to feed."

"Eh?" cried the captain, aghast. "Why, of course; I never thought of that."

"Dickenson did," said Lennox, laughing. "A thing like this touches him to the heart—I mean lower down."

"You hold your tongue, my fine fellow," growled Dickenson. "You're as bad as I am. I don't like the fighting, but I'm ready to do my share if you'll only feed me well. I feel as if I'd been losing flesh for weeks."

"And done you good," said Lennox seriously. "You were much too fat."

"Look here, Drew," growled the young man addressed; "do you want to quarrel?"

"Certainly not," was the reply. "I've had quite enough for one day."

Further conversation was prevented by their approach to the village, which was built at the foot of a precipitous kopje, the spot having been chosen originally for its fertility consequent upon the fact that a copious spring of fresh water rose high up among the rocks to form the little stream and gully at whose mouth the young officers had met with their fishing experience.

This village, known as Groenfontein, had been held now for nearly two months by the little force, the idea being that it was to be occupied for a day at the most, and vacated after the Boers had been driven off. But though this had been done at once, the enemy had, as Drew Lennox said, a disgracefully unmilitary way of coming back after they had been thoroughly beaten. They had come back here after the driving; others had come to help them from east, west, north, and south, and as soon as they were strengthened they had set to work to drive the British force away or capture it *en bloc*; but that was quite another thing.

For, as Dickenson said, the colonel's instructions were to drive and not be driven. So the Boers were driven as often as there was a chance; and then, as they kept on returning, the force had to stay, and did so, getting plenty of opportunities for making fresh drives, till the colonel felt that it was all labour in vain and waste of time.

Under these circumstances he sent messengers explaining the position and asking for instructions. But his despatches did not seem to have been delivered, for no orders came to him, and their bearers did not return. Consequently, like a sturdy British officer, he fell back upon his first command to hold the Boers in check at Groenfontein, soon finding that they held him in check as well, for even had he felt disposed to retire, it would have been impossible except at the cost of losing half his men; so he held on and waited for the relief which he felt would sooner or later come.

But it did not come sooner, and he relied on the later, making the best of things. Colonel Lindley's way of making the best of things was to return a contemptuous reply to the demands made from time to time for his surrender.

The first time this demand was made was when the enemy had him in front and rear. The envoys who came informed him that his position was perfectly hopeless, for he could not cross the river in face of the strong body the Boers had lining the banks; and that they had him in front, and if his people did not give up their arms they would be shot down to a man.

The colonel's answer to this was, "Very well, gentlemen; shoot away."

His officers were present, and Drew Lennox and Bob Dickenson exchanged glances at the word "gentlemen," for the embassy looked like anything but that; and they departed in an insolent, braggart way, and very soon after began to shoot, using up a great many cartridges, but doing very little harm. Then, growing weary, they gave up, and the colonel set one part of his men to work with the spade till dark, making rifle-pit and trench; while as soon as it was dark he despatched fully half of his force to occupy the precipitous mound at the back of the village, making a natural stronghold which he intended to connect with the camp by means of stone walls the next day, having a shrewd notion that if he did not the Boers would, for the mound commanded the place, and would soon make it untenable.

Captain Roby's company and another were sent to this duty, and the men were carefully posted—Lennox and Dickenson on the highest part, which was naturally the most windy and cold. Their orders, which they conveyed to the men, were to keep the strictest lookout, though the enemy had retired far enough away; for the Boers had at that early period of the war already acquired the credit of being slim and clever at ambush and night attack.

But the night was well advanced, and the two friends, after visiting post after post, were sitting huddled up in their greatcoats, longing for hot coffee or cigarettes, and feeling obliged to rub their sleepy and tired eyes from time to time, weary as they were with straining to see danger creeping up over the black, dark veldt, but straining in vain.

"B-r-r-r! What humbug it is to call this Africa!" growled Dickenson.

"What do you mean?" replied Lennox.

"Mean? Why, it's so cold. Where's your blazing heat and your sand? One might be at the North Pole. Ow! don't do that."

He started violently, for Lennox had suddenly stolen out a hand and pinched his arm sharply.

"Quiet! Listen!"

Dickenson drew his breath hard and strained his ears instead of his eyes.

"Well? Can't hear anything."

"Hist! Listen again."

There was a pause.

"Hear anything?"

"Yes; but I don't know what it is," said Dickenson, laying a hand behind one ear and leaning forward with his head on one side.

"What does it sound like?"

"Something like a heavy wagon coming along a road with its wheels muffled."

"Heavy wagon drawn by oxen?"

"Yes," replied Dickenson.

"Mightn't it be a big gun?"

"It might," said Dickenson dubiously; "but what, could a big gun be doing out there on the open veldt?"

"Lying still in its carriage, and letting itself be drawn to the place where it was to be mounted."

"Yes, of course it might be; but it couldn't."

"Why not? Bob, old fellow," whispered Lennox in an excited whisper, "I believe the Boers are stealing a march upon us."

"Well, they won't, because we're on the watch. But out with it: what is it you think?"

"They don't know that we are occupying the kopje to-night."

"No; we came after it was dark."

"Exactly. Well, they're bringing up a big gun to mount up here and give us a surprise in the morning."

"Phe-ew!" whistled Dickenson. "Oh, surely not!"

"I feel sure that they are."

"Well, let's send word on to the old man. Send one of the sergeants."

"And by the time he got there with his news, and reinforcements could be sent, the enemy would have the gun here."

"Let's tell Roby, then."

"Yes; come on."

In another minute they had told their officer their suspicions, and he hummed and ha'd a little after listening.

"It hardly seems likely," he said, "and I don't want to raise a false alarm. Besides, the outposts have given no notice; and hark! I can hear nothing."

"Now?"

They listened in the darkness, and it was as their captain suggested: all perfectly still.

"There," he said. "It would be horrible to rouse up the colonel on account of a cock-and-bull story."

"But it would be worse for him to be warned too late. There it is again; hark!" whispered Lennox, stretching out a hand in the direction farthest from the village.

"Can't hear anything," said the captain.

"I can," growled Dickenson softly.

"Yes, so can I now. It's a wagon whose drivers have missed their way, I should say. But we'll see."

"Or feel," grunted the captain. "It's as black as ink.—Here, Lennox, take a sergeant's guard and go forward softly to see if you can make anything out. I don't know, though; it may be as you say, and if it is—"

"We ought to bring in that gun," whispered Lennox.

"Yes, at all hazards. I don't know, though. There, take five-and-twenty of the lads, and act as seems best. If you can do it easily, force the drivers to come on, but don't run risks. If the Boers are in strength fall back at once. You understand?"

"Quite," said Lennox softly.

"Let me go with him, Roby?"

"No; I can't spare you."

"Yes, do; I can help him."

"He can do what there is to do himself, and would rather be alone, for it is only a reconnaissance."

"I should like him with me," said Lennox quietly, and he felt his arm nipped.

"Very well; but don't waste time. I can hear it quite plainly now. Mind, fall back at once if they are in force. I'll be well on the alert to cover you and your party."

The requisite number of men were soon under the young officer's orders, and they followed him softly down the rock-encumbered slope of the natural fortress—no easy task in the darkness; but the men were getting used to the gloom, and it was not long before the party was challenged by an outpost and received the word. They passed on, getting well round to the farther side of the kopje before they were challenged again.

"Glad you've come, sir," said the sentry; "I was just going to fire."

"Why?" asked Lennox softly.

"I can hear something coming out yonder in the darkness. You listen, sir. It's like a heavy wagon."

The man spoke in a whisper; then for some moments all was perfectly still.

"Can't hear it now, sir," whispered the sentry; "but I felt sure I heard something."

"Wait again," said Lennox softly; and there was a good five minutes' interval of waiting, but not a sound could be heard.

"Let's go forward, Bob," whispered Lennox; and after telling the sentry to be well upon the alert, he led his men slowly and cautiously straight away out into the black darkness of the veldt, but without hearing another sound till they were, as far as could be judged, a good two hundred yards from the last outpost, when the men were halted and stood in the black darkness listening once more, before swinging: round to the right and getting back by a curve to somewhere near the starting-place.

The next moment the young men joined hands and stood listening to an unmistakable sound away to their right and nearer to the kopje. The sound was distant enough to be very soft, but there it was, plainly enough—the calm, quiet crunching up of the food a span of oxen had eaten, indicative of the fact that they had been pulled up by their drivers and were utilising their waiting time by chewing the cud.

"Forward!" whispered Lennox, and his men crept after him without a sound, every one full of excitement, for the general idea was that they were about to surprise some convoy wagon that had gone astray.

A minute later the munching of the oxen sounded quite loudly, and the little party was brought to a halt by a deep, gruff voice saying in Boer Dutch:

"What a while you've been! How much higher can we get?"

"Fix bayonets!" cried Lennox sharply, and a yell of dismay arose, followed by a dozen random shots, as the metallic clinking of the keen, dagger-like weapons was heard against the muzzles of the men's rifles.

The shots fired seemed to cut the black darkness, and the exploded powder spread its dank, heavy fumes in the direction of the men's faces, but as far as Lennox could make out in the excitement of leading his party on in a charge, no one was hurt; and the next minute his little line was brought up short, several of the men littering angry ejaculations, and as many more bursting into a roar of laughter.

Chapter Four
Ways and Means

"Here, what in the name of wonder!" cried Dickenson angrily. "Yah! Keep those horns quiet, you beast."

"What is it?" cried Lennox excitedly.

"Roast-beef, sir—leastwise to-morrow, sir," cried one of the men. "We've bay'neted a team of oxen."

"Speak the truth, lad," cried another from Lennox's left. "We've been giving point in a gun-carriage."

"Silence in the ranks!" cried Lennox sternly as he felt about in the darkness, joined now by his comrade, and found that their charge had been checked by a big gun, its limber, and the span—six or eight and twenty oxen—several of the poor beasts having received thrusts from the men's bayonets.

It was a strange breastwork to act as a protection, but from behind its shelter a couple of volleys were sent in the direction of the flashes of light which indicated the whereabouts of the enemy, and this made them continue their flight, the surprise having been too great for their nerves; while the right interpretation was placed upon the adventure at once— to wit, that in ignorance of the fact that Colonel Lindley had done in the darkness exactly what might have been expected, and occupied the kopje, the Boers had brought up a heavy gun with the intention of mounting it before morning, and had failed.

"What's to be the next?" said Dickenson.

"Next?" cried Lennox. "You must cover us with three parts of the men while with the rest I try to get the gun right up to the kopje."

It was no easy task, for the driver and foreloper of the team had fled with the artillerymen and the rest of the Boers, while the pricked oxen were disposed to be unmanageable. But British soldiers are accustomed to struggle with difficulties of all kinds in war, and by the time the Boers had recovered somewhat from their surprise, and, urged by their leaders, were advancing again to try and recover the lost piece, the team of oxen were once more working together, and the ponderous gun was being slowly dragged onward towards the rocky eminence.

It was terribly hard work in the darkness; for the way, after about a hundred yards or so over level veldt, began to ascend, and blocks of granite seemed to be constantly rising from the ground to impede the progress of the oxen.

In spite of all, though, the gun and its limber were dragged on and on, while in the distance a line of tiny jets of fire kept on spurting out, showing that the enemy had recovered from the panic and were coming on, firing as they came, the bullets whizzing over the heads of our men, but doing no harm.

"Steady! steady! and as quietly as you can," said Lennox in warning tones, as he kept on directing and encouraging his men. "They are firing by guesswork.—Ah! that won't do any good," he muttered, for just as he was speaking Dickenson and his men, who had spread out widely, began to reply; "it will only show our weakness."

He looked forward again in the direction the oxen were being driven; but the kopje was invisible, and now he altered his opinion about the firing of Dickenson's detachment, for he felt that it would let the captain know what was going on, and bring up support.

He was quite right, for in a very little time Captain Roby had felt his way to them, learnt the cause of the firing, and carefully covered the retreat till the intricacies of the rocky ascent put a stop to further progress in the gloom, and a halt was called till morning.

The rest of the night passed in the midst of a terrible suspense, for though the Boer firing gradually died out, as if the leaders had at last awakened to the fact of its being a mere waste of ammunition, the British detachment, scattered here and there about the captured gun, lay in momentary expectation of the enemy creeping up and then making a rush.

"But they will not," said Lennox quietly. "They'll wait till morning, and creep up from stone to stone and bush to bush, trying to pick us off."

"You need not be so cock-sure about it," growled Dickenson. "They are in force, and must have known from our fire how few we were. A rush would do it."

"Yes; but they will not rush," replied Lennox. "They understand too well the meaning of the word *bayonet*. Cock-sure or no, they'll make no dash; but as soon as it begins to be light we shall have a hailstorm."

"Nonsense!" said Dickenson tetchily; "there's no sign of rain."

"I did not say rain," replied Lennox, "but hail—leaden hail from every bit of cover round."

"Oh, I see," said Dickenson. "Well, two sides can play at that game; and I fancy we have most cover here."

Lennox was quite right; for as soon as the first pale grey of a lovely dawn began to make objects stand up in an indistinct way upon the level veldt around the kopje, the sharp cracks of rifle after rifle began at every object that displayed movement upon the eminence, and the pattering of bullets among the rocks often preceded the reports of the Boer rifles.

But by this time Captain Roby had communicated with the colonel in the village, and had taken his steps, sending his men well out in the enemy's direction to take advantage of every scrap of cover to reply wherever it was necessary, which they did, their efforts, as the time went on, to some extent keeping the Boer fire down.

The colonel grasped the position at once and sent assistance, with the result that, in spite of terrible difficulties, by help of horse and mule to supplement the pulling powers of the ox-team, the big gun, limber, and an ammunition-wagon, which daylight showed lying deserted a quarter of a mile away among some bushes into which it had been dragged in the dark, were hauled to the flat top of the kopje, where they were surrounded with a rough but strong breastwork of the abundant stones, and by the men's breakfast-time a shell was sent well into the midst of a clump of bush which the Boers had made the centre of their advance.

A better shot could not have been made, for as soon as the shell had burst, the defenders of the kopje had the satisfaction of seeing that the greater part of the Boers' ponies had been gathered into shelter there, and a perfect stampede had begun, hundreds of horses, mounted and empty of saddle, streaming away in every direction except that in which the kopje lay.

There was no need for a second shell, for the sputtering rifle-fire ceased as if by magic, the Boers retiring, leaving the colonel's force at liberty to go on at leisure strengthening the emplacement of the enemy's heavy Creusot gun, and forming a magazine for the abundant supply of ammunition, also captured for its use.

The rest of the day was occupied, by as many of the men as could be spared, building up sangars (loose stone walls for breastworks) and contriving rifle-pits and cover to such an extent that already it would have taken a strong and determined force to make any impression; while, when the officers met at the mess that night and the matter was under discussion, the colonel smiled.

"Yes," he said, "pretty well for one day's work; but by the end of a week we shall have a little Gibraltar that will take all the men the Boers have in the field to capture—a regular stronghold, ready like a castle keep if we have to leave the village."

"And may that never be, colonel," said Captain Roby.

"Hear, hear!" cried every one present.

"So I say," said the colonel; "but we may at any time be ordered to occupy some other position. By the way, though, I should not dislike to send the Boer leader a letter of thanks for sending us that gun and a supply of oxen. How many must be killed?"

"Killed?" cried Captain Roby.

"Yes; several were bayoneted in that charge."

"Three only," replied the captain, "and they don't look much the worse for it. Their flesh seems to close up again like india-rubber. The vet says they will all heal up."

"Good," said the colonel. "Take it all together, I shall have a pleasant despatch to send to the general. The capture of the big gun; not a man killed, and only three wounded. How are they getting on, doctor?"

"Capitally. Nothing serious. But, by the way—" The doctor stopped and began to clean out his pipe.

"Yes, by the way?" said the colonel. "Nothing unpleasant to report, I hope?"

"Um—no," drawled the doctor. "A fresh patient with a touch of fever; but it wasn't that. I meant—that is, I wondered how you meant to send the despatch?"

"Ha! Yes," said the colonel thoughtfully; "how? I don't feel disposed to risk any more men, and I hear that the Kaffirs do not seem to be tempted by the pay offered them, although I have offered double what I gave before."

"That's bad," said the doctor. "Well, I suppose you can hold this place?"

"Tight!" said the colonel laconically.

"So long as provisions and ammunition hold out?" said Captain Roby tentatively.

"Yes," assented the colonel.

"And when they are ended," cried Dickenson, who had sat listening in silence, "we can try a bit of sport. There are herds of antelopes and flocks of guinea-fowl about, sir."

"I doubt it, Dickenson," said the colonel, smiling; "and I fancy that the most profitable form of sport for us will be that followed out by our mounted men."

"What's that, sir?" asked Dickenson.

"Stalking the enemy's convoys. These fellows have to be fed, hardy and self-supporting as they are. But there, we are pretty well supplied as yet, and the great thing is that our water-supply is never likely to fail."

The next morning the Boers made a fresh attack for the purpose of recapturing the gun or seizing the kopje where it was mounted. But this advance, like several more which followed, only resulted in a severe repulse, and at last their attacks formed part of a long blockade in which they hoped to succeed by starving the little British force into subjection.

Chapter Five
The Boer Prisoners

It was to this village and kopje, turned after its long occupation into what proved to be an impregnable stronghold—one which so far, to the Boers' cost, maintained its promise—that Drew Lennox and Bob Dickenson returned after their unfortunate fishing expedition, the colonel, a bluff, sun-burnt, stern-looking officer, meeting them with a frown as they came up. "How many men hurt, Roby?" he said.

"Only one, sir. Dickenson had his ear nicked by a bullet."

"Humph! Might have been worse, my lad," said the colonel. "Show it to the doctor.—Where are your fish, Lennox?"

"In the river, sir," said the young officer, with a shrug of the shoulders. "How was that?"

The young man briefly explained, and the colonel nodded his head.

"Look here," he said, "we want some change from our monotonous fare; but if you two had come back loaded with salmon I should have forbidden any further fishing—so of course I do now. I can't afford to have my officers setting themselves up as butts for the Boers to practise at."

"We have taken fifteen prisoners and their horses, sir," interposed Captain Roby, making an effort to turn aside the wrath of their chief.

"Yes, Mr Roby, I saw that you had some prisoners," replied the colonel meaningly; "but, excuse me, I had not finished addressing these two gentlemen."

"I beg pardon, sir."

"That will do," said the colonel. "There, I need say no more. Let's see the prisoners."

"I don't think I like fishing as a sport, Drew, old man," said Dickenson, rubbing his ear, and then wincing with pain. "Come on, and let's see the inspection of the enemy. But the boss needn't have been so gruff. We acted as bait, and he has caught fifteen Boers and their horses."

"And how are we to feed them all now we have got them?" said Lennox, with a quaint smile.

"Oh, that's what made the old man so waxy!" cried the other. "I see now. Well, let him set them up and have them shot."

"Of course; according to our merciless custom," said Lennox sarcastically; and directly after the two friends closed up to where the prisoners were being paraded, their horses, clever, wiry-looking little cobs, being led up behind them by some of the men.

It was almost the first time that the young men had been in such close contact with the sturdy, obstinate enemy they had so long kept at bay, and they stared eagerly at the rough, unshorn, ill-clad, farmer-like fellows, for the most part big-bearded, sun-tanned, and full of vigour, who met their gaze defiantly, but kept on directing uneasy glances at the other officers, more than once looking eagerly at their led horses as if mentally weighing whether by a bold rush they could reach their steeds, spring upon them, and gallop away.

But a glance round showed them the impossibility of such a proceeding, for they were unarmed and surrounded by men with fixed bayonets, while, in addition, every pony had an armed man holding its bridle; and as their shifty eyes were turned from one to another in a questioning way, the prevailing thought seemed to be that any such proceeding would be mad in the extreme, and could only result in their being shot down.

The inspection did not take long, and the colonel turned away to confer with the group of officers who followed him.

"The sooner we get rid of these fellows the better," he said, "for we can't keep them here. What shall I do?" he continued, in response to a question from the major of the regiment. "Make them take the oaths to be on parole not to bear arms against us again?"

"Ready for them to go and break their word," grumbled the major.

"Of course; after what has passed we can't trust them a bit. But we can't keep them here an hour; half-an-hour is too much. They will see far more of our weakness and the state of our defences in five minutes than I like."

He turned to the heavy, big-bearded man who seemed to be the leader, and asked if he would take the oath not to fight against the Queen again.

The man started and looked relieved, for he grasped all that was said to him—words which came while he was still in doubt as to what their fate was to be, his ideas tending towards a volley of rifles fired at ten paces.

The next minute he was interpreting the colonel's words to his comrades in misfortune, and with a meaning smile each man willingly made the promise in Dutch that he would take no further part in the war.

"Look here," said the colonel to their leader; "make them fully understand that if they are again taken in arms against the Queen—"

"They have no Queen," said the Boer leader surlily. "This is the Transvaal Republic."

"Indeed!" said the colonel sternly. "This is not the Transvaal Republic, but a part of the British Dominions now; and remember that you all owe allegiance to Her Majesty the Queen-Empress, whose laws you have now sworn to obey."

The man scowled.

"And if, as I was telling you, any of you are again found fighting against our troops, you will not be treated as people at war against us, but as rebels liable to be tried by a short drum-head court-martial, and shot out of hand. Do you understand?"

The man nodded.

"Make your companions fully understand it too."

The Boer leader hesitated as if about to speak, but the colonel turned upon him sharply.

"Quick, sir," he cried; "I have no time to waste. Tell your companions this, so that there may be no mistake."

The man stepped back, and his followers pressed round him talking eagerly, several of them understanding English to some extent, and for a few minutes they conversed together excitedly, till, with a shrug of the shoulders, the principal Boer turned and advanced to the colonel.

"Well," said the latter, "do they fully grasp all this?"

"Oh yes; they know," replied the man sourly.

"That will do, then," said the colonel. "No; stop. You are no longer our enemies, and we have treated you well; henceforth act as friends. Go back to your farms, and collect and bring here corn, oxen, and sheep, as much as you like, and I will buy it of you at a good price."

The Boer brightened up at this.

"In money?" he said. "Not in paper orders?"

"In hard cash, my suspicious friend," said the colonel, with a look of contempt; "but it's time you had learnt that our government paper is as good as Transvaal gold."

"We will be paid in gold," said the Boer, with a peculiar smile.

"That will do, then," said the colonel. "Now you can go, and the sooner you set to work to teach your fellow-countrymen to respect the British Government the better for you all. Now, off at once."

The Boer rejoined his companions, talked with them for a few minutes, and returned.

"Back again?" said the colonel. "Well, what is it?"

"We are waiting to go," said the Boer coolly.

"Very well; the way is open," said the colonel. "Off with you, and think you are lucky that we do not keep you as prisoners."

As he spoke he pointed out towards the open veldt; but the Boer shook his head.

"Not that way," he said. "We want to cross the spruit to join our friends."

The colonel hesitated.

"Well," he said, turning to the major, "perhaps it is not fair to send them out on the karoo."

"But if you let them join their friends they will be fighting against us again to-morrow."

"So they will be," said the colonel grimly, "if we send them in the other direction. You don't suppose I have any faith in their parole, do you?"

"I did not know," said the major.

"There, I will send a picket with you to see you safely to the ford," said the colonel. "Now, off at once, and bring the forage as soon as you can."

"To-morrow or next night," said the Boer, with a nod.

"Here, Roby, send a sergeant's guard to see these people past the outposts.—Now, my good fellow, time is valuable here. Follow that gentleman, and he will see that you are safely passed through our lines. Well, what now?"

"You haven't given him orders to return us our horses and our rifles."

"What!" cried the colonel.

"We can't get about without them," said the Boer coolly.

The colonel laughed.

"Well, of all the cool impudence!" he cried. "Why, you insolent dog!" he roared, "do you expect we are such children that we are going to give you the means of attacking us again directly you are safe?—Here, Roby, see these fellows out of the lines."

The colonel turned away and walked back to his quarters, followed by a torrent of abuse, which was promptly checked by Captain Roby, who gave his orders sharply, and the prisoners were marched off in front of the sergeant's guard with fixed bayonets.

But the incident was not quite at an end, for before a quarter of an hour had elapsed the crackling of rifle-fire was heard in the direction of the ford, towards which men were sent at once. The alarm soon died out on the cause being known, the sergeant reporting that he had approached the ford with the prisoners and displayed a flag of truce, which brought out a party of five or six dozen Boers upon the farther side of the river, into whose charge the prisoners were given. But no sooner were all across and seen to be talking to their friends than there was a rush for cover, and before the sergeant and the outposts stationed there could grasp what the movement meant the enemy's fire was opened upon them.

"Any one hurt, sergeant?" said Captain Roby.

"No, sir, wonderful to relate. Our lads were too sharp for them, and dropped at once. My heart rose to my mouth, sir, for I thought three of ours were hit; but it was only their sharpness, for they were returning the fire the next moment, and we kept it up as hot as the enemy did till they fell back."

"Quite time the Boers were taught the meaning of civilised war, Bob," said Lennox as they returned to their quarters.

"Quite; but I'm out of heart with them," replied Dickenson. "They're bad pupils—such a one-sided lot."

"What about the corn and sheep and beef those fellows are to bring to-morrow or next night?" said Lennox grimly.

"Well, what about it? I'm afraid they'll be too much offended with the colonel's treatment to come."

"Yes," said Lennox; "so am I."

Chapter Six
Pleasant Supplies

Matters looked anything but hopeful at Groenfontein, though the men were full of spirits and eager to respond to any of the attacks made by the Boers, who, with three commandos, thoroughly shut them in, joining hands and completely cutting off all communication.

Time was gliding on without any sign of help from outside, and the beleaguered party would have concluded that they were quite forgotten by their friends if they had not felt certain that the different generals were fully engaged elsewhere.

"Let's see," said Lennox one evening; "we've been attacked every day since our fishing-trip."

"That's right; and the Boers have been beaten every day for a week."

"And yet they are as impudent as over. They think that we shall surrender as soon as we grow a little more hungry."

"Then they'll be sold," said Dickenson, "for the hungrier I grow the more savage and full of fight I get. You know about the old saying of some fellow, that when he had had a good dinner a child might play with him?"

"Oh yes, I know," said Lennox. "Well, these children of the desert had better not try to play with me."

"Ought to have a notice on you, 'Take care; he bites'—eh?" said Lennox merrily.

"'M, yes; something of the kind. I say, I wish, though, I could sleep without dreaming."

"Can't you?"

"No; it's horrible. I go to sleep directly I lie down, and then the game begins. I'm at Christmas dinners or banquets or parties, and the tables are covered with good things. Then either they've got no taste in them, or else as soon as I try to cut a slice or take up a mouthful in a spoon it's either snatched or dragged away."

"Oh, don't talk about food," said Lennox impatiently; "it makes me feel sick. There's one comfort, though."

"Is there?" cried Dickenson excitedly. "Where? Give us a bit."

"Nonsense! I mean we have plenty of that beautiful spring water."

"Ugh!" cried Dickenson, with a shudder. "Cold and clear, unsustaining. I saw some water once through a microscope, and it was full of live things twizzling about in all directions. That's the sort of water we want now—something to eat in it as well as drink."

Lennox made an irritable gesture.

"Talk about something else, man," he cried. "You think of nothing but eating and drinking."

"That's true, old man. Well, I'll say no more about drinking; but I wonder how cold roast prisoner would taste?"

"Bob!" shouted Lennox.

"Well, what shall I talk about?"

"Look about you. See how beautiful the kopjes and mountains look in the distance this evening; they seem to glow with orange and rose and gold."

"There you go again! You're always praising up this horrid place."

"Well, isn't it beautiful? See how clear the air is."

"I dare say. But I don't want clear air; I'd rather it was thick as soup if it tasted like it."

"Soup! There you go again. Think of how lovely it is down by the river."

"With the Boers popping at you? I say, this ear of mine doesn't heal up."

"You don't mind the doctor's orders."

"So much fighting to do; haven't time."

"But you grant it is beautiful down by the river?"

"Yes, where only man is vile—very vile indeed; does nothing all day but try to commit murder. But there, it's of no use for you to argue; I think South Africa is horrible. Look at the miles of wretched dusty desert and stony waste. I don't know what we English want with it."

"Room for our colonists, and to develop the mines. Look at the diamonds."

"Look at our sparkling sea at home."

"Look at the gold."

"I like looking at a good golden furzy common in Surrey. It's of no use, Drew, my lad; it's a dismal, burning, freezing place."

"Why don't you throw it up and go home, then?"

"What! before we've beaten the Boers into a state of decency? No!"

Bob Dickenson's "No!" was emphatic enough for anything, and brought the conversation between the two young men to an end; for it was close upon the time for the mess dinner, which, whatever its shortcomings, as Bob Dickenson said, was jolly punctual, even if there was no tablecloth.

So they descended from where they had perched themselves close up to the big gun, where their commanding position gave them the opportunity for making a wide sweep round over the karoo, taking in, too, the wooded course of the river and the open country beyond in the possession of the Boers.

But they had seen no sign of an enemy or grazing horse; though they well knew that if a company of their men set off in any direction, before they had gone a quarter of a mile they would be pelted with bullets by an unseen foe.

They had seen the walls and rifle-pits which guarded the great gun so often that they hardly took their attention. All the same, though, soldier-like, Drew Lennox could not help thinking how naturally strong the kopje was, how easy it would be for two or three companies of infantry to hold it against a force of ten times their number, and what tremendous advantages the Boers had possessed in the nature of their country. For they had only had to sit down behind the natural fortifications and set an enemy at defiance.

"It's our turn now," Lennox said to himself, "and we could laugh at them for months if only we had a supply of food."

"Let's try this way," said Dickenson, bearing off to his left.

"What for? It's five times as hard as the regular track, and precipitous."

"Not so bad but what we can do it. We can let one another down if we come to one of the wall-like bits too big to jump."

"But it's labour for nothing. Only make you more hungry," added Lennox, with a laugh.

"Never mind; I want to make sure that an enemy could not steal up in the dark and surprise the men in charge of the gun. I'm always thinking that the Boers will steal a march on us and take it some day."

"You might save yourself the trouble as far as the climbing up is concerned. This is the worst bit; but they could do it, I feel sure, if our sentries were lax. I don't think they'd get by them, though."

"Well, let's have a good look what it is like, now all the crags are lit up."

They were lit up in a most wonderful way by the sun, which was just about to dip below the horizon, and turned every lightning-shivered mass of tumbled-together rock into a glowing state, making it look as if it was red-hot, while the rifts and cracks which had been formed here and there were lit up so that their generally dark depths could be searched by the eye.

"Do you know what this place looks like?" said Dickenson.

"The roughest spot in the world," replied Drew as he lowered himself down a perpendicular, precipitous bit which necessitated his hanging by his hands, and then dropping four or five feet.

"No! It's just as if the giants of old had made a furnace at the top of the kopje, and had been pouring the red-hot clinkers down the side."

"Or as if it was the slope of a volcano, and those were the masses of pumice which had fallen and rolled down."

"So that we look like a couple of flies walking amongst lumps of sugar. Well, yours is a good simile, but not so romantic as mine. That's a deep crack, Drew, old chap. Like to see how far in it goes?"

"No, thanks. I want my dinner," said Lennox.

"Dinner! Mealie cake and tough stewed horse."

"Wrong," said Lennox; "it's beef to-night, for I asked."

"Beef! Don't insult the muscle-giving food of a Briton by calling tough old draught-ox beef. I don't know but what I would rather have a bit of *cheval*—*chevril*, or whatever they call it—if it wasn't for that oily fat. But we might as well peep in that crack. Perhaps there's a cavern."

"Not to-day, Bob. It's close upon mess-time."

"Hark at him! Prefers food for the body to food for the mind. Very well. Go on; I'm at your heels."

They descended to the more level part of the granite-strewn eminence, acknowledged the salutes of the sentries they passed, and soon after reached the mean-looking collection of tin houses that formed the village—though there was very little tin visible, the only portion being a barricade or two formed of biscuit-tins, which had been made bullet-proof in building up a wall by filling them with earth or sand. The *tin* houses, according to the popular term, were really the common grey corrugated iron so easily riveted or screwed together into a hut, and forming outer and partition walls, and fairly rain-proof roofing, but as ugly in appearance as hot beneath the torrid sun.

Groenfontein consisted of a group of this class of house ranged about a wide market-square, while here and there outside were warehouses and sheds and a few farms.

Bob Dickenson said it was the ugliest and dirtiest place that ever called itself a town; and he was fairly right about the former. As to the latter, it might have been worse. Its greatest defect was the litter of old meat and other tins, while there were broken bottles enough to act as a defence when attacked by strangers.

The Boer inhabitants had for the most part fled; those who were left lived under the protection of the British force, which they preferred to being out on commando, using rifle, and risking their lives.

The empty houses left by the former inhabitants had at once been taken possession of for officers' and soldiers' quarters; the long warehouses and barns for stabling; and a big wool warehouse, happily containing many bales of wool, had been turned into mess and club room, the great bales making excellent couches, and others forming breastworks inside the windows and the big double doors.

Here the officers off duty lounged and rested, and here upon this particular night they were gathered round the social board to dine, each officer with his own servant; and it is worthy of remark that with officer and man, rifle, revolver, and sword were racked close at hand.

"Round the social board" is a most appropriate term, though not quite correct; for, while social in the highest degree, quite a brotherly spirit influencing the officers present, the board was really two, held together by a couple of cross-pieces and laid upon barrels, while the seats were of all kinds, from cartridge-boxes to up-ended flour-barrels, branded *Na.* and *Pa.* and *Va.*, and various other contractions of long-sounding United States names, which indicated where the fine white flour they once contained had been grown and ground.

The mess cook had done the best he could, and provided some excellent bread, but it was rather short in quantity. As to the meat, it was hot; but there were no dish-covers, which Bob Dickenson said did not matter in the least, for during the past few weeks they had been careful to draw a veil over the food.

But of water, such as needed no filtering, there was ample, ready for quaffing out of tin mug, silver flask, cup, or horn.

The Kopje Garrison | 51

"And the beauty of our tipple now is," said Bob, "that it never does a fellow the least harm."

It was a favourite remark of his, "an impromptu" that had been much admired. He made the remark again on this particular evening, but his tones sounded dismal.

"It's a great blessing, though," he added; "we might have none. Yes, capital water," he continued, draining his cup and setting it down with a rap on his part of the board. "Just think, Drew, old man, we might be forced to sit here drinking bad champagne."

"I don't want to drink bad or good champagne, old fellow," said Lennox; "but I do wish we had a barrel of good, honest, home-brewed British ale, with—"

"A brace of well-roasted pheasants between us two—eh?"

"No; I was going to say, a good crusty loaf and a cut off a fine old Stilton cheese."

"J-Ja!" sighed the next man.

"Never mind, gentlemen," said the colonel; "what we have will do to work upon. When we've done our work, and get back home, I'll be bound to say that John Bull will ask us to dinner oftener than will do us good. What do you say, doctor?"

"What do I say, Colonel Lindley?" cried the doctor, putting down his flask-cup. "I say this Spartan fare agrees with us all admirably. Look round the table, and see what splendid condition we are all in. A bit spare, but brown, wiry, and active as men can be. Never mind the food. You are all living a real life on the finest air I ever breathed. We are all pictures of health now; and where I have a wound to deal with it heals fast—a sure sign that the patient's flesh is in a perfect state."

"It's all very fine," said Bob Dickenson in a low voice to those about him. "Old Bolus keeps himself up to the mark by taking nips; that's why he's so well and strong."

"Nonsense!" said Lennox sharply. "I don't believe he ever touches spirits except as a medicine."

"Who said he did?" growled Dickenson.

"You, Bob; we all heard you," chorused several near.

"Take my oath I never mentioned spirits. I said *nips*."

"Well, you meant them," said Lennox.

"I didn't. Don't you jump at conclusions, Drew, old man. I meant nips of tonics. Old M.D. has got a lot of curious chemicals in that medicine-chest of his, and when he's a bit down he takes nips of them."

"I don't believe it," said a brother officer, laughing. "Old Emden, M.D.. take his own physic? Too clever for that!"

The darkness had closed in soon after the officers had taken their seats—early, after tropic fashion—and one of the messmen had lit four common-looking paraffin-lamps, which swung from the rafters, smelt vilely of bad spirit, and smoked and cast down a dismal light; but the men were in high spirits, chatting away, and the meal being ended, many of them had started pipes or rolled up cigarettes, when an orderly was seen to enter by the door nearest the colonel's seat and make quickly for his place.

There was a cessation of the conversation on the instant, and one motion made by every officer present—he glanced at the spot where his sword and revolver hung, while their servants turned their eyes to the rifle-stands and bandoliers, listening intently for the colonel's next order: for the coming of the orderly could only mean one thing under their circumstances—an advance of the Boers.

They were right. But the increased action of their pulses began to calm down again; for instead of standing up according to his wont and giving a few short, sharp orders, the colonel, after turning towards the orderly and hearing him out, merely raised his eyes and smiled.

"Wonders will never cease, gentlemen," he said, and he sent a soft, grey cloud of cigarette smoke upward towards the roof of the barn. "You all remember our prisoners, brought in after Lennox and Dickenson's fishing expedition?"

There was an eager chorus of "Yes" from all present save the two young officers mentioned, and they were too eager in listening to speak.

"Well, gentlemen, I told those men that the wisest thing they could do was to go back to their farms, give up fighting, and collect and bring into camp here a good supply of corn and beef."

"Yes, sir, I heard you," said Captain Roby, for the colonel paused to take two or three whiffs from his cigarette.

"Well, gentlemen, you will hardly credit the news I have received when you recall what took place, and be ready to place some faith in a Boer's sound common-sense."

"Why doesn't he speak out at once?" said Dickenson in a whisper. "Who wants all this rigmarole of a preface?"

"What is it, colonel?" said the major.

"That Boer, the leader of the little party of prisoners, evidently took my advice," continued the colonel; "and instead of rejoining his fighting friends, he has gone back to the ways of peace and trade, and they have just arrived at the outposts with a couple of wagon-loads of grain, a score of sheep, and ten oxen."

The news was received with a shout, and as soon as silence was obtained the colonel continued: "It seems incredible; but, after all, it is only the beginning of what must come to pass. For, once the Boer is convinced that it is of no use to fight, he will try his best to make all he can out of his enemies."

"Well, it's splendid news," said the major; "but what about its being some cunning trap?"

"That is what I am disposed to suspect," said the colonel; "so, quietly and without stir, double the outposts, send word to the men on the kopje to be on the alert, and let everything, without any display of force, be ready for what may come. You, Captain Roby, take half a company to meet our visitors, and bring the welcome provender into the market-place here."

"Bob," whispered Lennox, "if we could only go with Roby! There'll be a couple of score of the enemy hiding amongst those sacks."

"Get out!" responded Dickenson. "I never did see such an old cock-and-bull inventor as you are. It's stale, too. You're thinking of the old story of the fellows who took the castle by riding in a wagon loaded with grass and them underneath. Then it was driven in under the portcullis, which was dropped at the first alarm, and came down chop on the wagon and would go no farther, while the fellows hopped out through the grass and took the castle. Pooh! What's the good of being so suspicious? These Boers are tired of fighting, and they've taken the old man's advice about trade."

"I don't believe it," said Lennox firmly. "I wouldn't trust the Boers a bit."

"Well, don't believe it, then; but let's go and see what they've brought, all the same."

"Yes, certainly; but let's put the colonel on his guard."

"What! Go and tell him what you think?"

"Certainly."

"Thanks, no, dear boy. I have only one nose, and I want it."

"What do you mean?" said Lennox sharply.

"Don't want it snapped off, as they say. The idea of the cheek—going and teaching our military grandmother—father, I mean, how to suck eggs!"

"You never will believe till the thing's rammed down your throat," said Lennox angrily. "Well, come along as we have no orders."

And without further discussion the two young men buckled on their belts and followed Captain Roby, who, while the colonel's other instructions were being carried out, marched his men down to where some of the Boer party, well-guarded by the outposts, could be dimly seen squatted about or seated on the fronts of two well-loaded wagons, whose teams were tying down contentedly chewing the cud. Four more Boers kept the sheep and oxen in the rear of the wagons from straying away in search of a place to graze, for there was a tempting odour of fresh green herbage saluting their nostrils, along with the pleasant moisture rising from the trickling water hurrying away towards the gully where it found its way into the river.

"What do you say to telling Roby to set a man to probe the sacks with a fixed bayonet?"

"It would be wise," whispered back Lennox.

"Tchah!" sneered Dickenson. "How could a fellow exist under one of those sacks of corn? Why, they must weigh on to a couple of hundredweight."

"I don't care; there's some dodge, Bob, I'm sure."

"Artful dodge, of course. Here, let's see if we know the fellows again."

"Very well; but be on your guard."

"Bother! Roby and his men will mind we are not hurt."

As he spoke Dickenson led the way close up to the roughly-clad Boers about the wagons, where, in spite of the darkness, the face of their leader was easy to make out as he sat pulling away at a big German pipe well-filled with a most atrociously bad tobacco, evidently of home growth and make.

"Hullo, old chap!" said Dickenson heartily; "so you've thought better of it?"

The Boer looked at him sharply, and, recognising the speaker, favoured him with a nod.

"Brought us some provender?" continued Dickenson; and he received another nod.

"What have you got?"

The Boer wagged his head sidewise towards the wagons and herds, and went on smoking.

"Well done; that's better than trying to pot us. But, I say, what about your commando fellows? What will they say when you go back?"

The Boer took his pipe out of his mouth and stuffed a finger into the bowl to thrust down the loose tobacco.

"Nothing," he said shortly. "Not going back."

"What!" cried Lennox, joining in after pretty well satisfying himself that there could be no danger in the unarmed Boers and their wagons.

"What's what?" said the Boer sourly.

"You're not going back?" cried Dickenson, staring.

"Well, we can't go back, of course. If we tried they'd shoot us, wouldn't they?"

The reply seemed to be unanswerable, and Dickenson merely uttered a grunt, just as Captain Roby and his men marched up to form an escort for the little convoy.

"Well, commandant?" he said.

The Boer grunted. "Not commandant," he said; "field-cornet."

"Very well, field-cornet; how did you manage to get here?"

"'Cross the veldt," growled the man.

"Didn't you see any of your friends?"

"No," grumbled the Boer. "If we had we shouldn't be here. Have you got the money for what we've got?"

"No."

"Stop, then. We're not going on."

"But you must now. The colonel will give you an order."

"Paper?" said the Boer sharply.

"Yes."

"Then we don't go."

"Yes, you do, my obstinate friend. It will be an order to an official here, and he'll pay you a fair price at once—in gold."

"My price?"

"Oh, that I can't say," replied the captain. "But I promise you will be fairly dealt with."

The Boer put his burning pipe in his pocket, snatched off his battered slouch felt hat, and gave his shaggy head an angry rub, looking round at his companions as if for support, and then staring back at the way they had come, to see lanterns gleaming and the glint of bayonets dimly here and there, plainly showing him that retreat was out of the question. Then, like some bear at bay, he uttered what sounded like a low growl, though in fact it was only a remark to the man nearest to him, a similar growl coming in reply.

"Come, sir, no nonsense," said the captain sternly. "You have come to sell, I suppose?"

"I shouldn't be here if I hadn't," growled the Boer.

"Then come along. You cannot go back now. I have told you that you will be well treated. Please to recollect that if our colonel chose he could commando everything you have brought for the use of our force; but he prefers to treat all of your people who bring supplies as straightforward traders. Now come along."

The Boer grunted, glanced back once more, and at last, as if he had thoroughly grasped his position, said a few words to his nearest companions and passed the word to trek, when, in answer to the crack of the huge whip, the bullocks sprang to their places along the trek-tows, the wagons creaked and groaned, and the little convoy was escorted into the market-place, where, as soon as he saw him, the field-cornet made for the colonel's side and began like one with a grievance.

But the amount of cash to be paid was soon settled, and the Boer's objections died away. The only difficulty then left was about the Boers' stay.

"If we go back they'll shoot us," he said to the colonel. "We've brought you the provisions you asked for, and when you've eaten all you'll want more, and we'll go and fetch everything; but you must have us here now."

"My good sir," said the colonel, to the intense amusement of the officers assembled, who enjoyed seeing their chief, as they termed him, in a corner, "I have enough mouths to feed here; you must go back to the peaceable among your own people."

"Peaceable? There are none peaceable now. Look here: do you want to send us back to fight against you?" cried the Boer cornet indignantly.

"Certainly not," said the colonel; "and I would not advise you to, for your own sake."

"Then what are we to do? We got away with these loads of mealies, but it will be known to-morrow. We can't go back, and it's all your doing."

"Well, I confess that it is hard upon you," said the colonel; "but, as I have told you, I am not going to take the responsibility of feeding more mouths."

"But we've just brought you plenty."

"Which will soon be gone," cried the colonel.

"Oh, that's nothing," said the Boer, with a grin full of cunning; "we know where to get plenty more."

The colonel turned and looked at the major, who returned the look with interest, for these last words opened up plenty of possibilities for disposing of a terrible difficulty in the matter of supplies.

"I don't much like the idea, major," he said in a low tone.

"No; couldn't trust the fellow," was the reply. "May be a ruse."

"At the same time it may be simple fact," continued the colonel. "Of course he would be well aware of the whereabouts of stores, for the enemy always seem to have abundance. But no; it would be too great a risk."

"All the same, though," said the major, who afterwards confessed to visions of steaks and roast mutton floating before his mind, "the fellow would be forced to be honest with us, for he would be holding his life by a very thin thread."

"Exactly," said the colonel eagerly. "We could let him know that at the slightest suggestion of treachery we should shoot him and his companions without mercy."

"Make him understand that," said the major; and while the Boer party stood waiting and watching by the two wagons, which had been drawn into the square, a little council of war was held by the senior officers, in which the pros and cons were discussed.

"It's a dangerous proceeding," said the colonel, in conclusion; "but one thing is certain—we cannot hold this place long without food, and it is all-important that it should be held, so we must risk it. Perhaps the fellows are honest after all. If they are not—"

"Yes," said the major, giving his chief a meaning look; "if they are not—"

And the unfinished sentence was mentally taken up by the other officers, both Lennox and Dickenson looking it at one another, so to speak.

Then the colonel turned to the Boer cornet.

"Look here, sir," he said; "I am a man of few words, but please understand that I mean exactly what I say. You and your companions can stay here upon the condition that you are under military rule. Your duty will be to forage for provisions when required. You will be well treated, and have the same rations as the men; but you will only leave the place when my permission is given, and I warn you that if any of you are guilty of an act that suggests you are playing the spy, it will mean a spy's fate. You know what I mean?"

"Oh, of course I do," growled the Boer. "Just as if it was likely! You don't seem to have a very good opinion of us burghers."

"You have not given us cause to think well of you," said the colonel sternly. "Now we understand each other. But of course you will have to work with the men, and now you had better help to unload the wagons."

The cornet nodded, and turned to his companions, who had been watching anxiously at a little distance; and as soon as they heard the colonel's verdict they seemed at ease.

A few minutes later the regimental butchers had taken charge of one of the oxen and a couple of sheep, whose fate was soon decided in the shambles, and the men gathered round to cheer at the unwonted sight of the carcasses hung up to cool.

Meanwhile an end of one of the warehouses had been set apart for the new supply of grain, and the Boers worked readily enough with a batch of the soldiers at unloading and storing, with lanterns hung from the rafters to gleam on the bayonets of the appointed guard, the sergeant and his men keeping a strict lookout, in which they were imitated by the younger officers, Lennox and Dickenson waiting, as the latter laughingly said, for the smuggled-in Boers, who of course did not appear.

Lennox made it his business to stand close to the tail-board of one of the wagons, in which another lantern was hung, and with the sergeant he gave every sack a heavy punch as it was dragged to the edge ready for the Boers to shoulder and walk off into the magazine.

Seeing this, the Boer chief, now all smiles and good humour, made for the next sack, untied the tarred string which was tied round the mouth, opened it, and called to the sergeant to stand out of the light.

"I want the officers to see what beautiful corn it is," he said.

The sergeant reached up into the wagon-tilt to lift down the lantern from where he had hung it to one of the tilt-bows

"No, no," cried the Boer; "you needn't do that, boss. They can see. There," he cried, thrusting in both hands and scooping as much as he could grasp, and letting the glistening yellow grains fall trickling back in a rivulet again and again. "See that? Hard as shot. Smell it. Fresh. This year's harvest. I know where there's enough to feed four or five thousand men."

"Yes, it looks good," said Dickenson, helping himself to a handful, and putting a grain into his mouth. "Sweet as a nut, Drew, but as hard as flint. Fine work for the teeth."

"Yes," said the Boer, grinning. "You English can't grind that up with your teeth. Wait till it's boiled, though, or pounded up and made into mealie. Ha! Make yours skins shine like the Kaffirs'."

"You don't want these sacks back, I suppose?" said the sergeant who was superintending. "Because if you do I'd better have them emptied."

"Oh no, oh no," said the Boer. "Keep it as it is; it will be cleaner."

"Why are some of the sacks tied up with white string and some with black?" said Lennox suddenly.

"Came from different farms," said the Boer, who overheard the remark. "Here, I'll open that one; it's smaller corn."

He signed to one of his fellows to set down the sack he was about to shoulder, and opening it, he went through the same performance again, shovelling up the yellow grain with his hands. "Not quite so good as the other sort," he said; "it's smaller, but it yields better in the fields."

"Humph! I don't see much difference in it," said Lennox, taking up a few grains and following his friend's example.

"No?" said the Boer, chuckling as he scooped up a double handful and tossed it up, to shine like gold in the light. "You are not a farmer, and have not grown thousands of sacks of it. I have."

He drew the mouth of the sack together again and tied it with its white string, when it too was borne off through the open doorway to follow its predecessors.

"That roof sound?" said the Boer, pointing up at the corrugated iron sheeting.

"Oh yes, that's all right," said the sergeant.

"Good," said the Boer. "Pity to let rain come through on grain like that. Make it swell and shoot."

The first wagon was emptied and the second begun, the Boers working splendidly till it was nearly emptied; and then the cornet turned to Captain Roby.

"Don't you want some left out," he said, "to use at once?"

"Yes," said the captain; "leave out six, and we'll hand them over to the bakers and cooks."

Three of the white-tied and three of the black-tied sacks were selected by the field-cornet, who told his men to shoulder them, and they were borne off at once to the iron-roofed hut which was used as a store. Then the wagons being emptied, they were drawn on one side, and the captain turned to consult Lennox about what hut was to be apportioned to the Boers for quarters.

"Why not make them take to the wagons?" said Dickenson.

"Not a bad notion," replied Captain Roby; and just at that moment, well buttoned up in their greatcoats—for the night was cold—the colonel and major came round.

"Where are you going to quarter these men, Roby?" said the former.

"Mr Dickenson here, sir, has just suggested that they shall keep to their wagons."

"Of course," said the colonel; "couldn't be better. They'll be well under observation, major—eh?"

"Yes," said that officer shortly; and it was announced to the field-cornet that his party were to make these their quarters.

This was received with a smile of satisfaction, the Boers dividing into two parties, each going to a wagon quite as a matter of course, and taking a bag from where it hung.

Ten minutes later they had dipped as much fresh water as they required from the barrels that swung beneath, and were seated, knife in hand, eating the provisions they had brought with them, while when the colonel and major came round again it was to find the lanterns out, the Dutchmen in their movable quarters, some smoking, others giving loud announcement that they were asleep, and close at hand and with all well under observation a couple of sentries marching up and down.

"I think they're honest," said the colonel as the two officers walked away.

"I'm beginning to think so too," was the reply.

A short time before, Lennox and his companion had also taken a farewell glance at the bearers of so valuable an adjunct to the military larder, and Dickenson had made a similar remark to that of his chief, but in a more easy-going conversational way.

"Those chaps mean to be square, Drew, old man," he said.

"Think so?"

"Yes; so do you. What else could they mean?"

"To round upon us."

"How? What could they do?"

"Get back to their people and speak out, after spying out the weakness of the land."

"Pooh! What good would that do, you suspicious old scribe? Their account's right enough; they proved it by the plunder they brought and their eagerness to sack as much tin as they could for it."

"I don't know," said Lennox; "the Boers are very slim."

"Mentally—granted; but certainly not bodily, old man. Bah! Pitch it over; you suspect every thing and everybody. I know you believe I nobbled those last cigarettes of yours."

"So you did."

"Didn't," said Dickenson, throwing himself down upon the board which formed his bed, for they had returned to their quarters. "You haven't a bit of faith in a fellow."

"Well, the cigarettes were on that shelf the night before last, and the next morning they were gone."

"In smoke," said Dickenson, with a yawn.

"There, what did I say?"

"You said I took them, and I didn't; but I've a shrewd suspicion that I know who did smoke them."

"Who was it?" said Lennox shortly.

"You."

"I declare I didn't."

"Declare away, old man. I believe you went to sleep hungry."

"Oh yes, you may believe that, and add 'very' to it. Well, what then?"

"You went to sleep, began dreaming, and got up and smoked the lot in your sleep."

"You're five feet ten of foolishness," said Lennox testily as he lay down in his greatcoat.

"And you're an inch in height less of suspicion," said Dickenson, and he added a yawn.

"Well, hang the cigarettes! I am tired. I say, I'm glad we have no posts to visit to-night."

"Hubble, bubble, burr," —said Dickenson indistinctly.

"Bah! what a fellow you are to sleep!" said Lennox peevishly. "I wanted to talk to you about—about—about—"

Nothing; for in another moment he too was asleep and dreaming that the Boers had bounded out of their wagons, overcome the sentries, seized their rifles, and then gone on from post to post till all were well armed. After that they had crept in single file up the kopje, mastered the men in charge of the captured gun, and then tied the two trek-tows together and carried it off to their friends, though he could not quite settle how it was they got the two spans of oxen up among the rocks ready when required.

Not that this mattered, for when he woke in the morning at the reveille and looked out the oxen were absent certainly, being grazing in the river grass in charge of a guard; but the Boers were present, lighting a fire and getting their morning coffee ready, the pots beginning to send out a fragrant steam.

Chapter Seven
Friends on the Forage

There were too many "alarums and excursions" at Groenfontein for much more thought to be bestowed upon the friendly Boers, as the party of former prisoners were termed, in the days which ensued. "Nobody can say but what they are quiet, well-behaved chaps," Bob Dickenson said, "for they do scarcely anything but sit and smoke that horrible nasty-smelling tobacco of theirs all day long. They like to take it easy. They're safe, and get their rations. They don't have to fight, and I don't believe nine-tenths of the others do; but they are spurred on—sjambokked on to it. Pah! what a language! Sjambok! why can't they call it a whip?"

"But I don't trust them, all the same," said Lennox. "I quite hate that smiling field-cornet, who's always shifting and turning the corn-sacks to give them plenty of air, as he says, to keep the grain from heating."

"Why, he hasn't been at it again, has he?" said Dickenson, laughing.

"At it again?" said Lennox. "What do you mean?"

"Did he shout to you to come and look at it?"

"Yes; only this morning, when the colonel was going by. Asked us to go in and look, and shovelled up the yellow corn in one of the sacks. He made the colonel handle some of it, and pointed out that he was holding back the corn tied up with the white strings because it lasted better."

"What did the old man say?"

"Told him that, as the stock was getting so low, he and his men must make a raid and get some more."

"And what did Blackbeard say?"

"Grumbled and shook his head, and talked about the danger of being shot by his old friends if they were caught."

"Dodge, of course, to raise his price."

"That's what the colonel said; and he told him that there must be no nonsense—he was fed here and protected so that he should keep up the supply, and that he must start the day after to-morrow at the latest to buy up more and bring it in. Then, in a surly, unwilling way, he consented to go."

"Buy up some more?" said Dickenson, with a chuckle. "Yes, he'll buy a lot. Commando it, he'll call it."

That very day, growing weary of trying to starve out the garrison, the enemy made an attack from the south, and after a furious cannonading began to fall back in disorder, drawing out the mounted men and two troops of lancers in pursuit.

As they fell back the disorder seemed to become a rout; but Colonel Lindley had grown, through a sharp lesson or two, pretty watchful and ready to meet manoeuvre with manoeuvre. He saw almost directly that the enemy were overdoing their retreat; and he acted accordingly. Suspecting that it was a feint, he held his mounted troops in hand, and then made them fall back upon the village.

It was none too soon, his men being just in time to fall on the flank of one of the other two commandos, whose leaders had only waited till the first had drawn the British force well out of their entrenchments before one attacked from the east and the other drove back the defenders of the ford and crossed at once, but only to bring themselves well under the attention of their own captured gun on the kopje, its shells playing havoc amongst them, while the men of the colonel's regiment stood fast in their entrenchments. The result was that in less than an hour the last two commandos retired in disorder and with heavy loss.

"There," said Lennox as the events of the day were being discussed after the mess dinner, "you see, Bob, it doesn't do to trust the Boers."

"Pooh!" replied the young officer. "There are Boers and Boers, and one must trust them when they supply the larder. Good-luck to our lot, I say, and may they bring in another big supply. If they don't, we shall have to begin on those quadrupedal locomotives of horn, gristle, and skin they call spans. Ugh! how I do loathe trek ox!"

"Talking of that," said Lennox, "the cornet and his men ought to have been off to-night."

"Why?" said Dickenson, staring.

"Why? Because the enemy will be in such a state of confusion after the check they had to-day."

"To be sure; let's go and tell them so."

"I was nearly suggesting it to the colonel, but he would only have given me one of his looks. You know."

"Yes; make you feel as if you're nine or ten, even if he hadn't sarcastically hinted that you had not been asked for your advice. But I say, Drew, old fellow, I think you're right, and if Blackbeard thinks it would be best he'll go to the old man like a shot. No bashfulness in him."

Without further debate the two young men made their way across the market-square to the wagon where the Boers' dim lantern was swinging, passing two sentries on the way.

"Not much need for a light," observed Dickenson; "one might smell one's way to their den. Hang it all! if tobacco's poison those fellows ought to have been killed long ago."

The cornet was seated on the wagon-box, with his legs inside, talking in a low tone to his fellows who shared the wagon with him, and so intent that he did not hear the young officers' approach till Lennox spoke, when he sprang forward into the wagon, and his companions began to climb out at the back.

"Why, what's the matter with you?" said Dickenson laughingly as he stepped up and looked in. "Think some of your friends were coming to fetch you?"

"You crept up so quietly," grumbled the Boer, recovering himself, and calling gently to his companions to return.

"Quietly? Of course. You didn't want us to send a trumpeter before us to say we were coming, did you?"

"H'm! No. What were you doing? Listening to find out whether we were going to run away?"

"Psh! No!" cried Dickenson. "Here, Mr Lennox wants to say something to you."

"What about?" said the man huskily.

"I have been thinking that, as you are going on a foraging expedition," said Lennox, "you ought to go at once. It's a very dark night, and the enemy is completely demoralised by to-day's fight."

"Demoralised?" said the Boer.

"Well, scared—beaten—all in disorder."

"Oh," said the Boer, nodding his head like an elephant. "But what difference does that make?"

"They would not be so likely to notice your wagons going through their lines."

"Oh?" said the Boer.

"We think it would be a good chance for you."

"Does your general say so?"

"No; our *colonel* does not know that we have come."

"So! Yes, I see," said the Boer softly.

"We think you ought to take advantage of their disorder and get through to-night."

"Hah! Yes."

"You have only to go and see what the colonel says."

"Why don't you go?" said the Boer suspiciously.

"Because we think it would be better for you to go."

"And fall into the Boers' hands and be shot?"

"Bother!" cried Dickenson. "Why, you are as suspicious as—as—well, as some one I know. Now, my good fellow, don't you know that we've eaten the sheep?"

"Yes, I know that," said the Boer.

"Finished the last side of the last ox?"

"Yes, I know that too," replied the Boer, nodding his head slowly and sagely.

"And come down to the last ten sacks of the Indian corn?"

"Mealies? Yes, I know that too."

"Well, in the name of all that's sensible, why should we want to get you taken by your own people?"

"To be sure; I see now," said the cornet. "Better for us to get the wagons full again, and drive in some more sheep and oxen."

"Of course."

"Well, I don't know," said the man thoughtfully. "They will be all on the lookout, thinking that you will attack them in the night, and twice as watchful. I don't know, though. There is no moon to-night, and it will be black darkness."

"It is already," said Dickenson.

"Ha! Yes," said the Boer quietly, and he puffed at his pipe, which, after dropping in his fright, he had picked up, refilled, and relit at the lantern door. "Yes, that is a very good way. I shall go and tell the colonel that we will go to-night. You will come with me?"

"No," said Lennox; "the colonel does not like his young officers to interfere. It would be better for you to go."

"Your chief is right," said the Boer firmly. "He thinks and acts for himself. I do the same. I do not let my men tell me what I should do." He spoke meaningly, as if he were giving a side-blow at some one or other of his companions. "I think much and long, and when I have thought what is best I tell them what to do, and they do it. Yes, I will go to the colonel now and speak to him. Wait here."

"No," said Dickenson quietly. "Go, and we will come back and hear what the colonel thinks."

The Boer nodded, thrust his pipe in the folds of the tilt, after tapping out the ashes, and went off, the two officers following him at a distance before stopping short, till they heard him challenged by a sentry, after which they struck off to their left to pass by the corn store, and being challenged again and again as they made a short tour round by the officers' quarters, going on the farther side of the corrugated iron huts and the principal ones, four close together, which were shared by the colonel, the doctor, and some of the senior officers. As they passed the back of the colonel's quarters there was the faint murmur of voices, one of which sounded peculiarly gruff, Dickenson said.

"Nonsense! You couldn't distinguish any difference at this distance," said Lennox. "Come along; we don't want to play eavesdroppers."

"Certainly not on a wet night when the rain is rattling down on those roofs and pouring off the eaves in cascades," replied Dickenson; "but I never felt so strong a desire to listen before. Wonder what the old man is saying to our smoky friend."

"Talking to the point, you may be sure, my lad," replied Lennox. "I say, though, he is safe to tell Lindley that I suggested it."

"Well, what of that?"

"Suppose the expedition turns out a failure, and they don't get back with the forage?"

"Ha! Bad for you, old man," said Dickenson, chuckling. "Why, we shall all be ready to eat you. Pity, too, for you're horribly skinny."

"Out upon you for a gluttonous-minded cannibal," said Lennox merrily. "Well, there, I did it for the best. But I say, Bob, we've come all this way round the back of the houses here, and haven't been challenged once."

"What of that? There are sentries all round the market-square."

"Yes; but out here. Surely a man or two ought to be placed somewhere about?"

"Oh, hang it all, old fellow! the boys are harassed to death with keeping post. You can't have all our detachment playing at sentry-go. Come along. There's no fear of the enemy making a night attack: that's the only good thing in fighting Boers."

"I don't see the goodness," said Lennox rather gloomily.

"Ah, would you!" cried Dickenson. "None of that! It's bad enough to work hard, sleep hard, and eat hard."

"I always thought you liked to eat hard," said Lennox.

"Dear me: a joke!" said Dickenson. "Very bad one, but it's better than going into the dumps. As I was about to say, we've got trouble enough without your playing at being in low spirits."

"Go on. What were you going to say?"

"I was going to remark that the best of fighting the Boers is, that they won't stir towards coming at us without they've got the daylight to help them to shoot. We ought to do more in the way of night surprises. I like the mystery and excitement of that sort of thing."

"I don't," said Lennox shortly. "It always seems to me cowardly and un-English to steal upon sleeping people, rifle and bayonet in hand."

"Well, 'pon my word, we've got into a nice line of conversation," said Dickenson. "Here we are, back in the market-square, brilliantly lighted by two of the dimmest lanterns that were ever made, and sentries galore to take care of us. Wonder whether Blackbeard has finished his confab with the chief?"

"Let's go and see," said Lennox, and he walked straight across, answering the sentry's challenge, and finding the Boer back in his former place, seated upon the wagon-box, and conversing in a low tone with the men within.

He did not start when Lennox spoke to him this time, but swung himself deliberately round to face his questioner.

"Well," said the latter, "what did the colonel say?"

"He said it was a good thing, and that we should take our wagons, inspan, and be passed through the lines to-night."

"Oh, come," said Dickenson; "that's good! One to us."

"Yes," grunted the Boer after puffing away; "he said it was very good, and that we were to go."

"Then, why in the name of common-sense don't you get ready and go instead of sitting here smoking and talking?"

"Oh, we know, the colonel and I," said the man quietly. "We talked it over with the major and captains and another, and we all said that the Boers would be looking sharp out in the first part of the night, expecting to be attacked; but as they were not they would settle down, and that it would be best to wait till half the night had passed, and go then. There would be three hours' darkness, and that would be plenty of time to get well past the Boer laagers before the sun rose; so we are resting till then."

"That's right enough," said Dickenson, "so good-night, and luck go with you! Bring twice as many sheep this time."

"Yes, I know, captain," said the Boer. "And wheat and rice and coffee and sugar."

"Here, come along, Drew, old fellow; he's making my mouth water so dreadfully that I can't bear it."

"You will come and see us go?" said the Boer.

"No, thank you," replied Dickenson. "I hope to be sleeping like a sweet, innocent child.—You'll see them off, Drew?"

"No. I expect that they will be well on their way by the time I am roused up to visit posts.—Good-night, cornet. I hope to see you back safe."

"Oh yes, we shall be quite safe," said the man; "but perhaps it will be three or four days before we get back. Good-night, captains."

"Lieutenants!" cried Dickenson, and he took his comrade's arm, and they marched away to their quarters, heartily tired out, and ready to drop asleep on the instant as weary people really can.

Chapter Eight
"Run, Sir, for your Life!"

"Eh? Yes. All right," cried Lennox, starting up, ready dressed as he was, to find himself half-blinded by the light of the lantern held close over him. "Time, sergeant?"

"Well, not quite, sir; but I want you to come and have a look at something."

"Something wrong?" cried the young officer, taking his sword and belt, which were handed to him by the non-com, and rapidly buckling up.

"Well, sir, I don't know about wrong; but it don't look right."

"What is it?"

"Stealing corn, I call it, sir; and it's being done in a horrid messy way, too."

"What! from the stores?"

"Yes, sir," said the man; "but come and look."

"Ready," said Lennox, taking out and examining his revolver, and then thrusting it back into its holster.

The next minute, after a glance at Dickenson, who was sleeping peacefully enough, Lennox was following the sergeant, whose dim lantern shed a curious-looking halo in the black darkness. Then as they passed a sentry another idea flashed across the young officer's confused brain, brought forth by the sight of the guard, for on looking beyond the man there was no sign of the Boers' lantern hanging from the front bow of their wagon-tilts.

"What about the Boers?" he said sharply.

"Been gone about an hour, sir. I suppose it was all right? Captain Roby saw them start."

"Oh yes, it is quite right," said Lennox. "Now then, what about this corn? Some of the Kaffirs been at it?"

"What do you think, sir?" said the man, holding down the lantern to shed its light upon the ground, as they reached the open door of the store and showed a good sprinkling of the bright yellow grains scattered about to glisten in the pale light.

"Think? Well, it's plain enough," said Lennox. "Thieves have been here."

"Yes, sir. The open door took my notice at once. That chap ought to have seen it; but he didn't, or he'd have given the alarm."

"Go on," said Lennox, and he followed the man right into the barn-like building, to stop short in front of the first of the half-dozen or so of sacks at the end, this having been thrown down and cut right open, so that a quantity of the maize had gushed out and was running like fine shingle on to the floor.

"Kaffirs' work," said Lennox sharply.

"Well, sir, if I may give you my opinion I should say it was those Boers," said the sergeant gruffly.

"What!"

"Man must eat, sir, and it strikes me that they, in their easy-going way, thought it was as much theirs as ours, and helped theirselves to enough to last them till they could get more."

"Well, whoever has done it,"—began Lennox.

Then he stopped short, and took a step forward. "Here, sergeant," he cried, "hold the light higher."

This was done, and then the pair bent down quickly over the sacks, each uttering an angry ejaculation.

"Why, it's sheer mischief, sergeant," cried Lennox. "Done with a sharp knife evidently."

For the light now revealed something which the darkness had hitherto hidden from their notice. Another sack had been ripped up, apparently with a sharp knife, from top nearly to bottom. Another was in the same condition, and a little further investigation showed that every one had been cut, so that, on the farther side where all had been dark, there was a slope of the yellow grain which had flowed out, leaving the sacks one-third empty.

"Well, this is a rum go, sir," said the sergeant, scratching his head with his unoccupied hand. "They must have got a couple of sackfuls away."

"But why slit them up, when they could have shouldered a couple and carried them off?"

"Can't say, sir," said the sergeant.

Lennox turned back to the doorway, and his companion followed with the light.

"Hold it lower," said Lennox, and the man obeyed, showing the grain they had first noticed lying scattered about, while a little examination further showed the direction in which those who had carried it off had gone, leaving sign, as a tracker would call it, in the shape of a few grains which had fallen from the loads they carried.

"Follow 'em up, sir?" said the sergeant. "It would be easy enough if it keeps like this."

"Yes," said Lennox. "We should know then if it was the Boers."

The man stepped forward with the door of the lantern opened and the light held close to the ground, making the bright yellow grains stand out clearly enough as he went on, though at the end of a minute instead of being in little clusters they diminished to one here and another there, all, however, running in one direction for some fifty yards; and then the sergeant stopped.

"Seems rum, sir," he said.

"You mean that the Boers would not have been going in this direction?"

"That's so, sir. I'm beginning to think that it couldn't have been them."

"I'm glad of it," said Lennox, "for I want to feel that we can trust them. Who could it have been, then?"

"Some of the friendly natives, sir, I hope," replied the sergeant.

"But they wouldn't have come this way, sergeant. It looks more as if some of our own people had been at the corn."

"That's just what I was thinking, sir," replied the sergeant, "only I didn't want to say it."

"But that's impossible, sergeant. A man might have slit up the sacks out of spite, or from sheer mischief, but he wouldn't have carried off any."

"No, sir. He wouldn't, would he? Well, all I can say is that it's rather queer."

"Well, go on," said Lennox; and the sergeant went on, tracing the grain right out to the back of the corrugated iron huts that formed one side of the square, and then past the angle and along the next side, now losing the traces, but soon picking them up again, the hard, dry earth completely refusing to give any trace of the bearer's feet.

Then the next angle of the square was reached. turned, and the sergeant still passed on with the light.

"Gets thicker here," he whispered, and directly after he stopped and pointed down at two or three handfuls of the bright grain.

"Seem to have set down a basket here, sir," he said softly. "Shall I go on?"

"Go on? Yes, and trace the robbery home. The scoundrel who has tampered with the stores deserves the severest punishment."

The sergeant proceeded, but more slowly now, for he had only a grain here and a grain there to act as his guide; but these still pointed out the direction taken by the marauders, till the trackers came suddenly upon a good-sized patch.

"Tell you what, sir," whispered the sergeant; "there's only one chap in it, and he's got such a swag he's obliged to keep stopping to rest."

"Yes, that seems to be the case, sergeant," said Lennox, looking carefully about. "Let's see; we must be near the colonel's quarters," he whispered.

"That's right, sir. About twenty yards over yonder; and the fellows on sentry ought to have seen the light and challenged us by now."

"No," said Lennox; "the houses completely shut us off. Go on."

The light was held low down again and swung here and there in the direction that the marauder ought to have taken; but there was not a grain to be seen to indicate the track, and the sergeant had to hark back again and again without being able to find it.

"Rum thing, sir," he whispered. "He must have stopped here and found that his basket was leaking, and patched it up, for I can't see another grain anywhere."

"Neither can I, sergeant; but try again. Take a longer circle."

"Right, sir; but it does seem queer that he should have stopped to make all fast just behind the colonel's quarters."

"It seems to indicate that it was the work of some stranger; otherwise he would not have halted here."

"P'r'aps so, sir; but if he was a stranger how did he know where the corn store was?"

"Can't say, sergeant. Try away."

"Right, sir," said the man, proceeding slowly step by step, with the open lantern very close to the ground, and making a regular circle, in the hope of cutting the way at last by which the supposed thief had gone off after his last rest.

But minute succeeded minute without success, and Lennox was about to urge his companion onward in another direction, when the sergeant uttered a sharp ejaculation as if of alarm, jerking up the lantern as he started back, and in the same movement blew out the light and shut the lantern door with a loud snap.

Lennox, who was a couple of yards behind, sprang forward, unfastening the cover of his pistol-holster and catching his companion by the arm, while all around now was intensely dark.

"Enemy coming?" he whispered.

"Dunno yet, sir," panted the sergeant, whose voice sounded broken and strange. "Something awfully wrong, sir."

"Speak out, man! What do you mean?" whispered Lennox, whose heart now began to beat heavily.

"I've come upon something down here, sir."

"Ah! The thief—asleep?"

"No, sir," said the sergeant, and his fingers were heard fumbling with the fastening of the lantern.

"What are you doing, man? Why don't you speak?"

"Making sure the light's quite out, sir. Can't speak for a moment—feel choking."

"Then you hear the enemy approaching?"

"No, sir.—Ha! It's quite out! Now, sir, just you go down on one knee and feel."

"I don't understand you, sergeant," whispered Lennox; but all the same he bent down on one knee and felt about with his right hand, fully expecting to touch a heap of the stolen grain.

"No corn," he said at the end of a few seconds; "but what's this—sand?"

"Take a pinch up, and taste it, sir. I hope it is."

"Taste it?" said Lennox half-angrily.

"Yes, sir," said the sergeant out of the darkness, and the faint rustle he made and then a peculiar sound from his lips indicated that he was setting the example.

The young officer hesitated no longer, but gathering up a pinch of the dry sand from the ground, he just held it to the tip of his tongue.

"Why, sergeant," he whispered excitedly, "it's powder!"

"That's right, sir," replied the man. "Gunpowder—a train; a heavy train running right and left."

"Nonsense!"

"Truth, sir. I had the lantern close to it, and might have fired it if I'd dropped the lantern, as I nearly did."

"But what does it mean? Here, sergeant, that's what we have to see."

"Yes, sir," replied the sergeant in a hoarse whisper, "and don't you grasp it? One way it goes off towards the veldt—"

"And the other way towards the colonel's quarters," whispered Lennox. "Here, sergeant, there must be some desperate plot—a mine, perhaps, close up to that hut. Quick! Follow me."

The sergeant did not need the order, for he was already moving in the direction of the cluster of huts, but going upon his hands and knees, leaving the lantern behind and feeling his way, guiding himself by his fingers so as to keep in touch with the coarse, sand-like powder, which went on in an easily followed line towards the back of the colonel's hut.

It seemed long, but it was only a matter of a few seconds before they were both close up, feeling in the darkness for some trace of that which imagination had already supplied; and there it was in the darkness.

"Here's a bag, sergeant," whispered Lennox.

"A bag, sir? Here's five or six, and one emptied out, and—Run, sir, for your life! Look at that!"

For there was a flash of light from somewhere behind them, and as, with a bag of powder which he had caught up in his hand, Lennox turned round, he could see what appeared to be a fiery serpent speeding at a rapid rate towards where, half-paralysed, he stood.

Chapter Nine
Guy Fawkes Work

The light of the fired train had hardly flashed before the first sentry who saw it, fired, to be followed by one after another, till the bugles rang out, first one and then another, whose notes were still ringing when there was a muffled roar, then another, and another, till six had shaken the earth and a series of peculiar metallic clashes deafened all around.

But before the first sentry had raised his piece to his shoulder and drawn, the sergeant, seen in the brilliant light of the running train, seemed to have gone frantically mad.

"Chuck, sir, chuck!" he yelled, though Lennox needed no telling. The light which suddenly shone on the back of the cluster of sheet-iron huts had shown him what was necessary, and after raising the bag he had picked up with both hands high above his head, and hurling it as far as he could, he dashed at the others he could see packed close up against the colonel's hut, so that between him and the sergeant five had been torn from the ground and hurled in different directions outward from the buildings, leaving only the contents of a sixth and seventh bag which had been emptied in a heap connected with the long train before the others had been laid upon it in a little pile.

They were none too soon, for the last bag had hardly been hurled away with all the strength that the young officer could command, and while the sergeant was yelling to him to run, before the hissing fiery serpent was close upon them.

Fortunately the sergeant's crawling and the following trampling of the excited pair had broken up and crushed in the regularly laid train, scattering the powder in all directions, so that the rush of the hissing fire came momentarily to an end and gave place to a sputtering and sparkling here and there, giving Lennox and the sergeant time to rush a few yards away in headlong flight. There was a terrific scorching blast, and a tremendous push sent them staggering onward in a series of bounds before they fell headlong upon their faces; while at intervals explosion after explosion followed the fiery blast, the burning fragments setting off three of the other bags, fortunately away from where the pair had fallen.

The sergeant was the first to recover himself, and raising his face a little from the ground, he shouted, "Don't move, sir! Don't move! There's two or three more to go off yet."

Lennox said something, he did not know what, for he was half-stunned, the shock having had a peculiar bewildering effect. But at the second warning from his companion he began to grasp what it meant, and lay still without speaking; but he raised his head a little, to see that beneath the great canopy of foul-smelling smoke that overhung them the earth was covered with little sputtering dots of fire, either of which, if it came in contact, was sufficient to explode any powder that might remain.

But two bags had escaped, the explosive blast rising upward; and the danger being apparently at an end, the principal actors in the catastrophe roused to find officers hurrying to meet them, and men coming forward armed with pails of water to dash and scatter here and there till every spark was extinct and the remaining powder had been thoroughly drenched.

"Much hurt, old chap?" cried Dickenson, who was the first to reach his friend, and he supplemented his question by eagerly feeling Lennox all over.

"No! No: I think not," said Lennox, "except my head, and that feels hot and scorched. Can you see anything wrong?"

"Not yet; it's so dark. Here, let's take you to the doctor."

"No, no!" cried Lennox. "Not so bad as that. But tell me—what about the officers sleeping in those huts?"

"All right, I believe; but the backs of the houses are blown in, and the fellows at home were blown right out of their beds."

"No one hurt?"

"Oh yes; some of them are a bit hurt, but only bruised. But you? Oh, hang it all! somebody bring a light. Hi, there, a lantern!"

"No, no!" roared the colonel out of the darkness. "Are you mad? Who's that asking for a light?"

"Mr Dickenson, sir."

"Bah! Keep every light away. There may be another explosion."

The colonel gave a few sharp orders respecting being on the alert for an expected attack to follow this attempt—one that he felt to have been arranged to throw the little camp into confusion; and with all lights out, and a wide berth given to the neighbourhood of the headquarters, the troops stood ready to receive the on-coming Boers with fixed bayonets.

But an hour passed away, and the doubled outposts and those sent out to scout had nothing to report, while all remained dark and silent in the neighbourhood of the damaged huts.

Meanwhile Dickenson had hurried Lennox and the sergeant off to the doctor's quarters, where they were examined by that gentleman and his aids.

"Well, upon my word, you ought to congratulate yourself, Lennox."

"I do, sir," was the reply, made calmly enough.

"And you too, sergeant."

"Yes, sir," said the man stolidly.

"Why, my good fellow, you ought to have been blown all to pieces."

"Ought I, sir?"

"Of course you ought. It's a wonderful escape."

"Oh, I don't know, sir. What about my back hair, sir?"

"Singed off, what there was of it; and yours too, Lennox. Smart much?"

"Oh yes, horribly," said the latter.

"Oh, well, that will soon pass off. Threw yourselves down on your faces—eh?"

"No. We were knocked down."

"Good thing too," said the doctor. "Saved your eyes, and the hair about them. A wonderful escape, upon my word. Yes: you ought to have been blown to atoms.—Eh? What's that, sergeant?"

"I say we should have been, sir, if we hadn't scattered the powder-bags."

"Scattered the powder-bags?" said a voice from the door, and the colonel stepped into the circle of light spread by the doctor's lamp. "Tell me what you know about this explosion, Lennox. How came you to be there instead of visiting your posts?"

Lennox briefly explained, and the colonel stood frowning.

"I don't see all this very clearly," said the colonel. "Somebody stealing the corn, and you were tracing the thieves and came upon a train laid up to my quarters. There was a sentry there; what was he about?"

"No, sir: no sentry there," said Lennox.

"Nonsense! I gave orders for a man to be posted there, and it was done."

"I beg pardon, sir," said Lennox. "No one was there to challenge us."

"Indeed!" said the colonel.—"Who's that? Oh, Mr Dickenson, examine the place as soon as it is light. There was a man there, for I saw him myself. But now then, I cannot understand how the enemy can have stolen through the lines and carried the powder where it was found. What do you say, Lennox?"

"Nothing, sir. My head is so confused that I can hardly recall how it all happened."

"Of course. Well, you, sergeant. You said that you scattered the powder-bags."

"Yes, sir. Threw 'em about as far as we could."

"We?"

"Yes, sir. Mr Lennox and me."

"After the train was fired?"

"Oh yes, sir; it was coming on at a great rate."

"Humph! Then you did a very brave action."

"Oh no, sir," said the sergeant. "We were obliged to. Why, we should, as Dr Emden says, sir, have been blown all to bits if we hadn't. We were obliged to do something sharp."

"Yes," said the colonel dryly. "It was sharp work, sergeant, and you saved my life and the major's."

"Did we, sir? Very glad of it, sir."

"But about how the powder was conveyed there. I can see nothing for it but treachery within the camp.—Of course!—Those Boers!"

"But they had gone, sir," said Lennox.

"Yes, and left us a memento of their visit."

"Beg pardon, sir," said Dickenson.

"Yes? Go on, Mr Dickenson."

"I think I can see through the mystery."

"Then you have better eyes than I have," said the colonel. "Proceed."

"It was one of their tricks, sir," said Dickenson. "They came into camp with their wagons and waited their chance."

"But the powder, man, the powder?" said the colonel impatiently.

"So many bags of it, sir, each inside one of the sacks of maize; and the night they were to go away they slit their sacks open, took out the powder, and planted it at the back of your quarters, sir."

"That will do, Mr Dickenson," said the colonel dryly.

"Beg pardon, sir. I thought it a very likely explanation of the business."

"Too likely, Mr Dickenson," said the colonel, "for it is undoubtedly the right one. The misfortune is that the treacherous scoundrels have got away. Bah! They're worse than savages! Well, let us all be thankful for our escape. I thought I had taken every precaution I could, but one never knows. Then you will not have to go into hospital, Lennox?"

"Oh no, sir; I shall be all right in a few hours."

"And you, Colour-Sergeant James?"

"Beg pardon, sir?" said the blackened non-com, staring.

"I say, and you, *Colour-Sergeant* James," said the colonel, laying emphasis on the word colour. "You feel that you need not go into the infirmary?"

"Feel, sir?" cried the sergeant, drawing himself up as stiff as his rifle. "Beg pardon, sir, but that's quite cured me. I never felt so well in my life."

"I am glad of it, my man," said the colonel quietly.—"Yes?" he added as one of the junior officers came to the door.

"Two men come in from the kopje, sir: a message from the sergeant with the gun. There's a strong body of the enemy close up between us and the lines on the slope. The men had to go round a long way before they could get through."

"I'll come," said the colonel, and he hurried out to make some fresh arrangements, the effect of which was that as soon as it was light the action of the Boers was precipitated by a counter-attack, and after an hour's firing they were driven out of their cover, to run streaming across the veldt, their flight hastened by a few well-planted shells from the big gun and the rapid fire of the Maxim which swept the plain.

Chapter Ten
Tracking the Wagons

Lennox was well enough, when the sun was up, to accompany Dickenson to the examination of the scene of the explosion, but not in time to witness the discovery of two bags of unexploded powder, from where they had been hurled by Colour-Sergeant James, who was on the ground before it was light, as he explained to the two young officers.

"You were early, sergeant," said Lennox. "Yes, sir; to tell the truth, I was. You see, I couldn't sleep a wink."

"In so much pain?"

"Well, the back of my head did smart pretty tidy, I must say, sir, and I couldn't lay flat on my back as I generally do; but it wasn't that, sir—it was the thought of the step up. Just think of it, sir! Only been full sergeant two years, and a step up all at once like that."

"Well, you deserved it," said Lennox quietly. "Deserved it, sir? Well, what about you?"

"Oh, I dare say I shall get my promotion when I've earned it," said Lennox. "Now then, let's look round. You found two bags of the powder, then?"

"Yes, sir," said the man, pointing; "one down in that pit where they dug the soil for filling the biscuit-tins and baskets, and the other yonder behind that wall. The blast must have blown right over them."

"But how about the sentry the colonel said he saw here?" asked Lennox.

The man's countenance changed, a fierce frown distorting it.

"He was quite right, sir," said the sergeant, nodding his head. "They found him this morning at his post."

"Dead?" said Lennox in a hoarse whisper.

"Yes, sir—dead. Horrid! Some one must have crept up behind him with a blanket and thrown it over him while some one else used an iron bar. He couldn't have spoken a word after the first blow."

"But why do you say that?" said Dickenson. "I understand the sentry was found dead, but—"

"There was the blanket and the iron bar, sir—the one over him and the other at his side. I don't call that fair fighting, sir; do you?"

The answer consisted of a sharp drawing in of the breath; and the officers turned away to examine the mischief done by the explosion, the backs of two houses having been blown right in.

"Well," said Dickenson dryly, "it's awkward, because they've got to be made up again; but one can't say they're spoiled."

"Not spoiled?" said Lennox, looking wonderingly at the speaker.

"No; they were so horribly straight and blank and square before. They do look a little more picturesque now. Oh, he was a wicked wretch who invented corrugated iron!"

"Nonsense!" said Lennox.

"But it does keep the wet out well, sir," put in the sergeant. "I don't know what we should have done sometimes without it."

Further conversation was stopped by the coming towards camp of a couple of Boers bearing a white flag; but they were only allowed to approach within the first line of defence.

"Want to have a look at the mischief they have done," said Dickenson bitterly, "and they will not have a chance. My word, what they don't deserve!"

The permission they had come to ask was given, and they were turned back at once, to signal for their ambulance-wagons to approach, these being busy for quite an hour picking up the dead and wounded; while the murdered sentry was the only loss suffered by the defenders of Groenfontein and the kopje.

As soon as suspicion was firmly fixed upon the party of non-combatant Boers who had departed upon their mission to obtain fresh supplies, one of the first orders issued by the colonel was for a patrol of mounted men to go in pursuit and, if possible, bring them back.

"There is not much chance of overtaking them," he said to the officers present; "but with a couple of teams of slow-going oxen they cannot make their own pace. Then this is the last time I'll trust a Boer."

"The worst of it is," said the major, "that we have let them carry off those two spans of bullocks. Tut, tut, tut! Forty of them; tough as leather, of course, but toothsome when you have nothing else."

"Toothsome!" said Captain Roby, laughing. "A capital term, for the poor teeth of those who tried to eat them would have to work pretty hard—eh,—Dickenson?"

"Better than nothing," said the young lieutenant—a decision with which all agreed.

That day passed off without further attack from the enemy, who seemed to have drawn off to a distance; and as night fell the colonel became very anxious about the patrol, which had not returned. Dickenson, who had the credit of being the longest-sighted man in the regiment, had spent the day on the highest point of the kopje, armed with a powerful telescope, and from his point of vantage, where he could command the country in that wonderfully clear atmosphere for miles round, had swept every bit of plain, and searched bush and pile of granite again and again, till the darkness of evening began to fill up the bush like a flood of something fluid. When he could do no more he left the crew of the gun and began to descend by what he considered the nearest way to headquarters, and soon found it the longest, for he had delayed his return too long.

"Hang it all!" he muttered. "What a pile of shin-breaking rocks it is! I've a jolly good mind to go back and take the regular path; seems so stupid, though, now."

In this spirit he persevered, wandering in and out among the piled-up blocks, all of which seemed in the darkness to be exactly alike, often making him think that he was going over the same ground again and again. But he was still descending, for when he climbed up the next suitable place to try and get a view of the lights of the camp he could see them beneath him and certainly nearer than when he started.

"Shall manage it somehow," he muttered; "but, hang it! how hungry I am! There, I'll have a pipe."

He fumbled in his pocket as he stood in the lee of a block of granite, sheltered from the cold night wind, found the pipe, and raised it to his lips to blow through the stem, but stopped short with every sense on the alert, for from below to his left he heard a light chirp such as might have been given by a bird, but which he argued certainly was not, for he knew of no bird likely to utter such a note at that time of the evening, when the flood of darkness had risen and risen till it had filled up everything high above the highest kopje that dotted the plain.

"Couldn't be a signal, could it?" he said to himself. "Yes," he said directly after, for the chirp was answered from lower down.

Dickenson softly swung the case of his telescope round to his back out of the way, and took out his revolver without making a sound, listening intently the while, and at the end of a long minute he made out a low whispering close at hand; but he could not place it exactly, for the sounds seemed to be reflected back from the face of the rock directly in front of him.

"I wish it wasn't so dark," he said, and screwing up his lips, he tried to imitate the chirp, and so successfully that it was answered.

"Must be one of our sentries," he thought, and he hesitated as to his next proceeding.

"Don't want to challenge and raise a false alarm," he said; "but last night's work makes one so suspicious. I'll let them challenge me."

He turned to descend softly from where he had climbed to, and his foot slipped on the weather-worn stone, so that he made a loud scraping sound in saving himself from a fall; but not so loud that he was unable to hear the scuffling of feet close at hand, followed directly after by dead silence.

His finger was on the trigger of his pistol, and he was within an ace of firing in the direction of the noise, but refrained, and contented himself with walking as sharply as he could towards it with outstretched hands, for overhanging rocks made the place he was in darker than ever, and he was reduced to feeling his way. Then stopping short with a sense of danger being close at hand, he gave the customary challenge, to have it answered from behind him; and the next minute he was face to face with a sentry.

"I thought I heard something, sir," said the man. "Then it was you?"

"No, no," said Dickenson; "I heard it too—a low chirp like a bird."

"No, no, sir; not that—a sound as if some one slipped."

"Yes, that was I," said Dickenson; "but there was a chirp. Did you hear that?"

"Oh yes, I heard that, sir; and another one answered it."

"And then there was talking."

"Oh no, sir, I heard no talking. Sound like a bird; but I think it's a little guinea-piggy sort of thing. I believe they live in holes like rats, and come out and call to one another in the dark."

"Well, perhaps it may be; but keep a sharp lookout."

"I'll keep my ears well open, sir," said the man; "there's no seeing anything in a night like this."

The sentry was able to put his visitor in the right direction, and Dickenson went on, forgetting the incident and wondering how Lennox was getting on; then about what the colonel would say to his ill-success; and lastly, the needs of his being filled up all his thoughts, making him wonder what he should get from the mess in order to satisfy the ravenous hunger that troubled him after his long abstinence.

He reached the square at last, but not without being challenged three times over. Then making his way to the colonel's patched-up quarters, he was just in time to meet the patrol coming into the opening, their leader going straight to the mess-room, where the officers were gathered.

"Any luck?" said Dickenson. "I was on the lookout for you up yonder till I couldn't see."

"Yes, and no," said the officer. "Come on and you'll hear."

Dickenson followed his companion into the long, dreary-looking, ill-lighted barn, where they were both warmly welcomed; and the officer announced that he had gone as near the Boers' laagers as he could, drawing fire each time; but he had not been able to either overtake or trace the plotters till close upon evening, when on the return. They had found a sign, but there was so much crossing and recrossing that the best of scouts could have made nothing of it; and he concluded that the party he sought had got well away, when all at once they came upon the undoubted spoor of the two teams of oxen, followed it into the bush, and just at dusk came upon the two wagons in a bush-like patch among the trees.

"And what had the men to say for themselves?" said the colonel eagerly.

"The men had gone, sir," said the officer.

"Ah! Bolted at the sight of you?"

"Oh no, sir; they were gone."

"What! and left the wagons?"

"Yes, sir; they had left the wagons, but they had carried off the teams."

Chapter Eleven
The Colonel's Plans

The effects of the night alarm were dying out, for there was plenty to take the attention of the defenders of Groenfontein every day—days full of expectancy—for a Boer attack might take place at any moment, while every now and then some one at an outpost had a narrow escape; and two men were hit by long-range bullets, fired perhaps a mile away by some prowling Boer who elevated his piece and fired on chance at the buildings in the village.

"Sniping," the men termed it, and all efforts to suppress this cowardly way of carrying on the war were vain, for in most cases there was no chance of making out from what scrap of cover the shots had been despatched; while it became evident that, from sheer malignity, the undisciplined members of the enemy's force would crawl in the darkness to some clump of rocks, or into some ditch-like donga, or behind one of the many ant-hills, and lie there invisible, firing as he saw a chance, and only leaving it when the darkness came on again.

The rations issued grew poorer; but the men only laughed and chaffed, ridiculing one another and finding nicknames for them.

Colour-Sergeant James, the sturdy non-commissioned officer, the back of whose head still showed the blasting effects of the explosion which he had shared with Lennox, was known as the "Fat Boy," on account of the general shrinking that had gone on in his person till he seemed to be all bone and sinew, covered with a very brown skin; another man came to be known as the "Greyhound;" while Captain Roby's favourite corporal, an unpleasant-looking fellow, much disliked by Lennox and Dickenson for his smooth, servile ways, had grown so hollow-cheeked that he was always spoken of as the "Lantern," after being so dubbed by the joker of his company.

In fact, the men generally had been brought down to attenuation by the scarcity of their food; while their khaki uniforms were not uniform in the least, the men for the most part looking, as Bob Dickenson put it, "like scarecrows in their Sunday clothes."

"The lads are getting terribly thin, sergeant," said Lennox one day, after the men had been dismissed from parade.

"Oh, I don't know, sir," said the sergeant; "a bit fine, sir, but in magnificent condition. Look at the colour of them—regular good warm tan."

"But the Boers haven't tanned them, all the same, sergeant," put in Dickenson, who was listening.

"No, sir, and never will," said the sergeant proudly. "As to their being thin, that's nothing; they're as healthy as can be. A soldier don't want to be carrying a lot of unnecessary meat about with him; and as to fat, it only makes 'em short-winded. See how they can go at the double now, and come up smiling. They're all right, sir, and we can feed 'em up again fast enough when the work's done. Beg pardon, sir: any likelihood of a reinforcement soon?"

"You know just as much as I do, sergeant," said Lennox. "Our orders are to hold this place, and we've got to hold it. Some day I suppose the general will send and fetch us out; till then we shall have to do our best."

"Yes, sir, that's right; but I do wish the enemy would give us a real good chance of showing them what our lads are made of."

But the Boers had had too many of what Dickenson called "smacks in the face" during their open attacks, and seemed disposed now to give starvation a chance of doing the work for them. At least, that was the young officer's openly expressed opinion.

"But they're making a great mistake, Drew, my lad," he said one evening as he and his friend sat chatting together. "An Englishman takes a great deal of starving before he'll give in. They're only making the boys savage, and they'll reap the consequences one day. My word, though, what a blessing a good spring of water is!"

As he spoke he picked up the tin can standing upon the end of a flour-barrel that formed their table, had a good hearty drink, set it down again, and replaced his pipe between his lips. "I used to think that bitter beer was the only thing a man could drink with his pipe; but *tlat*! how good and fresh and cool this water is, and how the Boers must wish they had the run of it!"

"It helps us to set them at defiance," said Lennox. "They might well call the place 'Green Fountain.' It might be made a lovely spot if it wasn't for the Boer."

"Yes, I suppose anything would grow here in the heat and moisture. I suppose the spring comes gurgling up somewhere in the middle of the kopje."

"It must," said Lennox, "and then makes its way amongst the stones to spread out below there and flow on to the river."

"Seems rum, though," said Dickenson. "I never did understand why water should shoot up here at the highest part of a flat country. It ought to be found low down in the holes. What makes it shoot up?"

"The weight and pressure of the country round, I suppose," said Lennox. "Hullo! What does that mean?"

"Business," cried Dickenson, as both the young men sprang to their feet and seized belts and weapons. For the report of a rifle was followed by others, coming apparently from the direction of the kopje near to where the stream came rushing out between two rugged natural walls of piled-up stone. Every one was on the alert directly, fully in the expectation that the enemy we're about to act in non-accordance with their regular custom and make an attack in the dark.

But the firing ceased almost as suddenly as it had begun; and after a time the alarm was traced back to a sentry who had been on duty at the lower part of the west side of the kopje, near by where the water gushed up at the foot of a huge mass of granite, where the most precipitous part stretched upward half-way to the summit.

Captain Roby's company held the kopje that night, and consequently both of the young officers were present at the tracing of the cause of the alarm, when it seemed to have been proved that it was only false.

The sentry who fired was examined by Captain Roby, and was certain that he had not given any alarm without cause, for he said he had heard steps as of more than one person approaching him as if going to the water.

"And you challenged?" asked the captain.

"Yes, sir; and then all was quite quiet for a few moments, but I heard the sounds again as if they were coming closer to me, and I fired, and there was a rush of feet."

"A party of baboons going down to drink," said the captain contemptuously.

"There have been no baboons seen since we occupied the kopje," said Lennox.

"Perhaps not; but when they were driven off they must have gone somewhere, and what more likely than that they should come back to the spot where they could get water?—Come, my man, you felt frightened, didn't you?"

"Yes, sir," said the sentry; "I was a bit scared."

"And you think now that all you heard was a party of those big dog-like monkeys—eh?"

"No, sir; it was men, and only three or four."

"Ha! How do you know?"

"Because the baboons go on all fours, sir; and I could make out one man standing up as he ran off along the rocky bit of path."

"What! You saw one man?"

"Yes, sir."

"But it was dark?"

"I could see the figure of a man for a moment just against the sky, sir."

"But mightn't that have been one of the apes reared up for the time?"

"Oh no, sir," said the sentry. "I shouldn't mistake a monkey for a man; and besides, they don't wear boots."

"Ah! and do you say these people who came near you wore boots?"

"Well, it sounded like it, sir, for when I fired I could hear the leather squeak."

"Humph!" grunted Captain Roby; and Dickenson, who was full now of his adventure in what seemed to have been near the same place, spoke out:

"I think there's something in what he says:" and he related his own experience. "At the time, I was so occupied in getting back for something to eat that I forgot all about the matter after dinner. But now this has occurred I begin to feel that the chirping sounds I heard really were signals, and that I did hear voices talking together afterwards."

"Then it must have been Kaffirs sneaking there for water after it was dark."

"But the footsteps?" said Lennox.

"Well, Kaffirs have feet."

"But not boots," said Lennox quietly.

"I beg your pardon," said the captain warmly; "I could pick out a dozen of the black hangers-on who have boots which they have obtained from the men."

Just then an orderly arrived from the colonel to know what Captain Roby had made out respecting the alarm; and upon a full report being given, the colonel sent orders for Captain Roby to march his company to the foot of the kopje, surround it, and thoroughly search it from top to bottom.

This search was commenced as soon as it was light, the men having been led to the foot and stationed before day broke; and the arduous task seemed to be thoroughly enjoyed by the men, who, as they slowly ascended the rough cone, naturally closed in so that the prospect of missing any one hiding among the cracks and chasms grew less and less. To the soldiers it was like a game of hide-and-seek held upon a gigantic scale, and they shouted to one another in the excitement of the hunt. Every now and then a rift would be found which promised to be the entrance to a cavern such as abounded in many of the granite and ironstone piles; but in every instance, after the men had plunged in boldly with bayonets fixed, they found the holes empty and were brought up directly, not even finding a sign of the place having been occupied.

The officers advanced from four different places, but the incurvation of the mount, and its being only practicable for climbing here and there, caused Lennox and Dickenson to approach more rapidly than the others; hence it happened that by the time they were half-way to the top they were within talking distance, as they kept on trying to keep their men in line, and at the end of another hundred feet they were side by side, panting and hot from their efforts, and ready to give one another a hand or a leg up in difficult parts.

"Well, Drew, old man," cried Dickenson as they both paused to wipe their faces and give their men time to breathe, "nice job this! I suppose the old man meant it to give us an appetite for breakfast."

Lennox laughed.

"He ought to have given us a task to take away the sharpness; but it's all right. I shouldn't be at all surprised if we started two or three Kaffirs from some hole higher up."

"Why, what would they be doing there?"

"Keeping their gregarious home tidy for their tribe to come back to when we are gone."

"Well, plenty do live in these kopjes. Remember about that one up in the Matabele country that was full of cracks and passages, and had four or five caves one above another?"

"Oh yes, I remember it."

"This might be the same some day, but I believe it's all a reservoir of water inside."

"Or else solid, for there seems to be no door. We may find a way in yet; I shouldn't wonder."

"I should," said Dickenson; "and I believe after all now that the chirping I heard was made by some rat-like creature."

"The more I think about it," continued Lennox, "the more I feel ready to believe that two or three of the Kaffirs are here, and in communication with the Boers."

"What! acting as spies?"

Lennox nodded; he was still too short of breath to talk much.

"Well, now you come to talk like that, it does appear possible, for the Boers do seem to have known pretty well how and when to attack us."

"Exactly."

"Of course! Why, there was the night when they were bringing up the big gun. They must have had guides."

"Oh, if you come to that, they may have people with them who used to live here."

"Yes, they may have," said Dickenson; "but it isn't likely. Depend upon it, there are two or three Kaffirs somewhere about here, and we have them to thank for some of our misfortunes. If we do catch them they'll have it pretty sharp."

"Not they," said Lennox. "We shall treat them as prisoners of war."

"As spies," said Dickenson, "and you know their lot."

"Psh! The colonel would not shoot a set of poor ignorant blacks."

"Browns—browns, browns."

"For a reward they'd fight for us just as they may have been fighting for the Boers."

"But we don't want them to fight for us. If they'd try and feed us they'd be doing some good.—Yes, all right. Ahoy there!" shouted the speaker, for a hail came from higher up. "Forward, my lads; forward!"

This last to the men on either side, who had snapped at the chance of a few minutes' rest, after the fashion displayed by their officers.

The climbing advance went on again till the level patch at the top, which had been turned into a gun-platform, was reached, and the men halted in the bright sunshine, to group about the huge gun after they had been ordered to break off. They rested, enjoying the cool breeze and gazing eagerly about in search of enemies, seeing, however, nothing but the surrounding prospect all looking bright and peaceful in the morning sun.

"'Brayvo! Werry pretty!' as Sam Weller would have said," cried Dickenson as Captain Roby closed the field-glass he had been using and joined his junior officers, frowning and looking impatient.

"Look here, Mr Dickenson," he said sourly. "a little of that commonplace, slangy quotation may be tolerated sometimes after the mess dinner if it's witty—mind, I say if it's witty—but such language as this seems to me quite out of place, especially if spoken in the hearing of the men when on service."

"Yes, of course," replied Dickenson shortly; "but I took care that they were out of hearing."

"They are not out of hearing, sir," retorted Roby; "as Mr Lennox here will bear me witness, Sergeant James and Corporal May must have heard every word."

He turned to Lennox with a questioning look and waited for him to, as he termed it, bear witness.

"Well, really, I don't think they could have heard," said Lennox.

"What!" cried Roby indignantly. "Here, sergeant, you heard—you, Corporal May, you heard what Mr Dickenson said?"

"Yes, sir, everything," replied the corporal smartly.

"And you, sergeant?"

"I heard Mr Dickenson saying something, sir," replied the sergeant bluntly, "but I was looking along the gun here and did not catch a word."

"You mean you would not hear," cried the captain angrily.—"Look here, Mr Dickenson, don't let it occur again."

He jerked at the case of his field-glass and took it out again, then crossed to the other end of the roughly-made gun-platform and directed the telescope upon some object near the horizon.

The two subalterns exchanged glances.

"Mr Lennox—Mr Dickenson," said the latter in a low tone. "Poor old chap, he's regularly upset. Well, no wonder; wants his breakfast. I'm just as grumpy underneath for the same reason, but I keep it down—with my belt. Look here, Drew; go and prescribe for him. Tell him to buckle himself up a couple of holes tighter and he'll feel all the better."

"Hold your tongue! He isn't well, and he's put out about this mare's-nest hunt."

"Well, yes; we haven't done much good."

"Not a bit. How do you feel?"

"As if I should like to kick that time-serving corporal."

"What! the 'Lantern'? Yes: brute! Anything to curry favour with his master."

"Look here, don't forget. Mind I give old James two ounces of the best tobacco first time I have any—which I'm afraid will not be just yet."

"Mare's-nest," said Lennox thoughtfully. "Yes, I suppose it is a mare's-nest. Nobody could have been about here without being caught by the sentries."

"I don't know," said Dickenson, looking about him; "these niggers are very clever at hiding and sneaking about. I felt certain after what I had experienced that we should find a way into a passage and some caves. Here, 'tention; the general's coming back."

Captain Roby returned, replacing his glass, and gave a few sharp orders for the men to take their places once more and commence the descent, searching every crevice among the rocks as they went down.

This was carefully done, and the men reached the foot of the granite pile, formed up, and marched back to the market-place, where they were dismissed to their meagre breakfast, while the captain sought the colonel's quarters without a word to his subordinates.

"The doctor says fasting's very good for a man; but one man's meat, or want of it, is another man's poison, Drew, my boy, and starvation does not agree with Roby."

"No," replied Lennox. "I've noticed that he has been a bit queer for a week past."

"Say a fortnight, and I'll agree with you. Why, he has been like a bear with a sore head. Never said a civil word to any one, and I've heard him bully the poor boys shamefully."

"Yes; it is a pity, too, for they've behaved splendidly."

"Right you are. I always liked them, but I'm quite proud of the poor fellows now. I say though, hang it all! talking must be bad on an empty stomach. Lead on, my lord; the banquet waits."

"Banquet!" said Lennox, with a sigh.

"Yes. Oh, how tired I am of that mealie pap! It puts me in mind of Brahma fowls, and that maddens me."

"Why?"

"Because I used to keep some of the great, feather-breeched, lumbering things to send to poultry shows. Some one told me that Indian corn was a fine thing for them—made their plumage bright and gave them bone; so I ordered a lot."

"And did it answer the purpose?"

"Answer the purpose?" cried Dickenson indignantly. "Why, the beggars picked it up grain by grain and put it down again. Pampered Sybarites! Then the cock cocked his eye up at me and said, '*Tuck, tuck, tuck! Caro, waro, ware!*' which being interpreted from the Chick-chuck language which is alone spoken by the gallinaceous tribe, means, 'None of your larks: yellow pebbles for food? Not to-day, thankye!'"

"I say, Bob, what a boy you do keep!" said Lennox.

"The sweet youthfulness of my nature, lad. But, as I was telling you, the beggars wouldn't touch it, and I had to get our cook to boil it soft. Our mealie pap has just the same smell. That makes me think of being a real boy with my poultry pen: the Brahmas make me think of the young cockerels who did not feather well for show and were condemned to go to pot—that is to say, to the kitchen; and *that* brings up their legs and wings peppered and salted before broiling for breakfast, finished off with a sprinkle of Worcester sauce, and then—oh, luscious! oh, tender juiciness! Oh! hold me up, old man, or I shall faint. There, sniff! Can't you smell? Yes, of course; mealie pap in a tin, and—Oh, here's the colonel eating his. Roby will have to give his report now."

"Good—morning, gentlemen," said the colonel. "Just in time for breakfast. Well, what have you found?"

He had hardly asked the question before Captain Roby hurried in, to go up to his side at once and make his report.

"I'm sorry; but no more than I expected.—Here," he said, turning to his servant, after making a brave show of eating the meagre tin of Indian corn porridge; "bring me a little cocoa."

"Beg pardon, sir," said the man, bending over him from behind; "very sorry, but last of the cocoa was finished yesterday."

"Humph! Yes; I had forgotten," said the colonel, and he took up his spoon and began to play with the porridge remaining in his tin.

The breakfast was soon ended, and the officers made a show of chatting cheerfully together, while the colonel sat tapping the edge of his tin softly with his canteen spoon, looking thoughtfully into the bottom of the cleaned-out vessel the while. Then every eye was turned to him as he straightened himself up, for they judged that he was going to make some communication. They were right, for he threw down his spoon on the clothless board and said suddenly:

"Well, gentlemen, the French proverb says, *Il faut manger.*"

"Yes," said the doctor, with a grim smile; "but it is necessary to have something in the manger."

"Quite so, doctor," said the colonel, with a good-humoured nod; "so I may as well open a discussion on the position at once, and tell you that while Roby and his company have been searching the kopje the major and I have formed ourselves into a committee of ways and means, and gone round the stores.—Tell them, major."

The gentleman addressed shrugged his shoulders.

"There is so little to tell," he replied; "only that with about quarter-rations we can hold out for another week. That's all."

"Not all," said the colonel. "We have the horses as a last resource; but they are life to us in another way, and must be left till the very end."

Dead silence reigned, every man looking down at the rough table.

"Well, gentlemen," continued the colonel, "after giving every thought to our position I come to the conclusion that at all hazards I must hold this place."

"Hear, hear!" came from every lip.

"We are keeping three commandos fully employed, and that is something."

There was a sound like a murmur of satisfaction.

"I might determine," said the colonel, "to try and reach Rudolfsberg, and somehow or another we would cut our way there; but our losses would be terrible, and we should reach safety—some of us—with the feeling that we had not done our duty by holding Groenfontein at all hazards."

"That's quite right," said the major as his chief paused, and a murmur of assent followed the major's words.

"Then, gentlemen, that brings me back again to the French proverb. We must eat, so the first thing to do is to decide on which direction a raid is to be made: that means scouting, and the discovery of the nearest Boer store of provisions, with sheep and cattle. We are quite alone here, without the possibility of my words being heard, so I can speak out freely. Scouting parties must go out at once in the direction of each of the three commandos, and on the strength of their reports the expedition will be made."

"To-night?" said the major.

"Yes," replied the colonel. "Hush! Don't cheer! Let matters go on as if nothing fresh were on the way. We cannot afford to have our proceedings carried out of the lines by Kaffir spies."

Chapter Twelve
The Boer Advance

The scouting parties went out in three different directions after a long survey from the top of the kopje, the routes being marked out for the leaders in consultation with the colonel, who, glass in hand, selected the most likely routes to be followed so that the enemy might be avoided, and the more distant country reached where two or three Boer farms were known to be situated.

Then, with three of the best mounted men in each, they set off; and the colonel took especial care that no one of the many friendly—said to be friendly—natives who hung about the camp should follow. It was a necessary precaution, for the outposts stopped no less than a dozen men stealing through the long grass on both sides of the river, and, to their great disappointment, turned them back to go and squat down sulkily in such shade as they could find.

The instructions given were that at the latest the scouts were to be back at sundown, so as to give ample time for pointing out the route to be followed and preparations made for the raid to come.

Plenty of discussion ensued when the scouts had ridden off at a walk, opening out so as not to take the attention of the Boers; and as far as could be made out by the watchers there was not a sign of an enemy upon either of the hills.

The question of the discussion was which company of the regiment would be called upon to start upon the raid, the members of each hoping to be selected; and Captain Roby maintaining loudly, in a sharp, snappish way, that without doubt his company would be chosen, and turning fiercely upon any of his brother officers who differed from him.

"He's precious cock-sure, Drew," said Dickenson later on, as they strolled together up the steep sides of the kopje; "but we had our bit of work this morning, and it is not likely that the old man will send us."

"Of course not; but it was of no use to say anything. Our failure has had a strange effect upon the poor fellow, and a word would act upon him like fire upon tinder."

"Yes; but the starvation picnic has had its effect on other people too. Who's he that he should have the monopoly of getting into a passion about nothing? I say, though, as we were up there this morning I don't see what is the use of our going up again; there'll be no shade at the top, and we shall be half-roasted."

"Don't come, then," said Lennox quietly. "I'm going up to see if I can follow the scouts with a glass."

"Don't come?" cried Dickenson sharply. "Well, I like that! Here's another one touched by the sun. Old Roby is not to have the monopoly of getting into a fantigue."

"Nonsense! I'm not out of temper," said Lennox.

"Not out of temper? Well, upon my word! But I shall come all the same. I would now if it were ten times as hot."

"Very well," said Lennox, drawing his breath hard so as to command his temper, for he felt really ruffled now by the heat and his comrade's way of talking.

They climbed slowly on, step for step, till, as they zigzagged up into a good position which displayed the sun-bathed landscape shimmering in the heat, Lennox caught a glimpse of one of the scouting parties in the distance, and was about to draw his companion's attention to it when Dickenson suddenly caught at his arm and pointed to a glowing patch of the rock in the full blaze of the sun.

"Look," he said. "Big snake."

"Nonsense!" said Lennox angrily; "there are no snakes up here."

Their eyes met the next instant with so meaning a look in them that both burst out laughing, Dickenson holding out his hand, which was taken at once.

"I forgive old Roby," he said.

"So do I," said Lennox frankly. "Heat and hunger do upset a man's temper. See our fellows out there?"

He pointed in the direction where he had seen the mounted figures, feeling for his glass the while.

"Not our men," said Dickenson, following his example, and together they produced their glasses.

"Oh yes," said Lennox. "I am certain it was they."

"And I'm as certain it was not," cried Dickenson.

Their eyes met again; but this time they felt too serious to laugh, and were silent for some moments.

Dickenson then said frankly:

"Look here, old chap, there's something wrong with us. We've got the new complaint—the Robitis; and we'd better not argue about anything, or we shall have a fight. My temper feels as if it had got all the skin off."

"And I'm as irritable as Roby was this morning. Never mind. Can you make out the mounted men now?"

"No," said Dickenson after a pause. "Can you?"

"No. They're gone behind that patch of forest. There," he continued, closing his glass, "let's get up to the top and sit in the men's shelter; there'll be a bit of air up there."

He proved to be right, for a pleasant breeze, comparatively cool, was blowing on the other side of the mountain and tempering the glare of the sunshine, while they found that there was a bit of shade behind a turret-like projection standing out of the granite, looking as if it had been built up by human hands.

There they sat and watched for hours, scanning the veldt, which literally quivered in the heat; but they looked in vain for any movement on the part of the enemy, who had been disturbed by the scouts, and at last made up their minds to go down—truth to tell, moved by the same reason, the pangs of hunger asserting themselves in a way almost too painful to be borne.

"Let's go," said Dickenson; "they've got right away in safety. I believe the Boers are all asleep this hot day, and in the right of it: plenty to eat and nothing to do."

"Yes, let's go. I'm longing for a long cool drink down below there. Pst! What's that?"

"One of the fellows round there by the gun," said Dickenson.

"No," whispered Lennox decidedly; "it was close at hand. Did you hear it?"

"Yes. Sounded like the rock splitting in this fiery sunshine."

"More like a piece falling somewhere inside—beneath our feet—and I distinctly heard a soft, echoing rumble."

"Come along down, old man," said Dickenson. "It's too hot to be up here, and if we stop any longer we shall have something worse than being hungry—a bad touch of the sun. I feel quite ready to go off my head and imagine all sorts of things. For instance, there's a swimming before my eyes which makes me fancy I can see puffs of smoke rising out yonder, and a singing and cracking in my ears like distant firing."

"Where?" cried Lennox excitedly. "Yes, of course. I can see the puffs plainly, and hear the faint cracking of the fire. Bob, my lad, then that sharp sound we heard must have been the reverberation of a gun."

"Oh dear!" groaned Dickenson. "Come along down, and let's get our heads in the cool stream and drink like fishes."

"Don't be foolish! Get out your glass."

"To drink with?"

"No! Absurd! To watch the firing."

"There is no firing, man," cried Dickenson.

"There is, I tell you."

"Oh, he has got it too," groaned Dickenson. "Very well; all right—there is fighting going on out there a couple of miles away, and I can see the smoke and hear the cracking of the rifles. But come on down and let's have a drink of water all the same; there's plenty of that."

"You're saying that to humour me," said Lennox, with his glass to his eyes; "but I'm not half-delirious from sunstroke. Get out your glass and look. The Boers are coming on in a long extended line, and they must be driving in our scouts "

"You don't mean it, do you, old chap?" cried Dickenson, dragging out his glass.

"Yes; there's no mistake about it."

Crack! went a rifle from behind the projection, a few yards away; and directly after, as the two officers began scurrying down, the bugles were ringing out in the market-square, and the colonel gave his orders for supports to go out, check the Boer advance, and bring the scouting party or parties in.

Chapter Thirteen
Something in the Head

It was a narrow escape, but the nine men got safely back to quarters, but minus two of their horses. For the Boers had in every case been well upon the alert; their lines had not been pierced, and they followed up the retreating scouts till the searching fire from the kopje began to tell upon their long line of skirmishers, and then they sullenly drew back, but not before they had learnt that there were marksmen in the regiment at Groenfontein as well as in their own ranks.

"That's something, Drew," said Dickenson as he watched the slow movement of a light wagon drawn by mules. "But only to think of it: all that trouble for nothing—worse than nothing, for they have shot those two horses. Yes, worse than nothing," he continued, "for they would have been something for the pot."

Each of the scouting parties gave the same account of the state of affairs; that is to say, that though to all appearances the country round was clear of the enemy, a keen watch was being kept up, and, turn which way they would, Boers were ready to spring up in the most unexpected places to arrest their course and render it impossible to reach supplies and bring them in.

Their report cast a damp on the whole camp. For bad news travels fast, and this was soon known.

"Sounds bad," said Dickenson cheerfully, "and just like them. They are not going to run their heads into danger unless obliged. They mean to lie low and wait for us, then turn us back to starve and surrender."

"And they'll find that we shall take a great deal of starving first," replied Lennox bitterly. "But I don't agree with you altogether. I fully expect that, in spite of their failure to blow us up, it will not be long before they contrive something else."

"Well, we shall not quarrel about that, old man," said Dickenson cheerily. "If they do come on in some attack, every one here will be delighted to see them. We should enjoy a good honest fight. What I don't like is this going on shrinking and pulling the tongue farther through the buckle. If it goes on like this much longer I shall have to go to our saddler to punch a few more holes in my belt. I say, though, one feels better after that draught of water. I believe if I had stayed up yonder much longer I should have gone quite off my head, through fancying things, for it was only imagination after all."

A fresh company occupied the kopje that evening, and once more perfect silence reigned. There was one of the glorious displays of stars seen so often in those clear latitudes, when the great dome of heaven seems to be one mass of sparkling, encrusted gems.

Lennox had been standing outside his quarters for some time, enjoying the coolness, and shrinking from going in to where the hut was hot and stuffy and smelling strongly of the now extinguished paraffin-lamp, mingled with a dash of the burned tobacco in Dickenson's pipe.

"I say," said the latter, "hadn't you better come in and perch? Nothing like making your hay when the sun shines, and getting your forty winks while you can."

"Quite right," replied Lennox in a low, dreamy voice; "but it's very pleasant out here."

"That's true enough, no doubt, old man; but you'll be on duty to-morrow night out yonder, and you can go on star-gazing then. Yah! Oh—oh dear me, how sleepy I do feel!" he continued, yawning. "I'll bet a penny that I don't dream once. Regularly worn out, that's how I am. There, good-night if you won't come and lie down. I shall just allow myself half a—Oh, hang it! I do call that too bad!"

For ere he could finish his sentence a rifle cracked somewhere near the top of the kopje, followed by another and another; the bugles rang out, and from the continued firing it seemed evident that the Boers were going against their ordinary custom and making a night attack.

If they did, though, they were to find the camp ready for them, every man and officer springing to his place and waiting for orders—those given to Captain Roby being, as his men were so familiar with the spot, to take half a company and reinforce the detachment on the kopje.

They found that the firing had completely ceased by the time they were half-way up, and upon joining the officer in command there, to Captain Roby's great satisfaction, he found a similar scene being enacted to that which had taken place before him.

"Another false alarm, Roby," the officer said angrily. "Your fellows started the cock-and-bull nonsense, and it has become catching. The sentry here declares he saw a couple of figures coming down in the darkness, and he fired. The idiot! There is nothing, of course, and the colonel shall make an example of him."

Lennox was standing close up to the offender, and in spite of the darkness could make out that the man was shivering.

"Come, come," said the young officer in a half-whisper; "don't go on like that. You fancy you saw something?"

"I'm sure I did, sir," replied the sentry, grateful for a kind word after the severe bullying he had received for doing what he believed to be his duty. "I saw two of them, as plain as I can see you now. I was regularly took aback, sir, for I hadn't heard a sound; but as soon as I fired I could hear them rush off."

"You feel certain?"

"Yes, sir; and the captain says it was all fancy. If it was, sir, I know —"

"Know what?" said Lennox, impressed by the man's manner. "Speak out."

"Oh, I know, sir," said the man again, with a shudder.

"Well, speak out; don't be afraid."

"Enough to make any man feel afraid, sir," half whimpered the man. "I don't mind going into action, sir. I've shown afore now as I'd follow my officers anywhere."

"Of course you would, my lad," said Lennox, patting the young fellow encouragingly on the shoulder, for he could see that he was suffering from a shock, and, doubtless from abstinence and weakness, was half-hysterical.

"It's bad enough, sir, to be posted in the darkness upon a shelf like that over there, expecting every moment to get a bullet in you; but when it comes to anything like this, it makes a fellow feel like a coward."

"Who said coward?" said Dickenson, who had followed his companion and now came up.

"I did, sir," said the man through his chattering teeth.

"Where is he?" said Dickenson. "I should like to look at him. I haven't seen one lately."

"Here he is, sir," said the poor fellow, growing more agitated; "it's me."

"Get out!" cried Dickenson good-humouredly. "You're not a coward. There isn't such a thing in the regiment."

"Oh yes, there is, sir," whimpered the man. "It's all right, sir. I'm the chap: look at me."

"Stop a moment," said Lennox quickly; "aren't you one of the men who have been in the infirmary?"

"Yes, sir. This is the first time I've been on duty since."

"What was the matter with you?"

"Doctor said it was all on account of weakness, sir, but that I should be better back in the fresh air—in the ranks."

"And you feel weak now?"

"Yes, sir; horrid. I'm ashamed of myself for being such a coward. But I know now."

"Well, what do you know?" asked Lennox, more for the sake of calming the man than from curiosity.

"I thought I was going to get all right again and see the war through, if I didn't get an unlucky ball; but it's all over now. I've seen 'em, and it's a fetch."

"A what?" cried Dickenson, laughing.

"Don't laugh, sir, please;" said the man imploringly. "It's too awful. I see 'em as plain as I see you two gentlemen standing there."

"And who were they?" continued Dickenson; "the brothers Fetch?"

"No, sir; two old comrades of mine who 'listed down Plymouth way when I did. We used to be in the same football team. They both got it at Magersfontein, and they've come to tell me it's going to be my turn now."

"Bah!" growled Dickenson. "Did they say so?"

"No, sir; they didn't speak," said the man, shivering; "but there they were. I knew Tom Longford by his big short beard, and the other must have been Mike Lamb."

"Oh, here you are," said the captain of the company. "You can go back to quarters, and be ready to appear before the colonel in the morning."

"One moment, Captain Edwards," said Lennox gravely. "You'll excuse me for speaking. This man is only just off the sick list; he is evidently very ill."

"Oh yes, I know that, Mr Lennox," said the officer coldly; "he has a very bad complaint for a soldier. Look at him. Has he told you that he has seen a couple of ghosts?"

"Yes. He is weak from sickness and fasting, and imagined all that; but I feel perfectly certain that he has seen some one prowling about here."

"Ghosts?" said the captain mockingly.

"No; spies."

"Psh! It's a disease the men have got. Fancy. Every fellow on duty will be seeing the same thing now. There, that's enough of it."

"Look out!" cried Lennox angrily; and then in the same breath, "What's that?"

For there was a sharp, grating sound as of stone against stone, and then silence.

"Stand fast, every man," cried Lennox excitedly, seizing his revolver and looking along the broad, rugged shelf upon which they stood in the direction from which the sound had come.

"A lantern here," cried the captain as a sharp movement was heard, and half-a-dozen men at a word from their officer doubled along the shelf for a couple of dozen yards and then stood fast, while the other end of the path was blocked in the same way.

Lennox's heart was beating hard with excitement, and he started as he felt Dickenson grip his arm firmly.

Then all stood fast, listening, as they waited for the lantern to be brought. Quite ten minutes of painful silence elapsed before a couple of dim lights were seen approaching, the bearers having to come down from the gun-platform; and when the two non-commissioned officers who bore them approached, and in obedience to orders held them up, they displayed nothing but swarthy, eager-looking faces, and the piled-up rugged and weathered rocks on one side, the black darkness on the other.

"Come this way, sergeant," said Captain Edwards, and he, as officer in command of the detachment that night, led on, followed closely by Captain Roby and the two subalterns.

They went along in perfect silence, the lanterns here being alternately held up and down so that the rugged shelf and the piled-up masses of rock which formed the nearly perpendicular side of the kopje in that part might be carefully examined.

This was done twice over, the party passing each time where their men were blocking the ends of the shelf which had been selected for one of the posts.

"It's strange," said Captain Roby at last. "I can see no loose stone."

"No," said Captain Edwards. "It was just as if a good-sized block had slipped down from above. Let's have another look."

This was done, with no better result, and once more the party stood fast in the dim light, gazing in a puzzled way.

"Can any one suggest anything?" said Captain Roby.

There was silence for a few moments, and then Lennox caught hold of Dickenson's arm and gave it a meaning pressure as he turned to the two captains, who were close together.

"I have an idea," he whispered. "Give the orders loudly for the men to march off. Take them round to the south, and wait."

"What for?" said Captain Roby snappishly.

"I should like Dickenson and me to be left behind. I'll fire if there is anything."

"Oh, rubbish!" said Captain Roby contemptuously.

"No," said his brother officer quietly. "It is worth trying." Then turning to the two sergeants who bore the lanterns, he said, "When I say put out those lights, don't do it; cover them sharply with greatcoats."

Directly after he gave his first order, when the lanterns rattled, and all was dark.

Then followed the next orders, and tramp! tramp! tramp! the men marched away like a relieving guard, Lennox and Dickenson standing fast with their backs leaning against the rugged wall of rock, perfectly motionless in the black darkness, and looking outward and down at the faint light or two visible below in the camp.

As they drew back against the rock Lennox felt for his companion's hand, which gripped his directly, and so they stood waiting.

To them the silence seemed quite appalling, for they felt as if they were on the eve of some discovery—what, neither could have said; but upon comparing notes afterwards each said he felt convinced that something was about to happen, but paradoxically, at the same time, as if it never would; and when a quarter of an hour must have passed, the excitement grew more intense, as the pressure of their hot, wet hands told, for they felt then that whatever was about to happen must befall them then, if they were not interrupted by the return of their officers.

Each tried to telegraph to his companion the intensity of feeling from which he suffered, and after a fashion one did communicate to the other something of his sensations.

But nothing came to break the intense silence, and they stood with strained ears, now gazing up at the glittering stars, and now down through the darkness at the two feeble lights that they felt must be those outside the colonel's quarters in the market-square.

"I don't know how it was," said Lennox afterwards, "but just at the last I began somehow to think of being at the back of the colonel's hut that night just after Sergeant James had put out the light upon discovering the train."

"I felt that if the business went on much longer, something—some of my strings that were all on the strain—would crack," interrupted Dickenson.

"Yes," said Lennox; "I felt so too."

And this was how he was feeling—strained—till something seemed to be urging him to cry out or move in the midst of that intense period, when all at once he turned cold all down the back, for a long-drawn, dismal, howling wail rose in the distance, making him shudder just as he had seen the sentry quiver in his horror and dread.

"Bah! Hyena," he said to himself the next moment; and then a thrill ran through him as he felt Dickenson's grip increase suddenly with quite a painful pressure.

He responded to it directly, every nerve in his body quivering with the greater strain placed upon it by what was happening, till every nerve and muscle seemed to harden into steel. For the long expected—whatever it might prove to be—the mystery was about to unfold itself, and in his intense feeling it seemed to Lennox as if the glittering stars were flashing out more light.

It was only a noise, but a noise such as Lennox felt that he must hear—a low, dull, harsh, grating noise as of stone passing over stone; and though he could see nothing with his eyes, mentally he knew that one of the great time-bleached and weathered blocks of granite that helped to form the cyclopean face of the kopje wall had begun to turn as on a pivot.

This grating sound lasted for a few seconds only, and it came apparently from a couple of yards away to his right, as he stood with his back pressed against the rugged natural stones.

Then the noise ceased as suddenly as it had begun, and he listened, now holding his breath in the vain hope that it would silence the heavy, dull beating of his heart, whose throbs seemed to echo painfully in his brain.

He pressed Dickenson's hand again, to feel from the return grip how thoroughly his comrade was on the alert.

Then all was perfectly silent again, while a dull feeling of despair began to assert itself as he felt that they were going to hear no more.

At last, with head wrenched round to the right, his revolver feeling wet in his fingers and his eyes seeming to start with the strain of gazing along the shelf at the brilliant stars before him, his nerves literally jerked and he felt perfectly paralysed and unable to stir, for here, not six feet away, he could make out against the starry sky the dimly-marked silhouette of a heavily-built man.

Chapter Fourteen
A Strange Find

It seemed to Drew Lennox that he was staring helplessly at the dark shadowy shape for quite a minute—but it was only a matter of a few seconds—before, snatching his left hand from his companion's grasp, he let his revolver drop to the full extent of its lanyard, and sprang open-handed at the man.

The movement warned the latter of his danger, and turning sharply round from where he was watching the direction taken by the detachment, he made a desperate effort to catch the young officer by the throat.

But Lennox was springing at him, and the weight of his impact drove the man back for a yard or two; but he recovered himself, got a grip, and then a desperate struggle commenced at the edge of the rugged shelf of rock just where the kopje went down for some fifty feet almost perpendicularly, while a pile of heaped-up fragments which had lodged after falling from above stood out ready to receive the unfortunate who fell.

Neither spoke as they gripped, but stood panting heavily as if gathering breath for the terrible struggle that threatened death to one if not both combatants. They were not well matched. Lennox seemed to be slightly the taller, but he was young, slight, and not fully knit; while his adversary was broad-shouldered, and possessed limbs that were heavily coated with hardened muscles, so that in spite of the weight brought to bear in the young officer's sprint he recovered himself where a weaker man must have been driven backward to the ground.

Dickenson sprang forward to his comrade's help, but stopped short as he realised that in that narrow space there was only room for a struggle between two, and by interfering he would be more likely to hinder his friend than help. Hence it was that he stood waiting for his opportunity, listening to the hoarse breathing of the wrestlers and watching the faintly seen struggle—for capture on the one part, for ridding himself of his adversary by pushing him off the shelf on the other.

In a very few moments Lennox had recognised the fact that he was overmatched; but this only roused the stubborn bull-dog nature of the young Englishman, and setting his teeth hard, he brought to bear every feint and manoeuvre he had learnt at his old Devon school, where wrestling was popular, and in the struggles of the football field.

But all in vain: his adversary was far too heavy for him, and, to his rage and discomfiture, in spite of all his efforts he found one great arm tightening about his ribs with crushing pressure, while the man was bending down to lift him from the shelf, evidently to hurl him off into space.

The position was desperate, and in its brief moments Lennox did all that was in his power, tightening his grasp in the desperate resolve that if so savage a plan was carried out he would not go alone.

It might have been supposed that in his emergency-he would have called to Dickenson for help, but the fact was that his adversary so filled his thoughts that there was no room for his comrade's presence, and he struggled on, straining every muscle and nerve.

But, to repeat the previous assertion, he was completely overmatched by a desperate man; and, unless Dickenson could have interfered and saved him, Lennox's fate was to be thrown from the rocky ledge out into the black shadowy air, to fall heavily, crushed and broken, upon the stones below.

But fate favoured him at the last pinch, for as his enemy by sheer weight and pressure bore him back and then lifted him from the shelf preparatory to hurling him outward, Lennox suddenly gave up resisting, loosening his grasp so as to take fast hold round his enemy's neck, when the sudden cessation of resistance had the effect of throwing the latter off his balance just when he was very near the edge where he intended to plant his foot down and check his farther progress. The result was that he put his foot down a few inches too far, his heel pressing down upon the rock where his toes should have been, and before he could recover himself his foot was down over the side, while by a frantic wrench Lennox flung himself sidewise inward.

They fell sidewise upon the shelf, Lennox uppermost, his enemy half over the edge and gliding rapidly down, his weight drawing his adversary after him slowly, inch by inch, for the hitter's position debarred his making any successful effort to escape. For the enemy not only had him tightly clasped, but, feeling his disadvantage, had wrenched his face round so that he could savagely seize hold of the young officer's khaki jacket with his teeth. And there he hung on, doubtless intending to speak and declare that if he was to fall his enemy should share his fate. But no coherent words were uttered; nothing was to be made out but a savage growling as of some fierce wild beast.

The action took less time than the telling, and, fortunately for all, now was Dickenson's opportunity.

The darkness had prevented his seeing the whole of the varying phases of the struggle; but the latter part was plain enough, and fully grasping the position and the emergency of the case, he sprang upon the contending couple just at the right moment, adding his weight, which from his position of vantage completely checked the gradual gliding movement in which Lennox was being drawn onward to his death.

"Give up, you brute!" roared Dickenson now. "Surrender!"

For response the prostrate man, who was vainly striving to find foothold below the edge of the shelf, let go with one hand and quick as thought flung it over the speaker so that he got hold tightly by the tunic, growling fiercely the while.

"Yah! That's flesh!" roared Dickenson, and in his rage and pain he struck down heavily with his doubled fist. "You brute!" he cried. "Give up, or I'll shove you down."

The prisoner gave up struggling for a moment or two, and seemed to be trying to get a hold of some projecting stone.

"There," cried Dickenson, "let go. Give up; you're a prisoner. Leave off struggling, and I'll haul you back on to the shelf. It's no good to fight any more. That's right. You surrender, then? Mind, if you try any of your confounded Boer treachery I'll send a bullet through your skull."

Crack!

"Oh!"

The shot from a revolver, and a cry of pain from Dickenson, who at the same moment realised the fact that the prisoner's last movements had meant not giving up or getting a safer position on the ledge, but an effort to get at his revolver and fire at so close quarters that the condensed flame from the pistol's muzzle burned the young man's cheek, the bullet barely touching the skin as it flew off into space.

"Beast!" cried Dickenson savagely, and he struck wildly at the revolver as it was fired again, and fortunately diverted the clumsy attempt at an aim, but at the expense of his knuckles, two of which were cut against the chambers of the revolver.

As he uttered the word the young officer was recalling the fact that this made two shots, and he felt that in all probability there were four more to come. His hand was busy as well as his head, for he struck out again and again in an effort to get hold of the pistol; but he could not prevent the firing of another shot, which struck the rock beside him with a loud pat.

"Ha!" cried Dickenson in a tone full of satisfaction; "got you!" For his efforts in the darkness had been at last rewarded by his fingers coming in contact with the barrel of the little weapon, which he clasped tightly and held on to, in spite of jerk and snatch, feeling the barrel heat as it was fired again, and again, and again, but with the muzzle forced upward so that the bullets flew harmlessly away.

"That's better," growled Dickenson. "Now, you spiteful savage, will you give up—will you surrender?"

A savage growling was the only answer.

"You brute!" muttered Dickenson. "'Pon my word, if it wasn't for poor old Drew I believe I should let you go over, and see how you liked that.— Here, Drew," he cried aloud, "how is it? What are you doing?"

"Holding his left hand down. He has got hold of my revolver."

"Bless him for a beauty! Can you stop him?"

"I don't know yet; I'm so awkwardly situated. Can you keep us from going over?"

"Oh yes, I can do that. Here, I've got at my six-shooter now; hold still, and I'll put something through his head."

"No, no; we must take him alive," cried Lennox.

"It's all very fine, but he's going to take us dead. Better let me cripple him. Shall I light a match?"

"No, no. I've got tight hold of his wrist now, so that he can't use my revolver. Ha! Look out!"

"I shall have to shoot him," cried Dickenson; for, foiled in his effort to get hold of the fresh weapon, the man began to struggle again fiercely, heaving himself up and wrenching himself to right and left in a way that threatened to result in the whole party going over into the black gulf below.

Lennox uttered another warning cry.

"Take care?" growled Dickenson. "Who's to take care in the dark? Here, tell the brute in Dutch that if he doesn't give up I'll send a bullet through his head. He doesn't seem to understand plain English."

"Yes, he does, for he spoke in English just now."

This was too true, for just then the prisoner suddenly yelled out, "Dirck! Dirck! Help! The cursed rooineks have got me down."

"Oho! Then there are more than one of you, my beauty!" cried Dickenson. "Now then, this is a gag; hold still or I'll pull the trigger."

There was a clinking sound caused by the rattling of the desperate prisoner's teeth against the barrel of the pistol which Dickenson thrust into his mouth just as he was about to speak. But he wrenched his head round and began to struggle again so desperately that Lennox's temper got the upper hand and he began to grow merciless to a degree that tempted him to bid his comrade fire.

"Look here," roared Dickenson at the same moment, "I've had enough of this, my fine fellow. Surrender, or I'll fire without mercy."

"Ha!" ejaculated Lennox in a sigh of relief, for those six shots had not been fired in vain. The prisoner had unconsciously summoned assistance to complete his capture, and Lennox's sigh had been produced by the sight of a flash of light and the sound of hurrying feet, the two sergeants with their lanterns reaching the spot first, closely followed by the officers and men, who gazed down in wonder at the human knot composed of the wondrously tied up three lying at the edge of the precipice.

"Come on," shouted Dickenson. "We've caught the ghost. Don't let him go."

"Here, hold these, some one," cried Sergeant James, and as soon as he had got rid of his lantern he made fast, as a sailor would say, to the prisoner and held on, while, to use his words, his mate pulled out the prisoner's stings, for he had three—two revolvers (one of course discharged) and a keen-bladed sheath-knife, something like an American bowie.

Five minutes later the light of the held-up lanterns fell upon a fierce-looking, much bruised and battered, black-bearded Boer, lying upon the rocky shelf, tied hand and foot, his face so smeared and disfigured by blood that it acted like a mask.

"Carry him down at once," said Captain Roby; "he is evidently badly wounded."

"Not he," growled Dickenson savagely. "He hurt me more than I hurt him. He used pistol; I only used fist and punched him in the nose."

Sergeant James smiled grimly, and drawing a roll of bandage from his wallet, tore off a bit and wiped the blood from the prisoner's face.

"Hullo!" he cried.—"Hooray, Captain Roby, sir! This is our Boer friend who tried to blow us up."

Lennox stopped forward eagerly, and signed for the lantern to be lowered.

"Yes," he cried wonderingly; "that is the man."

"And no mistake," said Dickenson. "Come, I call this a good catch."

The other officers looked down at the dark eyes scowling up at them.

"Yes," he growled fiercely, "I am the man; and I'll do it yet."

"Perhaps your precious game may be stopped now, my good fellow," said Captain Roby meaningly.

"Yes," said Captain Edwards sternly. "You were treated well and generously the first time; this time you may find that the English officers can be stern as well as generous to a beaten enemy.—Well, Captain Roby," he continued, "there was no mistake, you see, about the alarm."

"So I see," said the latter officer coldly.

"The thing is, what was he doing here?"

"Playing the spy, or hiding and waiting for a chance to get away, I suppose."

"Well, you will take him down with you, and report to the colonel," said Captain Edwards.

"Stop a bit," cried Dickenson. "You haven't got the other."

"What other?" cried the two captains in a breath.

"This fellow's comrade."

"Has he one?"

"You heard what the private said about seeing two," cried Dickenson.

"Oh, the words of a man in a scare go for nothing," said Captain Roby contemptuously.

"Perhaps not; but this fellow was in no scare when he called for his companion—Dirck, did he call him, Lennox?"

"Yes, Dirck; and he must be somewhere close at hand. Look, Bob."

He touched his comrade's arm to draw his attention to the sneering smile on the prisoner's face.

"And where do you think his friend is?" said Captain Edwards.

"In the same place as this man came from. They have a hiding-place somewhere close by."

"Yes," cried Dickenson; "one that enables them to play a regular Jack-in-the-box trick."

"But how? Where?" said Captain Edwards.

"I don't know how, and I don't know where it is," replied Lennox, "but I do know that they have a hiding-place somewhere here amongst the rocks. This Boer was not here one minute; then we heard the creaking and grinding of a stone door close at hand, and he was standing out against the sky."

"Whereabouts?" said Captain Roby.

"About here," said Lennox, stepping to the rock close at hand. — "Bring the lantern, quick."

Sergeant James stepped forward with his and held it up for his officer, who began to examine the rock; but Dickenson paid no heed. He employed himself in watching the prostrate Boer attentively, and noticed that his eyes were being blinked violently, as if the man were in a great state of excitement. But he seemed to calm down rapidly as the young subaltern walked to and fro, holding the light up, then down, and always coming back to the starting-place.

"Well, can't you find it?" said Captain Roby, with a sneer.

"No," replied Lennox frankly. "I can see no signs of it."

"And are not likely to," replied Captain Roby, with a grunt indicative of the contempt he felt. "It's all absurd. What did you expect to find? A hidden Aladdin's cave, with genii keeping the door? — Here, Dickenson, you are a gentleman of fine imagination. Go and help him. Expand your lungs, and cry *Open Sesame!*"

"Why don't you," said Dickenson, "as you know Persian, or whatever it is, so well?"

Captain Roby was about to make an angry retort, but Captain Edwards now interfered.

"I don't think there is any hiding-place along here," he said. "There may be a rift or cave somewhere about the kopje, but certainly there does not seem to be one in this part."

"I am not satisfied," said Lennox, who was busy still directing the light in and out among the crevices of the rocks. "It hardly seems possible, but the natural form of the granite is in blocks which look as if they had been piled-up by the hand of man. Could any one of these be a rough door?"

"No; absurd," said Captain Roby. "There, we have captured our prisoner; let's get him down to the colonel."

"But what about his calling for Dirck to help him?" said Lennox eagerly.

"I did not hear him call for Dirck to help him," said Roby contemptuously.

"No, but we did," cried Lennox, as he went on tapping the granite blocks with the butt of his revolver, curiously watched the while by the prisoner, who was in complete ignorance of the fact that Dickenson, who stood half behind, was intently watching him in turn.

"Give it up, Lennox," said Captain Roby. "You are doing no good there."

"Burning!" cried Dickenson so suddenly that every one turned and stared.

"What is burning?" cried Captain Edwards.

"Drew Lennox is."

"Burning?"

"Hang it all, sir! have you forgotten all your childish games?" cried Dickenson impatiently. "'Hot boiled beans,' you know. Lennox is seeking, and he's burning."

"Am I?" cried Lennox excitedly, and the grim faces of the men thrown up by the lanterns grew eager and excited too.

"To be sure you are," said Dickenson.

"How do you know?"

"By my lord the prisoner's phiz here. He gave quite a twitch when you tapped that last rock but one."

"Ha!" cried Lennox; "then there is a way in here. I thought it sounded hollow."

He stepped back and began to tap the rough stone again to prove his words, every one now noticing that the rock gave out a dull, hollow tone; while, unable to contain himself, the prisoner, as he lay tightly bound upon his back, uttered a low, hissing sound as he drew in a deep breath.

"Here we are," cried Lennox, more excited than ever. "Sergeant, give some one else that lantern; take a man with you up there by the gun, and bring back a crowbar or two, and one of the engineers' picks."

The men went off at once, and while the party awaited their return Lennox went on examining the rough block of granite by which he stood, but looked in vain for any sign of hinge or fastening.

"I hope you are right, Lennox," said Captain Edwards, who had stepped to his side; and he spoke in a low voice.

"So do I," was the reply; "but I feel sure that there is, for there must be a hiding-place somewhere. Wait a bit, and we shall capture the prisoner's mate."

Lennox involuntarily glanced down at where the carefully bound Boer lay with the light shining full upon his eyes, and he could not repress a start as he saw the malignant flash that seemed to dart from them into his own. It affected him so that he ceased his examination for the moment, waiting impatiently till the distant sound of steps announced the return of the sergeant and the man bearing the implements he had sought.

"Got the crowbar?" cried Lennox eagerly.

"Yes, sir."

"Then bring it here. Thrust it in under the stone at this natural crevice."

"Why?" said Captain Roby sharply. — "Here, sergeant, try higher up."

But before the words were fully uttered the sergeant had driven the chisel-edge of the iron bar into the horizontal crevice about on a level with his knees, with the result that the men cheered so loudly that they drowned the angry curse which escaped the Boer's lips. For, to the surprise of all, no sooner had the sergeant pressed down the wedged-in bar than it acted as a lever would, lifting one corner of the stone so that it slipped away, the great block turning easily upon a central pivot, and leaving an opening some four feet high and just wide enough for a man to pass through.

"The light, sergeant. — Bayonets, my lads!" shouted Lennox, springing forward; but his cry was mingled with one from the prisoner, who yelled out:

"Fire, Dirck; fire! Never mind yourself; blow them all into the air."

It was an order which was full of suggestion, coming as it did so soon after the cowardly attempt to kill the colonel and his chief officers; but not a man shrank from the task before him, nor hesitated to take the risk, whatever it might be. Lennox was in first, closely followed by the sergeant, lantern in his left hand, iron bar in his right, ready to strike down the first man who resisted, while the light was directed here and there in eager search for bag or barrel that might contain the elements of destruction.

The lantern lit up one of the typical caverns of the country, so many of which have been utilised for strongholds by the Matabele, Mashona, and other chiefs, and Lennox found himself in a rift of the stone which ran right up overhead, a vast crack which the light of the lantern was too feeble to pierce, while away to the right ran a low-roofed passage, striking off almost at right angles, but only to *zigzag* farther on and die away in the darkness.

"Bayonets, lads!" cried Lennox again; "the other man must be down here."

"Look out!" cried Captain Roby, who was close behind. "Mind that open lantern there. Hi, sergeant! is there any sign of powder or dynamite?"

"No, sir," cried the non-com sharply, as he held the lantern as high as he could and made its light play in every direction. "All a bam to scare us, sir. No, no!" he yelled. "Keep back, every one. Up here, sir, in this hole. There's a bag that looks like those we found. Take the lantern, Mr Lennox, sir."

"No," cried the young officer; "keep it, and light me. The other fellow can't get away; we'll have him afterwards. Here we are," he continued, reaching up to a niche and drawing out a powder-bag. "Will you have it passed out, Mr Roby?"

"Yes: take hold, one of you.—Captain Edwards."

"Here you are."

"See that the powder-bag is put well out of the prisoner's reach. He is fast bound, but he might try to play us some trick."

"Yes, all right," said the captain; and then to the two men left on guard by the prisoner, "Keep a sharp eye on this man; don't let him stir."

"No, sir," was the reply; and then the order was given for the powder to be guarded.

As the captain returned it was to meet a man bearing out another bag, and he entered the cavern in time to see Lennox draw out another, and again another, till eight had been dragged out of the place into which they had been packed and carried out into the open air.

"Why, Lennox, man," he said laughingly, "you handle those bags as if they were tea. Aren't you afraid that some of them will explode?"

"Not he," said Dickenson, who was looking on and holding up the second lantern. "No danger. I'm here. I've been watching so that he shouldn't light a cigarette."

There was a titter from the men near, and Captain Roby cried impatiently, "Why, there's enough to have blown the top off the kopje and destroyed the big gun."

"Thoroughly, I should say, wedged-in there as it was," said Dickenson. "How much more is there, Lennox?"

"That's all," was the reply. "No, no. There's a great rift here to the right, full too."

"Hand it out, then, quickly," said Captain Roby. "Be careful there with your rifles; if a man lets his off by accident we shall all be blown to atoms."

"They'll take care," said Captain Edwards; "eh, my lads?"

"Rather, sir!" said the sergeant grimly; and all worked hard and carefully avoided the lanterns, till Lennox announced that the second rift had given out its last bag.

"Yes, that's all," he said; "but I want to know how they got it up here."

"They managed to get it up in the dark," said Captain Roby. "There, you may open a lantern now. Is there any sign of a train, Lennox?"

"Not the ghost of one. But I expect our friend meant to blow up the gun and do as much damage as he could besides. We were none too soon. Now what about the other? he must be in here somewhere. Shall I lead on, sir?"

"Yes," said Captain Roby sharply. "Take the sergeant with one lantern and ten men. I'll follow with the other lantern and ten more. You, Captain Edwards, keep a guard over the powder and the prisoner. Of course your men will be ready to receive any one trying to escape after avoiding our search."

"Right," was the answer; and sword in one hand, revolver in the other, Lennox and Dickenson began their advance into the maze-like cavern, closely followed by the sergeant holding the lantern well on high so that its rays kept on flashing from the men's bayonets

"Keep your eyes well skinned, Drew, old chap," whispered Dickenson, "and never mind your revolver. You're sure to miss in a place like this.— You behind, lads. The bayonet, mind, whenever our friend here makes a rush; he must be stopped."

There was a low murmur of assent from the men, and then, with eyes and bayonets gleaming strangely in the dancing light, the party moved steadily on into the weird darkness of the cave.

Chapter Fifteen
The Plot that Failed

The searchers' way was now a narrow crack such as might have been formed by some mighty convulsion of nature which tore apart a gigantic mass of stone, the fracture running here and there where veins of some softer material had yielded, to be separated sometimes only two or three feet, and at others opening out to form rugged chambers as much as twenty feet in extent, whose roofs ran up so high, that the dim light from the lanterns failed to reach them. Here and there were niches and crevices which were carefully searched in the expectation of their proving to be hiding-places; but the men, who forced their way in without hesitation, failed to obtain any result.

Upon reaching one which seemed to be the deepest, Dickenson, who was first to notice it, paused to shout, "Now, Dirck, old chap, come out and surrender before we fire."

"No, no," cried Lennox; "how do we know but what there may be quite a store of powder farther in?"

"But it looks such an awkward place," said Dickenson. "A fellow with a bayonet might keep a regiment at bay."

"Yes," said Lennox coolly; "it looks awkward, but come on."

As he spoke he pushed by, sword in hand, and began to explore the suspicious-looking rift.

"Oh, come; play fair," cried Dickenson. "I was first."

"Come along," said Lennox, with his voice sounding smothered.

"Oh, very well," grumbled Dickenson. "Bring the lantern, sergeant. We may as well see ourselves skewered."

He plunged in hastily, closely followed by the lantern-bearer, and as it seemed to be an extremely likely hiding-place, the rest of the party were halted ready to give assistance. But at the end of a minute the lantern had shown that it was a blind lead, and the explorers hurried back, and the advance was continued through narrow crack and rough opening, till the lights threw up the blank stone where the rift suddenly contracted.

"Why, here's the end of the cave!" cried Captain Roby. "We must have passed him somewhere."

"Then he is hiding somewhere high up on a shelf by the roof."

"No, no; look here," cried Lennox, stepping in advance. "Lantern—quick!"

Sergeant James stepped forward to where the young lieutenant was standing by a rough opening in the floor of the cavern, and upon the light being directed downward, to the surprise of all, the rugged branch of a small tree could be seen lowered down into a sloping position, with its boughs cut short off to form rough steps, their regularity suggesting that they were near akin in their growth to those of a fir, and affording good foot and hand hold to any one wishing to descend.

"We're on his track, sure enough," said Lennox, letting his blade hang from his wrist by the sword-knot, and beginning to descend quickly, the sergeant with the light closely following.

The next minute the leaders of the party were in a wide and spacious chamber, fairly level as to its floor, with the sides running into rugged niches and holes, all of which were well searched, without avail, a couple of men being left, sentry-like, at one which ran down like a sloping passage into some lower place.

Along this, as soon as the big chamber had proved to be empty, Lennox hurried. The descent was very steep and rugged, and necessitated his lowering himself down by his hands in two or three places, till a lower story, so to speak, was reached, in the shape of a vast chamber of the most irregular form, the whole party assembling about the entrance, where the lights were held-up, to show dimly what seemed to be huge, rounded lumps placed here and there upon heaps of broken stones or blocks which had fallen from the roof some ten or a dozen feet overhead, while at one end the top of the cave sloped down to join the rising floor.

"This seems to be the bottom of the cave," said Captain Roby. "Now, sharp, my lads. Keep that way out safe."

"Which?" said Dickenson. "Here's another hole in the floor. Lantern here. Yes, there's another private staircase with a flight of steps ready. This ought to be the well. Yes; come and listen. You can hear water rushing."

Sure enough, as they bent over the gloomy, mysterious-looking hole, up which a cool, moist breath of air arose, they could hear the gurgling rush of hurrying water, while the light held down showed the rugged bark of another tree ready for descent.

"Will you go down, Lennox?" said the captain.

"Oh yes, I'll go down," was the reply.

"Well, undress," said Dickenson banteringly. "It means a swim. Don't spoil your neat uniform."

"Will you go?" asked Lennox sharply.

"Oh yes, I'll go," said Dickenson.

"Thank you," replied Lennox through his set teeth.—"Here, sergeant, give me the lantern."

Catching it from the man, he planted his foot upon the first branch stump a foot below the edge of the yawning hole; but the moment he touched it a violent jerk was given to the tree-trunk, just as if it had been seized by some one below and wrenched round.

Lennox's position was so insecure, with one hand holding the lantern, that he was thrown off his balance, and he would have fallen headlong down but for the snatch he made at the sergeant, who also caught at him, slipped, and the two were nearly precipitated down the horrible place at the bottom of which the water was rushing with a hollow, echoing, whispering sound.

The tree saved them, the sergeant getting a firm hold; but between them the light of the lantern was shut off, hidden between the two men for the moment, and an attempt was made by Dickenson to reach and drag it up.

"I've got it," he cried. "Let it come. No, I haven't; mind."

For it had slipped through his fingers, and it went clattering down the rough, well-like place, striking against one of the projecting stumps of the tree-trunk, which turned it right over and threw it with an echoing crash against the wall, lit it up for a moment, and then the flame within was extinguished.

"Yah!" roared Captain Roby as the place was plunged into absolute darkness. "Here, bring up the other lantern."

There was silence, broken by panting and scuffling as of two men engaged in a struggle.

Then Sergeant James said hoarsely, "All right, sir?"

"Yes," panted Lennox, "but I thought I was gone."

"Who has got that other lantern?" asked the captain.

"It went out, sir," came in a husky tone from its bearer.

"Bah!" exclaimed Captain Roby. "Here, two of you make your way back to the top; be smart, and bring two more lanterns."

There was a low, hissing sound as of men all drawing in a deep breath at the same time, and before the captain could repeat his command a peculiar sound came up the hole.

"Look out!" cried Lennox. "Bayonets here! Some one is coming up."

Sergeant James sank upon his knees in the darkness, felt about for the edge of the hole, and then leaning over, seized hold of the tree-trunk, and whispered, "Some one's trying to drag it down, sir." Then in a stentorian voice: "Ahoy there! Fire straight down, my lads!"

There was a final jerk given to the trunk, next a grating and scratching sound against the wall, and then a rushing noise caused by the dislodging of a stone which fell with a crash, sending echoes repeating themselves far below, and after what seemed to be a measurable space of time there was a dull *plosh* as the stone plunged into water.

"Well," said Dickenson, breaking the silence as all about him stood breathlessly listening for the next sound, "I'm rather glad that wasn't I."

"Attention!" cried Captain Roby angrily as two or three of the men burst into a half-smothered guffaw. "Who has a match?"

"I have," said Dickenson, striking a wax vesta as he spoke, the bright flash being followed by the feeble little taper flame; "but it's nearly the last. Bring that lantern here."

There was a quick response, the bearer opening the door with fumbling fingers, and as he held the rapidly burning-down match Dickenson drew the pricker from his belt, held the light close, and began to operate on the wick of the little lamp inside the lantern.

"Only slipped down," he said. "Wick was too small. Hold the lantern still, man. That's better. I shall get it up directly."

The scratching of the sharp steel point sounded quite loudly on the socket of the lamp as the wick kept eluding the efforts made, and the faint light threw up the grim faces around in a strangely weird way, while not another sound was heard but the hissing rush of the water far below, till suddenly there was a sharp bang, the lantern was nearly knocked out of its holder's hand, and Dickenson yelled, "Oh Gemini!"

They were in utter darkness once more.

"Bah!" cried Roby. "How careless!"

"Burned down to my fingers," said Dickenson coolly out of the black darkness. "Do you know, I don't believe a bullet going into you hurts a bit more than being burned like that."

"For goodness' sake strike another match, Mr Dickenson," cried the captain angrily.

"Fumbling for it now, sir. Doesn't seem as if there are any more. Yes, here's one little joker hiding in a corner. Got him!"

Scr-r-r-itch! went the little match, and flashed into a bright flame which formed an arch in the air and disappeared down the yawning pit.

"Why, you left go!" cried Captain Roby.

"No wonder if I did, after burning my fingers so," grumbled Dickenson; "but I didn't, for I've got the wax here. Top jumped off."

Then there was a tinkling sound as he shook the little silver box he held.

"Hurrah!" he cried. "Here's one more. Ready with that lantern, my lad?"

"Yes, sir."

"Take the lamp out and let me try if I can get the wick up with the pricker before I strike the match."

The men's breathing could be heard as they stood, with every nerve on the strain, listening to the scraping, scratching sound made in the excitement and dread caused by the horrible darkness; for there was not a man present, from officer to the youngest private, who had much faith that they would find the way back to the mouth of the cavern.

"For goodness' sake mind you don't drop the match, Mr Dickenson," said the captain suddenly.

"Trust me, sir," said Dickenson coolly.—"Ah, would you slip back into the paraffin. Come out," he continued, apostrophising the wick he was pricking at. "Phew! How nasty it makes one's fingers smell! Bravo! Got him at last."

"Tut, tut, tut!" ejaculated the captain impatiently.

"Wait till I've opened the wick a little more. That's it! Here, what am I to wipe my fingers on?"

"Oh, never mind your fingers, man," cried Captain Roby.

"But they're quite slippery, sir."

"Rub 'em on my sleeve, sir," growled Sergeant James.

"Thankye, sergeant, but I've just polished them on my own."

Click! click! went the lamp as it was thrust back into the lantern, and there was once more the sound of men drawing their breath hard—a sound that was checked suddenly as the last match was heard to tinkle in the silver box.

"Got him!" said Dickenson audibly as he talked to himself. "Now then, ready with the lantern?" he said aloud.

"Yes, sir."

"Give me elbow-room, all of you."

There was the sound of men shrinking back.

"Now then," said Dickenson, "here goes I hope the head won't come off this time."

Fuzz! and directly after *fuzz!* but no light followed the rubbing of the match.

"Why, it has got no head," cried the striker in dismay, and at this announcement the men uttered a groan. "All right," cried Dickenson cheerily. "I was rubbing its tail instead of the head."

Cr-r-r-r-r-ch! went the match; there was a burst of flame, followed at a trifling interval by the steady glow of the tiny taper, and the young officer's fingers were lit up and seen to bear the flame to the lantern lamp, which caught at once and blazed up, when the door was shut with a click, and the men exhaled their pent-up breath in a hearty cheer.

"Well done!" said Captain Roby. "Here, I'll lead now; or would you like to continue what you began, Mr Lennox?"

The latter looked at him, and seemed to hesitate.

"Oh, very well," said Roby rather contemptuously. "I'll lead myself."

"No, no; you misunderstood me," cried Lennox as Dickenson turned upon him wonderingly. "I want to go on."

"I don't want to rob you of your charce," said Roby.—"Here, Mr Dickenson, what two men went back to fetch those lights?"

"Corporal May and Channings tried to feel their way, sir, but they found the job hopeless."

"But I gave orders."

"Yes, sir," said Dickenson; "but they could not find their way."

"I'll speak about this later on," said Roby. "Now then, Mr Lennox, are you ready?"

"Yes, sir," was the reply as the young officer stood waiting for Sergeant James, who had slipped off his scarf, passed it through the handle of the lantern, and was securing it to his waist.

"Then forward!" cried Roby.

"Better let me lead, sir, on account of the light," half-whispered the sergeant; "then you can be ready to give point at any one who comes at me."

"No," said Lennox firmly; "I must lead. Leave your rifle, and follow me, bayonet in hand."

He stepped to the mouth of the pit, tried the ladder-like contrivance, found it fairly firm, and began to descend as fast as he could; while, risking the strength of the wood, the sergeant stepped on as soon as there was room and followed, shedding the dancing light's rays on the weird-looking walls of the place.

Dickenson went next, and the captain followed, to find those in front waiting upon a fairly wide shelf, upon which the bottom of the tree was propped, while beneath it, and sloping now, the well-like pit went down into the black darkness, up from which the hollow, echoing rush of water came in a way which made some of the stoutest present shudder.

The shelf was at the mouth of a low archway which proved, upon the lantern being held up, to be the entrance to another of the ramifications of the great series of caves with which the kopje was honeycombed. Here within a few yards lay the first lantern, which had rebounded on falling and rolled down into a narrow crack in the flooring, a rift which ran from somewhere ahead, draining the interior of the cavern passage, and bearing a tiny stream of water to join the rushing waters below, these being undoubtedly the source of the perennial stream which issued from the foot of the kopje.

One of the men pounced upon the lantern at once, to find that, though the glass was much cracked, it was perfectly ready for use; and there was a short delay while it was relit without application to the one the sergeant had just detached, one of the men having now recalled that he had a tin box of matches nearly full.

The moment this was done Captain Roby gave the order to advance. He sent the lantern-bearers forward with orders to keep to right and left; and at the end of about a hundred feet, where the cavern chamber was beginning to contract, he called aloud for them to halt.

"Now, Mr Lennox," he cried, "advance with six men abreast in a line with the lights, and make ready to fire if the man in front does not surrender. Attention!"

His orders echoed along the roof of what seemed to be quite a narrow passage in front, and the men listened till the last echoes died out, when Captain Roby spoke again.

"Hoi, there, you Boer in hiding!" he cried. "Your comrade's a prisoner, and if you wish to save your life, surrender too."

The captain waited, but there was no reply, and the word was given to advance again, when suddenly from out of the darkness beyond the range of the lights there came the sharp, clear *click! click!* of a piece being cocked.

"There's the answer, Mr Lennox," said the captain. "Give your orders, and clear the place."

"No, stop; I surrender," came from a hoarse voice speaking in broken English. "Tell your men not to shoot."

"Come forward," cried Lennox, "and give up your piece."

He stepped towards the spot from whence the voice had come, to see the crossing lights of the two lanterns centre upon the broad, familiar face of one of the Boers who had been captured, and who had returned with the loaded wagons and the powder-bags, of which the last portion had been secured a short time before.

The man halted, and stood with his rifle presented at the young officer's breast.

The man halted, and stood with his rifle presented at the young officer's breast.

"One man can't fight against a hundred," he growled.

"Only with treachery and deceit," said Lennox sternly. "Give up your rifle, you cowardly dog."

"Not till you give your English word that I shall not be shot," replied the Boer.

"I'll give the order for you to be shot down if you don't give up your piece," cried Lennox angrily.

"You give the word that I shall only be a prisoner, or I'll shoot you through the heart," cried the Boer harshly.

"I give no word. Surrender unconditionally," cried Lennox, whose blood was up.

"Give your word, you miserable rooinek!" growled the Boer, whose teeth shone in the light, giving him the aspect of some fierce beast at bay. "Give your word. You're covered—your word of honour, or I'll fire."

"Fire!" shouted Captain Roby from behind; but the six men halted before obeying the ill-judged command. For, in response to the Boer's threat, Lennox had sprung forward to strike at the presented piece, the edge of his sword clicking loudly against the barrel of the rifle, turning it sufficiently aside to disorder the desperate man's aim, so that the bullet whistled by him and over the heads of his men, before sending a little shower of granite splinters and dust from the side of the cavern.

Before the Boer could fire again Lennox had him by the throat, and in another minute he was held up against the cavern wall by three men with their bayonets, while the sergeant wrested the rifle from his hands and tore away the man's well-filled bandolier.

"Ah!" he snarled; "cowards again. Always cowards, since the day when you ran away from us at Majuba."

"Hold your tongue, sir, before you are hurt by some of the men who know that they have one of the bravo miscreants before them who lay powder-mines ready to destroy those they dare not fight in the open field."

"Tell the dog I'll have him gagged as well as bound if he does not keep his tongue quiet," said Captain Roby, coming up.

The Boer laughed mockingly; and Captain Roby, who seemed unable to restrain the anger rising within him, turned away.

"See that he has no revolver, Lennox," he said hoarsely, "and try to find out whether he has any companions."

"He wouldn't say if he had," replied Lennox; "but we'll soon search and see. Sergeant James is making him fast. Yes, he had a revolver," he continued as he saw the sergeant take the weapon and thrust it inside his belt.

The next minute the prisoner was secure between two men, and the light-bearers went forward, to be brought to a standstill almost directly by the contraction of the cellar-like place, out of which there was no way in that direction.

Having satisfied themselves of this, the party hastened back to the tree, and stood looking about for a time, examining a few cracks and rifts, before the orders were given to mount to the upper cave—a risky and unpleasant task, for the tree-trunk was loose. The men, however, for the most part made light of it, and as soon as the big chamber was reached they proceeded to thoroughly examine that, when, to the delight of all, its real character of a hiding-place and storehouse belonging to one of the native tribes was revealed: for scores of huge woven baskets were piled-up, looking at a few yards' distance, with no better illumination than the military lamps, like masses of rock, but containing hundreds upon hundreds of bushels of hard, sweet corn, failing which there would soon have been only one chance of escape for the detachment, and that by a bold attempt to cut their way through.

The search was continued, but nothing more rewarded their efforts. There was the ample supply of corn, stored up by some tribe, and outside the bags of gunpowder hidden by the Boers, whose plan was quite evident, and thoroughly realised by all who had discovered the entrance—to blow up the great gun captured from them and destroy the stronghold that checked their advance.

Before long a sentry was marching up and down in front of that ingenious specimen of native work, the big stone entrance to the cave which ran so easily upon a pivot; while the detachment in charge of the big gun talked shudderingly of the risk they had unknowingly been running, for, given a little longer time and the right opportunity, their two crafty enemies would undoubtedly have fired their mine and blown the greater part of the kopje-top into the air.

"I was growing anxious over the long silence," said the colonel, smiling, after he had been made aware or the success attending the party that had hurried up at the alarm, and after he had examined the prisoners; "but you have done a splendid night's work—cleared away an impending danger, and secured a storehouse of corn sufficient for a whole month."

"A month or more," said Captain Roby.

"Ha! Then we can hold out and wait. But about these prisoners. Here, major, what do you say?"

"Humph!" ejaculated the major. "Two of the treacherous hounds who deceived us, and whom we let go to fetch us supplies."

"And came back to blow us up," said the colonel.

"Failed in that," said Captain Roby, "and then started another cold-blooded, treacherous plan."

"Yes," said the colonel, "based upon the knowledge they must have wrung from one of the native tribes they have oppressed. Well, gentlemen, we have two of the miscreant spies. What next?"

"The fate of spies," said Captain Roby. "I think it is due to our men that they should be shot."

"Kept prisoners till we can hand them over to the general, and let him decide," said the major. "What do you say, Edwards?"

"They are prisoners, and beaten," said the captain. "Yes, I side with you."

"Two against you, Roby," said the colonel.—"Well, Lennox—and you, Dickenson—you may as well give your opinion. What do you say, Dickenson?"

"I should like to see that black-haired brute tied up and flogged, sir."

"Should you?" said the colonel, smiling. "Well, I dare say he deserves it; but it is not the punishment we can give a prisoner, so your opinion will stand alone.—Well, Lennox?"

"Oh, it's all war, sir; and the fellows are half-savage peasants who hate us like poison. You can't shoot them, sir, for fighting their best—their way."

"No, Mr Lennox, I can't shoot them; but it will be a horrible nuisance to have to keep them as prisoners. I wish they had died fighting like brave men. As it is they will have to live prisoners till the war is at an end. Now then, about where to place them."

"Here, I know, sir," said Dickenson, laughing. "Shut them up in the kopje. They'll be quite at home there."

"No," said Lennox, joining in his comrade's merriment; "don't trust them there, sir. They're malicious enough to spend their time destroying all the corn."

"Well done, Lennox!" said the colonel emphatically. "I'm glad you spoke, for before anything was said I had determined to make their hiding-place their prison. You are right. That would not do at all.—Roby, you must have your prisoners placed in the safest hut that you can find, and let a sentry share their prison, for they must never be left alone. Now, gentlemen: bed."

Chapter Sixteen
The Lost Man

"Yes, sir, I'm very sorry, and feel that it's a great disgrace," said Colour-Sergeant James.

"Sorry!" said Captain Roby contemptuously.

"It's all I can be, sir," said the sergeant sadly. "I'm not going to defend myself."

"But how could you miss him when the roll was called?"

"I don't know, sir. I suppose it was all due to the excitement and being fagged out with what we'd gone through in that black hole."

"Black hole!" cried Roby. "You deserve the Black Hole yourself, sergeant."

"Yes, sir. I thought he answered, but the poor fellow must have lost his way somehow, and have got left behind."

"It's horrible," cried Roby. "I don't know what's to be done."

"Go in search of the poor fellow at once. It's enough to send a man out of his mind," broke in Lennox impatiently.

"I did not ask you for your opinion, Mr Lennox," said the captain coldly.—"Here, James, come with me to the colonel at once."

"Yes, sir," said the sergeant, and he followed his superior.

"What nonsense!" cried Dickenson. "Here, Drew, old man, let's go on up to the hole at once with half-a-dozen men and lanterns."

"That's what I wanted to do," said Lennox bitterly; "but I suppose it would be going against discipline."

"Going against your grandmother! Hesitate, when the poor fellow may be dying of fright? He is rather a chicken-hearted sort of a customer."

"So would you be if you lost yourself in that dismal hole."

"True, oh king! I should sit down in a fit of the horrors, and howl for my mother till I cried myself to sleep."

"No, you wouldn't, Bob. But old Roby does make me set up my bristles sometimes. I don't know what's come to him lately."

"I know what I should like to see come to him."

"What?"

"A good licking."

"Yes, to be followed by court-martial."

"Not if a Boer did it," said Dickenson, chuckling.

"What are you laughing at?"

"Thoughts, dear boy. Only thinking of what a lark it would be if he began bullying one of our prisoners—say Blackbeard—and the savage old Boer slipped into him with his fists. I shouldn't hurry to help him more than I could help."

"Don't humbug," said Lennox.

"I tell you I shouldn't. Look here, Drew, old chap, you haven't found me out yet. I'm not half such a nice young angel as you think."

"Hold your row; here's James." For the sergeant came hurrying in.— "Well?"

"Search party of twenty directly, gentlemen. Colonel sends word that you two are to come with us."

"Right," cried Lennox excitedly. "What did the colonel say?"

"'Poor fellow!' sir; and then he turned on the captain, sir."

"Yes," cried Dickenson eagerly, "What did he say to him?"

"Why the something or another hadn't he gone to look for Corporal May at once?"

"Bravo!" said Dickenson; and Lennox, who was buckling on his sword hurriedly, felt better.

"But how about you, James? Are you going to be degraded for neglect?" said Dickenson as they hurried out to join the men already assembled.

"No, sir," replied the sergeant, with a broad smile spreading over his manly countenance. "The colonel heard all I had to say in defence, and he just says, 'Bad job, sergeant—accident.'—You know his short way, sir?— Then, 'Be off and get your men together; find the poor fellow as soon as you can.'"

Captain Roby was just hurrying to a group of men waiting to make the start, when Sergeant James came up, carrying all the lanterns he could muster in a bunch. "Come, gentlemen," he said sharply; "make haste, please. Have you plenty of matches, sergeant?"

"Yes, sir."

"Fall in, my lads. Here, stop. No rifles; only your bayonets."

The firearms were returned to their quarters, and a couple of minutes later the search party were on their way to the kopje.

"Beg pardon, sir," said the sergeant, suddenly breaking from his place to address the captain; "wouldn't it be better to take a long rope with us?"

"What for?" said Roby angrily. "For the men to hold on by in case any one should be lost? Absurd!"

The sergeant was returning to his place, and Lennox and Dickenson exchanging glances, when the captain altered his mind.

"Yes," he said; "on second thoughts, we may as well take a coil. Hurry back and fetch one, sergeant."

The latter handed his bunch of lanterns to one of the men, and went off back to quarters at the double, while the party marched on.

"Fasting doesn't do old Cantankerous any good," said Dickenson in a half-whisper.

"Quiet! Quiet! He'll be hearing you and getting worse," said Lennox.

"Impossible!" grunted Dickenson. "He wants a week's good feeding or a fit of illness to do him good. He's going sour all over."

The sergeant did not overtake the party till they were close upon the entrance to the cave, where a sentry was pacing up and down; and now a sudden thought struck Roby.

"Here, sergeant," he cried angrily as the latter hurried up, rather breathless with his exertions. "How are we to get into the place? You haven't brought a crowbar to move the stone."

"No, sir. Left it hidden close by last night."

"Oh!" grunted Roby, halting the men; while the sergeant handed the coil of rope to one of them, who slipped it on over head and one shoulder, to wear it like a scarf; and James went on a few yards to a crack in the side of the rocky wall, thrust in his arm, drew out the bar, and trotted back to the opening, inserted the chisel, and raised the stone about an inch, when it turned upon its pivot directly.

"Wonderfully well made," said Dickenson. "One might have passed it a hundred times."

"Silence in the ranks!" cried Roby sternly; and the sergeant stepped into the dark hole at once, placed his hands one on either side of his lips, and gave a tremendous hail.

All listened to the shout, which went echoing through the passages and chambers of the cavern; but there was no reply, nor yet to half-a-dozen more hails.

"Tut, tut, tut!" ejaculated Roby. "I expected to find him waiting close to the entrance. Lanterns."

The men were already inside lighting them, eight being rapidly got ready; and once more the party began to traverse the weird place, but under far more favourable circumstances, the line of golden dots formed by the lanterns giving every one a far better opportunity of judging what the place was like.

At every turn in the crooked way a halt was called, and a fresh series of hails went echoing on before them; but not so much as a whisper of an answer greeted their ears.

"The poor fellow must have become tired out with waiting," said Captain Roby, "and dropped off to sleep."

"He sleeps pretty soundly, then," whispered Dickenson, who was in front with Lennox, following the sergeant, who carried the first lantern.

"Ought to have been woke up by that last shout, though," said Lennox. "What do you say, sergeant?"

"I'm afraid we shall come upon him soon regularly off his head, gentlemen," said the sergeant, "He isn't the pluckiest chap in his company."

"Don't talk like that, sergeant," said Lennox sharply. "It's enough to drive any poor fellow crazy to find himself shut up in a place like this and feel that he may never be found."

"Well, yes," added Dickenson, "it is; without counting all the horrors he'd conjure up about bogies and things coming after him in the dark."

"I dare say, sir," said the sergeant; "though I don't suppose there's anything worse here than bats."

"Halt! Now, all together," cried the captain from behind, and another series of shouts were given.

There was no response, and the party went spreading out and examining every nook as they passed through the echoing chambers, but found nothing.

"Is it likely that he did come out with us?" said Lennox as they neared the second well-like opening over the rushing water.

"Can't say, sir," said the sergeant. "The last I saw of him was when we were down in the lowest place, advancing to meet the second prisoner. I just had a squint of his face then by the lantern, and it looked like tallow."

"Effect of the light," said Dickenson.

"No, sir. It was the getting down that tree and hearing the water."

"That's it, sergeant," said the nearest man behind. "I never thought of it till you said that."

"Thought of what?" said the sergeant roughly.

"'Bout what Corporal May said to me."

"What was it?"

"That it was enough to scare any one getting down such a ladder as that, and if he'd known, he'd have seen the service anywhere before he'd have come."

"Yes, he looked regularly scared, gentlemen," said the sergeant; and then he stopped short, swinging his lantern over the hole before him and showing the top of the tree ladder, while the gurgling, echoing whisper of the running water seemed to fill the air with strange sounds. But these were drowned directly by a fresh burst of hails, which went echoing away.

"Forward!" said the captain at last. "Steady in front, there. Be careful how you go down, men."

"Don't be alarmed, dear Roby," whispered Dickenson. "Just as if we shouldn't be careful of our invaluable necks."

There was plenty of light now, for Lennox carried a lantern on going down after the sergeant, who had gone first, and stood at the bottom holding up his own, while four more were held over the yawning pit from the top. The men, too, were in better trim for the descent, knowing as they did the worst of what they had to encounter, so that they went down pluckily enough, in spite of the tree quivering and threatening to turn round, till it was held more steadily at both ends.

Then, as all crowded into the archway and hailed once more, their shouts seemed to return to them faintly from the arrow-shaped hollow, which from being broad at first went off nearly to a point, and more weirdly still from the continuation of the pit where the water ran.

"I'm beginning to be afraid he is not here," said the captain. "Open out, my lads, and thoroughly search every hollow and corner."

The men shouted again, with no result; and then they spread out like a fan and advanced, searching behind every stone, right on past the spot where the second Boer had been captured, and on once more till the cavern narrowed in and there was only room to creep.

"Hold the light closer, sergeant," said Lennox.

"See anything?" cried Roby from just behind him.

"Can't tell yet, sir.—What's that, sergeant?'

For answer the sergeant went down on his hands and knees and advanced, pushing his lantern before him.

"There, you needn't do that," said Roby impatiently. "The man's not here. It's a false alarm. He wasn't left behind, and we shall find him somewhere, when we get back to quarters. Come out, sergeant. I'm sick of this."

"But there's something here, sir."

"Eh? What is it?"

The sergeant thrust something behind him, and Lennox went down on hands and knees, reached into the narrow hole, which the sergeant nearly filled, and snatched the object from the man's hand.

"His helmet!" cried Lennox excitedly, and he too passed it back to where Roby and Dickenson were, and they examined the recovered headpiece.

"Oh, there's no doubt about it," said Dickenson. "Look here," he cried as Lennox and the sergeant came back; "what do you make of this?"

"Oh! it's the poor fellow's helmet, gentlemen," said the sergeant. "Look at his number, sir."

"Then where is he? Is there any opening in yonder?"

"Not room for a rat, sir. Seems as if he must have been left behind and felt his way in there to sleep. Look here, sir; I found these too."

The speaker held out a short black pipe with a little blackened, lately-smoked tobacco at the bottom, and a tin box containing plenty of matches.

"Why, he had all these and never said a word when I was so hard pushed," cried Dickenson.

"I expect he was in too much of a stoo to remember them, sir," said the sergeant. "He must have been precious queer, or he wouldn't have left these and his helmet behind."

"He was nearly off his chump, sergeant, with having to come down," said the man with the short memory.

"Then he has been here!" cried Captain Roby. "But where is he now?"

As if moved by one impulse, every one present turned sharply round to look in the direction of the archway beyond which the sloping continuation of the entrance-pit went on down to the running water. No one spoke, but all thought horrors; and Lennox acted, for, snatching a lantern from the nearest bearer, he ran as fast as the rugged floor would let him, back to the archway, took hold of the tree-trunk, and leaned over the horrible hole, swinging the light downward, while those who watched him, looking weird and strange in the distance, heard him shout loudly, and listened to hear, very faintly rising from far below, a faintly uttered, hollow moan.

Chapter Seventeen
Fishing with a Rope

"Forward!" cried Captain Roby loudly.

"Forward!" said a wonderfully exact echo from the pit, and the cavern chamber seemed to burst into strange, echoing repetitions of the confused trampling and rushing and thundering of feet, as, with the dancing lanterns, the men sprang forward to render help.

"He's down here," cried Lennox in excitement. "Silence, all of you!"

Captain Roby looked annoyed at the way in which his subaltern officer seemed to take the lead; but he said nothing then, only stood frowning, while in the midst of a breathless silence Lennox leaned over the dangerous-looking place and hailed again.

"Corporal! Are you down there?"

There was no response, and once more he hailed.

"Corporal May!"

This time there was a piteous moan.

"Oh! there's no doubt about it," cried Lennox. "Tie a lantern to the rope and lower it down. Let's see where he is."

"Thank you, Mr Lennox," said Roby coldly. "I will give the necessary orders."

"I beg pardon, sir," said Lennox, drawing back; but as he glanced aside he saw that the sergeant was busy with the end of the rope, fastening it to the handle of one of the lanterns, and the man who had slipped it off his shoulder was rapidly uncoiling the ring.

"Anybody got a flask?" said Dickenson. "We might send him down a reviver with the light."

But there was no reply, flasks being rarities at Groenfontein, and such as there were did not contain a drop. By this time the lantern was ready, and Sergeant James glanced at the captain, who signed to him to lower away.

Directly after, the descending lantern was lighting up the sides of the gulf, which were not six feet apart; but how far the great crack-like place extended they could not see, the light penetrating but a little distance, and then all was black darkness, out of which, from far below, there came up the murmuring, gurgling rush of the running water.

As for the lantern, as soon as it was lowered down it ceased swinging, coming with a sharp tap against smooth rock which went downward in a pretty regular slope, but so steep that the lantern lay upon its side and glided down as fast as the men could pay out the rope.

"I sha'n't have length enough, I'm afraid, sir," said the sergeant, who leaned over the edge.

"Then why didn't you bring more?" cried the captain angrily.

The sergeant was silent, and *grate! grate! grate!* the lantern went on down over the rock face, which sparkled with moisture, for an exceedingly thin sheet of water glistened and went on wearing it down as it probably had from the time the great kopje cavern was formed.

But still there was no sign of the missing man—nothing but glistening rock, and beyond that darkness.

"How much more rope have you?" said the sergeant in a whisper.

"'Bout a dozen feet," said the man who was passing it to him from behind.

"Swing the lantern to and fro," cried the captain sharply.

"It won't swing, sir," replied the sergeant. "If I try, it will only roll over on to its face."

"Never mind; you haven't tried. Now swing it," cried Roby.

"Bottom," cried the sergeant, for the lantern stopped short, and down beneath it there was a flash and a quivering reflection, showing that it was close to the flowing water.

"What is it resting on?" said Lennox eagerly, for he had forgotten the snub he had received and was all eagerness to help. "I didn't hear it click on rock."

"Just what I was thinking, sir," replied the sergeant, lifting the suspended lantern again and letting it descend once more.

"I wish to goodness, Mr Lennox, that you would not keep on interfering," cried Captain Roby angrily.—"Now, sergeant, what do you make out?"

"Rests on something soft, sir. No; it's hit against something hard. Why, it's metal—a buckle."

"I know," cried Lennox, forgetting himself again. "You've lowered it right down on to the poor fellow, and he's above the water."

"Mr—" began the captain angrily, but his words were drowned in the hearty cheer given by the men.—"Silence!" cried Captain Roby, and leaning over, he shouted down the horrible-looking pit.—"Unfasten the rope from the lantern," he said, "and tie it tightly round your breast. Don't be frightened now: we'll soon have you out."

There was no response.

"Tut, tut, tut!" went the captain again. "Some one will have to go down. Who'll volunteer?"

"I will, sir," cried Lennox excitedly, before any one else could answer.

The captain was silent for a few moments, and then, in a way that seemed to suggest that he had been trying to find some objection to giving his consent, "Very well, Mr Lennox," he said.—"Here, sergeant, haul up the light again."

This was rapidly done, the lantern set free, and the rope tied securely just beneath the young man's arms.

"How will you have the lantern, sir?" said the sergeant.

"I will see to that, James," said the captain. "Unfasten your belt, Mr Lennox, and pass it through the ring of the lantern so that it can hang to your waist and leave your hands free."

"Just as if we didn't know!" said the sergeant to himself as he helped in this arrangement.

"Sure the knot will not slip, sergeant?" said Lennox.

"Oh, it won't come undone, sir. If it moves at all, it will be to get tighter."

"That is what I meant. I want to breathe."

"Less talking there," said the captain. "Recollect that a man's life is in danger. If you feel any compunction about going, Mr Lennox, make way for one of the men."

"Ready, sir, and waiting for your orders," said Lennox quietly.

"Very well. Now then, lower away."

The sergeant took a firm hold of the rope, and whispered "Trust me, sir," to the explorer, who nodded and looked calmly enough in the sergeant's eyes, and gave way as he felt himself lifted off the stones upon which he stood and gently lowered down till he was half-hanging, half-sitting, against the sloping side of the rock. Then a few feet of the rope glided through the sergeant's hands, and Lennox stiffened himself out, to hang rigidly, feeling his back rest against the wet rock, over which he began to glide slowly, and then faster and faster as he was let down hand over hand, seeing nothing but the black darkness lit up like a quaint halo in front of him, and going down what he felt to be a terrible depth. He fought hard against one horrible thought which would trouble him: should he ever be pulled up again? And no sooner had he mastered this than another gruesome idea forced itself as it were out of the darkness in front, the words to his excited imagination seeming to be luminous: suppose the rope should break!

It is wonderful how much thought will compress itself into a minute. It was so here, these ideas repeating themselves again and again before the young man's feet touched something soft and yielding, and upon his stretching his legs wide he felt slippery rock.

"Hold on!" he shouted, and there was what sounded like a mocking chorus of "On—on—on—on!" beginning loudly and distinctly, and going right away into a faint whisper.

Turning himself a little on one side, Lennox bent outward so that the light of the lantern flashed from a narrow stream of water which, from the bubbles and foam, he could see was rushing towards him, to pass down under the ledge of rock upon which one foot rested; but now he was able to see what he wanted, and that was the missing corporal hanging face upward, but with head and neck over the edge of a block of stone which had checked his rapid slide down into the gulf, while the next moment the light showed that the poor fellow's legs were also hanging downward, the ledge being exceedingly narrow.

"Well?" cried Captain Roby. "Found him?"

"Yes, sir. Seems to be quite insensible. I can get my arms round him and hold him if you can haul us up. Will the rope bear us both?"

"No!" came in a roar from up above, every man, in his excitement, negativing the proposal.

"Silence, men!" cried the captain angrily. Then he shouted down, "It would be too risky. Here, I'll have the rope slackened, and you can untie it and make it fast round May's chest. I'll have him hauled up, and send the rope down again for you.—Slacken away, my lads."

The pressure on the rope ceased for a moment as it was slackened, and then it tightened with a jerk, and there was a loud, echoing splash as Lennox was plunged into rushing water to the waist, the sensation being as if he had been suddenly seized and was being dragged under into some great hole.

"Hold hard!" he roared, and the echoes seized upon the last word— "Hard—hard—hard!"—running right away again till it was a whisper.

"Why, what are you about?" cried Roby.

"Trying to save the light," panted Lennox. "There is no room to stand on the ledge with the poor fellow. Haul up a little more. My face is on a level with him now. Haul! haul! The water seems to suck me down. Ha!" he gasped; "that's better," and he wrenched himself round, catching at a piece of slippery rock that was against his waist, and looking for foothold, for a few moments in vain, till he saw a way out of his difficulty.

"How are you getting on?" cried the captain excitedly.

"I'm obliged to kneel right on the poor fellow," said Lennox; "there's so little room. He's alive—I can feel his heart beating. Keep the rope tight for a few minutes."

"Tight it is, sir," shouted Sergeant James.

"Look here, Lennox," cried Roby hoarsely: "can you unfasten the rope and tie it to the corporal? We can see nothing from up here."

"That's what I'm trying to find out, sir," replied Lennox.—"Yes, I think so."

"Think! You must be sure," cried Dickenson, whose voice sounded husky and strange. "Look here, I'm going to slide down to you."

"Silence!" roared the captain. "You will do nothing of the kind.—Look here, Lennox."

"I'm all attention, sir."

"If you can't do as I say I must send for another rope."

"No, no, it would be horrible to leave the poor fellow; he'd slip off the rock."

"Then you must stay with him."

"Very well, sir," said Lennox after a short pause.

"Ha! I think I can do it now I've found room to kneel."

"Bravo!" shouted Dickenson.

"Will you be silent, Mr Dickenson?" cried the captain.—"Now, Lennox, what are you doing?"

"Trying to get this knot undone, sir; it's so tight." At the end of a minute he cried, "I can't move the knot. I'm going to pass it over my head, and then make a noose and slip it round the corporal."

"Can you do that?"

"Yes, sir, I think so. Now slacken away all you can, but keep a tight hold in case I have to snatch at it again."

"Oh yes, they'll keep a tight hold.—Do you hear, Sergeant James?"

"Oh yes, sir, I hear," growled the sergeant, whose face glistened with the perspiration that streamed down from the gathering-place—his brow.

"How are you getting on?" cried the captain.

"Don't talk to me, please," panted Lennox. "I'm doing my best." There was a pause, and then, "I've got it off, and I'm going to pass it over his neck and shoulders now. It will compress his chest, but I can't help it."

"Don't study that; only get it fast. Ready?" continued the captain after another pause.

"Not quite yet. It is hard to get the loop over. I have to bend down to reach with one hand, and hold on with the other."

"Go on," said the captain.

A strange rustling sound came up, and then it seemed as if the rope was being flapped against the rock.

"Can't you do it?" shouted the captain.

"Not yet. I'm obliged to rest a minute."

"Oh dear! oh dear me!" panted Captain Roby in a tone of voice that seemed to suggest other words which indicated his idea that the young subaltern was very awkward.

"Got it at last!" came up. "I think so. Yes, I have him tight—right past his arms; he can't slip. Now, haul!"

"Haul!" echoed Captain Roby. "Quick!"

But Sergeant James knew better than that. The rope had to pass through his cautious hands, and he raised it gently.

"All right, sir?" he asked.

"Yes; haul," cried Lennox. "You have him now. Right; you're lifting him right off. I'll hold on to the rock. Be sharp, for it's a very awkward—"

The young subaltern's words were cut short at that moment by a most horrible, unearthly-sounding yell; for the tightening of the rope about the unfortunate corporal, and the steady strain as he was lifted from where he had lain so long, had the effect of arousing his dormant energies. Not realising that he was being helped, he had no sooner uttered his cry of horror than, as if suddenly galvanised into life, he began to struggle violently, tearing, kicking, and catching at something to hold on to for dear life.

Unfortunately, and consequent upon the slow way in which the rope was being drawn up, the first thing his right hand came in contact with was one of Lennox's arms round which his fingers fastened as if they were of steel. The next moment his right hand was joined by his left and he clung desperately, dragging the young officer from the slippery edge of rock, and before Lennox could raise a hand to help himself and hold on in turn, and cling desperately in the hope that after all perhaps the rope might bear them both, the corporal's spasmodic clasp ended as quickly as it came. Those at the top felt the strain on the rope less, and those who were gazing down unoccupied saw the light suddenly extinguished, heard a terrible, echoing splash, followed by suckings and whisperings that seemed as if they would have no end.

For Lennox did not rise again, the rush of water bearing him rapidly down into the very bowels of the cavernous mass of rock.

Chapter Eighteen
The Corporal Relates

The party at the head of the cavern stood for a few moments perfectly motionless, listening to the dying away of the strange gurglings and whispering echoes which followed the heavy splash, and then Dickenson uttered a wild cry of horror and despair.

"Pull!" he shouted. "Pull up!" and, spurred into action by his order, Sergeant James and the two men behind him who helped with the rope hauled away rapidly, till the rigid-looking form of the corporal rose out of the darkness into the light shed by the lanterns, to be seized by the sergeant and dragged into safety.

"Is he dead?" said Captain Roby hoarsely. "I dunno, sir," growled the sergeant, loosening the noose around the rigid sufferer, and then with a few quick drags unfastening the knot which had troubled Lennox in his helpless state.

"Silence a moment," cried the captain, "while I hail!" and he made the place echo with his repetitions of the subaltern's name.

There were answers enough, but given only by the mocking echoes; otherwise all below was still save the weird, rushing sound of the water.

"Here, what are you doing, Dickenson?" cried the captain, who suddenly became aware of the fact that the young lieutenant had seized the sergeant and was hindering him from securing the end of the rope about his chest.

"He's not going down: I am," cried Dickenson hoarsely.

"You?"

"Yes; I think I'm going to leave my friend in a hole like this?"

"Hole indeed!" thought the captain. Then aloud: "Let him go down, sergeant. Here, two lanterns this time;" and as the sergeant obeyed and began securing the rope about Dickenson, Roby seized and began unbuckling the young officer's belt, and himself passed the stiff leather through the ring-handles of a couple of lanterns, and rebuckled the belt, adjusting it so that Dickenson had a light on either side.

"Ready, sergeant?" said the young officer sharply.

"All right, sir; that'll hold you safe."

"What are you going to do, Dickenson?" said Roby, in a voice that did not sound like his own.

"I don't know," cried the young officer, with a curious hysterical ring in his voice. "Go down.—See when I get below.—Now then, quick!—Lower away.—Fast!"

He began gliding down the sharp slope directly after.

"Faster!" shouted Dickenson before he was half-way down; and the sergeant let the rope pass through his hands as quickly as he could with safety let it go, while the lanterns lit up the glistening sides with weirdly-strange, flickering rays, till the rope was nearly all out and Dickenson stopped with a sudden jerk.

"Got him?" shouted Roby.

"No!" came up in a despairing groan. "I'm on a dripping ledge. Lower me a few feet more till I call to you to stop."

The sergeant obeyed, and the call came directly after. For there was a splash and the lights disappeared—not extinguished, but they seemed to glide under a black projection that stood out plainly as a rugged edge against the light, which made the water flash and sparkle as it could be seen gliding swiftly by.

"Well?" shouted Roby again.

"Hold on with the rope," came up. "The water's close up to the foot of the lanterns. If you let it any lower they will go out."

"Right, sir," roared Sergeant James.

"Now," shouted Roby; "see him?"

"No; the water goes down here in a whirlpool, round and round, and I can feel it sucking at me to drag me below."

"Yes, sir; I can feel it along the rope. Look at my arms," growled the sergeant.

There was a quick glance directed at the sergeant, and those who were nearest could see that, while his arms jerked and kept giving a little, the rope was playing and quivering in the light.

"Can't you see anything?" cried Roby wildly.

"Place like a big well ground in the rock," came up in hollow tones; "the water all comes here, and goes down a great sink-hole. Shall I cut myself free and dive?"

"No!" came simultaneously, in a hoarse yell, from a dozen throats.

"Madness!" shouted Roby. "Look round again; he may be clinging to the rocks somewhere."

Dickenson uttered a strange, mocking laugh, so loud and thrilling that it made his hearers shudder.

"There's nothing but this hole, smoothed round by the water. I can see all round."

"Yah!" roared the sergeant. "Haul!" For suddenly his arms received a heavy jerk which bent him nearly double, and the light which glowed down by the water disappeared; while, but for the rush made to get a grip at the rope by Roby and a couple more men, the sergeant would have gone down.

As it was, the sudden snatch made dragged him back; and then, without further order, the men hauled quickly and excitedly at the rope till Dickenson's strangely distorted face appeared in the light.

"Hold on!" shouted the sergeant, and stooping down, he got his hands well under his young officer's armpits, made a heave with all his strength, and jerked him out of the horrible pit on to the hard rock.

Roby had helped by seizing the sergeant and dragging him back as soon as he had a good hold, and it was his captain's eyes that Dickenson's first met in a wild, despairing look, before, dripping with water from the chest downwards and the lights both extinguished, he sank upon his knees and dropped his face into his hands, no one stirring or speaking in the few brief moments which followed, but all noticing that the poor fellow's chest was heaving and that a spasmodic sob escaped his lips.

The silence was broken by the sergeant, who stood rubbing his wet hands down the sides of his trousers.

"Thought I was gone too," he said huskily.

His words reached Dickenson's understanding, but not their full extent. His hands dropped to his lap, and he looked up, gazing round in a strangely bewildered way, his lower lip quivering, and his voice sounding pathetically apologetic.

"Yes," he said feebly, "I thought I was gone. The water seemed to rise up round me suddenly to snatch me down. I did all I could—all I could, Roby, but it seemed to make me as weak as a child. Look at that—look at that!" he groaned, holding out one arm, which shook as if with the palsy. Then clasping his hands together he let them drop, and gazed away before him into the darkness through the arch, and said, as if to himself, "I did all I could, Drew, old lad—I did all I could."

"Dickenson," whispered Roby, bending over him. "Come, come, pull yourself together. Be a man."

The poor fellow turned his head sharply, and gazed wildly into the speaker's eyes.

"Yes, yes," he said, and drawing a deep breath, he eagerly snatched at the hand held out to him and stood up. "Bit of a shock to a fellow's nerves. I never felt like that when we went at the Boers. Thank you, sergeant. Thank you, my lads. I never felt like that."

"No," said the captain quickly. "It would have unmanned any one."

"Did me, sir," said Sergeant James. "And I never felt like that."

"Ha!" sighed Dickenson, giving himself a shake, and beginning to unbuckle his belt to get rid of the dripping lanterns. "I'm better now. Ought I to go down again, sir?"

"Go down again, man?" cried Roby. "Good heavens, no! It would be madness to send any one into that horrible pit.—Here, I had forgotten Corporal May. Where is he?"

"We laid him down in yonder, sir," said one of the men, indicating the interior of the cavern with a nod.

"Not dead?"

"No, sir, I don't think so," was the reply as the captain passed through the archway, followed by the sergeant, who snatched up a lantern; while Dickenson turned to the great pit, steadied himself by the tree-trunk which led up, and gazed into the black place.

"Poor old Drew!" he groaned softly. "If it had only been together—in some advance!"

And then, soldier-like, he drew himself up as if standing to attention, turned, and went to his duty again, walking pretty steadily after Roby to join them where the sergeant was down on one knee with his hand thrust inside the corporal's jacket.

"Heart's beating off and on, sir," growled James. "I don't think he's hurt. Seems to me like what the doctor called shock."

"Yes. What did he say?"

"I dunno, sir. Sort of queer stuff: sounded like foolishness. I'm afraid he's off his head.—Here, May—me, May, my lad. Hold up. You're all right now."

The man opened his eyes, stared at him wildly, and his lips quivered.

"What say?" he whispered.

"I say, hold up now."

"Hurts," moaned the poor fellow, beginning to rub his chest. "Have I been asleep?"

"I hope so, my lad," said Roby, "for you have been saved a good deal if you have."

"Ugh!" groaned the man, with a shiver. "Mind that light don't go out. Here," he cried fiercely, "what did you go and leave me for?"

"Who went away and left you?"

"I recklect now. It was horrid. I dursen't try and climb that tree again with the water all cissing up to get at me."

"What!" cried Roby sharply.

"It was when the orders were given to retire, sir. I kept letting first one chap go and then another till I was last, and then I stood at the bottom trying to make up my mind to follow, till the lights up atop seemed to go out all at once. Then I turned cold and sick and all faint-like, holding on by the tree, till there was a horrid rush and a splash as if something was coming up to get at me, and I couldn't help it—I turned and ran back through that archway place in the big hole, feeling sure that the water was coming to sweep me away. 'Fore I'd gone far in the black darkness I ketched my foot on a stone, pitched forward on to my head, and then I don't remember any more for ever so long. It was just as if some one had hit me over the head with the butt of a rifle."

"Where's the lump, then, or the cut?" said Sergeant James sourly.

"Somewhere up atop there, sergeant. I dunno. Feel; I can't move my arms, they're so stiff."

The sergeant raised his lantern and passed his hand over the man's head.

"Lump as big as half an egg there, sir," he said in a whisper.

"It's a bad cut, ain't it, sergeant?" said the corporal.

"No; big lump—bruise."

"Ah, I thought it was a cut; but I'd forgotten all about it when I come to again in the dark, and couldn't make it out. My head was all of a swim like, and I couldn't recklect anything about what had happened, nor make out where I was, only that I was in the dark. All I could understand was that my head was aching awful and swimming round and round, and I seemed to have been fast asleep for hours and hours, and that I had woke up. That was all."

"Well, go on," said the sergeant, in obedience to a hint from Roby.

"Yes, direckly," said the man. "I'm trying to think, but my head don't go right. It's just as if some sand had got into the works. Ah, it's coming now. It was like waking up and finding myself in the dark, and not knowing how I got there."

"Well, you said that before," said the sergeant gruffly.

"Did I, sergeant? Well, that's right; and I tried to get up, but I couldn't stand, my head swam so. Then I got on my hands and knees, and began to crawl to the ladder; and I went on and kept stopping on account of my head, till I knocked against my helmet and put it on, and began crawling again, thinking I must be where I'd lain down and gone to sleep. Then I went on again for ever so long till I could go no farther, for I was in a place where the rock came down over my head so that I could touch it; but it was all narrow-like, and I was so tired that I lay down, got out my pipe, lit up, and had a smoke."

"What next?" said the sergeant, exchanging glances with Roby and Dickenson, who were listening.

"That's all," said the man quietly. "So I'll just have a nap to set my head right. It's a touch of fever, I think."

"Stop a moment, my lad," said Roby. "Can't you recollect what came next?"

"No, sir," said the man drowsily. "Oh yes, I do. I know I began crawling again without my helmet after I'd smoked a pipe of tobacco—for the hard rim hurt my head—and went on and on for hours, till I thought I could hear water running; and then in a minute I was sure, and I made for it, for at that time I was so thirsty I'd have given anything for a drink to cool my hot, dry throat. Yes, it's all coming back now. I crept on till all at once the water falling sounded loud, and the next moment I was sinking down sidewise into a deep place where I was hanging across a stone to get at the water in the dark, and couldn't. It was just like a nightmare, sergeant, that it was, and I felt my head go down and my legs hanging till my back was ready to break, but I couldn't get away, and I lay and lay, till all at once I was snatched up, and that hurt me so that I yelled for help, and then the nightmare seemed to be gone and I was lying all asleep like till I saw you and the captain; and here I am, somewhere, and that's all."

It was all, for the corporal swooned away, and had to be lifted and carried up.

"Poor fellow!" said Captain Roby; "he'll be better when we get him out into the open air. See to him, my lads. If he cannot walk you must carry him."

The men closed round the corporal, while the captain and Dickenson walked back to where a couple of the men, looking sallow and half-scared with their task, stood holding one of the lanterns at the month of the water-chasm.

"Heard anything?" said the captain, in a low tone of voice which sounded as if he dreaded to hear his own words.

"Nothing, sir," was the reply; "only the water rushing down."

"It seems to me," —began the other, and then he paused.

"Yes: what? How does it seem to you?" asked the captain.

"Well, sir, as we stand listening here it sounds as if the hole down there gets choked every now and then with too much water, and then the place fills up more, and goes off again with a rush."

The captain made no reply, but stood with Dickenson gazing down into the chasm till there was a difference in the sound of its running out, when the latter caught at his companion, gripping his arm excitedly.

"Yes," he whispered hoarsely; "that's how it went while I was down there. Oh Roby! can't we do anything more?"

The captain was silent for some little time, and then he half-dragged his companion to the rough ladder.

"Come up," he said; "you know we can do no more by stopping thinking till one is almost wild with horror. Here, go up first."

It was like a sharp order, but Dickenson felt that it came from his officer's heart, and, with a shiver as much of horror as of cold from his drenched and clinging garments, he climbed to the next level and stood feeling half-stunned, and waiting while the sergeant climbed up and joined them with some rings of the rope upon his arm.

"May's going to try and climb up by himself, sir," said the sergeant in a low voice, "but I've made the rope fast round him to hold on by in case he slips. We don't want another accident."

The sight of the rope, and the sergeant's words, stirred Dickenson into speaking again.

"James," he said huskily, "don't you think something more might be done by one of us going down to the water again?"

"No, sir," replied the sergeant solemnly; "nothing, or I'd have been begging the captain to let me have another try long enough ago."

"Yes, of course, of course," said Dickenson warmly. "How are we to tell the colonel what has happened?"

The young officer relapsed into a dull, heavy fit of thinking, in which he saw, as if he were in a dream, the corporal helped out of the pit by means of the rope, and then go feebly along the cavern, to break down about half-way, when four men in two pairs crossed their wrists and, keeping step, bore him, lying horizontally, to the next ladder, up which he was assisted, after which he was borne once again by four more of the men; and as Drew's comrade came last with the captain, the procession made him nearly break down with misery and despair.

For, what with the slow, regular pacing, the lights carried in front, and the appearance of the man being carried, there was a horrible suggestion in it all of a military funeral, and for the time being it seemed to him that they had recovered his comrade and were carrying him out to his grave.

Chapter Nineteen
Not dead yet

The entrance at last, with the glorious light of the sun shining in, man after man drawing a heavy sighing breath of relief; and as they gathered outside on the shelf where the sentries were awaiting their coming, it seemed to every one there that for a few moments the world had never looked so bright and beautiful. Then down came the mental cloud of thought upon all, and they formed up solemnly, ready to march down.

"Well, Corporal May," said the captain, "do you think you can walk?"

"Yes, sir," replied the man. "My head's thick and confused-like, but every mouthful of this air I swallow seems to be pulling me round. I can walk, sir, but I may have to fall out and come slowly."

"Yes, yes, of course," said the captain, with whom the corporal had always been a petted favourite. "Don't hurry, my lad.—Sergeant, you and another man fall out too, if it is more than he can manage."

Then turning to the rest of the party, the captain glanced along the rank at the saddened faces which showed how great a favourite the young lieutenant had been, and something like a feeling of jealousy flashed through him as he began to think how it would have been if he had been the missing man. But the ungenerous thought died out as quickly as it had arisen, and he marched on with the men slowly, so as to make it easier for the corporal, till half the slope of the kopje had been zigzagged down, when he called a halt.

"Sit or lie about in the sunshine for ten minutes, my lads," he said, and the men gladly obeyed, dropping on the hot stones and tufts of brush, to begin talking together in a low voice, as they let their eyes wander over the prospect around, now looking, by contrast with the black horror through which they had passed, as if no more beautiful scene had ever met their eyes.

"How are you, Dickenson?" said the captain after they had sat together for a few minutes, drinking in the sunlight and air.

The young lieutenant started and looked at him strangely for a few moments before he spoke with a curious catch in his voice.

"Is it all true?" he said.

The captain's lips parted, but no words came; he only bowed his head slowly, and once more there was silence, till it was broken by Dickenson.

"Poor old Drew!" he said softly. "Well, I hope when my time comes I shall die in the same way."

"What!" cried the captain, with a look of horror which brought a grim smile to the subaltern's quivering lip.

"I did not mean that," he said sadly; "by a bullet, I hope, but doing what poor old Drew was doing—saving another man's life."

He turned his head on one side, reached out his hand, and picked from the sun-dried growth close at hand a little dull-red, star-like flower whose petals were hard and horny, one of the so-called everlasting tribe, and taking off his helmet, carefully tucked it in the lining.

"Off the kopje in which he died," said Dickenson, in reply to an inquiring look directed at him by the captain. "For his people at home if I live to get back. They'll like to have it."

Captain Roby said nothing aloud, but he thought, and his thoughts were something to this effect: "Who'd ever have thought it of this light-hearted, chaffing, joking fellow? Why, if they had been brothers he couldn't have taken it more to heart. Ha! I never liked the poor lad, and I don't think he liked me. There were times when I believe I hated him for—for—for—Well, why did I dislike him? Because other people liked him better than they did me, I suppose. Ah, well! like or not like, it's all over now."

He sat thinking for a few minutes longer, watching Dickenson furtively as he now kept turning himself a little this way and that way and changed his seat twice for a fresh piece of hot stone. Suddenly at his last change he caught the captain's eye, and said quite cheerfully:

"Getting a bit drier now." Then, seeing a surprised look in his brother officer's countenance, he said quietly, "I'm a soldier, sir, and we've no time for thinking if there's another comrade gone out of our ranks."

"No," said Roby laconically, and he held out his hand, in which Dickenson slowly laid his own, looking rather wistfully as he felt it pressed warmly. "I—I hope we shall be better friends in the future, Dickenson," said the captain rather awkwardly.

"I hope so too, sir," replied Dickenson, but there was more sadness than warmth in his tones as his hand was released.

"Yes; soldiers have no time for being otherwise.—There!"

The captain sprang up, and Dickenson stiffly followed his example.

"Fall in, my lads.—Well, corporal, how are you now?"

"Head's horrid bad, sir; but this bit of a rest has pulled me together. I should like to fall out when we get near the way down to the spring."

"Of course, my lad, of course.—Here, any one else like a drink?"

"Yes, sir," came in chorus from the rank.

"All of us, please, sir," added the sergeant.

"Very well, then; we'll fall out again for a few minutes when get down. 'Tention! Right face—march!"

The men went on, all the better for their rest, while the captain joined Dickenson in the rear, and marched step by step with him for some minutes in silence.

"What confoundedly bad walking it is down here!" he said at last. "Shakes a man all to pieces."

"I hadn't noticed it," said Dickenson, with something like a sigh.

"I say!"

Dickenson turned to look in the captain's face.

"Come straight to the chief with me, Dickenson. I don't like my job of telling him. He'll say I oughtn't to have let the poor fellow go down."

"I don't think he will," replied Dickenson, after a few moments' silence. "The old man's as hard as stone over a bit of want of discipline; but he's always just."

"Think so?" said the captain.

"Yes. Always just. I'll come with you, though I feel as weak as water now. But I shall be better still when we get down to the quarters; and it has got to be done."

No more was said till the bottom of the kopje was nearly reached, and at a word from the sergeant the men went off left incline down and down and in and out among the loose blocks of weathered and lichen-covered stone which had fallen from the precipices above, while, as glimpses kept appearing of the flashing, dancing water, the men began to increase their pace, till the two foremost leaped down from rock to rock, and one who had outpaced his comrade bounded down out of sight into the deep gully along which the limpid water ran.

"Oh!" exclaimed Dickenson, suddenly stopping short with his face distorted by a look of agony.

"What's the matter?" cried the captain anxiously. "Taken bad?"

"No, no. The men!" said the young officer huskily. "The water—the men are going to drink. That place in the cavern—it is, of course, where Groenfontein rises."

"Yes, of course," replied the captain; "but it is too late now."

He had hardly uttered the words before there was a yell of horror which made him stop short, for the foremost man came clambering back into sight, gesticulating, and they could see that he looked white and scared.

"Oh!" cried the captain. "It will be *sauve qui peut!* The Boers have surprised us, and the lads have nothing but their side-arms. Got your revolver? I've mine. Let's do the best we can. Cover, my lads, cover."

"No, no, no!" cried Dickenson in a choking voice. "I can't help it, Roby. I feel broken down. He has found poor Drew below there, washed out by the stream!"

"Come on," cried the captain, and in another few moments they were with the men, who were closing round their startled comrade.

"Couldn't help it." the poor fellow panted as his officers came within hearing. "I came upon him so sudden; I thought it was a ghost."

"Hold your tongue, fool!" growled the sergeant. "Fall in! Show some respect for your poor dead officer.—Beg pardon, gentlemen. They've found the lieutenant's body, and—thank Heaven we can—we can—Ur-r-r!" he ended, with a growl and a tug at the top button of his khaki jacket.

The men shuffled into their places and stood fast, imitating the action of their officers, who gravely doffed their helmets and stepped down into the hollow, where, upon a patch of green growth a few feet above the rippling water foaming and swirling in miniature cascades among the rocks, poor Lennox lay stretched out upon his back in the full sunshine, which had dried up the blood from a long cut upon his forehead, where it had trickled down one side of his face.

He looked pale and ghastly, and there was a discoloration about his mouth and on one cheek where he seemed to have been battered by striking against the stones amongst which he had been driven in his rush through the horrible subterranean channel of the stream; but otherwise he looked as peaceful as if he were asleep.

The captain stopped short, gazing at him, while Dickenson dropped lightly down till he was beside his comrade, and sank gently upon one knee, to bend lower, take hold of the right hand that lay across his chest, and then—"like a girl!" as he afterwards said—he unconsciously let fall two great scalding tears upon his comrade's cheek.

The effect was magical. Lennox's eyes opened wildly, to stare blankly in the lieutenant's face, and the latter sprang to his feet, flinging his helmet high over his head as he turned to the line of waiting men above him and roared out hoarsely:

"Hurrah! Cheer, boys, cheer!"

The shout that rang out was deafening for so small a detachment, and two more followed, louder still; while the next minute discipline was forgotten and the men came bounding down to group about the figure staring at them wildly as if not yet fully comprehending what it all meant, till the lookers-on began shaking hands with one another in their wild delight.

Then Dickenson saw the light of recognition dawn in his comrade's face, a faint smile appear about his mouth and the corners of his eyes, which gradually closed again; but his lips parted, and as Dickenson bent lower he heard faintly:

"Not dead yet, old man, but,"—His voice sounded very faint after he had paused a few moments, and then continued: "It was very near."

Chapter Twenty
All about it

The men forgot their thirst in the excitement of the incident, and as soon as Lennox showed signs of recovering a little from the state of exhaustion in which he lay, every one volunteered to be his bearer. But before he had been carried far he made signs for the men to stop, and upon being set down he took Dickenson's arm, and, leaning upon him heavily, marched slowly with the men for the rest of the way towards the colonel's quarters.

They were met, though, before they were half-way, their slow approach being seen and taken for a sign that there was something wrong; and colonel, major, doctor, and the other officers hurried to meet them and hear briefly what had occurred.

"Why, Lennox, my lad," cried the doctor after a short examination, "you ought to be dead. You must be a tough one. There, I'll see what I can do for you."

He took the young officer in his charge from that moment, and his first order was that his patient was to be left entirely alone, and, after partaking of a little refreshment, he was to rest and sleep for as many hours as he could.

"The poor fellow has had a terrible shock," he said to the colonel.

"Of course; but one naturally would like to know how he managed to escape."

"Very naturally, my dear sir; but his eyes tell me that if his brain is not allowed to recover its tone he'll have a bad attack of fever. A man can't go through such an experience as that without being terribly weakened. I want him to be led into thinking of everything else but his escape. I dare say after a few hours he will be wanting to talk excitedly about all he felt; but he mustn't. Not a question must be asked."

As it happened, the patient did exactly what the doctor wished: he slept, or, rather, sank into a state of stupor which lasted for many hours, came to his senses again, partook of a little food, and then dropped asleep once more; and this was repeated for days before he thoroughly recovered, and then began of his own volition to speak of his experience.

It was about a week after his mishap, in the evening, when Dickenson, just returned from a skirmish in which the Boers had been driven back, was seated beside his rough couch watching him intently.

"Don't sit staring at me like that, old fellow," said Lennox suddenly. "You look as if you thought I was going to die."

"Not you! You look a lot better to-night."

"I am, I know."

"How?" asked Dickenson laconically.

"Because I've begun to worry about not being on duty and helping."

"Yes; that's a good sign," said Dickenson. "Capital. Feel stronger?"

"Yes. It's just as if my strength has begun to come back all at once. Did you drive off the enemy to-day?"

"Famously. Gave them a regular licking."

"That's right. But tell me about Corporal May."

"Oh no, you're not to bother about that."

"Tell me about Corporal May," persisted Lennox.

"Doctor said you weren't to worry about such things."

"It isn't a worry now. I felt at first that if I thought much about that business in the cave I should go off my head; but I'm quite cool and comfortable now. Tell me—is he quite well again?"

"Not quite. He has had a touch of fever and been a bit loose in the knob, just as if he had been frightened out of his wits."

"Of course," said Lennox quietly. "I was nearly the same. I did not know at the time, but I do now. He is getting better, though?"

"Fast; only he's a bit of a humbug with it. I thought so, and the doctor endorses my ideas. He likes being ill and nursed and petted with the best food, so as to keep out of the hard work. I don't like the fellow a bit. There, you've talked enough now, so I'll be gone."

"No; stop," said Lennox. "Tell me about the stores of corn we found in that cave."

"Hang the cave! You're not to talk about it."

"Tell me about the grain," persisted Lennox.

"Oh, very well; we're going on eating it, for if it hadn't turned up as it did we should have been obliged to surrender or cut our way through."

"But there's plenty yet?"

"Oh yes, heaps; and we got about thirty sheep two days ago."

"Capital," said Lennox, rubbing his hands softly. "Now tell me—where is the grain stored?"

"Where the niggers put it when they collected it there."

"Not moved?"

"No. It couldn't be in a better place—a worse, I mean. Bother the cave! I wish you wouldn't keep on thinking about it."

"Very well, I won't. Tell me about the prisoners."

"Ah, that's better. The brutes! But there's nothing to tell about them. I wish they had got their deserts, but we none of us wanted to shoot them, though they did deserve it."

"Oh, I don't know," said Lennox. "They're a rough lot of countrymen, and they think that everything is fair in war, I suppose. Where are they?"

"Number 4 tin hut, and a fellow inside with them night and day. Then there's the sentry outside. Makes a lot of trouble for the men."

Lennox was silent for a few minutes before speaking again.

"I say, Bob."

"Yes?"

"Look at this cut on my forehead."

"I'm looking. Very pretty. It's healing fast now."

"Will it leave much of a scar?"

"I dare say it will," said Dickenson mockingly. "Add to your beauty. But you ought to have one on the other side to match it."

"I wasn't thinking about my looks," said Lennox, smiling.

"Gammon! You were."

"I suppose I must have been dashed against a block of stone."

"Good job, too. Doctor said it acted like a safety-valve, and its bleeding kept off fever."

"I suppose so. I must have been dashed against something with great force, though."

"Oh, never mind that. Will you leave off thinking about that cave?"

"No, I won't," said Lennox coolly. "I must think about it now; I can't help it."

"Then I'm off."

"Why?"

"Because you were getting better, and now you are trying to make yourself worse."

"Oh no, I'm not; and you are not going. Talking to you about it acts like a safety-valve, too. There, it's of no use for you to try and stop me, Bob, for if you go I shall think all the more. I've been wanting to tell you all about it for days."

"But the doctor said I was not to encourage you to talk about the horror."

"Well, you are not encouraging me; you are flopping on me like a wet blanket. I say, it was horrible, wasn't it?"

"No," said Dickenson angrily; "but this is."

Lennox was silent for a few minutes, and he lay so quiet that Dickenson leaned forward to gaze at him earnestly, "All right, Bob. I'm here, and getting awfully strong compared with what I was a week ago. I shall get up and come out to-morrow."

"You won't. You're too weak yet."

"Oh no, I'm not. I shall be on duty in two or three days, and as soon as I'm well enough I want you and the sergeant to come with me to have another exploration with lanterns and a rope."

"There, I knew it. You're going off your head again."

"Not a bit of it."

"Then why can't you leave the wretched cave alone?"

"Because it interests me. I mean to go down again at the end of the rope."

"Bah! You're mad as a hatter. I knew you'd bring it on."

"There, it's of no use. I want to tell you all about it."

"If you think I'm going to stop here and listen to a long rigmarole about that dreadful hole, you're mistaken; so hold your tongue."

"There's no long rigmarole, Bob. You know how the corporal yelled out and clutched at me."

"No; I only guessed at something of the kind," replied Dickenson unwillingly. "We could not see much."

"Well, in his horror at finding himself lifted he completely upset me. It was all in a moment: I felt myself gliding over the slimy stone, and then I was plunged into deep water and drawn right down."

"But you struck out and tried to rise?" said Dickenson, overcome now by his natural eagerness to know how his comrade escaped.

"Struck out—tried to rise!" cried Lennox, with a bitter laugh. "I have some recollection of struggling in black strangling darkness for what seemed an age, the water thundering the while in my ears, before all was blank."

"But you were horror-stricken, and felt that you must go on fighting for your life?"

"No," said Lennox quietly. "I felt nothing till the darkness suddenly turned to bright sunshine, and I have some recollection of being driven against stones and tossed here and there, till I dragged myself out of a shallow place among the rocks and up amongst the green growth. Then a curious drowsy feeling came over me, and all was blank again. That's all."

"But weren't you in agony—in horrible fear?"

"Yes, when I felt myself falling and tried to save myself."

"I mean afterwards, when you were being forced through, that horrible passage."

"What horrible passage?" said Lennox, with a faint smile.

"What horrible passage, man? Why, the tunnel, or channel, or whatever it is—the subterranean way of the stream under the kopje, in the bowels of the earth."

"I told you I was horrified for a moment and then I was choking in the water, till all seemed blank, and then I appeared to wake in the hot sunshine, where I was knocked about till I crawled out on to the bank."

"But didn't you suffer dreadfully?"

"No."

"Didn't you think about England and home, and all that?"

"No," said Lennox quietly.

"Weren't you in fearful agony as you fought for your life?"

"Not the slightest; and I don't think I struggled much."

"Well, upon my word!" cried Dickenson in a tone of disgust. "I like this!"

"Do you, Bob? I didn't."

"You didn't? Look here, Drew, I'm disgusted with you."

"Why?" said Lennox, opening his eyes wider.

"Because you're a miserable impostor—a regular humbug."

"What! don't you believe I went through all that?"

"Oh yes, I believe you went through all the—all the—all the hole; but there don't seem to have been anything else."

"Why, what else did you expect, old fellow?"

"What I've been asking you—pains and agonies and frightful sufferings and despairs, and that sort of thing; and there you were, pop down into the darkness, pop under the kopje, pop out into the sunshine, and pop—no, I mean, all over."

"Well, what would you have had me do? Stop underneath for a month?"

"No, of course not; but, hang it all! if it hadn't been that you got that cut on your forehead and a few scratches and chips, it was no worse than taking a dive."

"Not much," said Lennox, looking amused.

"Well, I really call it disgusting—a miserable imposition upon your friends."

"Why, Bob, you are talking in riddles, old fellow, or else my head's so weak still that I can't quite follow you."

"Then I'll try and make my meaning clear to your miserably weak comprehension, sir," cried Dickenson, with mock ferocity. "Here were you just taking a bit of a dive, and there were we, your friends, from the captain down to the latest-joined private, suffering—oh! I can't tell you what we suffered. I don't mean to say that Roby was breaking his heart because he thought there was an end of you; but poor old Sergeant James nearly went mad with despair, and the whole party was ready to plunge in after you so as to get drowned too."

"Did they take it like that, Bob?"

"Take it like that? Why, of course they did."

Lennox was silent for a few moments before he said softly, "And did poor old Bob Dickenson feel something like that?"

"Why, of course he did. Broke down and made a regular fool of himself, just like a great silly-looking girl—that is," he added hastily, "I mean, nearly—almost, you know."

"I'm very sorry, Bob," said Lennox gently, and his eyes looked large as he laid his hand upon his comrade's sleeve.

"Then you don't look it, sir. I say, don't you go and pitch such a lame tale as this into anybody else's ears. Here were we making a dead hero of you, and all the time—There, I've seen one of those little black and white Welsh birds—dippers, don't they call 'em?—do what you did, scores of times."

"In the dark, Bob?"

"Well—er—no—not in the dark, or of course I couldn't have seen it. There, that'll do. Talk about a set of fellows being sold by a lot of sentiment: we were that lot."

"The way of the world, Bob," said Lennox rather bitterly; "a fellow must die for people to find out that he's a bit of a hero. But please to recollect I did nothing; it was all accident."

"And an awfully bad accident too, old chap; only I don't see why the doctor need have prohibited your talking about the affair. We've all been thinking you went through untold horrors, when it was just nothing."

"Just nothing, Bob," said Lennox, looking at him with a wistful smile on his lip.

"Well, no; I won't say that, because of course it was as near as a toucher. For instance, the hole might have been too tight to let you through, and then—Ugh! Drew, old chap, don't let us talk about it any more. It's a hot day, and my face is wet with perspiration, but my spine feels as if it had turned to ice. Yes, it was as near as a toucher. I would rather drop into an ambush of the Boers a dozen times over than go through such a half-hour as that again."

Chapter Twenty One
Preparations

There was a splendid supply of corn in the great woven Kaffir baskets, and that and the captured flock of sheep did wonders; but there were many hungry mouths to feed, and the lookout was growing worse than ever. The Boers were fighting furiously all over the two states and keeping our men at bay, or else were flitting from place to place to be hunted down again, and keeping the British generals so busily at work that, though they tried hard, it was impossible to send help to the little detachment at Groenfontein, from which place they had received no news, neither were they able to get through a single despatch.

Many a long discussion took place amongst the soldiers about the state of affairs, in which Corporal May declared that it was a burning shame—that the generals only thought of saving their own skins, and didn't care a fig for the poor fellows on duty fighting for their lives.

Sergeant James was present, and he flushed up into a rage and bullied the corporal in the way that a sergeant can bully when he is put out. He told the corporal that he was a disgrace to the army; and he told the men that as long as a British officer could move to the help of his men who were in peril, he didn't care a snap of the fingers for his own life, but he moved.

Then it was the men's turn, and they spoke all together and as loudly as they could; but they only said one word, and that one word was "Hooray!" repeated a great many times over, with the result that Corporal May was fully of opinion that the men put more faith in the sergeant than they did in him, and, to use one of the men's expressions, "he sneaked off like a wet terrier with his tail between his legs."

Discussions took place also among the officers again and again after their miserable starvation mess, which was once more, in spite of all efforts to supplement it, reduced to a very low ebb. For the brave colonel was Spartan-like in his ways.

"I can't sit down to a better dinner than my brave lads are eating, gentlemen," he would say. "It's share and share alike with the Boers' hard knocks, so it's only fair that it should be the same with the good things of life."

"Yes, that's all very well, colonel," grumbled the major; "but where are those good things?"

"Ah, where are they?" said the colonel. "Never mind; we shall win yet. The Boers have done their worst to crack this hard nut, and we've kept them at bay, which is almost as good as a victory."

"But surely, sir," said Captain Roby impatiently, "help might have been sent to us before now. Has the general forgotten us?"

"No," said the colonel decisively. "I'm afraid that he has several detachments in the same condition as we are. That's why we do not get any help."

"Perhaps so, sir," said the captain bitterly. "but I'm getting very tired of this inaction."

"That sounds like a reproach to me, Roby," said the colonel gravely.

"Oh no, sir; I didn't mean that," said the captain.

"Your words expressed it sir. Come now, speak out. What would you do if you were in my place, with three strong commandos of the Boers forming a triangle with a kopje at each apex which they hold with guns?"

"I don't want to give an opinion, sir."

"But every one wishes that you should.—Eh, gentlemen?"

"Certainly," came in eager chorus.

"Well, if I must speak, I must, sir," said the captain, flushing.

"Yes, speak without fear or favour."

"Well, sir, all military history teaches us that generals with small armies, when surrounded by a greater force, have gained victories by attacking the enemy in detail."

"Yes, I see what you mean," said the colonel quietly. "You would have me attack and take first one kopje, then the second, and then the third?"

"Exactly, sir."

"Capital strategy. Mr Roby, if it could be done; but I cannot recall any case in which a general was situated as we are, with three very strong natural forts close at hand."

There was a murmur of assent, and Dickerson exchanged glances with Lennox, who was, with the exception of the scar on his forehead, none the worse for his terrible experience in the kopje cavern.

"You see, gentlemen," continued the colonel, who did not display the slightest resentment at Roby's remarks, "if the Boers were soldiers—men who could manoeuvre, attack, and carry entrenchments—they are so much stronger that they could have carried this place with ease. It would have meant severe loss, but in the end, if they had pushed matters to extremity, they must have won. As it is, they fight from cover—very easy work, when they have so many natural strongholds. I could take any of these; but while I was engaged with my men against one party, the other two would advance and take this place, with such stores as we have. Where should we be then?"

"Oh, but I'd leave half the men to defend the place, sir. Why, with a couple of companies, and a good time chosen for a surprise, I could take any of the enemy's laagers."

The colonel raised his eyebrows, and looked at the speaker curiously.

"You see, sir," continued Roby, speaking in a peculiarly excited way, "the men, as an Irishman would say, are spoiling for a fight, and we are getting weaker and weaker. In another fortnight we shall be quite helpless."

"I hope not, Mr Roby," said the colonel dryly. "Perhaps you would like to try some such experiment with a couple of companies?"

"I should, sir," cried the captain eagerly; and the other officers looked from one to the other wonderingly, and more wonderingly still when the colonel said calmly:

"Very well, Mr Roby. I will make my plans and observations as to which of the three laagers it would be more prudent to attack. If you do not succeed, you ought at least to be able to bring in some of the enemy's cattle."

That evening the colonel had a quiet council with the major, the latter being strongly opposed to the plan; but the colonel was firm.

"I do not expect much," he said, "but it will be reading the Boers a lesson, even if he fails, and do our men good, for all this inaction is telling upon them, as I have been noticing, to my sorrow, during the past three or four days. To be frank with you, Robson, I have been maturing something of the kind."

"But you will not give the command to Roby?" cried the major.

"Certainly not," said the colonel emphatically. "You will take the lead."

"Ha!" ejaculated the major.

"With Roby as second in command. I will talk with you after I have done a little scouting on my own account."

Two days elapsed, and Captain Roby had been talking a good deal in a rather injudicious way about its being just what he expected. The colonel had been out both nights with as many men as he could mount—just a small scouting party—seen all that he could as soon as it was daylight, and returned soon after sunrise each time after a brush with the enemy, who had discovered the approach to their lines and followed the retiring party up till they came within reach of the gun, when a few shells sent them scampering back.

It was on the third night that Captain Roby sat talking to his greatest intimates, and he repeated his injudicious remarks so bitterly that Captain Edwards said severely. "I can't sit here and listen to this, Roby. You must be off your head a little, and if you don't mind you'll be getting into serious trouble."

"Trouble? What do you mean, sir?" cried Roby. "I feel it is my duty to speak."

"And I feel it is not; and if I were Colonel Lindley I would not stand it."

He had hardly spoken when there was the crack of a rifle, followed by another and another. The men turned out ready for anything, fully expecting that the Boers were making an attack; but Dickenson came hurrying to the colonel with the report of what had happened.

The two prisoners had been waiting their opportunity, and rising against the sentry who shared their corrugated iron prison, had snatched his bayonet from his side and struck him down, with just enough life left in him afterwards to relate what had happened. Then slipping out, they had tried to assassinate the sentry on duty, but failed, for he was too much on the alert. He had fired at them, but they had both escaped into the darkness, under cover of which, and with their thorough knowledge of the country, they managed to get right away.

"Just like Lindley," said Roby contemptuous as soon as the alarm was over and the men had settled down again. "Any one but he would have made short work of those two fellows."

He had hardly spoken when an orderly came to the door of the hut where he, Captain Edwards, and two more were talking, and announced that the colonel desired to speak with Captain Roby directly. The latter sprang up and darted a fierce look at Captain Edwards.

"You have lost no time in telling tales," he said insolently.

"You are on the wrong track," said the gentleman addressed, angrily. "I have not seen the colonel to speak to since, and I have sent no message."

Roby turned on his heel wrathfully and went straight to the colonel's quarters, to face him and the major, who was with him.

To his intense astonishment and delight, the colonel made the announcement that the south-west laager was to be attempted by surprise that night by a hundred and fifty men with the bayonet alone, the major in command, Captain Roby second, and Captain Edwards and the two subalterns of Roby's company to complete the little force.

"When do we start, sir?" said Roby, with his heart beating fast.

"An hour before midnight," said the colonel; and the major added:

"Without any sound of preparation. The men will assemble, and every precaution must be taken that not one of the blacks gets wind of the attempt so as to warn the enemy of our approach."

"I have no more to add, Robson," said the colonel. "You know where to make your advance. Take the place if you can without firing a shot, but of course, if fire should be necessary, use your own discretion."

The whole business was done with the greatest absence of excitement. The three officers were warned at once; Captain Edwards looked delighted, but Dickenson began to demur.

"You are not fit to go, Drew," he said.

"I never felt more fit," was the reply, "and if you make any opposition you are no friend of mine."

"Very well," said Dickenson quietly; "but I feel that we're going to have a sharp bit of business, and I can't think that you are strong enough."

"I've told you that I am," said Lennox firmly. "The orders are that I go with the company, and the colonel would not send me if he did not know from his own opinion and the doctor's report that I am fit to be with the ranks."

There was a little whisper or two between Dickenson and Sergeant James.

"Oh, I don't know, sir," said the latter; "he has pulled round wonderfully during the last fortnight, and it isn't as if we were going on a long exhausting march. Just about six or seven miles through level veldt, sir, and in the cool of the night."

"Well, there is that," said Dickenson thoughtfully.

"And a good rest afterwards, sir, so as to make the advance, so I hear, just at the Boers' sleepiest time. Bah! It'll be a mere nothing if we can only get through their lines quietly. They'll never stand the bayonet; and I wouldn't wish for a smarter officer to follow than Mr Lennox."

"Nor a braver, James," said Dickenson quietly.

"Nor a braver, sir."

"If he is up to the mark for strength."

"Let him alone for that, sir," said the sergeant, with a chuckle. "I don't say Mr Lennox will be first, but I do say he won't be last; and the men'll follow him anywhere, as you know, sir, well."

"Yes," said Dickenson, drawing a deep breath; "and it's what we shall want to-night—a regular rush, and the bayonet home."

"That's it, sir; but I must go. The lads are half-mad with joy, and if I'm not handy we shall have them setting up a shout."

But of course there was no shout, the men who, to their great disgust, were to stay and hold the camp bidding good-luck to their more fortunate comrades without a sound; while more than once, with the remembrance of the dastardly murder that had just taken place, men whispered to their comrades something about not to forget what the cowardly Boers had done.

Exact to the time, just an hour before midnight, and in profound darkness—for the moon had set but a short time before—the men, with shouldered rifles, set off with springy step, Dickenson and Lennox, to whom the country was well known from shooting and fishing excursions they had made, leading the party, not a word being uttered in the ranks, and the tramp, tramp of feet sounding light and elastic as the lads followed through the open, undulating plain, well clear of the bush, there being hardly a stone to pass till they were within a mile of the little kopje where the Boers' laager lay.

There the broken country would begin, the land rising and being much encumbered with stones. But the place had been well surveyed by the major through his field-glass at daybreak two days before, and he had compared notes with Lennox, telling him what he had seen, and the young officer had drawn his attention to the presence of a patch of woodland that might be useful for a rallying-point should there be need. Captain Roby, too, had been well posted up; and after all that was necessary had been said, Lennox had joined his friend.

"Oh, we shall do it, Bob," he said. "What I wonder is, that it was not tried long enough ago."

"So do I," was the reply. "But, I say, speak out frankly: do you feel up to the work?"

"I feel as light and active as if I were going to a football match," was the reply.

"That's right," said Dickenson, with a sigh of relief.

"And you?"

"Just as if I were going to give the Boers a lesson and show them what a couple of light companies can do in a storming rush. There, save your breath for the use of your legs. Two hours' march, two hours' lie down, and then—"

"Yes, Bob;" said Lennox, drawing a deep breath, and feeling for the first time that they were going on a very serious mission; "and then?"

And then there was nothing heard but the light tramp—tramp—tramp—tramp of a hundred and fifty men and their leaders, not one of whom felt the slightest doubt as to his returning safe.

Chapter Twenty Two
For a Night Attack

It was a weird march in the silence and darkness, but the men were as elastic of spirits as if they had been on their way to some festivity. There may have been some exceptions, but extremely few; and Dickenson was not above suggesting one, not ill-naturedly, but in his anxiety for the success of the expedition, as he explained to Lennox in a whisper when they were talking over the merits of the different non-commissioned officers.

"I don't believe I shall ever make a good soldier, Drew," he said.

"What!" was the reply; and then, "Why?"

"Oh, I suppose I've got my whack of what some people call brute courage, for as soon as I get excited or hurt I never think of being afraid, but go it half-mad-like, wanting to do all the mischief I can to whoever it is that has hurt me; but what I shall always want will be the cool, calm chess-player's head that helps a man to take advantage of every move the enemy makes, and check him. I shall always be the fellow who shoves out his queen and castle and goes slashing into the adversary till he smashes him or gets too far to retreat, and is then smashed up himself."

"Well, be content with what you can do," said Lennox, "and trust to the cool-headed man as your leader. You'll be right enough in your way."

"Thankye. I say, how a trip like this makes you think of your men and what they can do!"

"Naturally," said Lennox.

"One of the things I've learnt is," continued Dickenson, "how much a regiment like ours depends on its non-commissioned officers."

"Of course," replied Lennox. "They're all long-experienced, highly-trained, picked men. See how they step into the breach sometimes when the leaders are down."

"By George, yes!" whispered Dickenson enthusiastically.—"Oh, bother that stone! Hff!—And I hope we sha'n't have them stepping into any breaches to-night."

"Why?"

"Why! Because we don't want the leaders to go down."

"No, of course not," said Lennox, laughing softly. "But, talking about non-commissioned officers, we're strong enough. Look at James."

"Oh yes; he's as good as a colonel in his way."

"And the other sergeants too."

"Capital, well-tried men," said Dickenson; "but I was thinking of the corporals."

"Well, there's hardly a man among them who mightn't be made a sergeant to-morrow."

"Hum!" said Dickenson.

"What do you mean?" cried Lennox shortly.

"What I say. Hum! Would you make that chap Corporal May a sergeant?"

"Well, no: I don't think I would."

"Don't think? Why, the fellow's as great a coward as he is a sneak."

"Don't make worse of the man than he is."

"I won't," said Dickenson. "I'll amend my charge. He's as great a sneak as he is a coward."

"Poor fellow! he mustn't come to you for his character."

"Poor fellow! Yes, that's what he is—an awfully poor fellow. Corporal May? Corporal *Mayn't*, it ought to be. No, he needn't come to me for his character. He'll have to go to Roby, who is trying his best to get him promoted. Asked me the other day whether I didn't think he was the next man for sergeant."

"What did you say?"

"Told Roby that he ought to be the very last."

"You did?"

"Of course: right out."

"What did Roby say?"

"Told me I was a fool—he didn't use that word, but he meant it—and then said downright that fortunately my opinion as to the men's qualities wasn't worth much."

"What did you say to that?"

"'Thankye;' that's all. Bah! It set me thinking about what a moll the fellow was in that cave business. It was sheer cowardice, old man. He confessed it, and through that your accident happened. I don't like Corporal May, and I wish to goodness he wasn't with us to-night. I'm hopeful, though."

"Hopeful? Of course. I dare say he'll behave very well."

"I daren't, old man; but I'm hopeful that he'll fall out with a sore foot or a sprained ankle through stumbling over a stone or bush. That's the sort of fellow who does—"

"Pst! We're talking too much," whispered Lennox, to turn the conversation, which troubled him, for inwardly he felt ready to endorse every word his comrade had uttered.

"Oh, I'm talking in a fly's whisper. What a fellow you are! Always ready to defend anybody."

"Pst!"

"There you go again with your *Pst*! Just like a sick locomotive."

"What's that?"

"I didn't hear anything. Oh yes, I do. That howl. There it goes again. One of those beautiful hyenas. I say, Drew."

"Yes?"

"My old people at home live in one of those aesthetic Surrey villages full of old maids and cranks who keep all kinds of useless dogs and cats. The old folks are awfully annoyed by them of a night. When I've been down there staying for a visit I've felt ready to jump out of bed and shell the neighbourhood with jugs, basins, and water-bottles. But *lex talionis*, as the lawyers call it—pay 'em back in their own coin. What a game it would be to take the old people home a nice pet hyena or a young jackal to serenade the village of a night!"

"There is an old proverb about cutting your nose off to be revenged upon your face. There, be quiet; I want to think of the work in hand."

"I don't," replied Dickenson; "not till we're going to begin, and then I'm on."

The night grew darker as they drew nearer to their goal, for a thin veil of cloud shut out the stars; but it was agreed that it was all the better for the advance. In fact, everything was favourable; for the British force had week by week grown less demonstrative, contenting itself with acting on the defensive, and the reconnoitring that had gone on during the past few days had been thoroughly masked by the attempts successfully made to carry off a few sheep, this being taken by the enemy as the real object of the excursions. For the Boers, after their long investment of Groenfontein and the way in which they had cut off all communications, were perfectly convinced that the garrison was rapidly growing weaker, and that as soon as ever their ammunition died out the prize would fall into their hands like so much ripe fruit.

They were thus lulled as it were into a state of security, which enabled the little surprise force to reach the place made for without encountering a single scout. Then, with the men still fresh, a halt was made where the character of the ground suddenly changed from open, rolling, bush-sprinkled veldt to a slight ascent dotted with rugged stones, which afforded excellent cover for a series of rushes if their approach were discovered before they were close up.

This was about a mile from the little low kopje where the Boers were laagered; and as soon as the word to halt had been whispered along the line the men lay down to rest for the two hours settled in the plans before making their final advance, while the first alarm of the sentries on guard was to be the signal for the bayonet-charge.

"I don't think we need say any more to the lads," whispered the major as the officers crept together for a few final words. "They all know that the striking of a match for a furtive pipe would be fatal to the expedition."

"Yes," said Captain Roby, "and to a good many of us. But the lads may be trusted."

"Yes, I believe so," said the major.

"There's one thing I should like to say, though," said Roby. "I've been thinking about it all the time we've been on the march."

"What is it, Roby?" said the major.—"Can you hear, Edwards—all of you?"

"Yes—yes," was murmured, for the officers' heads were pretty close together.

"I've been thinking," said Captain Roby, "that if we divided our force and attacked on two sides at once, the Boers would believe that we were in far greater force, and the panic would be the greater."

"Excellent advice," said the major, "if our numbers were double; but it would weaken our attack by half—oh, by far more than half. No, Roby, I shall keep to the original plan. We don't know enough of the kopje, and in the darkness we could not ensure making the attack at the same moment, nor yet in the weakest places. We must keep as we are. Get as close as we can without being discovered, and then the bugles must sound, and with a good British cheer we must be into them."

"Yes, yes, yes," was murmured, and Captain Roby was silent for a brief space.

"Very well, sir," he said coldly. "You know best."

"I don't know that, Roby," replied the major; "but I think that is the better plan—a sudden, sharply delivered surprise with the bayonet. The enemy will have no chance to fire much, and we shall be at such close quarters that they will be at a terrible disadvantage."

"Yes," said Captain Edwards as the major ceased speaking; "let them have their rear open to run, and let our task be to get them on the run. I agree with the major: no alterations now."

"No," said Dickenson in a low growl; "no swapping horses when you're crossing a stream."

"I have done," said Roby, and all settled down into silence, the officers resting like the men, but rising to creep along the line from time to time to whisper a word or two with the non-commissioned officers, whom they found thoroughly on the alert, ready to rouse up a man here and there who was coolly enough extended upon his back sleeping, to pass the time to the best advantage before it was time to fight.

Every now and then there came a doleful, despairing yelp from some hungry animal prowling about in search of prey, and mostly from the direction of the Boer laager, where food could be scented. Twice, too, from far off to their left, where the wide veldt extended, there came the distant, awe-inspiring, thunderous roar of a lion; but for the most part of the time the stillness around was most impressive, with sound travelling so easily in the clear air that the neighing of horses was plainly heard again and again, evidently coming from the Boer laager, unless, as Lennox suggested, a patrol might be scouting round. But as each time it came apparently from precisely the same place, the first idea was adopted, especially as it was exactly where the enemy's camp was marked down.

The two hours seemed very long to Lennox, who lay thinking of home, and of how little those he loved could realise the risky position he occupied that night. Dickenson was flat upon his back with his hands under his head, going over again the scene in the cavern where he was looking down the chasm and watching the movement of the light his friend had attached to his belt.

"Not a pleasant thing to think about," he said to himself, "but it makes me feel savage against that corporal, and it's getting my monkey up, for we've got to fight to-night as we never fought before. We've got to whip, as the Yankees say—'whip till we make the beggars run.' What a piece of impudence it does seem!" he said to himself a little later on. "Here we are, about a hundred and fifty hungry men, and I'll be bound to say there's about fifteen hundred of the enemy. But then they don't grasp it. They're beggars to sleep, and if we're lucky we shall be on to them before they know where they are. Oh, we shall do it;" and he lay thinking again of Corporal May, feeling like a boy once more; and he was just at the pitch when he muttered to himself, "What a pity it is that an officer must not strike one of his men!—for I should dearly like to punch that fellow's head.—Ha! here's the major. Never mind, there'll be other heads waiting over yonder, and I dare say I shall get all I want."

He turned over quickly, not to speak, but to grip his comrade's hand, for the word was being passed to fall in, and as he and Lennox gripped each other's hands hard and in silence, a soft, rustling movement was heard. For the men were springing to their feet and arranging their pouches and belts, before giving their rifles a thorough rub to get rid of the clinging clew.

"Fall in" was whispered, and the men took their places with hardly a sound.

"Fix bayonets!" was the next order, and a faint—very faint—metallic clicking ran along the lines, followed by a silence so deep that the breathing of the men could be heard.

"Forward!"

There was no need for more, and the officers led off, with the one idea of getting as close to the Boers as possible before they were discovered, and then charging home, keeping their men as much together as they could, and knowing full well that much must be left to chance.

The next minute the men were advancing softly in double line, opening out and closing up, as obstacles in the shape of stone and bush began to be frequent. But there was no hurry, no excitement. They had ample time, and when one portion of the force was a little entangled by a patch of bush thicker than usual, those on either side halted so as to keep touch, and in this way the first half-mile was passed, the only sound they heard being the neighing of a horse somewhere in front.

Chapter Twenty Three
The Advance

The horse's neigh was hailed with satisfaction by the officers, for it proved that they were going right; and soon after, this idea was endorsed and there was no more doubt as to their being aiming exactly, for right in front the darkness seemed to be intensified, and the advancing party could dimly see the rugged outline of the kopje marked against the sky.

Lennox drew a deep breath full of relief, for from what he could see there would be no terrible blundering and fighting their way up precipitous tracks, as the Boers' stronghold was nothing more than a vast mound, easy of ascent; though he did not doubt for a moment but that wherever the ground was fairly level the lower part would be strengthened by breastworks and row after row of wagons, from behind which the Boers would fire.

The advancing force tramped on as silently as ever, in spite of the impediments in their way; but there was no alarm, no scout sitting statue-like upon his active, wiry Basuto pony, and farther on no bandolier-belted sentry, rifle in hand, shouted the alarm. They might have been approaching a deserted camp for all the hindrance they met with.

It seemed to Lennox, just as others expressed it later on, that it was too good to be true, and the young officer's heart beat fast as, revolver in one hand, sword in the other, he stepped lightly on, prepared for a furious volley from the Boer rifles, being quite certain in his own mind that they must be going right into an ambush.

But no—all was safe: and they were so near that at any moment the bugles might sound, to be followed by the rousing cheer of the men in their dashing charge.

Suddenly there was a pause, and a thrill ran along the line, for there was something in the way not five yards from Lennox's position in the line.

"A sentry!" was whispered, and the line advanced again, for a burgher was lying across the way, fast asleep, and giving warning thereof through the nose—sleeping so hard that the men stepped right over him, he as unconscious as they were that other sentries were failing as much in their wearisome duty and being passed.

"It must be now," thought Lennox, as he could dimly make out, spreading to right and left, a line of wagons, but not closed up, for there were wide intervals between; and now a low, dull, crunching sound and the odour of bovine animals plainly announced that there were spans of oxen lying close by the wagons as if ready for some movement in the early morning for which their drivers had made preparations overnight.

As it happened, the interval between two of the wagons was fairly wide just opposite the spot where Lennox was in line with his men. Dickenson was off to his left, and Roby was leading.

In a whisper the major indicated that the men should close up and pass through this opening, but in the excitement of the moment he spoke too loudly, and from somewhere close, the guard having been passed in the darkness, a man started up and shouted:

"Who comes there?"

His answer was given by the loud call of a bugle, and as he fired his warning shot the major's voice was heard shouting, "Forward—bayonets!" and with a ringing cheer the men dashed on as best they could, making for the centre of the Boers' position, shouting, cheering again and again, and driving the yelling crowd of excited Boers who were springing up in all directions before them like a flock of sheep.

The confusion was awful: rifles were being fired here and there at random, and more often at the expense of friend than of foe; while wherever a knot of the enemy clustered together it was as often to come into contact with their own people as with the major's excited line, which dashed at them as soon as an opening could be found, with such effect that the Boers, thoroughly surprised, gave way in every direction, fleeing from bristling bayonets and overturning one another in their alarm.

It was terrible work, for the attacking line was so often arrested by impediments whose nature they could not stop to grasp, that it was soon broken up into little groups led by officers commissioned and non-commissioned. But still, after a fashion, they preserved the formation of an advancing wave sweeping over the kopje, and their discipline acted magnetically with its cohesion, drawing them together, while their enemies scattered more and more to avoid the bayonet as much as to find some shelter from which such of them as had their rifles could fire.

It was panic *in excelsis*, and though many fought bravely, using their pieces as clubs where they could not fire, the one line they followed was that of flight for the enclosure behind, where their horses were tethered; and in less than ten minutes the major's force had swept right through the Boer laager on to open ground, where, in response to bugle, whistle, and cry, they rallied, ready for rushing the enemy wherever they could see a knot gathering together to resist, or from which firing had begun.

Another five minutes, during which there was desperate work going on near what had been the centre of the attacking line, and the beating of horses' hoofs and trampling feet told that the Boers were in full flight in the direction of the next kopje, where their friends were in all probability sleeping in as much security as had been the case where the attack was made. And now, as soon as the major could get his men in hand, they dropped on one knee to empty the magazines of their rifles into the dimly seen cloud of flying men running and hiding for their lives, the volleys completely dissipating all thoughts of rallying to meet the attacking force; in fact, not a Boer stopped till the next kopje was reached and the news announced of their utter defeat.

It was quick but terrible work, for the men's bayonets had been busy. Their blood was up, and they felt that they were avenging weeks of cruel suffering, loss, and injury. But now that the wild excitement of the encounter was at an end, and they were firing with high trajectory at their panic-stricken foes, the bugle rang out "Cease firing!" and they gathered together, flinging up their helmets and catching them on their bayonets, and cheering themselves hoarse.

The next minute they were eagerly obeying orders, with the faint light of day beginning to appear in the east, and working with all their might to collect and give first aid to the wounded, whether he was comrade or enemy: no distinction was made; everything possible was done.

But before this Major Robson had selected the best runner of his men volunteering for the duty, and sent him off to Groenfontein bearing a hastily pencilled message written upon the leaf of his pocketbook:

"Boers utterly routed—kopje and laager taken. Many wounded; send help."

For the attacking force had not escaped unhurt, several having received bullet-wounds, as where the Boers could get a chance they fired well; but as far as could be made out in the first hurried examination not a man was dangerously injured, and in most of the cases their hurts were cuts and bruises given by the butts of rifles. As to the Boers, the majority of their hurts were bayonet-thrusts, in some cases the last injuries they would receive; but quite a score were suffering from the small bullet-holes made by the Mauser rifles fired by their friends in their random expenditure of ammunition, such of them as had been shot by our men lying far out on the veldt, having received their wounds during their hurried flight and not yet been brought in.

Many of the wounded Boers—there was not a single prisoner, orders having been given not to arrest their flight—looked on in wonder to see the easy-going, friendly way in which our soldiers gave them help. For it was a cheery "Hold up, old chap!" or "Oh, this is not bad; you'll soon be all right again."

"Here, Tommy, bring this Dutchman a drink of water."

For the fierce warrior was latent once again, and now it was the simple Briton, ready and eager to help his injured brother in the good old Samaritan mode.

There was other work in hand to do as soon as it was light enough—the roll to call—and there were missing men to be accounted for; while, as the officers responded to their names, there was no answer to that of Captain Roby.

"He was fighting away like a hero, sir, last time I saw him," said Sergeant James, whose frank, manly face was disfigured by a tremendous blow on the cheek.

"Search for him, my lads; he can't have been taken prisoner," said the major. "It's getting lighter now."

"Poor fellow! I hope he hasn't got it," said Dickenson to himself as he nursed a numbed arm nearly broken by a drive made with a rifle-butt.

Lennox was called, and Dickenson's eyes dilated and then seemed to contract, for there was no reply.

"Mr Lennox.—Who saw Mr Lennox last?"

There was no answer for some seconds, and then from where the wounded lay a feeble voice said, "I saw him running round one of the wagons, sir, just in the thick of the fight."

"He must be down," said the major sadly. "Look for him, my lads; he is somewhere on the ground we came along, lying perhaps amongst the Boers."

Dickenson groaned—perhaps it was from pain, for his injury throbbed, pangs running right up into the shoulder-joint, and then up the left side of his neck.

"Oh! don't say poor old Drew's down," he said to himself. "Just, too, when I was growling at him for not coming to look me up when I was hurt."

No one did say he was down but the young lieutenant's imagination, and he sat down on a rock and began watching the men coming and going after bringing in wounded men.

"Who said he saw Mr Lennox last?" cried Captain Edwards.

"I did," said the wounded man in a feeble, whining voice.

"Who's that?" said the major, stepping towards the man, who lay with his face disfigured by a smear of blood.

"I did, sir. Dodging round one of the wagons somewhere. It was where the Boers stood a bit, and I got hurt."

"Could you point out the place?"

"No, sir; it was all dark, and I'm hurt," said the man faintly.

"Give him some water," said the captain. "Your hurts shall be seen to soon, my lad. Cheer up, all of you; the major has sent for the ambulance-wagons, so you'll ride home."

"Hooray, and thanks, sir!" said the worst wounded man, and then he fainted.

Just then, as the first orange-tipped clouds were appearing far on high, four men were seen approaching, carrying a wounded man slung in Sergeant James's sash; and as soon as he caught sight of the injured man's face Major Robson hurried to meet the party.

"Roby! Tut, tut, tut!" he cried. "This is bad work. Not dead, sergeant?"

"No, sir; but he has it badly. Bullet at the top of his forehead; hit him full, and ploughed up through scalp; but as far as I can make out the bone's not broken."

"Lay him down, sergeant. How long will it be," he muttered, "before we get the doctor here? Where did you find him?"

"Lying out yonder all alone, beyond those rocks, sir," replied the sergeant.

"Water—bandage," said the major, and both were brought, and the best that could be done under the circumstances was effected by the major and Sergeant James, while the sufferer resisted strongly, every now and then muttering impatiently. Then irritably telling those who tended him to let him go to sleep, he closed his eyes, but only to open them again and stare vacantly, just as Dickenson, who had been away for another look round on his own account, came up and bent over him.

"Poor fellow!" muttered Dickenson sadly, and he laid his hand sympathetically upon that of the wounded captain.

"I don't think it's very serious," said the major. "Look here, Dickenson; we have no time to spare. Take enough men, and set half to round up all the bullocks and sheep you can see, while the others load up three or four wagons with what provisions you can find. Send off each wagon directly straight for camp, and the cattle too, while we gather and blow up all the ammunition and fire the wagons left. It will not be very long before the enemy will be coming back. Hurry."

Dickenson was turning to go when the major arrested him.

"Any news of Lennox?" he said.

"None, sir," said the lieutenant sadly.

But his words were nearly drowned by an angry cry from Roby: "The coward! The cur! He shall be cashiered for this."

"Go on, Dickenson," said the major; "the poor fellow's off his head. He doesn't mean you."

The lieutenant hurried away, and for the next half-hour the men worked like slaves, laying the wounded Boers well away from the laager, and their own injured men out on the side nearest Groenfontein; while Dickenson, in the most business-like manner, helped by Sergeant James, sent off a large drove of oxen, the big, heavy, lumbering animals herding together and trudging steadily away after a wagon with its regular span laden heavily with mealies, straight for Groenfontein. For a few Kaffirs turned up after the firing was over, evidently with ideas of loot, and ready to be impressed for foreloper, driver, or herdsmen to the big drove of beasts.

A few horses were rounded up as well, and followed the oxen; while, as fast as they could be got ready, three more provision-wagons were despatched, the whole making a long broken convoy on its way to the British camp.

By this time the men, working under the orders of Captain Edwards and the major, had got the Boers' ammunition-wagons together in one place behind a mass of rocks, on the farther side of the kopje, away from the wounded. Then the weapons that could be found were piled amongst the wagons in another place; and the troops were still working hard when the major bade them cease.

"We can do no more," he said; "we have no time. But oughtn't the ambulance-wagons to be here by now? The enemy can't be long; they're bound to attack. Ah, Dickenson, have you got all off?"

"All I could, sir, in the time."

"That's right. I want your men here. You'll be ready to help to get off the wounded as soon as the wagons come?"

Dickenson nodded, with his head averted from the speaker and his eyes wandering over the injured men.

"No news of Lennox?" he asked.

"None. I can't understand where the poor fellow is, unless he was carried off in the rush of the Boers' retreat. A thorough search has been made. Here, get up on the highest part of the kopje with your glass, and see if you can make out anything of the enemy."

The lieutenant was in the act of opening the case of his field-glass, when from where the wounded lay came another angry burst of exclamations from Roby, incoherent for the most part, but Dickenson heard plainly, "Coward—cowardly hound! To leave a man like that."

Dickenson turned a quick, inquiring look at the major.

"Delirium," said the latter sharply. "I don't know what the poor fellow has on his brain. Oh, if the ambulance fellows would only come! There, my dear boy, off with you and use that glass."

Chapter Twenty Four
The Sergeant in his Element

Dickenson dashed off and climbed the low kopje, zigzagging among rough stone walls, rifle-pits, and other shelter, and noting that, if the Boers came upon them before they could retreat, there was a strong position for the men from which they could keep the enemy at bay; and, soldier-like, he began calculating as to whether it would not have been wiser to decide on holding the place instead of hurrying back to Groenfontein, with the certainty of having to defend themselves and fight desperately on the way, small body as they were, to escape being surrounded and cut off.

To his great satisfaction, though, upon reaching the highest part of the mound and using his glass, there were only a few straggling parties of men dotting the open veldt, where everything stood out bright and clear in the light of the early morning. Some were mounted, others walking, and in two places there was a drove of horses, and all going in the direction of the next laager held by the Boers.

He stood with his glass steadied against a big stone and looked long, searching the veldt to right and left and looking vainly for the main body of the enemy retreating; but they were out of reach of his vision, or hidden amongst the bushes farther on. But even if the foremost had readied their friends, these latter were not riding out as yet to make reprisals, and, as far as he could judge, there was no risk of an attack for some time to come.

For a moment a feeling of satisfaction pervaded him, but the next his heart sank; and he lowered his glass to begin looking round the kopje where here and there lay the men who had fallen during the surprise.

"Where can poor old Drew be?" he almost groaned.

At that instant his eyes lit upon the figure of the major, waving his hand to him angrily as if to draw his attention; and raising his own to his lips, he shouted as loudly as he could, "Nothing in sight."

The major's voice came to him clearly enough, in company with another wave of the hand in the other direction: "Ambulance?"

Dickenson swung round his glass to direct it towards Groenfontein, and his spirits rose again, for right away beyond the long string of oxen and wagons, as if coming to meet them, he could make out three light wagons drawn by horses, and a knot of about twenty mounted men coming at a canter and fast leaving the wagons behind.

"Ha!" sighed Dickenson; "that's good. The colonel must have started them to meet us the moment the firing was heard."

He turned directly to shout his news to the watching major, who signed to him to come down; and he descended, meeting two men coming up, one of them carrying a field-glass.

"To watch for the enemy, sir," said the latter as they met. "Which is the best place?"

"Up yonder by that stone, my lad," replied Dickenson, pointing. "Any news of Mr Lennox?"

"No, sir; I can't understand it. I think I saw him running down the side of the kopje just as we were getting on, but it was so dark then I couldn't be sure."

"I can't understand his not being found," said Dickenson to himself, as he hurried down to where the major was posting the men in the best positions for resisting an attack, if one were made before the party could get away.

Dickenson's attention was soon too much taken up with work waiting, for the wounded had to be seen to. Rightly considering that before long the enemy would advance to try and retake their old position, the major gave orders that the Boer wounded be rearranged so that they were in shelter and safety; and then, as there was still no sign of danger, the few injured of the attacking force were borne to the nearest spot where the ambulance party could meet them. Then the final work of destruction began.

"Seems a thousand pities," said Captain Edwards, "badly as we want everything nearly here."

"Yes," said the major; "but we can take no more, and we can't leave the stores for the enemy.—Here, Dickenson, take Sergeant James and play engineer. I have had the trains laid and fuses placed ready. You two must fire them as soon as we are a few hundred yards away."

Dickenson shrugged his shoulders and said nothing.

"Take care, and make sure the fuses are burning; then hurry away. Don't run any risks, and don't let Sergeant James be foolhardy."

"I'll mind, sir," said Dickenson shortly.

"The wagons will be fired before we start, so that the wind will keep them going."

"What about the powder?" said Dickenson gruffly. "That is all together. There are three wagons wheeled down into the shelter of the rock, so that the blast will not reach the fire."

"It'll blow it right up," growled Dickenson.

"No," said the major; "the rocks will deflect it upwards. I've seen to that."

"Couldn't we make the mules carry off the wagons? All three ambulances will not be wanted."

"My dear boy, you mean well," said the major impatiently; "but pray be content with taking your orders. Edwards and I have thought all that out. The fire will not go near the wounded Boers, and the explosion will not touch the fire. As to carrying off these wagon-loads of cartridges that will not fit our rifles or guns, what is the use? Now, are you satisfied?"

"Quite, sir," said Dickenson. "I was only thinking that—"

"Don't think *that*, man; obey orders."

"Right, sir," said Dickenson stiffly, and he went off to look up Sergeant James. "Hang him!" growled the young officer. "It doesn't seem to be my work. Making a confounded powder-monkey of a fellow!"

He glanced up, and saw that the men were busy on high with the field-glass, but making no sign. Then he noted that the ambulance, with its escort, was coming on fast; and soon, after a little inquiry, he came upon the sergeant, busy with the men, every one with his rifle slung, linking wagons together with tent-cloth poles and wood boxes and barrels so that the conflagration might be sure to spread when once it was started, to which end the men worked with a will; but they did not hesitate to cram their wallets and pockets with eatables in any form they came across.

"Make a pretty good bonfire when it's started, sir," said the sergeant.

"Humph! Yes," said Dickenson. "But what are those two barrels?"

"Paraffin, sir, for the beggars' lamps."

"Well," said Dickenson grimly, "wouldn't it help the fire if you opened them, knocked in their heads, and bucketed out the spirit to fling it over the wagon-tilts?"

The men who heard his words gave a cheer, and without orders seized the casks, rolled them right to the end where the fire was to be started, drove in the heads with an axe, and for the next quarter of an hour two of the corporals were busy ladling out the spirit and flinging it all over three of the wagons and everything else inflammable that was near.

"Now pack the paraffin-casks full of that dry grass and hay," cried Dickenson, who had been superintending. "It will soak up the rest, and you can start the fire with them."

The men cheered again, and in a very short time the two barrels stood under the tail-boards of two wagons, only awaiting the flashing-off of a box of matches to start a fire that no efforts could check.

"Here is the ambulance party," cried Dickenson. "Come with me now, sergeant. Let your corporals finish what there is to do."

"I don't see that there's any more to do, sir," said the sergeant, wiping his wet face. "Want me, sir?"

"Yes; I've something to say. You will go down and see the wounded off. Oh dear! oh dear! I've been thinking of what we were doing, and not of poor Mr Lennox. You've heard nothing, I suppose?"

"Neither heard nor seen, sir," replied the sergeant. "Seems to me that, in his plucky way, he must have dashed at the enemy, got mixed, and they somehow swept him off."

"If they did," said Dickenson, "he'll be too sharp for them, and get away."

"That he will, sir."

"I was afraid the poor fellow was killed."

"Not he, sir," cried the sergeant. "He'd take a deal of killing. Besides, we should have found him and brought him in. He'll turn up somewhere."

"Ha! You make me feel better, James," said Dickenson. "It took all the spirit out of me. Now then, I've some bad news for you."

"Let's have it, sir. I've had so much that it runs away now like water off a duck's back."

"It has nothing to do with water, sergeant, but with fire."

"That all, sir? I see; I'm to stop till the detachment's well out of the way, and then fire the laager?"

"No," said Dickenson; "that will be done before the men have marched. You are to stop with me and light the fuses."

"To blow up the ammunition, sir? Well, I was wondering who was to do that."

The leader of the mounted escort had dropped from his panting horse.

"It's a risky job, sergeant."

"Pooh, sir! Nothing like advancing against a lot of hiding Boers waiting to pot you with their Mausers. Beg pardon, sir; who was Mauser?"

"I don't know, sergeant. I suppose he was the man who invented the Boer rifles."

"And a nice thing to be proud of, sir! I'm not a vicious sort of fellow, but I do feel sometimes as if I should like to see him set up as a mark, and a couple of score o' Boers busy trying how his invention worked."

"Come along," said the lieutenant.—"Then you don't mind the job?"

"Not I, sir. I always loved powder from a boy. Used to make little cannons out of big keys, filing the bottoms to make a touch-hole. I was a don at squibs and crackers; and the games we used to have laying trains and making blue devils! Ha! It was nice to be a boy!"

"Yes, sergeant; and now we've got something big to do. But there, you're used to it. Remember getting away the powder-bags with Mr Lennox?"

"Remember it, sir? Ha! But I was in a fright then."

"Of being blown up?"

"Well, sir, if you'll believe me, I never thought of myself at all. I was all in a stew for fear the powder should catch from the lantern and make an end of Mr Lennox."

"I believe you," said Dickenson; and they stopped at the spot where the ambulance-wagons had trotted up, and the leader of the mounted escort had dropped from his panting horse to speak to the major.

"Then you've done it, sir?"

"Yes, as you see. What message from the colonel?"

"Covering party advancing, sir, to help you in. You are to get all the provisions and cattle you can, and retire. But that I see you have done. Enemy near, sir?"

The major glanced at the top of the kopje before replying, and then said briefly, "Not yet."

Chapter Twenty Five
Another Explosion

The wounded men—a couple of dozen all told, many of the injuries being only slight—were rapidly lifted into the light wagons while the horses and mules were given water, and all went well, the more slightly hurt cheering and joking their bearers, and making light of their injuries in the excitement of the triumph.

"Mind my head, boys," said one; "it's been knocked crooked."

"And my leg's loose, you clumsy beggar; it's there somewhere. Don't leave it behind."

"I say, Joey, I've got a hole right through me; ain't it a lark!"

"Here, you, sir! Take care; that's my best 'elmet. I want it for a piller." And so on, and so on.

Only one man groaned dismally, and that was Corporal May.

"I say, mate; got it as bad as that?" said one of the bearers.

"Oh! worse—worse than that," moaned the corporal. "I'm a dead man."

"Are you, now?" said one of his fellows in the company. "I say, speak the truth, old chap; speak the truth."

"Oh!" groaned the corporal. "Why am I here—why am I here?"

"I dunno," said the bearer he looked at with piteous eyes. "I never was good at riddles, mate. Can't guess. Ask me another.—There you are, lifted as gently as a babby. You're only a slightly; I do know that."

The corporal was borne away, still groaning, and the man who had spoken last handed him some water.

"Cheer up, corporal," he said; "you'll be back in the ranks in a week."

Meanwhile the bearers were busy in the shelter where Captain Roby lay, flushed, fevered, and evidently in great pain, while his brother officers stood round him, eager to do anything to assuage his pangs and see him carefully borne to the wagon in which he was to travel.

"How are you, Roby?" said Dickenson, softly laying a powder-blackened hand upon the injured man's arm, while the bearers stood waiting to raise him.

The question and the touch acted electrically, Roby started; his eyes opened to their full extent, showing a ring of white all round the iris; and he made an effort to rise, but sank back.

"You coward—you miserable cad!" he cried. "You saw me shot down—I implored you to help me to the rear—and you chose that time to show your cowardly hate—you, an officer.—Coward! You ran—you turned and ran to save your beggarly life—coward!—coward! Oh, if I had strength!—I'll denounce you to the colonel. Cur!—coward!—cur!—I'll publish it for all the world to know."

Dickenson started at first, and then listened to the end.

"All right," he said coolly. "Don't forget when you write your book."

"Lift him, my lads, gently; we have no time to spare," said the major sternly; and as Roby was borne away, shouting hoarsely, "Coward!—cur!" Captain Edwards said sharply in a whisper, so that the men should not hear:

"Dickenson! Is this true?"

"Oh! I don't know," was the reply. "I recollect the bugle sounding, and then I was too busy to know what I did till it sounded 'Cease firing!' I know I was out of breath."

"Take no notice," said the major quickly. "The poor fellow's raving. Coward! Tchah! Be ready, Dickenson. You've found the sergeant?"

"All ready, sir."

In a very few minutes the ambulance-wagons were off again, with their attendants ordered to go at a steady walk, and, if an attack was made, to keep the red-cross flag well shown, and avoid the line of fire if possible.

And still there was no alarm given from the top of the kopje of the Boers' approach.

A short time was allowed for the ambulance to get ahead, during which the officers had another look at the Boer wounded, the major ordering water to be given to the men. Next a few sheaves of abandoned rifles were cast into the wagons to be burned, and a final look was given to the preparations already made for the destruction of the camp.

At last, while the long line of captured stores was crawling over the veldt, and a great number of the other oxen which had wandered off to graze were, according to their instinct, beginning to follow their companions as if to make for Groenfontein, the order was given for the men to fall in ready for the march back.

All was soon in order, and the major turned to Dickenson, who stood aside with Sergeant James, waiting to perform their dangerous task.

"I was going to appoint four more men to fire the wagons," said the major, "but with the preparations you have made the flames will spread rapidly, and you two can very well do it; and as soon as the fire has taken hold you can light the fuses yonder."

"Men signalling from the top of the kopje," said Captain Edwards.

"That means the enemy in sight," said the major coolly. "Signal to them to come down."

As the captain turned away to attend to his orders the major held out his hand to Dickenson.

"Do your work thoroughly," he said gravely, "and then follow as fast as you can. I will leave pickets behind to cover you."

Dickenson nodded, but said nothing, only stood fingering a box of matches in his pocket and watching the major hurrying down the encumbered slope of the kopje to join the men awaiting the order to march.

"Sentries on the top coming down, sir," growled the sergeant; and Dickenson nodded again, turning to watch the two men running actively along and leaping from stone to stone, till they were pretty close to the drawn-up force, when the bugle rang out, the voices of the officers were heard, and the retiring party went off at a good swinging march.

Dickenson watched them for a few minutes without a word, while the sergeant stood with his rifle grounded and his hands resting upon the muzzle, perfectly calm and soldierly, patiently waiting for his orders, just as if he and the sergeant were to follow as a sort of rear-guard instead of to fulfil about as dangerous a task as could fall to the lot of a man, knowing too, as he did, that the enemy had been signalled as advancing—a body of men armed with the most deadly and far-reaching rifles of modern times.

"About time now, sergeant," said Dickenson coolly.

"Yes, sir; 'bout right now, I should think."

"I want them to have a fair start first," continued Dickenson; "and I can't help feeling a little uneasy about the enemy's wounded, for there will be an awful explosion."

"Oh, they'll be all right, sir. Make 'em jump, perhaps, and think they're going to be swept away."

"I wish they were farther off," said Dickenson; and then he uttered an ejaculation as he started aside, an example followed by the sergeant, who chuckled a little as he exclaimed:

"Wish 'em farther off, sir? So do I."

For, following directly one after the other, two shots were fired from the shelter where the wounded Boers had been carefully laid in safety, a couple of them having evidently retained their rifles, laying them under cover till they could find an opportunity to use them.

"That's nice and friendly, James," said Dickenson coolly. "Forward!—under cover."

"I feel ashamed to run, sir," said the sergeant fiercely.

"Look sharp!" cried Dickenson, for two more bullets whistled by them. "I don't like bolting, but it seems too bad to be shot down by the men we have been getting into safety."

"And fidgeted about, sir," said the sergeant grimly. "I wish you'd give me orders to chance it and go back and give those blackguards one apiece with their own rifles. It must have been them the captain meant when he was letting go about cowards and curs."

"Very likely, poor fellow!" said Dickenson, marching coolly on till they were covered from the Boers' fire. "There, they may fire away now to their hearts' content," he continued, as he halted at the end of the prepared wagons. "Wind's just right—eh?"

"Beautiful, sir; and as soon as the blaze begins to make it hot you'll find the breeze'll grow stiffer. It's a great pity, though."

"Yes; I wish we had all this at Groenfontein."

"So do I, sir; but wishing's no good. I meant, though, it's a pity it isn't dark. We should have a splendid blaze."

"We shall have a splendid cloud of black smoke, sergeant," said Dickenson, taking out his box of matches. "Ready?"

"Ready, sir," replied the sergeant, and each held his match-box as low down in the paraffin-barrel as the saturated hay would permit, struck a match, and had to drop it at once and start back, for there was a flash of the evaporating gas, followed by a puff of brownish-black, evil-odoured smoke, which floated upward directly.

"Bah! Horrible!" cried Dickenson, coughing. "My word, sergeant! there's not much doubt about the Boers' camp blazing."

"Serve 'em right, sir, for using such nasty, common, dangerous paraffin. Here comes the wind, sir: what did I say?"

For the soft breeze came with a heavier puff, which made the forked tongues of flame plunging up amongst the thick smoke begin to roar, and in a very few seconds the fire was rushing through one of the tilted wagons as if it were a huge horizontal chimney.

"Did you get singed, sergeant?"

"No, sir. It just felt a bit hot. Hullo! what's that?"

For a horrible shrieking and yelling arose from the direction of the wounded Boers.

"The crippled men," said Dickenson. "They're afraid they are going to be burned to death. We ought to go and shout to them that there's nothing to fear."

"Yes, sir, it would be nice and kind," cried the sergeant sarcastically; "only if we tried they wouldn't let us—they'd shoot us down before we were half-way there."

"Yes, I'm afraid so," said Dickenson, who stared almost in wonder at the terrific rate at which the fire was roaring up and sweeping along, threatening, as wagon after wagon caught, to cover the kopje with flame.

"Perhaps, sir," said the sergeant, with a grim smile, "it would be a comfort to the poor fellows' nerves if we sent up the ammunition-wagons now."

"Whether it would or not, sergeant, we must be sharp and do it, or with these flakes of fire floating about we shall not dare to go near our fuse."

"That's what I'm thinking, sir," said the sergeant.

"Forward, then;" and the pair went on at the double to the spot where the train was laid, the fuses being some distance from the ammunition-wagons, and on lower ground sheltered by great stones.

The next minute the pair were down on one knee sheltering their match-boxes from the wind behind a big rock, with the train well in view, for those who laid it had not scrupled to use an abundance of powder.

"I did not reckon about this wind," said Dickenson. "As fast as one of us strikes a light it will be blown out."

"That's right, sir."

"And we shall never get the fuse started."

"We must try, sir."

"Yes," said Dickenson. "Here, it must be one man's job to fire the train; the explosion will send off the next wagon."

"And no mistake, sir. We ought to have had a lantern to light the fuse at. But you get lower down, sir, and I'll set off the whole box of matches I've got here, chuck it into the train, and drop behind this big stone."

"That seems to be the only way to get it done," replied Dickenson.

"Yes, I'm sure of it, sir," said the sergeant.

"All right, then; run down and get behind that piece of rock. I'll do it directly."

"No, no, sir; let me do it," pleaded the sergeant.

"'Tention!" roared Dickenson. "Quick! No time to lose. Off at once."

The sergeant's lips parted as if he were about to say something, but Dickenson gave him a stern look and pointed downward towards the stone, when discipline ruled, and the man doubled away to it, grumbling and growling till he was lying down panting as if he were out of breath.

"I could have done it better myself," he said hoarsely; and then, "Oh, poor lad, poor lad! If—if—"

There was a sharp crack, followed by a pause filled up by the shrieking and yelling of the wounded Boers. Then the sergeant felt that he must raise his head and see how matters were going on; but he refrained, for there was a peculiar hissing noise. Dickenson had taken about twenty matches out of the box he carried, held them ready, and ignoring the fuse, he struck the bundle vigorously, stretched out his hand, which was almost licked by the flash of flame, and applied it to the thickly-laid train.

For a few moments there was no result, the wind nearly blowing out the blazing splints; but just as the young man was hesitating about getting out more matches—*phitt*! There was a flash as the powder caught and the flame began to run in its zigzag course right along the ground towards the nearest ammunition-wagon.

Turning sharply, Dickenson laid his hands upon a block of loose stone, vaulted over it, and dropped flat upon his face, conscious the while of the piteous cries of the wounded men.

The next instant there was a tremendous concussion, the stone giving him a violent blow, and as the sky above seemed to blaze there was a roar like thunder, then a perceptible pause, another roar, again a pause, and another roar.

Then for a few moments the young officer lay deafened and feeling stunned, till beneath the pall of smoke which hung over him he opened his eyes and saw the sergeant kneeling by his side with his lips moving.

Dickenson stared at him wonderingly, while he saw the horrified look in the man's face and its workings as he kept on moving his lips, and finally half-raised his young officer and laid him down again.

"What's the matter?" said Dickenson—at least he thought he did—he felt as if he had said so; but somehow he could not hear himself speak for the crashing sound of many bells ringing all together.

He did not for the moment realise what had happened, but like a flash the power of thinking came back, and drawing a deep breath, he tried to get up, but could hardly stir. Something seemed to hold him down.

"Give me your hand, sergeant," he said, but still no words seemed to come, and he repeated what he wished to speak; but before he had completed his sentence, he grasped the fact that the sergeant's manner had changed, for he rose up, felt behind him, looked at him again, and seemed to speak, for his lips moved.

"Are you hurt?" Dickenson said, in the same way.

The sergeant's lips moved and he shook his head, looking the while as if he were not hurt in the least.

"Then why don't you speak?" said Dickenson.

The man smiled and pointed to his ears.

"The explosion has deafened you?" said Dickenson dumbly, for still he could not hear a word. "What do you mean? Oh, I see."

For the sergeant clapped him on the chest, and then placing his shoulder against the stone, he seemed to be exerting all his strength to force it uphill a little, succeeding so well that the next moment Dickenson felt himself slip, glided clear of the sergeant's legs, and rose to his own, while the man leaped aside and the great block slipped two or three yards before it stopped.

"Then I was caught by the stone?" said Dickenson wonderingly. "I felt it move."

He felt sure now that he had said those words; but in his confused state, suffering as he was from the shock, he could only wonder why the sergeant should begin feeling him over, and, apparently satisfied that nothing was broken, begin hurrying him along in the direction taken by the retreating force, which, now that the dense cloud of smoke was lifting, he could see steadily marching away in the distance, but with a group of about a dozen lingering behind.

Just then the sergeant stopped, unslung his rifle, placed his helmet on the top, and held it up as high as he could, till Dickenson saw a similar signal made by the party away ahead.

"They know we're all right," said Dickenson, still, as it seemed, dumbly: and the sergeant nodded and smiled.

"It was an awful crash. I mean they were terrible crashes, sergeant."

There was another nod, and after a glance back the sergeant hurried him along a little faster.

"Can you—no, of course you can't—hear whether the Boers are calling out now?"

The sergeant shook his head.

"Poor wretches!" said Dickenson. "But they were too far off to be hurt."

The sergeant nodded.

"Here, I can't understand this," said Dickenson.

"You pointed to your ears and signified to me that the explosions had made you as deaf as a post."

The sergeant turned to him, looking as if he were trying to check a broad grin, as he pointed to his officer's ears. That made all clear.

"Why, it is I who am deaf," cried Dickenson excitedly; and almost at the same moment something seemed to go *crack, crack* in his head, and his hearing had come back, with everything that followed sounding painfully loud.

"And no wonder, sir," said the sergeant. "It was pretty sharp. My ears are singing now. Does it hurt you where you were nipped by the stone?"

"Feels a bit pinched, that's all."

"And you're all right beside, sir?"

"Yes, I think so, sergeant."

"That's good. Well, sir, you did it."

"What! blew up the wagons? Yes, sergeant, I suppose we've done our work satisfactorily. But do you think the Boers would be hurt?"

"If they were, sir, it was not bad enough to make them stop singing out for help. I heard them quite plainly after the explosions. Can you walk a little faster, sir?"

"Oh yes, I think so. I'm quite right, all but this singing noise in my ears. I say, though, what about the enemy?"

"I don't know anything about them, sir; the kopje hides them for the present, but once they make out how few we are, I expect they'll come on with a rush; and the worst of it is, they're mounted. But it'll be all right, sir. The colonel said he was sending out a covering party to help us in, didn't he?"

"Yes," replied Dickenson.

"Oh, we shall keep them off. They'll begin sniping as soon as they get a chance, but they'll never make a big attack in the open field like we're going over now."

A very little while after they overtook the party hanging back till they came up, Captain Edwards being with the men, ready to congratulate them on the admirable way in which their task had been carried out.

The brisk walking over the veldt in the clear, bright air rapidly dissipated Dickenson's unpleasant sensations, and when the main body was overtaken the young officer would have felt quite himself again if it had not been for the dull, heavy sense of misery which asserted itself: for constantly now came the ever-increasing belief that he must accept the worst about his comrade, something in his depressed state seeming to repeat to him the terrible truth—that poor Drew Lennox must be dead.

He found himself at last side by side with the major, who as they went on began to question him about his friend's disappearance, and he frowned when Dickenson gravely told him his fears.

"No, no," said the major; "we must hope for better things than that. He'll turn up again, Dickenson. We must not have our successful raid discounted by such a misfortune.—Eh, what's that?"

"Boers in sight, sir," said Sergeant James. "Mounted men coming on fast."

"Humph! Too soon," said the major, and he proceeded to make the best of matters. The ambulance party was signalled to hurry forward, and a message sent to the little rear-guard with the store wagons and cattle to press forward with their convoy to the fullest extent. Then, as the mounted Boers came galloping on and divided in two parties, right and left, to head off the convoy, the eager men were halted, faced outward, and, waiting their time till the galloping enemy were nearly level at about three hundred yards' distance, so accurate a fire was brought to bear that saddles were emptied and horses went down rapidly. Five minutes of this was sufficient for the enemy, the men swerving off in a course right away from the firing lines, and, when out of reach of the bullets, beginning to retreat.

"Has that settled them?" said Captain Edwards.

"No," said the major; "only made them savage. They'll begin to try the range of their rifles upon us now. Open out and hurry your men on, for the scoundrels are terribly good shots."

The speaker was quite right, for before long bullets began to sing in the air, strike up the dust, and ricochet over the heads of the men, to find a billet more than once in the trembling body of some unfortunate ox. But fighting in an open plain was not one of the Boers' strong points; the cover was scarce, they had their horses with them, and the little British party was always on the move and getting nearer home. Several bold attempts were made to head them off, but they were thwarted again and again; but in spite of his success, the major began to grow frantic.

"Look at those blundering oxen, Dickenson," he cried. "It's a regular funeral pace over what will be our funerals—the brutes! We shall have to get on and leave them to their fate. I'll try a little longer, though. I say, we must be half-way now."

"Yes; but unfortunately there's a fresh body of the enemy coming up at a gallop," said Dickenson, who had paused to sweep the veldt with his field-glass. "Yes, twice as many as are out here."

"What!" cried the major. "Well, there's no help for it; we shall have to leave the cattle behind. Send a man forward to tell the convoy guard to halt till we come up, and let the cattle take their chance."

"The men with the wagons too, sir?"

"No," cried the major; "not till we're at the last pinch. We must try and save them."

The messenger was sent off at the double; and as the retreating party marched on, the major continued to use his glass, shaking his head in his annoyance from time to time as he saw the Boer reinforcements closing up.

"Oh!" he groaned, "if we only had a lancer regiment somewhere on our flank, just to manoeuvre and keep out of sight till their chance came for a charge. Make them run—eh, Edwards?"

"Yes," said the captain dryly; "but unfortunately we have no lancer regiment on our flank."

"No," replied the major; "and we must make the best of it."

"Beg pardon, sir," said Sergeant James to Dickenson; "but don't it seem a pity?"

"What? To have got so far and not be able to get back unhurt?"

"I was thinking of the cattle, sir," replied the sergeant gloomily. "Hungry and low as the poor lads are with the want of meat, it seems a sin to forsake all that raw roast-beef. It's enough to make the men mutiny."

"Not quite, sergeant," replied his officer as he tramped steadily on. "But look forward; it doesn't seem to make any difference. The baggage-guard has halted, but the oxen are marching on, following the wagons steadily enough."

"Yes, sir; as the old lines used to say that I learnt at school, 'It is their nature too.'"

"I suppose the enemy will divide, take a long reach round, and get ahead of the convoy."

"Yes, sir, that'll be their game. They'll make for that patch of wood and rocks in front, occupy it, and force us to make a what-you-may-call-it."

"Détour?" said Dickenson.

"That's it, sir."

"Yes," said Dickenson thoughtfully; "they'll be able—mounted—to make it before we can."

But the major seemed to think differently, for he sent fresh men on to hurry the convoy, his intention being to occupy the rough patch of a few acres in extent, hoping to keep the enemy at bay from there till the promised help came from Groenfontein.

"Yes, I know," he said impatiently when Dickenson joined him for a few minutes to receive fresh orders. "It's distant, and we shall be without water; but it must be done. They must not even stampede the cattle."

"The major says the cattle must be saved, sergeant," said Dickenson as he doubled and rejoined his little company.

"Does he, sir?" said the sergeant cheerfully. "Very well, sir, then we must do it. Beg pardon, sir; might be as well for you to go on and say a few words to the lads to cheer them up."

"They're doing wonderfully well, sergeant."

"That's true, sir; but we want 'em to do better. They don't see the worst of it. It's all very well to appeal to a soldier's heart and his honour, and that sort of thing; but this is a special time."

"What do you mean? This is no time for making speeches to the brave fellows."

"Of course not, sir. But just you say in your merry, laughing way something about the beggars wanting to get our beef, and you'll see what the lads can do. Taking a bone from a hungry dog'll be nothing to it. The lads'll shoot as they never shot before, for there isn't one of them that isn't thinking of roast and boiled."

Dickenson laughed, and went on at once along the little column, saying his few words somewhat on the plan the sergeant had suggested, and it sent a thrill through the little force. They had just come up with the convoy guard, who heard what he said, and somehow or other—how, it is as well not to inquire—several of the great lumbering beasts began to bellow angrily and broke into a trot, which probably being comprehended by the drove in front, they too broke into a trot, which in turn was taken up by the spans in the wagons, and the whole line was in motion.

The drivers and forelopers who led the way made for the cover, and at the word of order that passed along the line the men doubled, cheering loudly the while, and sending the bullocks blundering along in a cloud of dust.

"Steady, there! Steady!" shouted the major. "Never mind the cattle. The lads will be winded, and unable to shoot."

"Yes," panted Captain Edwards; for while this had been going on, the enemy, now tripled in number, were repeating their former evolution, and two clouds of them taking a wide sweep round were nearly abreast of the little force, evidently on their way to seize the patch of bush as a shelter for their horses while they dismounted, occupied the cover, and dealt destruction to those who came on.

The major saw the uselessness of his manoeuvre now, and was almost ready to give it up; but still he had hopes.

"The cattle will screen our advance," he said, "and the enemy are bound to ride right round on account of cover for their horses. I believe even now that we can get to this side as soon as the Boers get to the other, and we must clear the bush at the point of the bayonet."

The men soon knew what was required of them, and they kept on steadily at the double. But minute by minute it grew more evident that the fast, strong ponies of the enemy, long as the sweep being taken on either side proved to be, must get to the cover first; and, to the despair of the officers, while they were still far distant in the deceiving, clear air, they saw the two big clouds of the enemy, as if moved by one order like a well-trained brigade of cavalry, swing round right and left and dash for the thick patch of dwarf trees dotted with rocks.

"We're done, sergeant," said Dickenson breathlessly.

"Yes, sir," said the man coolly; "they've six legs to our two. I'm sorry about that beef, for I'd set my mind on a good meal at last."

At that moment the bugle rang out, for it was madness to press on, and the men, disappointed of their bayonet-charge to clear the little open wood, began to draw breath ready for their next order to turn off right or left and continue the retreat out of rifle-fire as soon as they could.

"Oh, it's maddening!" cried Dickenson passionately as he unfastened the cover of his revolver holster.

"Oh no, sir," said Sergeant James. "Case for a cool head. You'll see now how neatly the major will get us out of fire and take us round. I wish, though, that our covering party had been within reach."

An order rang out directly for the party to advance left incline, which meant the giving up of their loot, and the men went on with set teeth as they saw the two great clouds of Boers growing darker as they pressed in for the patch of trees; and then there was a cheer bursting from every throat—a cheer that was more like a hoarse yell, for from both ends of the little wood, still some five hundred yards away, there was a puff of smoke, followed by the rattle of a Maxim-gun on the right, a small field-piece, shrapnel charged, on the left, and directly after a couple of volleys given by well-concealed men.

The effect was instantaneous: riders and fallen horses and men were struggling in wild confusion, falling and being trampled down, and those unhurt yelling in wild panic to get clear. And all the while, as fast as they could fire, the hidden covering party in the wood were supplementing the Maxim and gun fire by emptying their magazines into the two horror-stricken mobs. For they were nothing better, as in a selfish kind of madness to escape they dragged their horses' heads round and lashed and beat at them with the butts of their rifles, to begin frantically galloping back by the way they came.

But the worst of their misfortune had not come. Each wing had to gallop for some distance within shot of the major's little force, which poured in volley after volley before "Cease firing!" was sounded, the Boers having continued their flight right away, evidently making for their ruined laager, leaving horse and man dotting the veldt.

The men were too busy congratulating each other upon their victory, and helping to round up the cattle scared by the firing, to pay much heed at first to the wounded enemy; but as soon as a dozen of the best riders were mounted on some of the Bechuana ponies which, minus their riders, had begun to contentedly browse on such green herbage as could be found, the major set a party to work bringing the wounded Boers into the shade.

"Their own people will see to them as soon as we are gone," said the major. "What do you make out, Edwards?" he continued to that officer, who was scanning the retreating enemy through his glass.

"They seem to me to be gathering together for another advance," said Captain Edwards.

"No," said the major, "they will not do that. This has been too severe a lesson for them. They'll wait till we are gone, and then come to see to their killed and wounded. That was a sudden turn in the state of affairs."

"Ha!" replied Captain Edwards. "I was beginning to wonder how many of us would get back to Groenfontein."

"Yes," said the major; "so was I."

In a very short time the ambulance party and the convoy, with its great train of cattle, were once more on their way to the camp, well-guarded by half the party Colonel Lindley had so opportunely sent to the help of the expedition, the rest, with the major's little force, following more deliberately, keeping on the alert for another attack from the Boers, who waited till their foes were quitting the field before coming slowly on. But not for a new encounter; their aim now was only to carry off their wounded comrades and bury their dead.

"Yes," said the major, "they have had one of the sharpest lessons we have given them during the war. We suffered enough in carrying the kopje by surprise; this time we have not lost a man."

These last words haunted Dickenson all the way back to the camp, which was reached in safety, the men being tremendously cheered by the comrades they had left behind. But in spite of his elation with the grand addition to their supplies and the two great triumphs achieved by his men, the colonel looked terribly down-hearted at the long array of wounded men; while with regard to Lennox he shook his head.

"A sad loss," he said. "I looked upon Drew Lennox as one of the smartest young fellows in the corps. It's very hard that misfortune should have befallen him now."

"But you think he'll get back to us, sir?" said Dickenson excitedly.

The colonel gave him a quick look.

"I hope so, Mr Dickenson; I hope so," he said. "There, cheer up," he added. "We shall soon see."

Chapter Twenty Six
"A Coward!—a Cur!"

It was about an hour later, when the wounded had been seen to by the surgeon—who reported very favourably on the men, whose injuries were for the most part the result of blows from rifle-butts received in the struggle on the kopje—that two of the scouts who had been left to watch the Boers came in with a sufferer dangerously injured by a rifle-bullet.

Dickenson's heart gave a throb as he saw the men, and being off duty, he hurried to meet them, in the hope and belief that they had found Lennox. But it was one of their companions.

The men's report was that the Boers had come steadily on as the British force retreated, and had then been busily engaged collecting their dead and wounded, paying no heed to the little outpost watching them till their task was done, when, as the last of their wagons moved off, they began firing again, till one of the outposts fell, and the others remained too well covered, staying till the firing had ceased, and then hurrying back.

"Poor old Lennox!" said Dickenson to himself. Then, seeing that Sergeant James was watching him, he shook his head.

"I was hoping that they were bringing in Mr Lennox, sir," said the sergeant gloomily. "Of course, seeing the temper the enemy is in after their defeat, it would be like getting some of our fellows murdered if the colonel gave me leave to go out with a white flag."

"I'm afraid so too," said Dickenson.

"But what about as soon as it's dark, sir? Think the colonel would let us go to make a better search? He must be near the Boers' laager where we missed him."

"I was thinking something of the sort," said Dickenson. "Will you go with me, James?"

"Will I go with you, sir?" cried the sergeant. "Wouldn't I go through anything to try and get him back? You'll ask the colonel to name me, sir?"

"If he gives consent," said Dickenson warmly. "He'll tell me to take two or three men, and of course I shall pick you for one."

"Thankye, sir; and don't you be down-hearted. You're fagged now, sir, with all we've done since we started, and that explosion gave you a horrid shaking up. You go to your quarters, sir, as soon as the colonel has given leave, and lie down—flat on your back, sir—and sleep till it's time for starting. I'll have the others ready, and I'll rouse you up, sir."

"Very well, sergeant," said the young officer. "I must own to being a bit down."

As soon as the sergeant had left him, the young officer went to the colonel's quarters and asked to see him.

"Come in, Dickenson," said the chief, and he held out his hand. "Thank you, my lad," he said. "I've heard all about what you've done. Very good indeed. I sha'n't forget it in my despatch, but when it will get to headquarters is more than I can tell. I'm glad you have come. What can I do for you?"

Dickenson stated his wishes, and the colonel looked grave.

"I don't know what to say, Dickenson," he replied. "It would be a very risky task. I have scouts out, but I doubt whether they'll be able to tell whether the enemy is still holding the kopje. If he is, you will run a terrible risk. I've just lost one of my most promising young officers; I can't spare another."

"I was afraid you would say so, sir. But Drew Lennox and I have always been regular chums together, and it seems horrible to settle down quietly here in safety and do nothing to try and find him."

"It does, my dear sir; but we soldiers have to make sacrifices in the cause of duty."

"Yes, sir; but we've had a splendid bit of luck since last night. Can't you strain a point?"

The colonel smiled.

"Well, it's hardly fair to call it luck, Dickenson," he said. "I think some of it's due to good management. Eh?"

"Yes, sir; you are quite right."

"Well there, then, if you'll promise me to run no risks with the lads, and return if you find the enemy still at the kopje, I'll give you leave to take a sergeant and a couple of men and go."

Dickenson looked pleased and yet disappointed.

"We might find him somewhere near, sir, even if the Boers are there," he said.

"In the darkness of a moonless night, with men on the *qui vive* ready to fire at the slightest sound?"

"We got well into the laager last night, sir, with a hundred and fifty men," said Dickenson in tones of protest.

"But you wouldn't get in to-night with one, and such an enterprise against either of the other laagers would now be impossible. There, I can make no further concessions, for all your sakes, so be content."

"You are right, sir, and I am wrong," replied Dickenson quietly.

"You will retire, then, directly you find the place occupied?"

"Yes, sir."

"Go, then, as soon as it is dark. You can pick two men who can ride, take three of the captured Bechuana ponies, and one can hold them while the others search."

"Thank you, sir."

"But I have no hope of your finding him, Dickenson. This is solely from a desire that we may feel we have done all we can do in such a case. Now I am busy. You have been up all night, and nearly been killed. Go and lie down for a few hours' sleep."

The young officer left the colonel's presence, and had no trouble in finding the sergeant, for he was watching for his return, and heard with eagerness the result.

"Ride? Capital, sir; make us fresher for our work. We shall find him. I don't believe he's dead. Now you'll take a rest, sir. I'll have the ponies ready, and the men."

Dickenson gave him the names of the two men he would like to take, but had to give up one.

"Can't sit a horse, sir; hangs on its back like a stuffed image. Now Jeffson, sir, was a gentleman's groom. Ride anything. I wonder he isn't in the cavalry."

"Very well, then; warn Jeffson. There, I am done up, sergeant. I trust you to rouse me as soon as it's dark."

"Right, sir. But one word, sir."

"What is it?"

"Captain Roby, sir. Keeps off his head, sir. Going on awfully. Doctor Emden says it's due to the bullet striking his skull."

"Dangerous?" said Dickenson anxiously.

"Oh no, sir; but he keeps on saying things that it's bad for the men to hear; and that Corporal May, he's nearly as bad. He thinks he's worse. He's within hearing, and every time the captain says anything, Master Corporal May begins wagging his head and crying, and tells the chaps about him that it's all right."

"Poor fellow! There, I'll go and see them before I lie down."

"No, sir; please, don't," said the sergeant earnestly. "You've done quite enough for one day."

"Confound it, man! don't dictate to me," cried Dickenson testily.

"Certainly not, sir. Beg your pardon, sir; but we've got a heavy job on to-night, and it's my duty to warn you as an old soldier."

"What do you mean?"

"I mean, sir, that I've had twenty years' experience, and you've had two, sir. A man can only do so much; when he has done that and tries to do more, he shuts up all at once. I don't want you to shut up, sir, to-night. I want you to lead us to where we can find Mr Lennox."

"Of course, sergeant. I know you always mean well. Don't take any notice of my snappish way."

"Not a bit, sir," said the man, smiling. "It's only a sign that, though you don't know it, you're just ready to shut up."

"But, hang it all, man!" said the young officer, with a return of his irritable manner, "I only want to just see my brother officer for a few minutes."

"Yes, sir, I know," said the sergeant stubbornly; "but you're better away. He's right off his head, and abusing everybody. If you go he'll say things to you that will upset you more than three hours' sleep will wipe out."

"Oh, I know what you mean now—what he said before—about my being a coward and leaving him in the lurch."

"Something of that sort, sir," replied the sergeant.

"Poor fellow! Well, perhaps it would be as well, for very little seems to put me out. It was the shock of the explosion, I expect. There, sergeant, I'll go and lie down."

"I'll bring you a bit of something to eat, sir, when I come. There's plenty now."

"Ah, to be sure; do," said the young man. "But I could touch nothing yet. Remember: as soon as it is quite dark."

"Yes, sir; as soon as it is quite dark."

Dickenson strode away, and the sergeant uttered a grunt of satisfaction.

"Poor fellow!" he muttered. "It would have made him turn upon the captain. Nobody likes to be called a coward even by a crank. It would have regularly upset him for the work. Now then, I'll just give those two fellows the word, and then pick out the ponies. Next I'll lie down till the roast's ready. We'll all three have a good square meal, and sleep again till it's time to call Mr Dickenson and give him his corn. After that, good-luck to us! We must bring that poor young fellow in, alive or dead, and I'm afraid it's that last."

Meanwhile Dickenson had sought his quarters, slipped off his accoutrements and blackened tunic, and thrown himself upon his rough bed. It was early in the afternoon, with the sun pouring down its burning rays on the iron roofing of his hut, and the flies swarming about the place.

As a matter of course over-tired, his nerves overwrought with the excitement of what he had gone through, and his head throbbing painfully, he could not go to sleep. Every time he closed his eyes his ears began to sing after the same fashion as they did directly following the explosion, and after tossing wearily from side to side for quite an hour, he sat up, feeling feverish and miserable.

"I'm making myself worse," he thought. "I know: I'll go down to the side of the stream, bathe my burning head and face, and try and find a shady place amongst the rocks."

He proceeded to put his plan into execution, resuming his blackened khaki jacket and belts, and started off, to find a pleasant breeze blowing, and, in spite of the afternoon sunshine, the heat much more bearable than inside his hut. His way led him in the direction of the rough hospital, and as he drew near, to his surprise he heard Captain Roby's voice speaking angrily, and Dickenson checked himself and bore off to his right so as to go close by the open door.

"Poor fellow!" he said. "I must see how he is."

He went into the large open hut in which the captain had been placed by the doctor's orders, because it was one in which the sides had been taken off so as to ensure a good current of air. As the young officer entered he caught sight of two others of the injured lying at one end, and noted that the wounded corporal was one.

Both men were lying on their backs, perfectly calm and quiet; but Roby was tossing his hands about impatiently and turning his head from side to side, his eyes wide open, and he fixed them fiercely upon his brother officer as he entered.

"How does he seem, my lad?" said Dickenson to the attendant, who was moistening the captain's bandages from time to time.

"Badly, sir. Quite off his head."

"Ah! Cur!—coward!" cried Roby, glaring at him. "Coward, I say! To leave me like that and run."

"Nonsense, old fellow!" said Dickenson, affected just as the sergeant had said he would be; and his voice sounded irritable in the extreme as he continued, "Drop that. You said so before."

"Who's that?" cried Roby, with his eyes becoming fixed.

"Me, old fellow—Dickenson. Not a coward though."

"Who said you were?"

"Why, you did, over and over again."

"A lie! No. I said Lennox. Ah! To run for his miserable life—a coward—a cur!"

"What!" cried Dickenson angrily; but Roby lay silent as if exhausted, and, to the young officer's horror and disgust, a womanly sob came from the corporal's rough pallet at the end of the hut, and in a whining voice he moaned:

"Yes, sir; he don't mean you, but Mr Lennox, sir. I saw him run, and it's all true."

Chapter Twenty Seven
"There's Nothing like the Truth"

Bob Dickenson's jaw dropped as he stood staring for some moments at the corporal—as if he could not quite believe his ears. It seemed to him that this had something to do with the explosion, and that his hearing apparatus was still wrong, twisting and distorting matters, or else that the excitement of the past night and his exertions had combined with the aforesaid explosion to make him stupid and confused.

But all the same he felt that he could think and weigh and compare Roby's words with those of the corporal, and experienced the sensation of a tremendous effervescence of rage bubbling up within his breast and rising higher and higher to his lips till it burst forth in words hot with indignation.

"Why," he roared, "you miserable, snivelling—lying—Oh, tut, tut, tut! what a fool I am, quarrelling with a man off his head!—Here, orderly," he continued, turning to the hospital attendant, "this fellow May doesn't know what he's saying."

"So I keep on telling him, sir," said the man sharply; "but he will keep at it. Here's poor Captain Roby regularly off his chump, and bursting out every now and then calling everybody a coward, and, as if that ain't bad enough, Corporal May goes on encouraging him by saying *Amen* every time."

"I don't," cried the corporal, in a very vigorous tone for one so badly injured; "and look here, if you make false charges against me I'll report you to the doctor next time he comes round, and to the colonel too."

"What!" cried the orderly fiercely. "Yes, you'd better! Recollect you're down now, and it's my turn. I've had plenty of your nastiness, Mr Jack-in-office Corporal, for a year past, when I was in the ranks. You ain't a corporal now, but in hospital; and if you say much more and don't lie quiet I'll roll up a pad of lint and stuff that in your mouth."

"You daren't," cried the corporal, speaking the simple truth defiantly, and without a trace of his previous whining tone.

"Oh yes, I dare," said the attendant, with a grin. "Doctor's orders were that, as you were put in here when you oughtn't to be, I was to be sure and keep you quiet so as you shouldn't disturb the captain, and I'm blessed if I don't keep you quiet, so there."

"You daren't," cried the corporal tauntingly.

"What! Just you say that again and I will. Look here, my fine fellow. In comes Dr Emden. 'What's this, orderly?' he says. 'How dare you gag this man?'

"'Couldn't keep him quiet, sir,' I says. 'He's been raving awful, and lying, and egging the captain on to keep saying Mr Dickenson and Mr Lennox is cowards.'"

"I wasn't lying," cried the corporal, with a return of his whimpering tone. "What Captain Roby says is all true. I saw Mr Lennox sneak off like a cur with his tail between his legs."

"Cur yourself, you lying scoundrel!" cried Dickenson.—"Here, orderly, I'll hold him. Where's that gag?"

"Oh! Ow!" wailed the corporal. "Here, if you touch me I'll cry for help."

"You won't be able to," said the orderly, making a pretended rush at the doctor's chest of hospital requirements.

"Bah! Quiet, orderly. Let the scoundrel alone. He's off his head and doesn't know what he's saying, poor wretch."

"Begging your pardon, sir," said the attendant, "the captain don't; but this chap does. I haven't seen what I have amongst the sick and wounded without picking up a little, and I say Master Corporal here's doing a bit o' sham Abram to keep himself safe."

"Oh, nonsense," said Dickenson shortly. "You're getting as bad as the poor fellow himself. The doctor would have seen in a minute."

"I don't know, sir," whispered the attendant, glancing at the corporal, who lay with his eyes half-closed and his ears twitching. "He's pretty cunning. Had a crack or two with a rifle-stock, I think, but only just so much as would make another man savage. You'll see; he'll be sent back into the ranks in a couple of days or so."

"No, no, orderly," said Dickenson. "I prefer to believe he's a bit delirious."

"Well, sir, I hope he is," said the man, "for everybody's sake, including his own. I don't know, though," he continued, following the lieutenant outside after the latter had laid his hand upon Roby's burning forehead, and been called a coward and a cur for his pains; "I've got my knife into Master

Corporal May for old grudges, and I should rather like Mr Lennox to hear him say what he does about him. Corporal May would get it rather hot."

"That will do," said Dickenson; "the man's in such a state of mental excitement that his captain's ravings impress him and he thinks it is all true. There, you, as a hospital attendant, must learn to be patient with the poor fellows under your charge."

"I am, sir," said the man sturdily. "Ask the doctor, sir. I'm doing my best, for it's sore work sometimes with the poor chaps who are regularly bad and feel that they are going home—I mean the long home, sir. I've got six or seven little things—bits of hair, and a silver ring, and a lucky shilling, and such-like, along with messages to take back with me for the poor fellows' mothers and sisters and gals; and please goodness I ever get back to the old country from this blessed bean-feast we're having, I'm going to take those messages and things to them they're for, even if I have to walk."

"Ha!" said the young officer, laying his hand on the man's shoulder and gripping him firmly, for there was a huskiness in his words now, and he sniffed and passed his hand across his nose.

"Can't help it, sir. I'm hard enough over the jobs, but it touches a man when it comes to sewing 'em up in their blankets ready for you know what. Makes you think of them at home."

"Yes," said Dickenson, in quite an altered tone. "There, you know me. When we get back and you're going to deliver your messages, if you let me know, orderly, I'll see that you don't have to walk." Dickenson turned sharply to walk away, but came back. "Try and keep the captain from making those outrageous charges, my lad."

"I do, sir; but he will keep on."

"Well, go on cooling his bandages, and he'll go off to sleep."

"I hope so, sir," replied the man. "But what about Corporal May?"

"Serve him the same, of course," said Dickenson, and he hurried away, with Roby's words ringing in his ears.

"Chap wants to be a sort of angel for this work," said the orderly as he fumbled about his slight garments. "Hankychy, hankychy, where are yer? Washed you out clean in the little river this morning and dried you on a hot stone."

"What are you looking for, mate?" said the third patient in the hut feebly—a man who, with a shattered arm-bone, was lying very still.

"Hankychy," said the orderly gruffly. "Lost it."

"Here it is. You lent it to me to wipe my face and keep off the flies."

"Did I? So I did. All right, mate; keep it. Mind you don't hurt the flies. Like a drink o' water?"

"Ah-h!" sighed the injured man. That was all, but it meant so much.

There was a pleasant, trickling, tinkling sound in the heated hut as the orderly took a tin and dipped it in an iron bucket. The next minute he was down on one knee with an arm under the sufferer's shoulders, raising him as gently as if the task was being done by a woman. Then the tin was held to the poor fellow's lips, and the orderly smiled as he saw the avidity with which it was emptied.

"Good as a drop of beer—eh?" he said.

"Beer?" replied the patient, returning the smile. "Ha! Not bad in its way; but I never tasted a pint so good as that."

"Oh! Ah!" said the orderly grimly. "Wait till you get all right again, and you'll alter your tune."

"Get right again?" whispered the man, so that the corporal should not hear. "Think I shall?"

"What! with nothing else the matter but a broken bone? Why, of course."

"Ah!" sighed the poor fellow, with a look of relief. "I'm a bit down, mate, with having so little to eat, and it makes me think. Thankye; that's done me a lot o' good."

He settled down upon the sack which formed his couch, and the orderly rose to take back the tin, not seeing that Corporal May's eyes were fixed upon the vessel, which he watched eagerly, as if expecting to see it refilled and brought to him. But the orderly merely set it down, and made a vicious blow at a buzzing fly.

"Well, what have I done?" whined the corporal.

"Done? Heverythink you shouldn't have done," said the orderly. "Look here, corp'ral; next time the barber cuts your hair, you ask him to take a bit off the end of your tongue. It's too long, mate."

"Do you want me to report you to the doctor for refusing to bring me a drink?"

"Not I," said the orderly coolly. "The chief's got quite enough to do without listening to the men's complaints."

"Then bring me a drink of water directly."

"All right," said the man good-humouredly; "but you'd better not."

"Better not? Why?"

"Because it only makes you cry. Runs out of your eyes again in big drops, just as it does out of another fellow's skin in perspiration. Strikes me, corp'ral, that you were meant for a gal."

"You won't be happy till you've been reported, my man," said the patient.

"And I sha'n't be happy then, mate. Want a drink o' water?"

"Yes; but things are managed here so that the patients have to beg and pray for it."

"And then they gets it," said the orderly good-humouredly as he dipped the tin again; "and that's more than you can say about what most chaps begs and prays for. There you are."

"Well, help me up," said the corporal.

"Yah! Sit up. You can."

"Oh!" groaned the man in a peculiar way which sounded as if he were not satisfied with its effectiveness, and so turned it into a whine.

"Won't do with me, corp'ral," said the man. "You gammoned the doctor, but you haven't took me in a bit."

"Only wait!" said the patient in a miserable whining tone this time. "How cowardly! What a shame for such as you to be put in charge of wounded men!"

"Wounded!" said the orderly, laughing. "Why, your skin is as whole as mine is. You've frightened yourself into the belief that you're very bad."

"Ah! you'll alter your tone when I've reported you."

"Look here, corp'ral; it strikes me that, with the row that's coming on about you and the captain charging the officers with being cowards, there's going to be such a shine and court-martial that you'll have your work cut out to take care of yourself. Here, put your arm over my shoulder, and up you come."

"Eh?" said the corporal in a much more natural tone.

"Eh—what?"

"About the court-martial?"

"Oh, I don't know. I only said what I thought," said the orderly, winking to himself. "Now then, up you come. Mind the water."

He supported the corporal gently enough, and helped him to raise the water to his lips, watching him as he drained it, and then lowered him gently down and knelt, still looking at him, till the corporal gazed back at him wonderingly.

"What are you staring at?" he said sharply.

"You, old man."

"Why?"

"I was thinking. Your knocks have made you quite off your head."

"That they haven't. I'm as clear over everything as you are."

"Oh no," said the orderly. "You're quite off your chump, and don't know what you're saying."

"You're a fool," said the corporal angrily.

"Tell me something I don't know, old chap. Fool? Why, of course I was, to 'list and come out for a holiday like this. Oh yes, plenty of us feels what fools we've been; but we're making the best of it—like men. D'yer hear—like men? I say, the captain's regularly raving, ain't he?"

"Well, er—yes—no."

"Oh, he is; and you'd better own up and be cracked too. You don't know what you've been saying about Mr Lennox."

The corporal hesitated, looking up in the orderly's eyes curiously, and seeming as if he was thinking deeply of the man's words and debating in himself about the position he was going to occupy if an inquiry did follow the captain's charges. He was not long in deciding, but he forgot to whine as he said, "Off my head? Delirious? Not a bit. I saw all the captain said, and I'm as clear as you are. I shall stick to it. There's nothing like the truth."

"Oh yes, there is," said the orderly, chuckling; "a thoroughly good thumping lie's wonderfully like it sometimes—so much like it that it puzzles people to tell t'other from which."

"Look here, orderly; do you mean to tell me I'm a liar?" said the corporal angrily.

"Not I. 'Tain't no business of mine; only it strikes me that there's going to be a regular row about this. People as go righting don't like to be called cowards. It hurts anybody, but when it comes to be said of a soldier it's like skinning him. There, I must go and wet the captain's lint."

Saying which, the orderly rose and went to captain Roby's side to moisten the hot bandages, so that their rapid evaporation might produce a feeling of coolness to his fevered head.

Chapter Twenty Eight
A Find

Dickenson walked frowning away from the hospital hut, thinking of the manner in which Roby had shifted the charge of cowardice from his shoulders to Lennox's, and a sigh of misery escaped from his breast as he made for the side of the bubbling stream.

"Poor fellow!" he said to himself. "I'm afraid that he's where being called coward or brave man won't affect him."

He reached the beautiful, clear stream, lay down and drank like some wild animal, and then began bathing his temples, the water setting him thinking of Lennox's adventures by its source, and clearing his head so much that when he rose at last and began to walk back to his quarters he felt wonderfully refreshed.

This state of feeling increased to such a degree that when he once more lay down after taking off his hot jacket, the heat from the roof, the buzzing of the flies, and the noises out in the village square mingled together into a whole that seemed slumber-inviting, and in less than ten minutes he was plunged in a deep, heavy, restful sleep, which seemed to him to have lasted about a quarter of an hour, when he was touched upon the shoulder by a firm hand, and sprang up to gaze at the light of a lantern and at nothing else.

"Close upon starting-time, sir," said the sergeant out of the darkness behind the lamp.

For a few moments Dickenson was silent, and the sergeant spoke again.

"Time to rouse up, sir."

"Yes, of course," said the young officer, getting slowly upon his feet, and having hard work to suppress a groan.

"Bit stiff, sir?"

"Yes; arm and back. I can hardly move. But it will soon go off."

"Oh yes, sir. It was that big stone nipping you after the blow-up."

"I expect so," said Dickenson, struggling into his jacket. "Ha! It's getting better already. Where are the ponies?"

"Round by the tethering-line, sir; but you've got to have a bit of supper first."

"Oh, I want no supper. I've no appetite now."

"Armoured train won't work, sir, without filling up the furnace," said the sergeant sternly; "and the ponies are not quite ready."

"You promised to have them ready, sergeant."

"So I did, sir; but we want all we can out of them to-night. We may have to ride for our lives; so I managed to beg a feed of mealies apiece for them. There's a snack of hot meat ready in the mess hut, sir, and the colonel would like to see you before you start."

"Yes," said Dickenson, finishing buckling on his sword, and slipping the lanyard cord of his revolver about his neck.

He hurried then to the mess-room, where a piece of well-broiled steak, freshly cut from one of the oxen, was brought by the cook, emitting an aroma agreeable enough; but it did not tempt the young officer, whose one idea was to mount and ride away for the kopje. Certainly it was not only like fresh meat—very tough—but it possessed the toughness of years piled-up by an ox whose life had been passed helping to drag a tow-rope on trek. So half of it was left, and the young man sought the colonel's quarters.

"Ha!" he said. "Ready to start, then?"

"Yes, sir."

"Well, I must leave all to your discretion, Dickenson," he said. "Recollect you promised me that if there was any sign of the kopje being still occupied you would stop at once and return."

"Yes; I have not forgotten, sir."

"That's enough, then. Keep your eyes well open for danger. I'd give anything to recover Lennox, but I cannot afford to give the lives of more of my men."

Dickenson frowned.

"You mean, sir, that you do not believe he is still alive."

"I don't know what to say, Dickenson," said the colonel, beginning to walk up and down the hut. "You have heard this ugly report?"

"Yes, sir; and I don't believe it."

"I cannot believe it," said the colonel; "but Captain Roby keeps on repeating it to the doctor and the major; while that man who was wounded, too, endorses all his captain says. It sounds monstrous."

"Don't believe it, sir," cried Dickenson excitedly.

"I have told you that I cannot believe it," said the colonel; "but Mr Lennox is missing, and it looks horribly corroborative of Roby's tale. There, go and find him—if you can. We can't add that to our other misfortunes; it would be a disgrace to us all."

"You mean, sir," said Dickenson coldly, "if Drew Lennox had—has—well, I suppose I must say it—run away?"

"Exactly."

"Well, sir, I don't feel in the least afraid. He is either a prisoner, lying badly wounded somewhere about the kopje, or—dead."

He said the last word in a husky tone, and then started violently.

"What is it, man?" cried the colonel excitedly, for the young officer seemed as if he were suffering from some violent spasm. "Are you hurt?"

"Something seemed to hurt me, sir," said the young man; "but it was only a thought."

"A thought?"

"Yes, sir," was the reply. "I was wondering whether it was possible."

"Whether what was possible?" said the colonel impatiently. "Don't speak in riddles, man."

"No, sir. It came like a flash. Suppose the poor fellow was somewhere near the spot where we exploded the ammunition?"

"Fancy," said the colonel coldly. "There must have been plenty of places round about the part you attacked without Lennox being there. There, lose no time; find him, and bring him back."

"He half believes that wretched story put about by Roby," said Dickenson to himself as he walked stiffly away, depressed in mind as well as body, and anything but fit for his journey, as he began to feel more and more. But he made an effort, stepped out boldly in spite of a sharp, catching pain, and answered briskly to the sentries' challenges as he passed into the light shed by the lanterns here and there.

"Ready, sir?" said a voice suddenly.

"Yes; quite. The sooner we're off the better."

"The ponies are waiting, sir; and I've got the password, and know exactly where the outposts are if I can hit them off in the dark, for it's twice as black as it was last night."

"Then it will be a bad time for our search."

"Search, sir?" said the sergeant bluntly. "We're going to do no searching to-night."

"What!" cried Dickenson.

"It's impossible, sir. All we can do is to get as close as we can to the kopje and find out whether the enemy is still there. Then we must wait for daylight. If the place is clear, it will be all easy going; if the Boers are still there we must have a hasty ride round, if we can, before we are discovered."

"Very well," said Dickenson slowly as they walked on to the lines where the ponies were tethered, mounted, and went off at a walk, the sergeant and Dickenson side by side and the two men close behind; while the slight, cob-like Bechuana ponies upon which they were mounted seemed to need no guiding, but kept to the track which brought them again upon outposts, where their riders were challenged, gave the word, and then went steadily on at a walk right away across the open veldt.

"Ponies know their way, sir," said the sergeant after they had ridden about a mile. "I'll be bound to say, if we let them, they'll take us right by that patch of scrub where the enemy had his surprise, and then go straight away for the kopje."

"So much the better, sergeant," said Dickenson, who spoke unwillingly, his body full of pain as his mind was of thought.

"Will you give the order for us to load?"

"Load?" said Dickenson in a tone expressing his surprise. "Oh! of course;" and he gave the necessary command, taking the rifle handed to him by one of the men as they rode on. "I was thinking of our chances of finding the Boers out scouting. I suppose it is quite possible that we may run against a patrol."

"More than likely, sir. They'll be eager enough to find out some way of paying back what we gave them to-day."

"Of course, and—What does this mean?" whispered Dickenson, for his pony stopped short, as did the others, the sergeant's mount uttering a sharp, challenging neigh and beginning to fidget.

"Means danger, sir," whispered the sergeant. "We loaded none too soon."

There was nothing for it but to sit fast, peering into the wall of darkness that surrounded them, trying vainly to make out the approaching danger, every man listening intently. Fully ten minutes elapsed, and not a sound was heard. The ponies, well-trained by the Boers to stand, remained for a time perfectly motionless, till all at once, just as Dickenson was about to whisper to the sergeant that their mounts had probably only been startled by some wild animal of the desert, one of them impatiently stretched out its neck (drawing the hand holding the reins forward), snuffed at the earth, and began to crop at the stunted brush through which they were passing. The others immediately followed suit, and, letting them have their own way, the party sat once more listening in vain.

Then came a surprise. All at once, from what Dickenson judged to be some fifty feet away, there was the peculiar *ruff! ruff! ruff! ruff!* of some one walking slowly through the low scrub, which there was not unlike walking over a heather-covered track.

"Stand," cried the lieutenant sharply, "or we fire."

"No. Hold hard," cried a familiar voice. "Who goes there? Dickenson, is that you?"

"Lennox! Thank Heaven!"

The steps quickened till he who made them came staggering up to the lieutenant's pony, at which he caught, but reached short, stumbled, and fell.

The sergeant was off his pony in a moment, handing the reins to a companion, and helping the lost man to rise.

"Are you all right?" said Dickenson excitedly as he reached down, felt for, and firmly grasped his friend's wet, cold hand.

"All right?" said Lennox bitterly. "Well, as all right as a man can be who was about to lie down utterly exhausted, when he heard your pony."

"But are you wounded?"

"No; only been nearly strangled and torn to pieces. But don't ask me questions. Water!" A water-bottle was handed to the poor fellow, and they heard him drink with avidity. Then ceasing for a short space, he said, "I was just going to lie down and give it up, for I was completely lost." He began drinking again, and then, with a deep breath of relief: "Whose is this?"

"Mine, sir," said the sergeant, and he took the bottle from the trembling outstretched hand which offered it.

"Thankye, sergeant," sighed the exhausted man. "It does one good to hear your voice again. Are we far from Groenfontein?"

"About three miles," said Dickenson.

"Ah!" said Lennox, with a groan. "Then I can't do it."

"Yes, you can," said Dickenson warmly. "Here, hold on by the nag's mane while I dismount. We'll get you into the saddle, and walk the pony home."

"Excuse me, sir; I'm dismounted," said the sergeant, "and I'd rather walk, please."

"Thank you, James," said Dickenson. "I'll take your offer, for I'm nearly done up myself."

"You keep still, then, sir.—Dismount, my lads, and help to get Mr Lennox into the saddle.—Rest on me, sir; I've got you. Sure you're not wounded, sir?"

There was no reply; but the sergeant, who had passed his arm round his young officer's waist, felt him subside, and if the hold had not been tightened he would have sunk to the ground.

"Got him?" cried Dickenson.

"Yes, sir; all right. Fainted."

"Fainted?"

"Yes, sir. Regular exhaustion, I suppose. We'll get him into the saddle, and I think the best way will be for me to got up behind and hold him on, for he's regularly given up now that he has fallen among friends."

"But the pony: will it carry you both?"

"Oh yes, sir—at a walk. They're plucky little beasts, sir. But we've got him, sir, and that's what I didn't expect. I suppose we mustn't cheer?"

"Cheer? No," said Dickenson excitedly. "Look here, sergeant; I'm a bit crippled, but I'll have him in front of me."

"But he's on my pony now, sir, with the lads holding him. Had we better drag him down again? He's precious limp, sir; and I'm afraid he's hurt worse than he said."

"Very well; keep as you are," said Dickenson hurriedly; and, almost unseen, the sergeant mounted behind his charge and began to feel about him for the best way of making the poor fellow as comfortable as possible.

"He's got his sword all right, sir, but his revolver's gone. Stop a moment," continued the sergeant, fumbling in the darkness; "there's the lanyard, but his hat's gone too. There, I've got him nicely now. Mount, my lads."

There was a rustling sound as the men sprang into their saddles again.

"Ready?" said Dickenson.

"Yes, sir."

"Stop a moment. How are we to find our way back?"

"We shall have to trust to the ponies, sir," said the sergeant. "Let's see; we have turned their heads round over this job. We must leave it to them; they'll find their way back, thinking they're going to get some more mealies. Trust them for that."

"Forward at a walk!" said Dickenson. "Tut, tut, sergeant! It's as black as pitch. If a breeze would only spring up."

"Dessay it will, sir, before long."

"How does Mr Lennox seem?"

"Head's resting on my clasped hands, sir, and he's sleeping like a baby—regular fagged out."

It was a slow and toilsome march; but the party were in the highest of spirits, and, in the hope of seeing the lights at Groenfontein at the end of an hour or so, they kept on, only pausing now and again to listen for danger and to rearrange Lennox, whose silence began to alarm his friend. But the sergeant assured him that the poor fellow was sleeping heavily, and they went on again with a dark mental cloud coming over Dickenson's exhilaration as he thought of the unpleasant news that awaited his friend.

"But a word from him will set that right," he said to himself. "Poor fellow! He must be done up to sleep like that. Why, he never even asked how we got on after the fight."

Chapter Twenty Nine
In Difficulties

On and on at the ponies' slow walk through the short scrub or over the bare plain, with the clever little animals seeming to instinctively avoid every stone that was invisible to the riders in the intense darkness. Every now and then a halt was made, one of which their steeds immediately took advantage by beginning to browse on such tender shoots as took their fancy, and again and again the whispered questions were asked:

"How does he seem, sergeant?"

"Fast asleep, sir."

"Hadn't you better let one of the men take your place?"

"Oh no, sir; I'm all right, and so's he."

"Can either of you hear anything?"

"No, sir; only the ponies cropping the bush." Then a faint, "We ought to be getting near home, sergeant."

"Yes, sir."

"Can we do anything more?"

"No, sir; only wish for a row of gas-lamps along a straight road, and it ain't any good to wish for that."

"I can see nothing, sergeant, and the sky seems blacker than the earth."

"Both about the same, sir, I think."

"It is so unfortunate, sergeant, just at a time like this."

"Oh, I don't know, sir; one ought to make the best of things, and weigh one against another."

"What do you mean?"

"Well, sir, we're bothered a good deal with the darkness, and we're obliged to do what a human man don't like to do—trust to a dumb animal instead of himself. Of course that's bad; but then, on the other side, we're not running up against any of the enemy, and instead of hunting for hours after a long ride and then not finding what we come for, here we are not having a long dangerous ride at all, and him we wanted to find tumbling right atop of us and in a way of speaking, saying, 'Looking for me, my lads? Here I am!'"

"Yes, we have been very fortunate," said Dickenson.

"Fortunate, sir? I call it downright lucky."

"Of course—it is. But can we do no more?"

"Not that I see, sir—feel, I mean. We might camp down and let the horses feed till daylight."

"Oh no; let us keep on."

"Very well, sir; then there really is nothing we can do but trust to the ponies. They somehow seem to see in the dark."

"Forward, then!"

At the end of another half-hour they drew rein again, and almost precisely the same conversation took place, with the exception that Dickenson declared at the end that they must have lost their way.

"Well, sir," replied the sergeant dryly, "it's hardly fair to say that, sir."

"What do you mean?" said Dickenson tartly.

"Begging your pardon, sir, one can't lose what we've never had. It's been a regular game of Blindman's buff to me, sir, ever since we left the last post."

Dickenson was silent, for he felt that he had nothing to say but "Forward!" so he said that, and the ponies moved on again.

"We must be going wrong, sergeant," said Dickenson at last. "We have left Groenfontein to the right."

"No, sir; I think not," replied the man. "If we had, we should have broken our shins against the big kopje and been challenged by our men."

"Then we've passed it to the left."

"No, sir. If we had we should have come upon the little river, and the ponies would have been kicking up the stones."

"Then where are we?" said the lieutenant impatiently.

"That's just what I'm trying to find out, sir. I wouldn't care if I knew which was the north, because then one could say which was the south."

"Psh! It all comes of trusting to the ponies."

"Yes, sir; but that's one comfort," said the sergeant. "We know they're honest and would not lead us wrong. Poor brutes! they're doing their best."

"I'm beginning to feel hopelessly lost, sergeant. I believe we keep going on and on in a circle."

"Well, sir, we might be doing worse, because it must be daylight by-and-by."

"Not for hours," said Dickenson impatiently. "We are, as I said, hopelessly lost."

"Hardly," said the sergeant to himself, "for here we are." Then aloud he once more proposed that they should bivouac till daybreak.

"No," said the leader decisively. "We'll keep on. We must have been coming in the right direction, and, after all, I dare say Groenfontein is close at hand."

He was just about to give the order to march again when the long, snappish, disappointed howl of a jackal was heard, and the ponies ceased grazing and threw up their muzzles; while as Dickenson leaned forward to give his mount an encouraging pat he could feel that the timid creature's ears were thrust right forward.

"Always seems to me, sir," said the sergeant gently, "that the wild things out in these plains never get enough to eat. Hark at that brute."

He had hardly spoken when from out in the same direction as the jackal's cry, but much farther away, came the tremendous barking roar of a lion, making the ponies draw a deep breath and shiver.

"Well," said Dickenson, "that can't be our way. It must be open country yonder. It's all chance now, but we needn't run into danger and scare our mounts. We'll face right round and go as far as we can judge in the opposite direction to where that cry came from."

"Yes, sir; and it will make the ponies step out."

The sergeant was quite right, for the timid animals responded to the touch of the rein, immediately stepped out at the word "Forward!" and then broke into a trot, which had to be checked.

The roar was not heard again, but the yelps of the jackals were; and the party went on and on till suddenly the cautious little beasts began to swerve here and there, picking their way amongst stones which lay pretty thickly.

"This is quite fresh, sergeant," said Dickenson.

"Yes, sir. I was wondering whether we had hit upon the river-bank."

"Ah!" cried Dickenson eagerly, just as his pony stopped short, sighed, and began to browse without reaching down, the others seeming to do the same.

"But there's no river here, sir," continued the sergeant.

"How do you know?"

"Ponies say so, sir. If there'd been a river running by here, they'd be making for it to get a drink."

"Yes, of course. Here, sergeant, I can touch high boughs."

"Same here, sir."

"But there's no wood in our way."

"What about the patch where our men surprised the Boers yesterday, sir?"

"To be sure. Why, sergeant, we must have wandered there."

"That's it, sir, for all I'm worth."

"Ha!" said Dickenson, with a sigh of relief. "Then now we have something tangible, and can easily lay our course for Groenfontein." The sergeant coughed a little, short, sharp, dry cough, and said nothing. "Well, don't you think so?"

"Can't say I do, sir. I wish I did."

"Why, hang it, man! it's simple enough. Here's the coppice, and Groenfontein must lie—"

Dickenson stopped short and gave his ear a rub, full of vexation.

"Yes, sir, that's it," said the sergeant dryly; "this is the patch of wood, but which side of it we're looking at, or trying to look at, I don't know for the life of me. It seems to me that we're just as likely to strike off straight for the Boers' laager as for home. I don't know how you see it, sir."

"See, man!" cried Dickenson angrily. "It's of no use; I only wish I could see. We can do nothing. I was thinking that we had only to skirt round this place, and then face to our left and go straight on, and we should soon reach home."

"Yes, sir; I thought something of that sort at first, but I don't now. May I say a word, sir?"

"Yes; go on. I should be glad if you would."

"Well, sir, it's like this; whenever one's in the dark one's pretty well sure to go wrong, for there's only one right way to about fifty that are not."

"Yes, of course."

"Then won't it be best to wait till the day begins to show in the east, and rest and graze the ponies for a bit? Better for Mr Lennox too."

"You're right, sergeant; and it would have been better if I had given the order to do so at first.—Here, dismount, my lads, and hobble your cobs.— Here, I'll help you to get Mr Lennox down, sergeant. Stop a moment; let's try and find a patch of heath or grass or something first.—Hullo! what's here?" he cried a minute later, after dismounting and feeling about.

"What have you found, sir?"

"Ruts—wheel-marks made, of course, by our guns or their limbers. Can't we tell our way by those?"

"No, sir. It makes things a bit simpler; but we had a gun and wagon at each end, and we can't tell in the dark which end this is. If we start again by this we're just as likely to make straight off for the Boer camp as for ours."

"Yes; we'll wait for daylight, sergeant," said Dickenson. "We're all tired out, so let's have two or three hours' rest."

A few minutes later Lennox, still plunged in a stupor-like sleep, was lifted from the sergeant's pony, and at once subsided into the bed of short scrub found for him; the ponies, well hobbled, were cropping the tender parts of the bushes; and the weary party were sitting down.

There was silence for a few minutes, and then the sergeant spoke in a whisper.

"Think it would be safe for the men to light a pipe, sir?"

"Hum! Yes," said Dickenson, "if they light the match to start their pipes under a held-out jacket and in the shelter of one of the big stones."

He repented directly he had given the consent, on account of the risk.

"But, poor follows!" he said, "this will be the second night they have been out on the veldt, and it will help to keep them awake."

Lennox was at the end of a couple of hours sleeping as heavily as ever. Dickenson had seated himself close by him so that he could lay a hand upon his forehead from time to time; and he judged that the poor fellow must be in pain, for each time there was a sharp wincing, accompanied by a deep sigh, which resulted in the touch being laid on more lightly. It was only to satisfy himself in the darkness that his comrade was sleeping and not sinking into some horrible state of lethargy; and finding at last that there was no apparent need for his anxiety, the watcher directed his attention to listening for sounds out upon the veldt, and divided the time by making surmises as to the experiences through which Lennox must have passed.

Captured and escaped! That was the conclusion to which he always came, and he wished that Lennox would wake up and enliven the tedium of the dark watch by relating all that he had gone through.

The lion made itself heard again and again, but at greater distances; and the prowling jackals and hyenas seemed to follow, for their cries grew fainter and fainter and then died out into the solemn silence of the veldt, which somehow appeared to the listener as if it were connected with an intense feeling of cold.

Then all at once, as Dickenson turned himself wearily and in pain from the crushing he had received when the stone slipped, he became conscious of something dark close by, and his hand went involuntarily to his revolver.

The next minute he realised that what he saw was not darker, but the sky behind it lighter, and he sprang to his feet.

"You, sergeant?" he said.

"Yes, sir," was whispered back. "Be careful; one never knows who may be near. The light's coming fast."

Coming so fast that at the end of a quarter of an hour Dickenson could dimly make out the steep kopje by Groenfontein away to his left, and the low, hill-like laager that they had destroyed twenty-four hours before low down on the opposite horizon.

"Why, sergeant," he whispered eagerly, "if we had started again in the dark we should have gone right off to where the Boers might have been."

"Yes, sir, and away from home. That's the worst of being in the dark."

"As soon as it's a little lighter," whispered Dickenson, "we had better carefully examine this place. It is quite possible that there may be a patrol of the enemy occupying it, as we have done."

"Yes, sir, likely as not, for—"

The sergeant clapped his hand over his lips and dropped down upon his knees, snatching at his officer's jacket to make him follow his example.

There was need enough, for all at once there was something loudly uttered in Dutch, replied to by another speaker, the voices coming from the other side of the woodland patch.

In another minute there was quite a burst of talking, and, making signs to his two companions, the sergeant stepped softly to where the ponies were browsing and led them in amongst the trees, which stood up densely, until they were well hidden.

The next idea was to lift Lennox well under cover; but he was not touched, for he was still sleeping, and already so well hidden that it would not have been possible for any one to see him if passing round outside the trees and the thin belt of scrub.

"Get well down there, my lads," said Dickenson then. "We'll try and hold this little clump of stones if they do find us. If they do, we must give them a wild shout and a volley. They need not know how few we are."

The men crouched down among the stones while the pale grey dawn was broadening, and waited in the full expectation of being discovered; for though a mounted patrol might in passing fail to see the men, the chances were that it would be impossible to go by without catching sight of the ponies.

It was evident enough to the listeners that the Boer party had passed the night in this shelter, and that they must have been sleeping without a watch being kept; otherwise, in spite of the quiet movements of Dickenson and his men, their arrival must have been heard; and now, as they crouched there, rifle in hand, all waited in the hope that the party would ride off at once in the direction of the ruined laager.

But Dickenson waited in vain, for the crackling of burning sticks told that the enemy did not intend to start till they had made their breakfast, and the young officer's brain was busily employed debating as to whether it would not be better to try and drive them off with a surprise volley, putting them to flight in a panic. Under the circumstances he took the non-commissioned officer into consultation.

"If you think it's best, sir," said the sergeant, "do it; but you can't get much of a volley out of four rifles, and if you follow it up by emptying your magazines there'll be no panic, for they'll know what that means."

"What do you advise, then?"

"Waiting, sir. We're only four. There's Mr Lennox, but that seems like bringing us down to two instead of making us five. As we are we're in a strong position, and they may ride right away without seeing us; and that's what we want, I take it, for we don't want to fight—we want to get Mr Lennox safely back. If they don't ride straight off, and are coming round here and see us, we can try the panic plan while they're mounted. They're pretty well sure to scatter then. If we fire now they're not mounted, they'll take to cover, and that'll be bad, sir."

"Yes. It means a long, dull time," replied Dickenson. "We'll wait, sergeant; but how long it will be before they know we're here I'm sure

I don't know. I've been expecting to hear one of the ponies neigh every moment, and that will be fatal."

"Oh, I don't know, sir. You never can tell. They may take fright even then after the startlings we've given them. They're brave enough chaps so long as they're fighting from behind stones, or in ambush, or when they think they've got the whip-hand of us; but a surprise, or the thought that we're getting round their flank and into their rear, is more than they can stand."

"Silence!" whispered Dickenson. "I think they're on the move."

But they were not, and the sun was well up before sundry sounds pointed to the fact that the enemy were preparing to start.

For sundry familiar cries were heard, such as a man would address to a fidgety horse which declined to have its saddle-girth tightened. The men were laughing and chatting, too, until a stern order rang out, one which was followed by the trampling of horses—so many that the sergeant turned and gave a significant glance at Dickenson.

"Now then, which way?" thought the latter. "If they come round this side they must see us, and they are bound to, for here lies their laager."

He was right, for the trampling came nearer, and it was quite evident that the little party were riding round in shelter of the patch of wood, so as to get it between them and the English camp before striking straight away.

They were only about a dozen yards distant, dimly seen through the intervening trees, and Dickenson was in the act of glancing right and left at his men when a chill ran through him. For Lennox, who had lain perfectly still in the shadow beneath the bush where he had been laid, suddenly began to mutter in a low, excited tone, indicating that he was just about waking up. It was impossible to warn him, even if he had been in a condition to be warned; and to attempt to stir so as to clap a hand over his lips must have resulted in being seen.

There was nothing for it but to crouch there in silence with hearts beating, and a general feeling that in another few seconds the order must come to fire.

The moments seemed to be drawn out to minutes as the Boers rode on, lessening their distance and talking loudly in a sort of formation two or three abreast, till the front pair were level, when one of them raised his hand to shade his eyes, and drew his comrade's attention to something in the distance.

"It's a party of the rooineks," he said in his Dutch patois; "or some of our horses left from that wretched surprise yesterday."

"I shall never do it in the dark," said Lennox half-aloud, and Dickenson's heart seemed to cease beating.

"What do you say, behind there?" cried the first speaker sharply, but without turning his head.

"I say they're rooineks," said one of the three who came next.

"Yes, they're rooineks, sure enough," said the first Boer; "but that's not what you said just now."

"Yes, I did," was the surly answer; "but every one here's talking at once."

"Yes," growled the first speaker. "Silence, there! Halt!"

The men reined up in a group, while the first man, who seemed to be in command, dragged out a much-battered field-glass, focussed it, and tried to fix the distant objects. But his horse was fresh and fidgety, waiting to be off.

"Stand still!" cried the Boer savagely, and he caught up the reins he had dropped on the neck of his mount and gave them a savage jerk which made the unfortunate animal plunge, sending the rest into disorder, so that it was another minute before steadiness was restored.—"Mind what you're about, there," cried the leader. "Keep close to the bushes. Do you want to be seen?"

He raised his glasses to his eyes again for a few seconds, closed them, and thrust them back into their case.

"There's too much haze there," he said. "Can't see, but I feel sure they're some of our ponies grazing."

"Going to round them up and take them back with us?"

"I would if I was sure," was the reply, "but after yesterday's work we can't afford to run risks. Curse them! They've got enough of our stores to keep them alive for another month."

Every man was gazing away into the distance, little suspecting that only a few yards away four magazine-rifles were covering them, and that at a word they would begin to void their charges, with the result that at least half-a-dozen of them, perhaps more, would drop from their saddles, possibly never to rise again. And all this while the little British party crouched there with, to use the untrue familiar expression, their hearts in their mouths, watching their enemies, but stealing a glance from time to time at the shadowy spot beneath the thick bush, wondering one and all what the young lieutenant would say next.

"He must give the order to fire," said the sergeant to himself as he covered the leader. "We shall have Mr Lennox speaking out louder directly and asking where he is."

The sergeant was quite right, for all of a sudden Lennox exclaimed:

"Why, it's light! Here, where am I?"

But it was directly after the Boer leader had shouted the order to advance, and the little body of active Bechuana ponies sprang forward, eager to begin cantering over the plain, not a man the worse for his narrow escape, as they burst out chatting together, Lennox's exclamation passing quite unnoticed, even if heard.

"Ha!" ejaculated Dickenson, exhaling his long-pent-up breath. "I doubt if any of them will be nearer their end again during the war."

And then, after making sure that the Boer party were going off at a sharp canter, and that the risk of speaking or being seen was at an end, he crawled quickly to where Lennox lay upon his back, his eyes once more closed, and sleeping as soundly as if he had never roused up into consciousness since early in the night.

"Lennox—Drew," whispered Dickenson, catching him by the arm, but only eliciting a low, incoherent muttering. "Well, you can sleep!"

"It's not quite natural, sir," said the sergeant. "He must have been hurt somewhere, and the sooner the doctor has a look at him the better."

"Yes," said Dickenson thoughtfully.—"That was a close shave, sergeant."

"Yes, sir—for the enemy. If we had fired they'd have gone off like frightened sheep, I feel sure now."

"Yes, I think so too. But we must not stir yet."

"No, sir; I'd give those fellows time to get out of sight. We don't want them to see us. If they did, they'd come swooping down to try and cut us off. What do you say to trying if we can make out what's wrong with Mr Lennox? I think he must have been hit in the head."

"Yes; let's look," said Dickenson: and after planting a sentry to keep a sharp lookout from a sheltered spot on each side of the little woodland patch, he set to work, with the sergeant's help, to carefully examine his rescued comrade, but without the slightest result, save finding that his head was a good deal swollen in one part, and, lower down, his left shoulder was puffed up, and apparently excessively tender from either a blow or wrench.

"It's beyond us," said Dickenson, with a sigh. "We'll make a start now, and get him into the doctor's hands."

"Yes, sir; we might make a start now," said the sergeant. "Wait a few minutes, sir, while I saddle up the ponies. I'll be quite ready before you call the sentries, sir."

"I'll try and wake Mr Lennox, then," said Dickenson, "and we'll get him on to the pony first."

"I wouldn't, sir, if you'll excuse me," said the sergeant. "If he's half-insensible like that from a hurt to his head, it'll be best to let him wake up of himself."

In a very short time he was once more on a pony, with the sergeant keeping him in his place.

"Perhaps so," said the young officer; "but I don't like his being so stupefied as this."

The preparations were soon made, and the sergeant led the horses together, just as Dickenson rose from Lennox's side, took out his glass, and joined the sentry on their side.

"Can you make out anything?" he said.

"Only the same little cluster as the Boers did, sir. I think it's ponies grazing."

He had hardly spoken before there was a hail from the other side of the little wood.

"What is it?" shouted the sergeant.

"Boers coming along fast. I think it's the same lot coming back. Yes, it must be," cried the sentry. "I've just come across their pot and kettle and things. This must be their camp."

"Over here," shouted Dickenson. "Now, sergeant, we must mount and be off, for we shall not have such luck again."

"No, sir," said the sergeant gruffly. "Will you help, sir?"

Dickenson's answer was to hurry to his friend's side, and in a very short time he was once more on a pony, with the sergeant keeping him in his place; while the others sprang into their saddles and rode off, manoeuvring so as to keep the enemy well on the other side of the woodland clump, and managing so well that they did not even see them for a time, the Boers riding back toward their old bivouac; and for a while there seemed to be no danger.

But it was terribly slow work keeping to a walk. Twice over the pony on which Lennox was mounted was pressed into an amble, but the shaking seemed to distress the injured man, and the walking pace was resumed, till all at once there was ample evidence that they had been seen, a distant crack and puff of smoke following a whistling sound overhead, and directly after the dust was struck up pretty close to one of the ponies' hoofs.

"The game has begun, sergeant," said Dickenson calmly.

"Yes, sir. Shall we dismount and give them a taste back?"

"We out here on the open veldt, and they under cover quite out of sight? No; press on as fast as we can, straight for Groenfontein. They must have it all their own way now."

"Hadn't we better try a canter again, sir?"

"Yes, sergeant, if we are to save his life. Forward!"

They were nearly half a mile on their way, and slowly increasing the distance; but it was quite time to take energetic action, for, to Dickenson's dismay, the Boers were not going to content themselves with long shots, and all at once ten or a dozen appeared round one end of the little wood, spreading out as they galloped, and coming straight for them in an open line.

Chapter Thirty
His Dues

Burdened as the little party was with an insensible man, escape by trusting to the speed of their active little mounts was quite out of the question; and, young officer though he was, Dickenson was old enough in experience to know what to do.

About a couple of hundred yards ahead was a scattered patch of the pleasant form of South African growth known locally, from its catching qualities, as the Wait-a-bit-thorn, and as rapidly as they could go Dickenson led his men to that, finding, as he expected, just enough cover in the midst of a perfectly bare plain, if not to shelter lying-down men, at least to blur and confuse the enemy's marksmen. Here he gave the order, "Dismount!" Lennox was laid flat upon his back, to lie without motion, and each man took the best shelter he could; while the ponies, not being trained like the modern trooper to lie down, were left to graze and take care of themselves.

The Boers came galloping on, to find, on a small scale, how much difference there was between attacking in the open and defending a well-sheltered position. But they had it yet to learn; and, evidently anticipating an easy victory, they galloped forward bravely enough, fully intending to hold the party up and expecting surrender at once.

Dickenson waited till they were well within range before giving the order to fire, adding sternly the instruction that not a single cartridge was to be wasted, no shot being fired till the holder of the rifle felt sure.

The order was succeeded by utter silence, broken only by the thudding of hoofs, and then *crack*! from the sergeant's piece, a puff of greyish-white smoke, and one of the enemy's ponies went down upon its knees, pitching the rider over its head, and rolled over upon one side, kicking wildly, and trying twice before it was able to rise to its feet, when it stood, poor beast! with hanging head; while its rider was seen crawling away, to stop at last and begin firing.

Crack! again, and one of the Boers fell forward on the neck of his mount and dropped his rifle, while his frightened pony galloped on, swerving off to the right.

Crack! crack! two more shots were fired without apparent effect, and then two more at intervals, each with good, or bad, effect. In one case the rider threw up his arms and, as his pony tore on, fell over sidewise, to drop with his foot tight in the stirrup, and was dragged about a hundred yards before he was freed and his mount galloped away.

The other shot took effect upon a pony, which stopped dead, to stand shivering, in spite of the way in which the Boer belaboured it with his rifle, seeming to pound at it with the butt to force it along. But it was all in vain— the poor brute's war was over, and it slowly subsided, its rider springing off sidewise, to drop on one knee, as he tried to shelter himself behind the animal; but he was not quick enough, for Dickenson's rifle was resting upon a tuft of thorn, perfectly steady, as he covered his enemy. *Crack!* and another tiny puff of smoke. The noise and the greyish vapour were nothings out in that vast veldt, but they meant the exit of a man from the troublous scene.

They meant more; for, as he saw the effect, the leader of the Boers shouted an order, and his men swerved off right and left, presenting their ponies' flanks to the British marksmen, who fired rapidly now, and with so good aim that two more ponies were badly hit, their riders leaping off to begin running after their comrades as hard as they could, while a third man fell over to one side, lay still for a few moments, and then struggled into a sitting position and held up his hands.

"Don't fire at him!" cried Dickenson excitedly, and none too soon, for one of the men was taking aim.

"Ha!" said the sergeant grimly as the Boers galloped back. "That'll take some of the bounce out of the gentlemen. One of them told us that our men didn't know how to shoot. I dare say if we'd had their training we might be able to bring down springboks as well as they can."

"Yes; capital, capital, my lads!—Well, sergeant, I think we may go on again."

"No, sir, no!" cried the man excitedly. "They don't know when they're beaten. Look at that."

For as he spoke the two little parties joined up again into one, sprang off their ponies, and imitated Dickenson's manoeuvre, lying down and beginning to shoot at long-range.

"I don't think they'll hurt us at that distance, sergeant," said Dickenson.

"They'll hurt us if they can hit us, sir," replied the man; "but it's a long way, and with their hands all of a shake from such a bit as they've just gone through."

All the same, though, the bullets began to whistle overhead; then one struck the ground about ten yards in front of the sergeant and ricocheted, passing so near that the whiz was startling.

"That was well meant," he said coolly; "but I don't believe the chap who sent it could do it again."

"Look at that poor fellow," said Dickenson suddenly.

"'Fraid of being hit by us or them, sir," replied the sergeant. "Not a very pleasant place."

For the Boer who had thrown up his hands in token of surrender had begun to crawl slowly and painfully to their right, evidently to get well out of the line of fire. The man was evidently hit badly, for he kept on sinking down flat on his face, and four times over a curious sensation of regret came over Dickenson, mingled with a desire to go to his help with such surgical aid as he could supply. But each time, just as he was going to suggest it to the sergeant, the man rose on all fours again and crawled farther away.

"I don't think he's much hurt, sir. Going pretty strong now."

The sergeant had hardly spoken before Dickenson uttered an ejaculation, for the wounded man suddenly dropped down flat again and rolled over, showing as one hand came into sight that he still grasped his rifle; and then he was completely hidden, as if he had sunk into some slight depression.

"Dead!" sighed Dickenson solemnly.

"Looks like it, sir," said the sergeant quietly.

"Or exhausted by his efforts," said Dickenson. "Look here, sergeant, a man's a man."

"'For a' that, and a' that,' as the song says," muttered the sergeant to himself.

"Whether he's one of our men or an enemy. I can't lie here, able to help, without going to his help."

"No, no, sir; you mustn't stir," cried the sergeant excitedly. "If you begin to move there'll be a shower of bullets cutting up the ground about you. It's a good hundred and fifty yards to crawl."

"I can't help that." said Dickenson quietly. "I must do it."

"But think of yourself, sir," said the sergeant.

"A man in my position can't think of himself, sergeant."

"Well, think of us, sir."

"I shall, sergeant."

"Ha!" cried the sergeant, in a tone full of exultation. "And think of your friend, sir. He wants help as bad as that chap, and you ought to think of him first."

For just then they heard Lennox talking hurriedly, and on Dickenson looking back over his shoulder he could see his comrade's hands moving in the air, as if he were preparing to struggle up.

Dickenson began to turn hurriedly to creep back to where Lennox lay, with one of the ponies grazing calmly enough close by, when the hands fell again, and the young officer lay perfectly still.

"He has dropped to sleep again, and may be quiet for an hour. Sergeant, I'm going to crawl out to that wounded Boer."

"Very well, sir; you're my officer, and my duty is to obey. I'm very sorry, Mr Dickenson. It's a good two hundred yards, sir, and I believe it's a bit of slimmery. He crawled there to be out of shot."

Whiz-z-z! crack! A puff of smoke and then a rush of hoofs, for the pony which had been grazing so calmly close by where Lennox lay went tearing over the veldt for about fifty yards, when, with two of its companions trotting after it as if to see what was the matter, it pitched suddenly upon its head, rolled over with its legs kicking as if it were galloping in the air, and then they fell and all was over, the two others turning and trotting back, to begin grazing once again.

"That's bad," said Dickenson sadly. "We couldn't spare that pony. Why, sergeant, they can shoot! I didn't think they could have done it at this range."

"What! not at two hundred yards, sir?"

"Two hundred, man? It's a thousand."

"Why, you don't see it, sir," cried the sergeant excitedly. "It wasn't the enemy out yonder sent that bullet home."

"Not the enemy out there?" cried Dickenson.

"No, sir. It was your dead man who fired that shot."

"What?"

"Don't feel so sorry for him, sir, do you, now?"

As the sergeant was asking this question, the soldier who lay off to their left, and who had not discharged his piece for some time, fired simultaneously with a shot which came from the direction where the wounded Boer lay.

"Ah!" cried the sergeant excitedly. "Can you see him from there?"

"No," growled the man; "but I saw something move, and let go on the chance of hitting him, but only cut up the sand "

"Don't take your eye from the spot, my lad," cried Dickenson sharply. "Never mind a fresh cartridge. Trust to your magazine."

"Yes, sir; that's what I'm doing," was the reply.

"Hadn't we all better do the same, sir?" asked the sergeant.

"Yes," said Dickenson angrily.

"I doubt whether we can keep his fire down, though, sir. He's got us now."

"Not yet—the brute!" cried Dickenson through his teeth.

"He'll have the other two safe, sir."

"Other two?" cried Dickenson wonderingly.

"What! don't you see, sir? There's another of the ponies hit."

"Good gracious!" cried Dickenson, in such a homely, grandmotherly style that, in spite of their perilous position, the sergeant could not help smiling.

But his face was as hard as an iron mask directly, as he saw the look of anguish in his young officer's face, Dickenson having just seen the second pony standing with drooping head and all four legs widely separated, rocking to and fro for a few moments, before dropping heavily, perfectly dead.

Crack! came again from the same place, and another of the grazing ponies flung up its head, neighing shrilly, before springing forward to gallop for a couple of hundred yards and then fall.

And crack! again, and its following puff of smoke, making the fourth pony start and begin to limp for a few yards with its off foreleg broken; and crack! once more, and the sound of a sharp rap caused by another bullet striking the suffering beast right in the middle of the shoulder-blade, when it dropped dead instantly, pierced through the heart.

"Best shot yet, sir," said the sergeant grimly; "put the poor beast out of its misery. Now," he muttered to himself, "we know what we've got to expect if we don't stop his little game."

"Every man watch below where the smoke rose," said Dickenson slowly and sternly. "That man can't see without exposing himself in some way. Yes; be on the alert. Look! he's pressing the sand away to right and left with the barrel of his rifle. Mind, don't fire till you've got a thoroughly good chance."

No one spoke, but all lay flat upon their chests, watching the moving right and left of a gun-barrel which was directed towards them, but pointing so that if fired a bullet would have gone over their heads. It was hard to see; but the sun glinted from its polished surface from time to time, and moment by moment they noted that it was becoming more horizontal.

Every man's sight was strained to the utmost; every nerve was on the quiver; so that not one of the four felt that he could trust himself to shoot when the crucial moment came.

It came more quickly than they expected; for, after a few moments of intense strain, the barrel was suddenly depressed, till through the clear air the watchers distinctly saw a tiny hole and nothing more. Then all at once the sun glinted from something else—a something that flashed brightly for one instant, and was then obscured by smoke—the smoke that darted from the little, just perceptible orifice of the small-bore Mauser and that which shot out from four British rifles, to combine into one slowly rising cloud; while as the commingled reports of five rifles, friendly and inimical, died away, to the surprise of Dickenson and his men they saw the figure of a big swarthy Boer staggering towards them with both hands pressed to his face. The next moment he was lying just in front of his hiding-place, stretched out—dead.

Chapter Thirty One
Safe at Last

"Ha!" ejaculated Dickenson, with a sigh of relief, and he turned away to creep to where Lennox lay, finding him still plunged in the same state of stupor.

"One ought to lay him in the shade," he thought; but there was very little that he could do beyond drawing a few pieces of the thorn bush together to hang over his face. He then took out his handkerchief to lay over the bush, but hastily snatched it away again. "Bah!" he muttered. "It's like making a white bull's-eye for them to fire at."

Then he crept back to his position, with the bullets still whizzing overhead or striking up the dust, and he almost wondered that no one had been hit.

"I hope Mr Lennox is better, sir," said the sergeant respectfully.

"I see no difference, sergeant. But what does that mean?"

"What we used to call 'stalking horse,' sir, down in the Essex marshes. Creeping up under the shelter of their mounts."

"Then they are getting nearer?"

"Yes, sir. Don't you think we might begin to pay them back? We could hit their ponies if we couldn't hit them."

"Yes, sergeant, soon," replied the young officer, carefully scanning the enemy's approach; "but I think I'd let them get a hundred yards, or even two, nearer before we begin. The business is simplified."

"Is it, sir?"

"I mean, there's no question of retreating now that the ponies are gone. It's either fight to the last, or surrender."

"You mean, sir, that there were three things to do?"

"Yes; and now it's one of two."

"Isn't it only one, sir? I think the lads feel as I do, right-down savage, and ready to fight to the last."

"Very well," said Dickenson; "then we'll fight to the last."

The sergeant smiled, and then for a time all lay perfectly still, fully expecting that one or other of the many bullets which came whizzing by would find its billet; but though there were several very narrow escapes, no one was hit, and though the enemy in front had greatly lessened the distance, their bullets struck no nearer. But the men grew very impatient under the terrible strain, and all three kept on turning their heads to watch their officer, who lay frowning, his rifle in front and his chin supported by his folded arms.

"Ah!" came at last, in an involuntary sigh of relief from all three, as they saw Dickenson alter his position after the enemy had made a fresh and perceptible decrease in the distance between them by urging their ponies forward, the men's legs being strongly marked, giving the ponies the appearance of being furnished with another pair, as their riders stood taking aim and resting their rifles across the saddles.

But no order to fire came from Dickenson, who still remained quiet. Then all at once:

"Sergeant," he said, "I've practised a great deal with the sporting rifle, but done very little of this sort of thing myself. I'm going to try now if I can't stop this miserable sneaking approach of the enemy."

The men gave a hearty cheer.

"I'm sorry for the poor ponies," he said, "for I think this range will be well within the power of the service arm."

"Yes, sir, quite," said the sergeant promptly.

Dickenson was silent once again, and they saw him taking a long, careful aim at the nearest Boer. The effect of his shot was that the pony he had aimed at sprang forward, leaving a Boer visible, facing them in astonishment before he turned to run.

"Fire!" said Dickenson, and three shots followed almost instantaneously, while the running Boer was seen lying upon the earth.

"Be ready!" said Dickenson, aiming now at another of the ponies, and paying no heed to six or seven replies from the exasperated Boers.

The pony now fired at reared up, and in the clear sunshine the man who was aiming across it was seen to be crushed down by the poor animal's fall, and he did not rise again.

Once more Dickenson's rifle rang out, and he shifted it back now to his right, to fire his fourth shot almost without aiming. As the smoke cleared away by the time the young officer had replaced the exploded cartridges, one pony could be seen struggling on the ground, another was galloping away, while two men were crawling backward on hands and knees.

"It seems like butchery, sergeant," said Dickenson, taking another long aim before firing again. "Missed!"

"No, sir: I saw the pony start," said the sergeant eagerly. "There, look at him!"

For the two men cheered on seeing the pony limp for a few yards and then fall, just beyond where his master was lying stretched out on his face.

"Poor brute!" said Dickenson in a low voice.

"He didn't say it was butchery when that chap was knocking down our mounts at quarter this distance," said the sergeant to himself. "But, my word, he can shoot! I shouldn't like to change places with the Boers when he's behind a rifle."

Just then the men cheered, for three more of the enemy who had been stalking them were seen to spring into the saddle, lie flat down over their willing mounts, and gallop away as hard as they could to join their comrades.

"Well, we've stopped that game for the present, sergeant," said Dickenson. "Perhaps we may be able to keep them off till night.—But that's a long way off," he said to himself, "and we've to fight against this scorching heat and the hunger and thirst."

"Hope so, sir," said the sergeant, in response to what he had heard; "but—"

He ceased speaking, and pointed in the direction of the patch of scrub forest where they had passed the night.

Dickenson shaded his eyes and uttered an ejaculation. Then after another long glance: "Ten—twenty—thirty," he said, as he watched two lines of mounted men cantering out from behind the patch right and left. "Why, there must be quite thirty more."

"I should say forty of 'em, sir."

"Why, sergeant, they're moving out to surround us."

"Yes, sir," said the sergeant coolly; "but you won't surrender?"

"Not while the cartridges last."

"Well, there's enough to account for the lot, sir, if we hand in ours and you do the firing."

The young officer burst into a forced laugh.

"Why, sergeant," he cried, "what do you take me for?"

"Soldier of the Queen, sir, ready to show the enemy that our march at the Jubilee wasn't all meant for show."

Dickenson was silent for a time.

"Ha!" he said at last, with a sigh. "I want to prove that; but there are times when holding out ceases to be justifiable—fighting becomes mere butchery."

"Yes, sir, when forty or fifty men surround four and a wounded one, shoot down their mounts so as they can't retreat, and then try and butcher them. It's all on their side, sir, not ours; and the men think as I do."

Dickenson was silent again, lying there with his teeth set and a peculiar hard look in his eyes, such as a man in the flower of his youth and strength might show when he knows the time is fast approaching for everything to end. Meanwhile the two fresh parties that had come on the scene were galloping hard to join the enclosing wings of the first comers, who stood fast, fully grasping what was to follow, and keeping the attention of their prey by firing a shot now and then, not one of which had the slightest effect.

"Oh for some water!" groaned Dickenson at last. "Poor Mr Lennox! How he must suffer!"

"Not he, sir. He's in that state that when he wakes up he'll know nothing about what has taken place. It's you that ought to have the drink, to steady your hand for what is to come."

Dickenson made no reply aloud, but he thought bitterly, "When he wakes up—when he wakes up! Where will it be: the Boer prison camp, or in the other world?"

The sergeant and the men now relapsed into a moody silence, as they lay, rifle in hand, with the sun beating down in increasing force, and a terrible thirst assailing them. Dickenson looked at their scowling faces, and a sudden impression attacked him that a feeling of resentment had arisen against him for not surrendering now that they were in such a hopeless condition. This increased till he could bear it no longer, and edging himself closer to the sergeant, he spoke to him upon the subject, with the result that the man broke into a harsh laugh.

"Don't you go thinking anything of that sort, sir, because you're wrong. Oh yes, they look savage enough, but it's only because they feel ugly. We're all three what you may call dangerous, sir. The lads want to get at the enemy to make them pay for what we're suffering. Here, you ask them yourself what they think about surrendering."

Dickenson did not hesitate, but left the sergeant, to crawl to the man beyond him, when just as he was close up a well-directed bullet struck up the sand and stones within a few inches of the man's face, half-blinding him for a time and making him forget discipline and the proximity of his officer, as he raged out a torrent of expletives against the Boer who had fired that shot.

"Let me look at your face, my lad," said Dickenson. "Are you much hurt?"

"Hurt, sir? No! It's only just as if some one had chucked a handful of dust into my eyes."

"Let me see."

A few deft applications of a finger removed the trouble from the man's eyes, and he smiled again, and then listened attentively to his officer's questions.

"Oh, it's as you think best, sir," he said at last; "but I wouldn't give up. We don't want to. All we're thinking about is giving the enemy another sickening for what they've done."

Dickenson crawled away to the other man—away to his right—to find him literally glowering when spoken to.

"What do the others say, sir—the sergeant and my comrade?"

"Never mind them," replied Dickenson. "I want to know how you feel."

"Well, sir," was the reply, "about an hour ago I felt regular sick of it, and that it would be about like throwing our lives away to hold out."

"That it would be better to surrender and chance our fate in a Boer prison?"

"Something of that sort, sir."

"And how do you feel now?"

"Just as if they've regularly got my dander up, sir. I only want to shoot as long as we've got a cartridge left. I'd give up then, for they'd never wait for us to get at them with the bayonet."

Dickenson said no more, but returned to his old place, watching the galloping Boers, who had now gone far enough to carry out their plans, and were stopping by twos to dismount and wait, this being continued till the little English party formed the centre of a very wide circle. Then a signal was made from the starting-point, and firing commenced.

Fortunately for the party it was at a tremendously long-range, for, after the way in which the enemy had suffered in regard to their ponies, they elected to keep what they considered to be outside the reach of the British rifles; and no reply was made, Dickenson declining to try and hit the poor beasts which formed the Boer shelter in a way which would only inflict a painful wound without disabling them from their masters' service.

"It would be waste of our cartridges, sergeant," he said.

"Yes, sir," was the reply; "perhaps it's best to wait. They'll be tempted into getting closer after a bit. Getting tired of it if they don't hit us, and make us put up a white flag for the doctor. Look at them. Oh, it's nonsense firing at such a distance. Their rifles carry right enough, but it's all guesswork; they can't take an aim."

The sergeant was right enough; but the bullets were dangerous, and they came now pretty rapidly from all round, striking with a vicious *phit!* which was terribly straining to the nerves. And all the time the heat of the sun grew more painful. There was not a breath of air; and the pull's of smoke when the enemy fired looked dim and distant, as if seen through a haze.

The sergeant made some allusion to the fact.

"Looks as if there was a change coming. There, sir, you can hardly see that man and horse."

"No," said Dickenson sadly, "but I think it's from the state of our eyes. I feel giddy, and mine are quite dim."

"Perhaps it is that, sir," said the sergeant. "Things look quite muddled up to me. Now turn a little and look yonder, out Groenfontein way."

Dickenson turned wearily, and winced, for three bullets came almost simultaneously, two with their vicious *whiz-z!* the other to cut up the ground and ricochet.

"Not hit, sir?" said the sergeant anxiously.

"No; but one shot was very near. Yes, I see what you mean: the Boers are mounting out in that direction. They're coming closer. We shall perhaps have a chance now," he cried, with more animation.

It seemed, though, that they were going to retire as they came, the circle being opened on the Groenfontein side and the men retiring in twos, to go on increasing in two groups, firing rapidly the while; but, to the surprise of the beleaguered party, the bullets ceased to whiz in their direction.

A dead silence fell upon the group, no one daring to speak the hope that was in him for fear of exciting his companions by an idea that might after all prove only to be imagination. Then all spoke together, and there was an excited cheer.

"Yes," cried Dickenson; "there's help coming. The Boers are retiring fast."

"Why, of course, sir," said the sergeant confidently. "The colonel would be sure to send out to see why we didn't come back. There's a lot of our fellows out yonder that the enemy is firing at, and we can't see them for the haze. It is haze, and not giddiness and our eyes.'

"No, sergeant; we can see clearly enough. I can make out the advance of the relief party. Wait five minutes, and I'll see what a few signal-shots will do."

But before the time mentioned the Boers could be seen steadily retreating, and the puffs of smoke from the firing of an advancing party could be made out. Signals followed, and but a short time elapsed before the Boers were driven off and the rescued party were reviving under the influence of the water proffered from the relief party's bottles.

The return to Groenfontein commenced at once, with Lennox carried by four men by means of scarfs; but he was not the only man who needed this aid, four more being hit during the return, the driven-off Boers hanging at a safe distance on flank and rear, sniping at every chance with the longest of shots, till the outposts were reached, and a cheer welcomed the rescued men as they marched in.

The motion through the air had gradually revived Lennox, so much so that when the party was met by the colonel and officers the young lieutenant was able to reply to a question or two before the doctor intervened.

"Leave him to me for a bit," he said, and had Lennox borne toward the hut where Roby and the corporal were lying, Dickenson following close behind.

"The colonel did not shake hands with him," said the young officer to himself, "and the major never spoke. Surely they don't think—"

He got no farther, for they had reached the hut, when, to the surprise of all, Roby wrenched himself round to glare at Lennox being carried in, and then in a harsh, excited voice he cried:

"Lennox here? Coward! Cur!—coward! How dare you show your face again?"

And at these words Corporal May wagged his head slowly from side to side and uttered a weary groan.

Chapter Thirty Two
An Unpleasant Business

"Why, Roby!" cried Lennox, after standing for some moments gazing wildly at his brother officer, and then going close up to his rough resting-place. "For goodness' sake, don't talk in that way!"

"Coward! Cur! To run away and leave me like that!" cried Roby.

Lennox stared at him with his eyes dilating, and then he turned sharply and looked from Dickenson to the doctor and back again, ending by clapping his hands to his forehead and holding his breath before gazing wildly at Roby once more as if doubting that the torrent of reproaches he listened to were real.

"Am I off my head a little, doctor?—the sun, and that dreadful thirst. Am I mad?"

"Mad? No, my lad; but you're in a parlous state.—Here, orderly, I must have Mr Lennox in the next hut. He is exciting Captain Roby horribly."

"Yes; horribly," said Lennox. "Poor fellow! Is he so bad as that?"

"Oh yes, he's bad enough," said the doctor gruffly.

"Corporal May, too," said Lennox, with a troubled look at the other patients occupying the hut. "Are you much hurt, May?"

For answer the man glared at him and turned his face away, making Lennox wince again and look at the other patient. But he was lying fast asleep.

"Rather a queer welcome," said the young officer, turning now to Dickenson, and once more his eyes dilated with a wondering look. "Why, Bob, you're not going to call me a coward too?"

"Likely!" said the young man gruffly.

"Don't stand talking to him, Mr Dickenson," said the doctor sharply.—"Here, lean on the orderly, sir; he'll help you into the next hut. I want to try and diagnose your case."

"Yes—please if it's necessary," said Lennox, catching at the orderly as if attacked by vertigo.—"Thank you, old fellow," he whispered huskily as

Dickenson started forward and caught him by the other arm. "Not much the matter. Gone through a good deal. Faint. The sun. Touch of stroke, I think."

He hung heavily upon the pair, who assisted him out into the next hut, while Roby's accusation was reiterated, the words ringing in his ears: "Coward!—cur!—runaway!" till he was out of sight, when Roby sank back exhausted.

"Don't question him, and don't let him talk about what he has gone through," said the doctor a short time later, when he had made his fresh patient as comfortable as circumstances would allow, and he was growing drowsy from the sedative administered. "It's not sunstroke, but a mingling of the results of exposure and overdoing it altogether. I don't quite understand it yet, and I want to get at the truth without asking him."

"Oh doctor! don't you join in thinking the poor fellow has been behaving in a cowardly way."

"Tchah! Rubbish! What is it to me, sir, how the man has been behaving? He's all wrong, isn't he?"

"Yes; terribly."

"Very well, then, I've got to put him all right. If he has committed any breach of discipline you can court-martial him when I've done."

"But, hang it all, doctor!" cried Dickenson fiercely, "you don't believe he's a coward?"

"Humph! Very evident you don't, my lad," said the doctor grimly.

"Of course not."

"That's right; then stick to it. I like to see a man back up his friend."

"Who wouldn't back him up?" cried Dickenson.

"Oh, I don't know. It's very evident that Roby won't."

"Roby's as mad as a March hare," cried Dickenson.

"Well, not quite; but he's a bit queer in his head, and I'm afraid I shall have to perform rather a crucial operation upon him. I don't want to if I can help it, out here. It requires skilled help, and I should like some one to share the responsibility."

"Internally injured?" asked Dickenson.

"Oh no. The bullet that ploughed up his forehead is pressing a piece of bone down slightly on the brain."

"Slightly!" said Dickenson, with a laugh. "Turned it right over, I think."

"Yes, you fellows who know nothing about your construction do get a good many absurd ideas in your head. Here, talk softly; I want to get at the cause of his trouble. He's not wounded."

"Why, his skull's ploughed up, and the bone pressing on his brain."

"Do you mean that for a joke—a bit of chaff, Mr Dickenson?" said the doctor stiffly.

"A joke, sir? Is this a subject to joke about?" replied Dickenson.

"Certainly not, sir; but you thoughtless young fellows are ready to laugh at anything."

"Well, sir, you're wrong. Roby and I were never very great friends, but I'm not such a brute as to laugh and sneer when the poor fellow's down."

"Who was talking about Captain Roby?"

"You were, sir. You told me that his brain was suffering from pressure, and then you went on to say that you wanted to get at the cause of his hurt."

"Bah! Tchah! Nonsense, man! I was talking then about Lennox."

"I beg your pardon, sir."

"Oh, all right, my lad. Now then; I'm talking about Lennox now. I say I want to get at the cause of his trouble without questioning him and setting his poor feverish brain working. Tell me how you found him."

Dickenson briefly explained.

"Humph! Utterly exhausted; been suffering from the sun, thirst, and evidently after exerting himself tremendously. Been in a complete stupor more than sleep, you say?"

"Yes."

"Well, it's very strange," said the doctor thoughtfully. "He was in the assault, wasn't he?"

"Oh yes, of course."

"Well, human nature's a queer thing, Dickenson, my lad."

"Yes, sir; very," said the young man gruffly, "or Roby wouldn't behave like this and set that sneak May off on the same track."

"And," continued the doctor testily, as if he did not like being interrupted, "the more I examine into man's nature the more curious and contradictory I find it—I mean, in the mental faculties."

"I suppose so, sir.—What's he aiming at?" added the young officer to himself.

"Now, look here, Dickenson, my lad; between ourselves, that was rather a horrible bit of business, eh?—that attack in the half-darkness."

"Well, sir, it wasn't quite like an *al fresco* ball," said Dickenson gruffly.

"Of course not. Bayoneting and bludgeoning with rifle-butts?"

Dickenson nodded.

"And all on the top of the excitement of the march and the long waiting to begin?"

"Just so, sir," said Dickenson.

"Enough to over-excite a young fellow's brain?"

"Well—yes, sir; it's not at all cheerful work But, really, I don't see what you mean."

"Just this, my dear boy, and, as I said, between ourselves. You don't think, do you. that just in the midst of the fight poor Lennox was seized with what you vulgar young fellows call a fit of blue funk, do you?"

"No, sir, I do not," said Dickenson stiffly. "Certainly not."

"Lost his nerve?"

"No, sir."

"I've lost mine before now, my lad, over a very serious operation—when I was young, you know."

"May be, sir; but Drew Lennox is not the sort of fellow for that."

"As a rule, say."

"Yes, as a rule, sir, without a single exception."

"And took fright and ran?"

"Rubbish, sir! He couldn't."

"Just as Roby says?"

"Roby's mad."

"And as Corporal May holds to in corroboration?"

"No, sir, no; and I should like to see Corporal May flogged."

"Rather an unpleasant sight, my lad," said the doctor quietly, "even when a culprit richly deserves it. But about Lennox. He might, though as a rule brave as a lion, have had a seizure like that."

"No, he mightn't sir," said Dickenson stoutly.

"You don't know, my lad."

"Oh yes, I do, sir. I know Drew Lennox by heart."

"But there is such a thing as panic, my lad."

"Not with him, sir."

"I say yes, my lad. Recollect that he had a terrible shock a little while ago." Dickenson's lips parted. "He was plunged into that awful hole in the dark, and whirled through some underground tunnel. Why, sir, I went and looked at the place myself with Sergeant James, and he let down a lantern for me to see. I tell you what it is; I'm as hard as most men, through going about amongst horrors, but that black pit made me feel wet inside my hands. I wonder the poor fellow retained his reason."

"But he got the better of that, sir," said Dickenson hoarsely.

"How do you know, sir? He seemed better; but a man can't go through such things as that without their leaving some weakening of the mental force."

"Doctor, don't talk like that, for goodness' sake!"

"I must, my lad, because I think—mind you, I say I think—"

"Doctor, if you begin to think Drew Lennox is a coward I'll never respect you again," cried Dickenson angrily.

"I don't think he's a coward, my dear boy," said the doctor, laying his hand upon the young officer's arm. "I think he's as brave a lad as ever stepped, and I like him; but no man is perfect, and the result of that horrible plunge into the bowels of the earth shook him so that in that fierce fight he grew for a bit very weak indeed."

"Impossible, doctor!" cried the young man fiercely.

"Quite possible," said the doctor, pressing his companion's arm; "and now let me finish. I tell you, I like Drew Lennox, and if I am right I shall think none the less of him."

"*Ur-r-r-r!*" growled Dickenson.

"It is between ourselves, mind, and it is only my theory. He lost his nerve in the middle of that fight—had a fit of panic, and, as Roby and the corporal say (very cruelly and bitterly), ran for his life—bolted."

"I'll never believe it, sir."

"Well, remain a heretic if you like; but that's my theory."

"I tell you, sir—"

"Wait a minute, my lad; I haven't done. I suggest that he had this seizure—"

"And I swear he had not!"

"Wait till I've finished, boy," said the doctor sternly.

Dickenson stood with his brow knit and his fists clenched, almost writhing in his anger; and the doctor went on:

"I suggest, my dear boy, that he had this fit of panic and was aware that it must be known, when, after running right away—"

"Yes, sir; go on," said Dickenson savagely—"after running away—"

"He came quite to himself, felt that he would be branded as a coward by all who knew him, and then, in a mad fit of despair—"

"Yes, sir—and then?"

"You told me that he came back without his revolver."

"Yes, sir," said Dickenson mockingly—"and then he didn't blow his brains out."

"No," said the doctor quietly, "for he had lost his pistol, perhaps in the fight; but it seems to me, Dickenson, that in his agony of shame, despair, and madness, he tried to hang himself."

"Tried to do what?" roared Dickenson.

"What I say, my dear boy," said the doctor gravely.

"I say, doctor, have you been too much in the sun?" said Dickenson, with a forced laugh, one which sounded painful in the extreme.

"No, my dear fellow; I am perfectly calm, and everything points to the fact—his state when you found him, sorrowful, repentant, and utterly exhausted by his sufferings in his struggles to get back to face it out like a man."

"Doctor, you are raving. His appearance was all compatible with a struggle, fighting with the Boers—a prisoner bravely fighting for his escape. Everything points to your fact? Nonsense, sir—absurd!"

"You're a brave, true-hearted fellow, Dickenson, my lad, and I like you none the less for being so rude to me in your defence of your poor friend. He must be sleeping now after the dose I gave him. Come with me, and I'll give you a surprise."

"Not such a one as you have already given me, doctor," said the young man bitterly.

"We shall see," said the doctor quietly; and the next minute he was standing by Lennox's side, carefully lifting a moistened bandage laid close to his neck.

Dickenson uttered a faint cry of horror. For deeply marked in his friend's terribly swollen neck there was a deep blue mark such as would have been caused by a tightened cord, and in places the skin was torn away, leaving visible the eroded flesh.

"Oh doctor!" groaned Dickenson, trembling violently.

"Hold up, my dear boy," whispered his companion. "No one knows of it but my orderly, you, and myself. It will soon heal up, and I shall not feel it my duty to mention it to a soul."

Chapter Thirty Three
The Tale he told

"Look here, Roby," said Dickenson, three or four days later, when, having a little time on his hands—the Boers, consequent upon their late defeat, having been very quiet—he went in to sit with the captain of his company, finding him calm and composed, and ready to talk about the injury to his head, which seemed to be healing fast.

"Precious lucky for me, Dickenson," he said; "an inch lower and there would have been promotion for somebody. Narrow escape, wasn't it?"

"Awfully."

"Such a nuisance, too, lying up in this oven. I tell Emden that I should get better much faster if he'd let me get up and go about; but he will not listen."

"Of course not; you're best where you are. You couldn't wear your helmet."

"My word, no! Head's awfully tender. It makes me frightfully wild sometimes when I think of the cowardly way in which that cur Lennox—"

"Hold hard!" cried Dickenson, frowning. "Look here, Roby; you got that crotchet into your head in the delirium that followed your wound. You're getting better now and talk like a sane man, so just drop that nonsense."

"Nonsense?"

"Yes; horrible nonsense. Have you thought of the mischief you are doing by making such a charge?"

"Thought till my head has seemed on fire. He'll have to leave the regiment, and a good job too."

"Of course, over a craze."

"Craze, sir? It's a simple fact—the honest truth. Ask Corporal May there.—It's true, isn't it, May?"

"Oh yes, sir; it's true enough," said the corporal, "though I'm sorry enough to have to say it of my officer."

"It doesn't seem like it, sir," said Dickenson in a voice full of exasperation.

"No, sir; you think so because you always were Mr Lennox's friend. But it ain't my business, and I don't want to speak about it. I never do unless I'm obliged."

"You—you worm!" cried Dickenson, for he could think of nothing better to say. "Have you ever thought it would have been much better, after your bit of fright in the cavern, if Mr Lennox had left you to take your chance, instead of risking his life to save yours?"

"No, sir; I ain't never thought that," whined the man; "but I was very grateful to him for what he did, and that's what keeps me back and makes me feel so ill speaking about him. I wouldn't say a word, sir, but you see I must speak the truth."

"Speak the truth!" growled Dickenson as he turned angrily away. "Look here, Roby, if I stop here much longer I shall get myself into trouble for kicking a patient. Now, once more, look here. You've done an awful lot of mischief by what you said when your fit of delirium was on you, and you're in such a weak state now that as soon as you begin thinking about Lennox you make yourself worse by bringing the crazy feeling back again."

"Crazy feeling? Bah! I know what I'm saying. A coward! I wish the old days were back. I'd call him out and shoot him."

"No, you wouldn't, for you'd have to wait till the doctor took you off his list, and by that time you'd be quite back in your right senses."

"Robert Dickenson!" cried Roby, flushing scarlet, and his features growing convulsed.

"Yes, that's my name; but I'm not going to submit to a bullying from the doctor for exciting his patient. Good-bye. Make haste and get well. I can't stop here."

"Stay where you are," shouted Roby furiously. "Drew Lennox is—"

"My friend," muttered Dickenson, rushing out. "Poor fellow! I suppose he believes it; but he doesn't know how bad he is. It's queer. That idea regularly maddens him. Hullo! here's the boss."

"Ah, Dickenson, my lad! Been to cheer up Roby?"

"Yes, sir; I've been to cheer him up a bit," said Dickenson.

"That's right. Getting on nicely, isn't he?"

"Ye-es."

"What do you mean with your spun-out 'yes'?"

"I thought he seemed a little queer in the head yet."

"Oh yes, and that will last for a while, no doubt. But he's mending wonderfully, and I'm beginning to hope that there will be no need for the operation: nature is doing the work herself."

"That's right, sir," said Dickenson dryly. "I'd encourage her to go on."

The doctor smiled.

"Going to see Lennox?"

"If I may."

"Oh yes, you may go now. He's getting on too: picking up strength. Don't let him talk too much, and don't mention a word about that report of Roby's."

"Certainly not," said Dickenson; and the doctor passing on, the young officer entered the next hut, to find his friend looking hollow-eyed and pulled down, the nerves at the corners of his eyes twitching as he slept.

Dickenson sat down upon a box watching him, and it was as if his presence there acted upon the patient, who, at the end of a few minutes, opened his eyes and smiled.

"How strange!" he said, holding out his hand.

"What's strange?"

"I was dreaming about you. How long have you been there?"

"Five or ten minutes."

"How are things going on?"

"Pretty quiet."

"No news of relief?"

"Not the slightest. We seem to be quite forgotten out here in this corner."

"Oh—no," said Lennox; "we're not forgotten. The country is so big, and our men are kept busy in other directions."

He turned as he spoke to got into an easier position, and then winced, uttering an ejaculation indicating the pain he felt.

"Why didn't you speak, and let me help you?" said Dickenson.

"Because I want to be independent. It was nothing. Only my neck; it's awfully sore still."

Dickenson winced now in turn. A chill ran through him, and his forehead contracted with pain; but Lennox did not grasp the feeling of horror and misery which ran through his friend.

"I shall be precious glad when it's better," continued Lennox. "Did I tell you how it got in this state?"

"No. Don't talk about it," said Dickenson shortly.

"Why not? I'm all right now. Have I been raving at all?"

"Not that I have heard."

"I wonder at it, for until this morning I've felt half my time as if I were in a nightmare."

"Look here; the doctor said that you were to be kept perfectly quiet, and that I was not to encourage you to talk."

"Good old man. Well, I'm as quiet as a mouse, and you are not going to encourage me to talk. I haven't felt inclined to, either, since I got back. I don't suppose it has been so, but I've felt as if all the veins in my head were swollen up, and it has made me stupid and strange, and as if I couldn't say what I wanted, and I haven't tried to speak for fear I should wander away. But I say, Bob, did I go in to see Roby lying wounded when I came back?"

"Yes."

"Ah, then that wasn't imagination. It's like something seen through a mist. It has all been like looking through glass cloudy and thick over since we rushed the Boers."

"Look here," said Dickenson, rising; "I must go now."

"Nonsense; you've only just come. Sit down, man; you won't hurt me. Do me good.—That's right. I want to ask you something."

"No, no; you'd better not talk."

"What nonsense! I'm beginning to suffer now from what fine people call *ennui*. Not much in my way, old fellow. You're doing me good. I say, look here. Something has been bothering me like in my dreams. You say I did go in to see poor Roby?"

"Yes; but look here, Drew, old man," cried Dickenson, "if you get on that topic I must go."

"No, no; stay. I want to separate the fancy from the real. I've got an idea in my head that Roby turned upon me in a fit of raving, and called me a coward and a cur for running away and leaving him. Did I dream that?"

"No," said Dickenson huskily. "He has been a good deal off his head. He did shout something of that sort at you."

"Poor fellow!" said Lennox quietly. "But how horrible! Shot in the forehead, wasn't he?"

"Bullet ploughed open the top of his head."

"I didn't see what was wrong with him in the rush. I can remember now, quite clearly, seeing him go down, with his face streaming with blood."

"You recollect that?" said Dickenson excitedly, in spite of himself.

"Oh yes. The light was coming fast, and we were near where a lot of the Boers were making for their mounts to get them away. One big fellow was leading his pony, and as poor Roby was straggling blindly about, this Boer ran at him, holding his rein in one hand, his rifle in the other, and I saw him shorten it with his right to turn it into a club to bring it down on Roby's head."

"All!" cried Dickenson, with increasing excitement, and he waited by Lennox, who ceased speaking, and lay gazing calmly at the door. Then all the doctor's warnings were forgotten, and the visitor said hoarsely, "Well, go on. Why don't you speak?"

"Oh, I don't want to begin blowing about what I did," said Lennox quietly.

"But I want to hear," said Dickenson. "Go on—the Boer raised his rifle to bash it down on Roby's head. What then?"

"Well, he didn't. I was obliged to cut him down. Then the pony jerked itself free and galloped off."

"And you ran to catch it?" cried Dickenson excitedly.

"Nonsense!" said Lennox, laughing. "Why should I do that? What did I want with the pony, unless it might have been to get poor Roby across its back? But I never thought of it. I only thought of getting him on mine."

"And did you?" cried Dickenson.

"Of course I did. I wanted to carry him to the rear, poor fellow."

"Ha!" ejaculated Dickenson.

"Well, don't shout. What an excitable beggar you are?"

"Go on, then. You keep giving it to me in little bits. What then?"

"Oh, I got him on my back, and it was horrible His wound bled so."

"But you carried him?"

"Yes, ever so far; till that happened."

"Yes! What?"

Lennox touched his neck, and his hearer literally ground his teeth in rage.

"Will—you—speak out?" he cried.

"Will you take things a little more coolly?" said Lennox quietly. "Didn't Emden say I was to be kept quiet?"

"Of course; of course," said Dickenson hurriedly. "But you don't know, old chap, what I'm suffering. I'm in a raging thirst for the truth—I want to take one big draught, and you keep on giving me tiny drops in a doll's teaspoon."

"It's because I hate talking about it. I don't want to brag about carrying a wounded man on my back with a pack of Boers on horseback chivvying me. Besides, I'm a bit misty over what did happen. An upset like that takes it out of a fellow. Since I've been lying here this morning thinking it over the wonder to me is that I'm still alive."

Dickenson pressed his teeth together, making a brave effort to keep back the words which strove to escape, and he was rewarded for his reticence by his comrade continuing quietly:

"It all happened in a twinkling. Roby was balanced on my back, and I was trying to get away from the retreating Boers, sword in one hand, revolver in the other; and I kept two off who passed me by pointing my pistol at them, when another came down with a rush, made a snatch at the lanyard, and, almost before I could realise what was happening, poor Roby was down and I was jerked off my feet and dragged along the rough ground, bumping, choking, and strangling. For the brute had made a snatch at my revolver, caught the lanyard, and held on, with the slip-noose tight between the collar of my jacket and my chin, and his pony cantering hard. I can just remember the idea flashing to my brain that this must be something like the lassoing of an animal by a cowboy or one of those South American half-breeds, and then I was seeing dazzling lights and clouds that seemed to be tinged with blood; and after that all was dark for I can't tell how long, before I began to come to, and found myself right away on the veldt, with the sun beating down upon my head, and a raging thirst nearly driving me mad. I suppose I was mad, or nearly so," continued Lennox after a brief pause, "for my head was all in a whirl, and I kept on seeing Boers dragging me over the veldt by the neck, and hearing horses galloping round me, all of which was fancy, of course; for at times I was sensible, and knew that I was lying somewhere out in the great veldt where all was silent, the horses I heard being in my head. Then I seemed to go to sleep and dream that I was being dragged by the neck again, on and on for ever."

"Horrible," panted Dickenson.

"Yes, old fellow, it was rather nasty; but I suppose a great part of it was fancy, and even now I can't get it into shape, for everything was so dull and dreamy and confused. All I can tell you more is, that I woke up once, feeling a little more sensible, and began to feel about me. Then I knew that my sword was by my side and my hand numb and throbbing, for the sword-knot was tight about my wrist. I managed to get that loosened, and after a good deal of difficulty sheathed my sword, after which I began to feel for my revolver, and got hold of the cord, which passed through my hand till I felt that it was broken—snapped off or cut. That was all I could do then, and I suppose I fainted. But I must have come to again and struggled up, moved by a blind sort of instinct to get back to Groenfontein. I say I suppose that, for all the rest is a muddle of dreams and confusion. The doctor says you and a party came and found me wandering about in the dark, and of course I must have been making some blind kind of effort to get back to camp. I say, old fellow, I ought to have been dead, I suppose?"

"Of course you ought, sir," said the doctor, stepping in to lay a hand upon the poor fellow's brow. "Humph! Not so feverish as you ought to be, chattering like that."

"Then you've heard, doctor?" cried Dickenson excitedly.

"I heard talking, sir, where there ought to be none," replied the doctor sharply.

"But did you hear that your precious theory was all wrong?"

"No, sir; I did not," said the doctor sharply. "I based my theory upon what seemed to be facts, and facts they were. I told you that my patient here was suffering from the tightening of a ligature about his neck."

"And quite correct, too, doctor," said Lennox, holding out his hand. "I suppose if that lanyard had not broken I shouldn't be alive here to talk about it."

"Your theory, my dear boy, is as correct as mine," said the doctor, taking his patient's hand, but not to shake it, for he proceeded to feel Lennox's pulse in the most business-like manner, nodding his head with satisfaction.

"Much better than I expected," he said. "But you must be quiet now. I was horrified when I came by and heard such a jabbering going on. Let's see: where are your duds?"

He went to the corner of the hut, where the orderly had placed the patient's uniform, everything as neatly folded as if it had been new instead of tattered and torn; while above, on a peg, hung belts, sword, pouches, and the strong cord-like lanyard stiffened and strained about the noose and slipping knots, while the other end was broken and frayed where the spring snap had been.

"Humph!" said the doctor. "I wonder this cord didn't snap at once with the drag made upon it. All the same I don't suppose you were dragged very far."

He looked at his patient inquiringly, but Lennox shook his head slowly.

"It may have been for half-an-hour, doctor, or only for a minute. I can't tell."

"Probabilities are in favour of the minute, sir," said the doctor. "Well, it's a strange case. I never had but one injury in my experience approaching it, and that was when an artillery driver was dragged over the plain by his horses. A shell burst close to the team, and this man somehow got the reins twisted about his neck, and he was dragged for about a mile before he was released."

"Much hurt?" said Dickenson.

"Yes," said the doctor, with a short nod of the head. "He was very much hurt indeed."

"And I was not, doctor?" said Lennox, smiling.

"Oh no, not in the least," said the doctor sarcastically. "You only wanted your face washed and you'd have been all right in a few hours, no doubt. I've done nothing for you. The old story. Why, let me tell you, sir, when you were brought in I began to wonder whether I was going to pull you round."

"As you have, doctor, and I am most grateful."

Lennox held out both hands as he spoke, his right being still swollen and painful; and this time the doctor took them non-professionally, to hold them for a few moments.

"Of course you are, my dear boy, and I'm heartily glad to see you getting on so well; but, upon my word, I do sometimes feel ready to abuse some of our rough ones. I save their lives, and they take it all as a matter of course—give one not the slightest credit. But there, from sheer ignorance of course. You're getting right fast, and I'll tell you why: it's because you're in a fine, vigorous state of health. You fellows have no chance of over-indulging yourselves in eating and drinking."

"Not a bit, doctor," said Dickenson, making a wry face.

"Oh yes, I know," said the doctor. "You have to go through a good many privations, but you're none the worse. Primeval man used to have hard work to live; civilised man is pampered and spoiled with luxuries."

"Especially civilised man engaged in the South African campaign against the Boers," said Dickenson, while his comrade's eyes lit up with mirth.

"Sneer away, my fine fellow; but though it's precious unpleasant, fasting does no man any harm. Now, look here, sir; if we were in barracks at home you fellows would be indulging in mess dinners and wines and cigars, and sodas and brandies, and some of you in liqueurs, and you wouldn't be half so well, not in half such good training, as you are now."

"The doctor hates a good cigar, Drew, and loathes wine," said Dickenson sarcastically.

"No, he doesn't, boys; the doctor's as weak as most men are when they have plenty of good things before them. But my theory's right. Now, look at the men. Poor fellows! they've had a hard time of it; but look at them when they are wounded. I tell you, sir, that I open my eyes widely and stare at the cures I make of awful wounds. I might think it was all due to my professional experience, but I'm not such an idiot. It's all due to the healthy state the men are in, and the glorious climate."

"And what about the fever, doctor?" said Lennox.

"Ah, that's another thing, my dear boy. When the poor fellows are shut up in a horribly crowded, unhealthy camp, and are forced to drink water that is nothing less than poisonous, they go down fast. So they would anywhere. But see how we've got on here—the camp kept clean, and an abundant supply of delicious water bubbling out of that kopje. Then—Bless my heart! I forbade talking, and here I am giving you fellows a lecture on hygiene.—Come along with me, Dickenson.—You, Lennox, go to sleep if you can. No more talking to-day."

The doctor literally drove Dickenson before him, and hooked him by the arm as soon as they were outside.

"I'm very glad we settled for that idea of mine to be private, Dickenson, my dear boy. But it did look horribly like it."

"Perhaps," said the young man. "But you give it up now?"

"Certainly," said the doctor.

"And you give up the idea too about his running away?"

"Of course."

"Then the sooner you give Roby something that will bring him to his senses the better."

"I wish I could; but the poor fellow seems to have got it stamped into his brain."

"Yes; and the worst of it is he doesn't talk like a man touched in the head."

"No, he does not; though he is, without doubt."

"Can't you talk quietly to the chief? There's he and the major and Edwards take it all as a matter of course. They don't give poor old Drew the credit for all that he has done since we were here, but believe all the evil. It's abominable."

"*Esprit de corps*, Dickenson, my lad."

"Yes, that's all right enough; but they turn silent and cold as soon as the poor fellow's name is mentioned; while that isn't the worst of it."

"What is, then?" said the doctor.

"The men sing the tune their officers have pitched, and that miserable sneak, Corporal May, sings chorus. Oh! it's bad, sir; bad. Fancy: there was the poor fellow knocked over when trying to save his captain's life, and the man he helped to save turns upon him like this."

"Yes, it is bad," said the doctor; "but, like many more bad things, it dies out."

"What! the credit of being a coward, doctor? No; it grows. *Ur-r-r!*" growled the speaker. "I should like to ram all that Corporal May has said down his throat. He'd find it nastier physic than any you ever gave him, doctor. I say, I'm not a vindictive fellow, but when I keep hearing these things about a man I like, it makes me boil. Do you think there's any chance of the corporal getting worse?"

"No," said the doctor sternly; "he hasn't much the matter with him, only a few bruises. But if he did die it would be worse still for poor Lennox."

"No! How?"

"Because he'd leave the poison behind him. There, I'll do all I can with the colonel; but all the officers believe Roby, and that Lennox was seized with a fit of panic. There's only one way for him to clear it away."

"Exchange? How can he?"

"Exchange? Nonsense! Get strong, return to his company, and show every one that he is not the coward they think."

"There's something in that, certainly," said Dickenson sadly; "but he'll want opportunities. Suppose he had the chance to save the major's life; how do we know that he too wouldn't set it about that Lennox was more cowardly still? Saving lives doesn't seem to pay."

"Nonsense, my lad! You're speaking bitterly now."

"Enough to make me, sir. It isn't only Roby; Lennox saved Corporal May as well."

"Never mind that You tell Lennox to try again. Third time, they say, never fails."

"Humph!" said Dickenson. "Well, we shall see."

"Yes," said the doctor; "we shall see."

Chapter Thirty Four
The Mud that Stuck

"It's a bad business, Mr Lennox," said the colonel sternly, some weeks later, when matters looked very dreary again in the camp, for the supplies of provisions had once more begun to grow very short, and the constant strain of petty attacks had affected officers and men to a degree that made them morose and bitter in the extreme.

"But surely, sir, you don't believe this of me?" said Lennox, flushing.

"As a man, no, Mr Lennox; but as your commanding officer I am placed in a very awkward position. The captain of your company makes the most terrible charge against you that could be made against a young officer."

"But under what circumstances? He was suffering from a serious injury to the head; he was delirious at the time."

"But he is not delirious now, Mr Lennox, and that which he accused you of in a state of wild frenzy he maintains, now that he is recovering fast, in cold blood."

"Yes, sir; it seems cold-blooded enough after what I did for him."

"Unfortunately he maintains that this is all an invention on your part."

"And my being dragged away for some distance by one of the Boers, sir?"

"Yes; he declares that he was not insensible for some time after his hurt, and that had what you say occurred he must have seen it."

"Then it is his word against mine, sir?" said Lennox.

"Unfortunately it is not, Lennox," said the colonel gravely. "If it were only that I should feel very differently situated. Your conduct during the war has been so gallant that, without the slightest hesitation, I should side with you and set down all that Captain Roby has said to a hallucination caused by the injury to his head. But, you see, there is the testimony of Corporal May, who declares that he witnessed your conduct—conduct which I feel bound to say seems, when weighed by your previous actions, perfectly inexplicable."

"Then I am to consider, sir, on the testimony of this man, that I am unworthy of holding a commission in Her Majesty's service?" said Lennox bitterly.

"Stop," said the colonel. "Don't be rash, and say things of which you may repent, Lennox."

"An innocent man defending himself against such a charge, sir, cannot always weigh his words. Look at my position, sir. I am fit now to return to my duty, and I find a marked coldness on the part of my brother officers and a peculiarity in the looks of the men which shows me plainly enough that they believe it true."

"I have noticed it myself," said the colonel. "save in two instances. Mr Dickenson is downright in his defence of you; and I freely tell you for your comfort that the bravest non-commissioned officer in the regiment, when I was speaking to him on the subject, laughed the charge to scorn, and— confound him!—he had the insolence to tell me he'd as soon believe that I would run away as believe it of you."

"Ha!" ejaculated Lennox, with his eyes brightening. "Sergeant James?"

"Yes; Sergeant James. A fine, staunch fellow, Lennox. He'll have his commission by-and-by if I can help it on."

"Well, sir," said Lennox slowly, "I suppose it is of no use to fight against fate. Am I to consider myself under arrest?"

"Certainly not," said the colonel firmly. "This is no time for dealing with such a matter. I have enough on my hands to keep the enemy at a distance, and I want every one's help. But as soon as we are relieved—if we ever are—I am bound, unless Captain Roby and the corporal retract all they have said and attribute it to delirium—I am bound, I say, to call the attention of my superiors to the matter. I shall do so unwillingly, but I must. Out of respect to your brother officers, and for your sake as well, I cannot let this matter slide. It would be blasting your career as a soldier—for you could not retain your commission in this regiment."

"No, sir," said Lennox slowly, "nor exchange into another. But it seems hard, sir."

"Yes, Lennox, speaking to you not as your colonel but as a friend, terribly hard."

"Then the sooner I am arrested and tried by court-martial, sir, the better. I was ready to return to my duty, but to go on with every one in the regiment looking upon me as a coward is more than I could bear." The colonel was silent. "Have I your leave, sir, to go back to my quarters?" said Lennox at last.

"Not yet," said the colonel. "Look here, Lennox; this wretched charge has been made, and I cannot tell my officers and men what they shall and what they shall not believe. An inquiry must take place—by-and-by. Till it is held, the task rests with you to prove to your brother officers and the men that they have misjudged you."

"And to you, sir," said Lennox coldly.

"I do not judge you yet, Lennox," said the colonel gravely. "I am waiting."

"And how am I to prove, sir, that I am not what they think me?"

The colonel shrugged his shoulders and smiled sadly.

"You need not go and publish what I say, Lennox," he replied; "but I have very good reason to believe that the Boers are heartily sick of waiting for us to surrender, and that they have received orders to make an end of our resistance."

"Indeed, sir?"

"They have been receiving reinforcements, and the blacks bring word in that they have now two more guns. There will be plenty of chances for you to show that you are no coward, and that before many hours are past."

"Do you mean, sir, that I can take my place in the company?"

"I do."

"Thank you, sir. Something within me seems to urge me to hold aloof, for the coldness I have experienced since the doctor said I was fit for service is unbearable."

"Would not standing upon your dignity, Lennox, and letting your comrades face the enemy, look worse than manfully taking your place side by side with the men who are going forward to risk wounds or death?"

"Yes, sir; much," said Lennox, flushing. "I will live it down."

"Shake hands, Lennox," said the colonel, holding out his own. "Now I feel that you have been misjudged. Those were the words of a brave man. Mind this: the matter must be properly heard by-and-by, but let it remain in abeyance. Go and live it down."

The young officer had something more to say, but the words would not come; and the colonel, after a glance at him, turned to a despatch he had been writing, and began to read it over as if in ignorance of his visitor's emotion.

"Oh, by the way, Lennox, one word before you go. About this man May. Have you ever given him any cause to dislike you?"

"No, sir, I think not. I must own to always having felt a dislike to him."

"Indeed," said the colonel sharply. "Why?"

"I would rather you did not ask me, sir."

"Speak out, man!" said the colonel sternly.

"Well, sir, I have never liked him since he obtained his promotion."

"Why?"

"I did not think he deserved it so well as some of the other men of his standing."

"Humph! Let me see; he was promoted on Captain Roby's recommendation."

"Yes, sir; he was always a favourite with his captain."

"Have you been a bit tyrannical—overbearing?"

"I have only done my duty by him, sir. Certainly I have been rather sharp with him when I have noticed a disposition on his part to hang back."

"Perhaps he has never forgiven you for saving his life," said the colonel, smiling.

"Oh, surely not, sir."

"I don't know," said the colonel. "But think a minute."

"I was certainly very sharp with him that time when we explored the cavern, for that was one of the occasions when he hung back as if scared. But no, no, sir; I will not suspect the man of accusing me as he has through spite. He believes he saw me run, no doubt. But I did not."

"There, Lennox, you've had a long interview, and I have my despatch to write up. I have plenty to worry my head without your miserable business. Now, no rashness, mind; but I shall expect to hear of you leading your men in the very front."

"If they will follow me, sir, I shall be there," said Lennox quietly. "If they will not I shall go alone."

Chapter Thirty Five
Company at Dinner

"Why didn't you tell me you were going to have it out with the chief?" said Dickenson, encountering his comrade directly he had left the colonel's quarters.

"Because you told me never to mention the wretched business again."

"Did I? Oh, that was when I was in a wax. Well, what does the old man say?"

"That I am to go on as if nothing had happened."

"That's good. Well, what else?"

"Take my place in my company, and wait till we're relieved, and then be ready for a court-martial."

"That's good too, for no one can prove you guilty. What else?"

"Keep well in the front, and get myself killed as soon as I can."

"If he said that, he's a brute!" cried Dickenson. "Gammon! I don't believe the old man would say such a thing. But look here, I'm precious glad. This means you're going to live it down."

Lennox nodded. "Here," he said, "let's go into our hut."

"No, not yet. I want to walk up and down in the fresh air a bit."

"But the sun is terribly hot."

"Do you good," said Dickenson abruptly. "Let's go right to the end and back three or four times."

"Bah!" said Lennox. "You want to do this so as to ostentatiously show that you mean to keep friends with me."

"Suppose I do. I've a right to, haven't I?"

"Not to give me pain. It does. Help me to live it down quietly."

"Very well; if you like it better. But I say, you'll show up in the mess-room to-night?"

"Why should I?"

"Because the place is wretched and the fare's—beastly. There, that doesn't sound nice, but I must say it."

"I had rather stay away. It would only provoke what I should feel cruelly, and I could not resent it."

"No, but I could; and if any one insults you by sending you to Coventry, I'll provoke him. I suppose I mustn't punch my superior officer's head, but off duty I can tell him what I think of him, and I'll let him have it hot and strong."

"Then I shall stay away."

"No, you sha'n't. I will instead."

"That would be worse, Bob. Look here; I want you to help me to live this charge down, to treat it with quiet contempt. If you make yourself so fierce a partisan you will keep the wound sore and prevent it from healing up."

"Very well, then; I'll give it a good chance. There, I promise you I won't show my temper a bit; only play fair."

"In what way?"

"Don't turn upon me afterwards and call me a coward for not taking your part."

"Never fear. I don't want you to get into hot water for my sake."

"My dear boy," said Dickenson, chuckling like a cuckoo in a coppice in early spring, "that's impossible."

"Why?"

"Because I'm in hot water now with everybody, and have been ever since."

"I am sorry."

"And I am glad—jolly glad. Oh, don't I wish there was duelling still!"

"Haven't you killed enough men to satisfy you?" said Lennox sadly.

"More than enough. I don't want to kill brother officers, only to give them lessons in manly faith. But bother that! I say: you promise to come and take your place this evening?"

"Yes; I promise," said Lennox quietly.

"Then I'll tell you something. Roby's coming too."

"Roby!"

"Yes; for the first time since he got his wound."

Lennox was silent.

"There, I'm not going to try and teach you, old fellow," continued Dickenson; "but if I were you I should ignore everything, unless the boys do as they should do—meet you like men."

"Well," said Lennox, "we shall see."

That dinner-time came all too soon for Lennox, who had sat in his shabby quarters thinking how wondrously quiet everything was, and whether after what the colonel had hinted it was the calm preceding the storm.

"Come along," cried Dickenson, thrusting his head into the hut.

Lennox felt his heart sink as he thought of the coming meeting, for this was the first time he had approached the mess-room since the night of the attack upon the kopje. He winced, too, a little as he passed two sentries, who seemed, he thought, to look curiously at him. But the next moment his companion's rather boisterous prattle fell upon deaf ears, for just in front, on their way to the mess-room, were Roby and the doctor walking arm in arm, and then they disappeared through the door.

"Oh, won't I punish the provisions when the war is over!" said Dickenson. *Sniff, sniff!* "Ah! I know you, my friend, in spite of the roasting. I'd a deal rather be outside you than you inside me. And yet it's all prejudice, Drew, old man, for the horse is the cleanest and most particular of vegetable-feeding beasts, and the pig is the nastiest—cannibalistic and vile."

They passed through the door together, to find the colonel present, and the other officers about to take their places. Roby had evidently not been prepared for this, and he looked half-stunned when the doctor turned from him, advanced to Lennox, and shook hands.

"I wish we had a better dinner in honour of my two convalescents."

"This is insufferable," said Roby in a voice choking with anger.

"Let that wait, doctor," said the colonel.

"Come along, Lennox," cried Dickenson, after darting a furious glance at Roby. "Very, very glad to see you once more in your place."

No one else spoke for a few moments, and the dinner was about to be commenced, when Roby suddenly rose to his feet.

"Colonel Lindley," he said, in a husky voice full of rage, "are you aware who is present here this evening?"

"Yes, Captain Roby," said the colonel sternly. "I desired Mr Lennox, now that he is convalescent, to return to his usual place at the mess-table."

Roby's jaw dropped, and he stared at the officers around as if silently asking them whether he heard aright. But every man averted his eyes and assumed to be busy commencing the miserable meal.

"Well!" exclaimed Roby at last; and then in a tone which expressed his utter astonishment: "Well."

"Sit down, Captain Roby," continued the colonel, raising his eyebrows as he saw that his subordinate was still standing

"I beg your pardon, sir," said Roby stiffly, after looking round in vain for something in the way of moral support from his brother officers, who all sat frowning at their portions.

"Yes?" said the colonel calmly.

"I have no wish to be insubordinate, but, speaking on behalf of all present here, I desire to say that we feel it impossible to remain at the table in company with one who—"

"That will do," said the colonel, fixing Dickenson with his eyes, for that individual had suddenly given vent to a sound that was neither sigh, grunt, ejaculation, nor snort, but something that might have been the result of all these combined.

"I beg your pardon, sir?" said Roby hotly.

"I said that would do, Captain Roby," replied the colonel. "I did not gather that you had been elected to speak for your brother officers upon a subject about which I consider myself to be the proper arbiter. Moreover, if any officer feels himself aggrieved respecting any one whom I elect to join us at the mess-table, I am always open to hear his complaint."

"But really, sir," began Roby indignantly, "this is an assembly of honourable gentlemen."

"With an exception," growled Dickenson.

"Yes," cried Roby passionately, "with an exception—I may add, two exceptions."

"Look here, Captain Roby," cried Dickenson, springing up, "do you mean this as an insult to me?"

"Silence!" cried the colonel, rising in turn. "Mr Dickenson, resume your seat."

Dickenson dropped down so heavily that the empty cartridge-box that formed his seat cracked as if about to collapse.

"Captain Roby," said the colonel, "I beg that you will say no more now upon this painful subject. Resume your seat, sir."

"Sir," said Roby, "I must ask your permission to leave the mess-table. Whatever my brother officers may choose to do, I absolutely refuse to sit at the same table with a—"

"Stop!" roared Dickenson, springing up again in a furious passion. "If you dare to call my friend Lennox a coward again, court-martial or no court-martial, I'll knock you down."

Every man now sprang to his feet as if startled by the sudden verbal shell which had fallen amongst them. Then there was a dead silence, till Lennox said huskily, "Will you give me your permission to return to my quarters, sir?"

"No, Mr Lennox," said the colonel quietly. "Take your places again, gentlemen.—Captain Roby—Mr Lennox—if we are alive and uninjured in the morning I will see you both at my quarters with respect to this painful business. To-night we have other matters to arrange. I have just received trustworthy information that another reinforcement has reached the enemy. I have doubled the number of scouts sent out, and as soon as we have dined we have all our work to do in completing our arrangements to meet what the Boers intend for their final attack. Gentlemen, sit down. Our duty to our country first; minor matters of discipline after."

There was a low buzz of excitement as every man resumed his seat, Roby alone hesitating, but dropping sharply back into his place in unwilling obedience to a sharp tug given at his tunic by the officers on either side.

"What about your promise?" said Lennox in a whisper to Dickenson.

"Hang my promise!" growled his comrade. "Do you take me for a stump?"

Chapter Thirty Six
"What a Brick!"

Every one burst into the hurried flow of conversation that now followed the colonel's announcement, the excitement growing at the thought of the dreary siege at last coming to an end, while, to judge from the remarks, the feeling at the table was one of relief at the prospect of at last trying final conclusions with the Boers.

"Yes," said Captain Edwards to those near him, "I am heartily glad. Let them come on and give us a chance of some real fighting. All this miserable sniping and lurking behind stones has been barbarous. People say that the Boers are patriotic and brave: let them act like soldiers and give us a chance."

The conversation grew more and more exciting, till the meagre repast was at an end, when the colonel rose and walked round to the back of Dickenson's seat.

"Come to my quarters," he said quietly, and he walked out, followed by the young subaltern.

The stars were out, shining brightly, and all looked peaceful and grand as the colonel led on to his hut, with Dickenson stringing himself up for the encounter he was about to have with his chief. and growing more and more determined and stubborn as the moment approached.

"I don't care," he said to himself. "I'll tell him I'll challenge Roby, whether it's allowed or not;" and then he felt as if some one had thrown cold water in his face, for the colonel said quietly:

"What a grand night, Dickenson! I wonder what our friends are doing at home, and whether they are thinking about us."

Dickenson stared at him, but it was too dark for him to distinguish the play of his officer's countenance.

"No light," said the colonel as he turned into his quarters. "Have you a match?"

"Yes, sir," said the young officer rather gruffly, and the little silver box he took from his pocket tinkled softly as he searched for a match and struck it, the flash showing the colonel turning up the lamp wick.

"That's right," he said; "light it."

A minute later the mean-looking hut, with its camp table, lamp, and stools, was lit up, and the colonel seated himself.

"I've very few words to say, Dickenson," he said kindly, "but those are about your conduct to-night. You are young, hot-headed, and unwise."

"Can't help it, sir. My nature," said the young man shortly.

"I suppose so. But of course you are aware that you have been guilty of a great breach of etiquette, and that your conduct cannot be passed over very lightly."

"I suppose not, sir. I'm ready to take my punishment."

"Yes," said the colonel; and then, after a pause, "You seem to attach yourself more than ever to Mr Lennox since this affair."

"Yes, sir; we are very old friends. I should not be his friend if I did not stick to him now he is under a cloud."

"Rather unwise, is it not? You see, you cut yourself apart from your brother officers, who are bound to stand aloof till Mr Lennox has cleared himself."

"I'm sorry not to be friendly with them, sir," said Dickenson sturdily; "and if there is any cutting apart, it is their doing, not mine. I am ready to do my duty in every way, sir; but I must stand by my friend."

"Then you have perfect faith in his innocence?"

"Perfect, sir; and so would you have if you knew him as well as I do."

"I do know him pretty well, Dickenson," said the colonel quietly. "Well, I suppose you know that I ought to be very severe with you?"

"Yes, sir, of course."

"And that I was bound to summon you to come to my quarters?"

"Or put me under arrest, sir."

"I cannot spare any of my officers to-night, Dickenson, so I suppose it must be deferred till after the attack."

"Thank you, sir. I don't want to be out of the fight."

"I suppose not. By the way, have you seen much of Roby since he has been about again?"

"Oh yes; a great deal, sir, on purpose. I've been trying to get him into a better frame of mind."

"Well, I must say that you have not succeeded very well."

"Horribly, sir. I thought he'd think differently as his wound healed up; but he is worse than ever."

"Now then," said the colonel, "tell me frankly what you think of Captain Roby's state."

"I think he puzzles me, sir. One hour I think he is as mad as a hatter—"

"Say as mad."

"Yes, sir; one hour he's as mad as mad, and the next he's perfectly sane."

"Perfectly sane, I should say, Dickenson," said the colonel.

"Yes, sir, in all things but one, and over that he's just like that fellow in the story."

"What fellow in what story?" said the colonel coldly.

"That Mr Dick, sir, who couldn't write anything without getting King Charles's head into it."

"I see; and you think Captain Roby cannot help getting what he considers to be Lennox's cowardice into *his* head?"

"Exactly, sir."

"Humph! Well, there may be something in that. There, I have no more to say to you now. No rashness to-night, but do your best with your men. I'd rather hear that you saved one of our lads than killed half-a-dozen Boers."

"I understand, sir."

"Understand this too. If you have any conversation with your brother officers, say I have had you here to give you a severe reproof for the present, and that probably something more will follow when we have crushed the Boers. If they crush us you will get off. That will do, Dickenson. I expect our friends will visit us to-night, though more probably it will be just before daylight. Ask the major to step here as you go. By the way, you and Lennox were at school together?"

"Yes, sir; and at Sandhurst too."

"Well, I hope he has as good an opinion of you as you have of him. Good-night for the present."

"Good-night, sir," said the young man as he went out into the starlight to deliver his message.—"Well, I hope we shall win to-night, for the chief's sake! Hang it all," he muttered, "what a brick he is!"

Chapter Thirty Seven
To Clear the Kopje

As a rule, the garrison at Groenfontein after the posting of the watch settled itself down for a quiet night's rest, for experience had taught that there was very little to fear in the shape of a night attack. This was foreign at first to the Boers' idea of warfare. They knew well enough that they were strongest in defence, and acted accordingly. Every place they held was turned into a hive of cells, in which they lurked, stings ready. It was generally some kopje covered with loose stones, cracks, and crevices, while the open portions were soon made formidable with loopholed walls of loosely built-up stones. If their resting-place was in the more open country, it was a laager whose walls were the wagons, banked up and strengthened with stakes, thorn bushes, and a terrible entanglement of barbed galvanised iron wire.

Attacks had been made on the fortified village and the kopje at early morning, but never pushed home; and all through the occupation the tactics of the general in command had been the harassing of the British regiment with shell fire and clever marksmanship from cover, so constant and so dangerous that the wonder to the English officers was that the enemy had not long before fired their last cartridge away.

But upon this particular night something more was fully expected. The English scouting parties had brought in the information respecting the reinforcements to the Boer corps, so that when a Zulu, who had been a very faithful hanger-on to the British force, came in full of eagerness that afternoon to announce that the Boers meant to attack in force, the colonel, though always ready to doubt the information received and the possibility of the black spies' surmises being correct, felt that he was warranted in making every preparation; and this was set about in a calm, matter-of-fact way.

Judging that the attack would be in the form of a surprise directed at the kopje, possession of which would render the village perfectly untenable, the two field-guns posted in the most commanding position in the village were hauled up to appointed places on the kopje to strengthen the big captured gun, and the major portion of the troops were marched up to the well-fortified lines there, the colonel intending to hold the rocky elevation himself, leaving the defence of the village to the major, who was to keep the enemy who attacked in play there as long as seemed necessary, and then retire along the well-fortified path which connected village and kopje, where the principal stand was to be made.

The great natural advantages of the rocky mount had not been neglected. From the first the colonel had looked upon it as a little inland Gibraltar in which he could bid defiance to ten times the number of the enemy that had been attacking him, so long as food and ammunition lasted; and to this end he had, directly after the discovery of the entrance to the cavern, supplemented the stores found there by removing all they had from the village, and making additions from time to time whenever suitable captures were made; while, greatest prize of all, there was the inexhaustible supply of pure cold water, easily enough obtainable as soon as proper arrangements were made.

Hence it was that the little English force was always ready, the plans for the defence arranged, and nothing remained to be done but for the various defenders to march quietly to their appointed places.

Consequently, after the watch-setting, the orders were given, and party after party moved silently through the soft darkness, till by the brilliant starlight each battery was manned and the trenches which commanded the probable approaches to the kopje lined, while the same precautions were taken in the village, where wall and hut had been carefully loopholed; and then all was ready. The men lay down in their greatcoats and blankets to snatch such sleep as they could get, as it was anticipated that several hours would probably elapse before the attack—if any—was made.

"I was in hopes," said Dickenson when all was ready, "that we should be up yonder, ready to cover the gunners. It would be a treat to play Boer and show them what firing from behind stones is like. Something new for them."

"But we shall not stay here very long if they do come," replied Lennox.

"No; we understand all that. Been drilled into us pretty well. But it strikes me that, according to the good old fashion of nothing occurring so likely as the unexpected, if they do come it will not be to where we are waiting, but from somewhere else."

"Where else can they come from?" said Lennox sharply.

"Oh, don't ask me," said Dickenson, laughing. "I'm not a Boer: how can I tell? They'll have hatched out some dodge. Got a balloon all the way from Komati Poort, perhaps, and about three o'clock they'll have it right over the top of the kopje, and if we had been up there I dare say we should have found them sliding down ropes like spiders."

"Highly probable," said Lennox dryly.

"Ah, you may jest; but you see if they don't come crawling right close up like so many slugs on a wet night. The first thing we shall know will be that they are there."

"Ah, now you are talking sense."

"But I don't guarantee that it's going to be like that," said Dickenson quickly, "so don't be disappointed."

"I shall not be. I'm ready for anything."

"Good, lad. That's the way to deal with the Boers. I've learnt that: for they certainly are the trickiest fellows going. I say—"

"Hadn't you better leave off talking now?"

"Only whispering. I was going to say that the major's here with us, and has put Edwards in command of both companies."

"But Roby's with him?"

"Yes; but Edwards is boss. I shouldn't have felt comfortable with our convalescent at the head of affairs."

"You need not have minded. Roby's as brave as he is high."

"May be; but he has that bee in his bonnet still. I half believe that old Emden's wrong after all."

"In what way?"

"He said the bullet just ploughed through Roby's scalp and pressed down a bit of bone. I believe he has the bullet in his head."

"Absurd!" said Lennox.

"Oh no. Likely enough. They came buzzing along, too, like swarming bees. That would account for what he said about you."

"Be quiet," said Lennox sharply. "If the enemy comes to-night I want to fight, and not to think about that."

"All right. I hope they will come; it will be a waste of sleep if they don't. Bah!" he added after a long-drawn yawn. "They won't come—they know better. These nigger spies see a few men on ponies, and away they run to say they've seen a big commando, and hold out their hands for the pay. Take my word for it, there'll be no fighting to-night."

It seemed as if Dickenson was right in his surmise, for the time glided on, with the stars rising to the zenith and beginning to decline. The heavens had never seemed more beautiful, being one grand dome of sparkling incrustations. The atmosphere was so clear that it seemed to those who lay back watching as if the dazzling points of light formed by the stars of the first magnitude stood out alone in the midst of the transparent darkness, while the shape of the kopje was plainly marked out against the vivid sky.

"Too light for them," said Dickenson after a long pause.

"They will not come till morning.—Who's this?"

"Roby."

He it was, the tall figure in a greatcoat coming close up to stop and speak to Sergeant James about being watchful, and then passing on without a word to his juniors. Roby came in the same quiet, furtive manner three times over during the night, twice being in company with Captain Edwards, who stopped to have a few words with Lennox and Dickenson as to the probability of an attack; but Roby stood aloof.

"And a good job too," said Dickenson after the last occasion. "I don't want to be malicious, though it seems so, about a man who has just got over a bad hurt; but I do hope the Boers will come, and that he will be wounded again—"

"Shame!" said Lennox angrily.

"Perhaps so; but you might have let me finish—wounded again; not a bullet wound, but a good cut that will bleed well and take the bad blood out of him. We should hear no more of his fancies."

"Drop that," said Lennox sternly; and then, to change the conversation, "Surely it must be getting near daybreak."

"Oh no; not yet. Let's have another walk round, and a word with the men."

This, one of many, was carried out, the young officers finding that there were no sleepers, the men not on the watch having, from the expectation that if there were an attack it would be about daybreak, instinctively roused up, every one being fully on the alert.

Lennox winced more than ever now as he stood in the trench they expected to be the likeliest, from its position, for the attack, for its capture would give the enemy a good point for further advances; and Captain Edwards had pointed it out to the major as being likely to be rushed, with the consequence that this part was the most strongly held, and the supporting party placed near.

And now, as Dickenson began whispering to his men, Lennox felt more bitterly than ever how thoroughly Roby's charge had gone home. For whenever he spoke to one of the watch the answer was abrupt and cold, while with his companion the men were eager and ready to be questioned.

Everything possible had been done to guard against surprise, and the communication with the chain of outposts was constant; but the surprise came from where it was least expected, and just when the friends were standing together in the redoubt, with Dickenson grudgingly owning that the stars were perhaps not so bright.

"The night has passed more quickly than I expected it would," whispered Lennox. "Can't you feel what a chill there is in the air?"

"Ugh—yes!" said Dickenson, with a shiver. "It's quite frosty out here."

"And a hot cup of coffee would be a blessing," said Captain Edwards, who, with Roby, had returned again.

"Yes," said Dickenson; "a good fire would warm us up."

"There it is, then," said Captain Edwards excitedly, for without a warning from the outposts, between which the Boers had crawled in the darkness unheard, a tremendous burst of firing was opened upon the kopje, the enemy having made their way up by inches till they were well within reach of the defending lines—so close, in fact, that for the time being the big guns were useless, their fire at such close quarters being as likely to injure friend as foe.

"Stand fast, my lads!" cried Captain Edwards. "We shall have them here directly.—Now, gentlemen, you know what to do. Ah! I thought so;" for a scattering fire was opened by the outposts, who, according to their instructions, began to fall back to take their places in the line ready to resist the attack upon the village.

Lennox felt stunned by the suddenness of the attack, and ready to confess that their trained troops were in nowise equal to the enemy in the matter of cunning; for, as if by magic, the wild fire ran completely round the kopje, which, contrary to expectation, had become the main object of attack, and in a short time the flashing of the rifles and the continuous rattle told plainly enough that by their clever ruse the Boers had completely surrounded the kopje, cutting the British force in two.

Certainly a portion of them had been led between two fires—between that of the village and that from the eminence; but the British fire was hindered by the danger of injuring their friends, and in a very short time the major grasped the fact that it was waste of energy to try and defend the village, which was only lightly attacked, and quite time for him to retire and lead his men to the support of the colonel.

His orders had hardly been given to the various centres to fall back from the trenches and houses held, when the agreed-upon signal flew up from the top of the kopje in a long line of light, followed by the bursting of a rocket, whose stars lit up the cloud of smoke rising round the mount.

Everything had been so well planned beforehand that there was not the slightest confusion: the men fell back steadily to the village square, leaving the Boers still firing out of the darkness into the defensive lines; and then, as steadily as if in a review, the advance was made to cut through the investing crowd, which, facing the other way, was keeping up a tremendous fire.

The signal for the advance was given with another rocket fired from the square as a warning to the colonel to cease firing on their side; and then the men steadily commenced their arduous task, the leading company going on in rushes, seizing the shelters, pouring in volleys, and driving the Boers before them and to right and left, in spite of their determined resistance to hold that which they had surprised by rising, as it were, as Sergeant James afterwards said, right out of the earth.

The holders of the village under the major numbered pretty well half of the total force remaining to the colonel, and, led by the major himself, two companies went at the strong force of the enemy drawn across their way, like a wedge, in spite of the concentrated fire delivered by the desperate men, who had to give way. The second body was under Captain Edwards, and Roby and Lennox and Dickenson had the dangerous post of bringing on the single company that formed the rear-guard.

In the wild excitement of those minutes Lennox was conscious of cheering his men on.

The start was made without a man down. Three or four had slight wounds, but in the rear-guard not a man had been hit, while for some distance after quitting the redoubt they were still exempt. But the leading company was beginning to suffer badly: men kept on falling or staggering out to seek shelter in trench, rifle-pit, or behind boulder, and for a while the battle raged fiercely and but little progress was made, a crowd of the enemy pressing up from either side to take the places of those who fell or were beaten back, till the order was given in a lull to fix bayonets.

Then for a few brief moments the firing near at hand almost ceased, so that the metallic rattle of the little daggers being affixed to the rifle muzzles was plainly heard, to be followed by a hearty British cheer given by every throat from van to rear, the men's voices sounding full of exultation as, with the bugle ringing out, they dashed forward.

There was no working forward by inch or by foot now; the Boers gave way at once, and the broad column dashed on, dealing death and destruction to all who, in a half-hearted way, opposed their progress. It was quick work, for there was less than a couple of hundred yards to cover to be through the Boer line and reach the shelter of the rough stone walls and huge boulders which formed on that side the first defences of the kopje.

In the wild excitement of those minutes Lennox was conscious of cheering his men on, as with bayonets at the ready they dashed on toward the main body, driving back the Boers who were trying to close in again after being beaten back by the first rushes. Men were trampled under foot in the half-darkness, friends and foes alike, for it was a horrible business; but the men, in their wild excitement, cheered and cheered again till they were brought up by the first rugged wall and received with another burst of cheers from the holders of the bristling line of rifles and bayonets who were lining it.

"Through with you—over with you!" shouted the major.—"Here, help those poor fellows in.—Where's Captain Edwards?"

"Here he is," panted Dickenson, as he half-carried, half-dragged his brother officer to an opening in the wall.

"Tut, tut, tut!" ejaculated the major. "Here, Captain Roby, take full lead there on the left. Captain Roby!—Who has seen Captain Roby?"

"I did," said Captain Edwards faintly. "Shot down at the same time as I was."

"Ah-h!" roared the major. Then excitedly: "Where about?"

"A hundred yards away, perhaps. Shot down leading the left company in the charge. I—I was trying to help him along when I went down too."

"Killed?" said the major.

"No; bullet through the thigh."

"We must fetch him in. Here; volunteers!"

Lennox leaped on to the wall in the pale grey light of the fast-coming day, and as he stood there, stooping ready to leap down, fully a score of rifles sent forth their deadly pencil-like balls from where to right and left the Boers were crouching.

Down he went, to pitch head first, and a sound like a fierce snarling ran along the sheltered side of the stone wall; but as the men saw him spring to his feet again and begin to run they were silent for a few moments, as if in doubt as to what their young lieutenant meant; for Dickenson sprang on to the wall, trying hard to balance himself on the loose top where bullets kept on spattering, as he roared out, with his voice plainly heard above the rattle of the Boers' rifles, "Look at the coward! Running away again! Volunteers, come on!"

There was a curious hysterical ring in his loud laugh as, with the bullets whirring and whistling about him and a cross fire concentrated upon where he stood, he too leaped down, to begin running, while a burly-looking sergeant literally rolled over the wall, followed by two more men from the rear company, all plainly seen now dashing towards where Lennox was running here and there among the dead and wounded which dotted the sloping ground, before stopping suddenly to go down on one knee and begin lifting a wounded man upon his shoulder.

"Well," cried the major, "he's the queerest coward I ever saw. I wish the colonel was here."

His words brought forth a tremendous cheer from all who heard them, but the major turned upon the men angrily.

"Shoot, you rascals, shoot!" he cried; "right and left. Keep down the savages' fire if you can."

For, unmoved by the gallant actions going on in front, brave men setting death at defiance—as scores of others had done all through the war—in the noble endeavour to save a wounded man's life, dozens of the Boers began firing at the rescue party, heedless of the fact that their bullets crossed the narrow way traversed by the little force in their dash from the village to the kopje, and now horribly dotted by the wounded and dying of both sides who had fallen in the desperate encounter.

Yells and shouts arose from both sides as the bullets took effect among friends; but in their mad hate against those whom they called the British rooineks, the Boers fired on. Fortunately, for the most part the wielders of the Mauser were not calmly lying down behind stones, with rests for their rifles, but were crowded together, nervous, agitated, and breathless with running, so that their bullets were badly aimed during the first minute or two. Directly after, they were startled by the hail poured upon them from the whole line of men behind the great wall—a hail of lead beneath which many fell never to rise again, while the greater part devoted themselves to seeking cover, crawling anywhere to get under the shelter of some stone.

The roar, then, that greeted the little party struggling back was not from British throats but from British rifles, which for the time being thoroughly kept down the enemy's fire, till Lennox and Dickenson bore the insensible form of Roby right up to the wall, followed by Sergeant James and his two companions, each carrying a wounded comrade on his back.

And now, without ceasing their firing, the line cheered till all were hoarse, while four men sprang over to Roby's help, the others being tumbled over, to be seized by willing hands.

It was quite time, for both Lennox and Dickenson were spent—the former sinking upon his knees to hold on by one of the stones; Dickenson bending forward to try and wave one hand, but dropping suddenly across Roby's knees.

"Wounded?" cried the major excitedly, as he bent over Lennox directly he was lifted in, the last of the four.

Lennox opened his fast-closing eyes and stretched out his right hand to feel for Dickenson's, in vain. Then, with a sigh, he looked up at the major and touched his left arm, his breast, and his neck. "Yes," he said faintly, "the coward has it now."

"Bearers here," cried the major, and he turned to direct his men, for he was needed.

The Boers were coming on again in short rushes, regardless of the terrific fire poured upon them in the faint light of day, and a perfect hail of bullets was flying to and fro. And not only facing the village, but all round the kopje, where the enemy had in several places secured a footing and were utilising the stone defences prepared by the colonel's men, but of course from the reverse side. It had this good effect, though; it condensed the British force, giving them less ground to defend; and for the next two hours wherever a Boer dared to show enough of himself to form a spot at which to aim, a bullet came.

The losses were terrible on both sides, for the attack was as brave as the defence; and even when the two small guns were brought into action, to send shells hurtling wherever the continually increasing enemy were seen to approach in clusters, the attack went on.

"It's of no use, major," said the colonel at last, as they stood together; "they mean to have the place."

"What!" said the latter officer fiercely. "You don't mean surrender?"

"My dear fellow, no: not while there's a cartridge left."

"Ha!" sighed the major. "You gave me quite a turn."

"I meant, if this keeps on we shall lose as many men as if we brought it to a head. Besides, they'll hold on to the parts they've got, and keep creeping nearer."

"You mean the bayonet at once?"

"Exactly," said the colonel. "Off with you; take one side and I'll take the other. We must clear the kopje before the heat comes on."

"Yes," said the major, with a grim smile; "and the lads must want their breakfast now."

The men in each trench rolled up their sleeves as they heard the order given to fix bayonets again, and, leaping over the defences, rushed forward, to be staggered a little by the enemy's fire; then, with a cheer, on they went, the sun glistening upon the line of pointed steel.

It was more than the Boers could bear; defence after defence was vacated, and, soon after, the result of charge after charge was followed by a headlong flight which soon spread into a panic. It was *"Sauve qui peut,"* uttered in Boer Dutch; while the failure of the daring attack was completed fast by the emptying of the rifle magazines among flying men, and the shots from the three guns, which had their opportunity at last.

A stand was made in the village, which was obstinately held for a time by two big commandos which had come upon the ground too late to be of much service; but in spite of a pom-pom, a Maxim, and a heavy howitzer, the big gun on the top of the kopje silenced their fire before sundown, by which time their heaviest piece was destroyed, the village burning, and the two commandos in full flight.

Then came the flag of truce for permission to carry off the wounded and bury the many dead.

It was about this time that Doctor Emden looked to the colonel and said:

"Awful! Poor fellows! I don't know where to turn to first."

Chapter Thirty Eight
The Doctor's Diplomacy

It was a couple of days later, when the kopje was dotted with the rough shelters that the uninjured men had worked hard to erect from the ruins of the village, the principal being for the benefit of the wounded. The position was the same, or nearly the same, as it had been before. The Boers had retreated to their laagers, which were more strongly held than ever, and the investment was kept up with more savage determination; while the defenders had only the kopje to hold now, the village being a desolation, and the colonel's forces sadly reduced.

The doctor was in better spirits, and showed it, for he had managed to get something like order in his arrangements for his wounded men. But the colonel and the major were in lower spirits, and did not show it, for matters looked very black indeed, relief seeming farther off than ever.

"My last orders were to hold this place," said the colonel to the major, "and I'm going to hold it."

"Of course! Keep on. Every day we shall be having another man or two back in the ranks. Ah! here is Emden.—Well, how are the lads?"

"Getting on splendidly. My dear sirs, I have heard people abuse the Mauser as a diabolical weapon. Nothing of the sort; it is one of the most humane. The wounds are small, cleanly cut, and, so long as a bone is not touched, begin to heal with wonderful rapidity. Come and have a look round."

"Yes; we have come on purpose," said the colonel. "By the way, though, before we go into the officers' shelter, I wish you had contrived differently about Roby and Lennox. It seemed very short-sighted, after what has occurred, to place them next to one another."

"My dear sir," cried the doctor, "I did all I could to try and save the poor fellows' lives as they were carried in to me, without thinking about their squabbles and quarrels and rank."

"Yes, yes; of course, doctor. I beg your pardon. You have done wonders."

"Thankye! Done my best, of course. But don't you worry about those two; they'll be all right. Come and see."

"But about the men? Nothing more serious, I hope."

"N-n-no. Had to take that fellow's leg off to save his life."

"What poor fellow? Oh yes—Corporal May?"

"Yes. He objected strongly, but it had to be done. He threatens to commence an action against me when he gets home—so I hear."

They had been moving towards the shelter of corrugated iron beneath which the officers lay, each of whom greeted them with a smile. They were all badly wounded, but looked restful and contented, as wounded men do who have achieved a victory.

Roby seemed to be the most cheerful, and he beckoned to the colonel to come closer, while the doctor cocked his eye rather drolly and in a way that the chief did not understand.

"Well, Roby," said the colonel, "you look better."

"Well, for a man who has had the top of his head rasped by a bullet and got a hole right through his leg, I call myself a wonder."

"Does your wound pain you much?"

"Quite enough; but there, I don't mind. We've whipped."

"Yes," said the colonel, smiling; "we've whipped, thanks to every one's gallant behaviour. You did splendidly, Roby."

"Did my best, sir," said the captain quietly. "But I'm not quite as I should like to be," he continued confidentially. "Don't take any notice. I can't quite understand about my hurt on the head."

"Indeed?" said the colonel, frowning.

"I recollect, of course, getting the stinging pain in my leg, and going down, and then it seemed to me that one of the Boers kicked me at the top of the forehead with his heavy boot, and I was trampled on. After that I fainted, and didn't come to until the firing was going on and Lennox came running through it to pick me up. Colonel, that's about the bravest thing that has been done since we've been here."

"Quite," said the colonel, watching the speaker curiously.

"I want you to promise me that you'll mention it well in your despatch about the taking of the laager."

"If I ever get a despatch to headquarters it shall contain that, I promise you."

"Thank you," said Roby warmly, and with the tears now in his eyes. "I say, colonel, I'm sorry I went down; but the doctor says the lads got back after another skirmish, with plenty of cattle and stores."

"Yes," said the colonel; "it was a splendid addition to our supplies and—"

"Stop! stop! please, colonel," said the doctor. "Roby's weak yet."

"Oh no, doctor."

"My dear fellow, I say yes; and I say," said the doctor, bending down to whisper to his patient, "Lennox and Dickenson are both very feeble. Think of them."

Roby took the doctor's hand and pressed it, accompanying the pressure with a significant look.

"Thank you for coming, colonel," he said, "and you too, major. Emden's an awful tyrant when he gets us on our backs."

"Right," said the doctor. "Nero was nothing to me.—Now, gentlemen, just a word or two with the rest of my nursery folk, and then I must order you off."

The colonel nodded, passed on to Captain Edwards, and said a word or two; the same followed at Dickenson's side, where the young officer, forgetful of his wounds, gave his chief a look full of exultation, receiving a good-humoured nod in return, and Dickenson turned his face sidewise with a sigh of content.

"Wait a bit," he said to himself. "I'll have it out with the old man as soon as I get better. He's bound to ask poor old Drew's pardon. But fancy Roby turning like this."

Meanwhile the colonel had passed on to Lennox's side, to find him far the greatest sufferer of the party present, and unable to do more than smile his thanks and lie back, extremely weak, but with a look of calm restfulness in his eyes that told that there was nothing mental to trouble him and keep him back.

"What do you think of them, colonel?" said the doctor as soon as they were outside.

"All much better than I expected," said the colonel.

"But what about Roby? He is quite delirious from his wound, is he not?"

"Perfectly calm, sir, with his *mens* much more *Sana* than his *corpus*. I thought he was all wrong at first, but he's only weak—pulse regular, temperature as cool as a hot iron roof will let it be." (Note: *Mens sana in corpore sano.*)

"But, hang it all, doctor! his head's all in a muddle about storming the little kopje and getting the cattle and stores away."

"Yes; that's the comical part of it. He's a bit mixed, and in his present state I let him think what he likes, so long as it is not likely to do him any harm."

"But really, Doctor Emden, I fail to follow your reasoning," said the colonel rather stiffly.

"Never mind, colonel; leave it. I don't follow all your military manoeuvres, so I leave them to you. Let the cobbler stick to his last. There, man, don't look mystified. Let me explain. Roby had bad concussion of the brain from that first shot. There was no fracture, but the bone was, so to speak, a little dented down, and the consequence was that, though he rapidly recovered his health bodily, he did not get his mental balance quite right at the same time."

"Then you think that charge of his against Lennox was a trifling aberration that's now over. I hope you are right, doctor; but—"

"But me no buts," said the doctor. "I stake my reputation upon it. Surely, man, you can see the proof? The poor fellow showed you that he has not the slightest recollection now of what has been going on since the expedition to the laager."

"To be sure," said the major. "I see now. That explains it. He talked as if he thought this was the result of being shot down there."

"To be sure he does. He thinks, too, that Edwards is wounded from a skirmish with the Boers during the retreat."

"Then there was no nonsense, no unreality, in his display of interest in poor Lennox?"

"Not a bit. He's delighted with the poor fellow's gallantry, and talks to me about how much he owes him."

"But his charge of cowardice?"

"Wind, my dear sir; wind. Let it blow away. If any one were to tell him of it now he would stare with astonishment and ask you if you meant to insult him. Take my word for it, the hallucination has completely passed away. The fresh wound, with its loss by haemorrhage, and the reaction, has acted antagonistically to his mental trouble. He has, so to speak, stepped mentally from the attack on the Boers to their attack on us, and as soon as he recovers his strength he'll be as good a man as ever."

"But when we tell him about his charge?" said the colonel.

"Why tell him, sir? Let it rest. If it ever comes out by accident, that's quite another thing. The trouble has settled itself, as some troubles will."

"I wish this one would," said the major, "for I'm getting very sick of being penned up here on very reduced rations. Have they quite forgotten us at headquarters?"

"No," said the colonel. "Their hands are full.—Meanwhile, doctor, our ranks are very thin, so as fast as you can send the poor lads back to the ranks, let us have them again. The Boers will not let us rest like this for long."

Chapter Thirty Nine
At Last!

But the Boers had received so severe a lesson that they did leave the garrison severely alone for nearly a month, save that there were often sharp encounters between patrols and the foraging parties which made a dash whenever there was a chance of capturing something for the military larder.

It had come to the colonel holding a private council, at which the doctor was present to give his opinion how long it would be before the wounded men would be sufficiently strong to undertake a night march and then push on to try and join hands with the nearest post held by our forces.

"If we could feed the lads as they ought to be fed, in about a month," replied the doctor quietly. "Going on as we are now—never." The colonel started from his seat. "Do you mean this, Emden?" he said excitedly. "The men's appearance speaks for itself. It is all the healthy can do to keep body and soul together; the wounded are at a standstill."

"No, no," said the colonel warmly; "all of our officers, though certainly weak, have returned to their duty."

"Yes," said the doctor; "but then they all partook more of a certain essence than the men do. The poor fellows had done marvellously well, and the more educated, better-class fellows compare wonderfully well with those of a lower station; but there is that difference."

"And pray what is the wonderful essence, doctor?" said Captain Edwards, smiling.

"*Esprit de corps,* my dear sir," said the doctor.

"Well," cried the colonel, "then you have settled it, doctor. We are not going to surrender."

"No!" came in chorus.

"We can't go and leave our weak ones behind."

"No!" came with double the force.

"We are too much reduced in available men to run any risks." There was no reply to this, and the colonel continued: "Then there is nothing else to be done, gentlemen, but take up another hole in our belts, keep on sending messages when we can get a Kaffir runner, and wait patiently for help."

As the officers sauntered away from the rough hut which had been built in a niche for the colonel, Roby was limping along with the aid of a stick and Lennox's arm, while Dickenson was rolling up a cigarette composed of the very last dust of his tobacco, ready to hand it to the captain, who suffered a good deal still from the bullet wound, the missile having passed right through his thigh. They had to pass two of their men, seated upon a rock in a shady corner, one of them being minus his right leg, which had been removed half-way between knee and hip; the other was recovering very slowly from a bullet wound in the face, an injury which had mended very slowly and kept him low-spirited, fretful, and ready to affect the companionship of one as fretful and as great a sufferer as himself. The group of officers stopped to say a few kind words to the men, and then, having nothing hopeful to hold out for their comfort, passed on.

"See that Captain Roby?" said the one-legged man.

"Of course I do."

"Well, I did have some hopes of him as being a man, but he isn't. He's a sneak, that's what he is—a sneak."

"Better not let him hear you say so," said the other.

"Tell him if you like."

"Tell him yourself."

"You know how he let on about Mr Lennox running away in the fight?"

"Oh yes, of course; but it was all a mistake. He was off his head, Captain Roby was."

"Tchah! Not he. It was all true, but the captain wouldn't hold to it. They hang together, these officers, and make things up, so that when their turn comes to be in trouble the others back them. I was out here the other day, and old Roby came doing the civil and asking me how I was, so I rounded upon him about giving up saying Mr Lennox was a coward. What do you think he says?"

"Said you were cracked."

"Yes; only he said mad. What do you think of that?"

"That he ought to have said you were a sneak and a cur," said the man, getting up and walking away, but only to stop and turn round. "Look here, corporal," he said; "take a bit of advice. Drop that altogether, or some day the chaps may turn upon you and forget that you're a crippled man, and give you what you don't like."

"Why?" cried Corporal May wrathfully.

"Because every one of us thinks Mr Lennox is about the pluckiest fellow in the regiment, and would follow him into the hottest fire the enemy could get up."

Affairs, after gliding sluggishly along for months, began to move swiftly now. Two weeks after there was an announcement that a Kaffir, a despatch-runner, had reached the kopje, and he was hurried before the officers, to prove to be the Zulu who had brought in the warning of the last attack. He had fresh news now—that once more the Boers had been reinforced, and that they had received three heavy guns. Preparations were again made for the reception of the enemy, but the men moved about looking grave and stern. The old hopeful elasticity seemed gone Dickenson noted this, and called Lennox's attention to it.

"Yes," he said; "but the first shouts will rouse them, and they'll fight as well as ever."

"Of course," said Dickenson. "Still, one can't help feeling dull."

There was no attack that night; but the scouts had reports to make of the advance of the enemy from all the laagers, and the next morning soon after sunrise half-a-dozen Boers rode up under the white flag—their leader being blindfolded and led into the colonel's presence, with the other officers gathered round.

"I have come from our general with a message," said the Boer officer shortly. "He knows that you are all nearly starved, and that the kopje is covered with sick and wounded. He tells me to say he does not wish to attack and shoot you all down, though you deserve it. He says he will be merciful, and gives you ten minutes to consider whether you will haul down and surrender. What am I to tell him?"

"Tell the officer who sent you that we do not want ten seconds to consider, and that we do not know how to haul down the British colours. Let him come here and drag them down himself."

"What do you mean?" said the man roughly, and opening his eyes wider than was his wont in wonder.

"War!" cried the colonel sternly, and he signalled to those who had brought the messenger to re-tie the bandage across his eyes and lead him back through the lines.

Two hours later a heavy gun began the attack, one which was to be no night surprise entailing a heavy loss to the assailants, but a slow, deliberate shelling of the gallantly defended place to destruction; while now the difficulty was felt by the garrison for the first time of how to reply, for the new guns which had come upon the scene were served with smokeless powder, and the best glasses failed to show whence the bursting shells had come.

The officers had nothing to do on the kopje but keep going about among their men in the trenches and behind the walls, to say a few encouraging words and insist upon them not exposing themselves, for it was waste of cartridges to use a rifle; while the firing from the big gun and its smaller brothers too was infrequent for the reasons above given. Hence it fell about that more than once the officers paid what may be called visits from time to time, just to exchange a few words, and on one of these occasions Captain Roby, who walked fairly well with a stick, joined Lennox and Dickenson.

"This is cheerful," he said. "Did you over know anything more exasperating?"

"Horrible!" said the two young men in a breath. "What's the chief going to do?" added Dickenson.

"I've just come from him," replied Roby. "Nothing. What can he do but hold the dogs of war in leash until the Boers think they have shelled us enough, and come on?"

"Nothing, of course," said Dickenson, carrying on the captain's simile; "but the dogs are grinding their teeth, and when the enemy does come, by Jingo! he'll find them pretty sharp."

Hour after hour the Boers kept on throwing heavy shells on to the kopje, while the shelter was so good that not a single life was lost; but the casualties from the shattering shells provided the doctor and his aids with quite sufficient work, and it was with a sigh of relief that he ceased attending to the last man brought in, for with darkness the firing ceased.

Then came the night full of alarms with the terrible anxiety and expectation of the assault which did not come. For, as it proved, the Boers had been furnished with too awful a lesson in the former attack to venture upon another surprise, with its many accidents and risks to themselves. They preferred to wait for daylight, and with the first pale streaks of dawn the bombarding began once more, and went on briskly till an hour after sunrise, when the lookouts from the top of the kopje passed the words, "Here they come."

Just about the same time the scouts came running in bearing the same warning, and now the kopje guns began to play their parts more effectively.

For from three directions, covered by their own pieces, quite a cloud of the Boers could be seen approaching fast to get within rifle-range, dismount, and then begin a careful skirmishing advance, seizing every spot that afforded cover, completely surrounding the defenders, and searching the kopje from side to side with a terrific fire.

This was vigorously replied to; but the advance was never for a moment checked, the manoeuvring of the enemy being excellent, and their skill in keeping hidden and crawling from place to place exasperating to the defenders, for in spite of careful aiming and deliberation the Boer losses were remarkably small.

"They mean it this time, Bob," said Lennox sadly.

"Yes, they mean it; and somehow I don't feel up to the work at all. I didn't know I was so weak. Feel your wounds much?"

"Horribly. I can only use my glass and watch the stubborn brutes coming on."

"Same here. I've had six shots at 'em, and then I handed the rifle back to the Tommy who lent it to me."

"How many times did you hit?" asked Lennox.

Dickenson looked round to see if either of the men could hear him, and then he whispered softly, "Not once."

Lennox took no notice, for he was resting his field-glass upon the rough top of the stone wall, looking outward over the veldt.

"Well, didn't you hear what I said?"

"Yes. Don't worry," replied Lennox shortly. "Here, quick!" he cried excitedly. "Take your glass and look straight away yonder to the left of the laager we took."

"Eh? Yes! All right. I see. Here, send word to the chief. They're coming on fast now, three clouds of them. Reinforcements. Why don't those fellows make the big gun begin to talk?"

"Because they can see what I can, Bob," cried Lennox joyously. "Look again. Lance-tips glittering in the sun. Our men. Hurrah! Strong bodies of cavalry. Why, Bob, they'll catch the enemy in the open now. The siege is up. Hush! Don't shout."

"Why, man? It will encourage the lads."

"And warn the enemy that help is coming. Five minutes more ignorance will be worth anything to the relief force. I'll go to the chief at once."

There was no need. Almost at that moment the colonel had caught sight of the lance-tips through his glass; but quite ten minutes more—minutes crowded with excitement—elapsed before the attacking party were aware of the danger in their rear, and then came the terrible reverse. Boers began running back to where their ponies were being held out of rifle-shot, but running in vain, for the British cavalry were there first, spurring their steeds and stampeding the ponies, sending them in all directions prior to charging through and through the retreating parties, and keeping up the pursuit until recalled.

Others of the relief force had meanwhile been aiming at the three laagers, into which the infantry dashed, the first warning of this received at the kopje being through the cessation of the shelling, for the guns were either silenced or put out of action, the whole of the Boer force literally melting away.

It was one of the most brilliant episodes of the war; and that night, the supplies having come up, the relief party were hoarse with cheering the men whom they dubbed British heroes, and all was festivity and joy.

No, not all; for during the long watches of that night, with the stars looking piercingly through the cold, clear air, parties were out, British and Boer, searching far and wide, and the ambulance-wagons creaked and rattled with their terrible loads, while Doctor Emden, the doctors of the relief expedition, and those working for the Boers were busy till morning.

It was Lennox and his comrade who, being still only invalids, had the forethought to make their way at sunrise to where the doctor had been working all the night, and they found him lying utterly exhausted upon an old greatcoat, fast asleep.

Lennox touched him gently, and he sprang up.

"Yes, all right," he said; "I'll come. How many this time?—Eh? What! you, my dear boys? Hurt?"

"No, no, doctor; drink this," said Lennox gently, and he held out a steaming tin.

"Coffee! Eureka!" cried the doctor. "My dear boy, I began to think I was never to taste the—ha, delicious!—infusion of the berry—again. Ha! Another? Yes, please. No; wake up and give it to that poor fellow there. He has been working with me all the night.—That's right," said the doctor, after seeing his wishes fulfilled. "Ah, it's all very well for you, my fine fellows, who have the rush and dash and wild excitement of battle, but it's horrible for us who have all the cold-blooded horrors afterwards. You have the show and credit too, and the rewards."

"But we have the wounds too, doctor," said Lennox.

"To be sure, my dear boy; to be sure. Don't take any notice of what I say. I'm worn out. We get our rewards too, in the shape of the brave fellows' thanks. But if those people at home who shout for war only knew what it means when the fight is over, they'd alter their tune. But I say, this day's work ought to bring it to an end."

It did, in the Groenfontein district; and for Colonel Lindley's battle-scarred, hunger-weakened veterans there came a time of rest and peace.

By way of postscript to this narrative of South African adventure, here is the letter received from Mark Roby by Drew Lennox soon after the voyage home and the ovation which he and his comrades had received in their march through London streets:

My Dear Lennox,—I have just seen the *Gazette*, and am of course delighted to find the word "Major" prefixed to my name. I do not write out of vanity; it is from the sincere desire to be one of the first to congratulate my brave old companion in arms, Drew Lennox, V.C. Bravo! You deserved it. May I live to see you a general, with a lot more orders on your breast. But there is something more I want to say. I dined with Bob Dickenson and old Sawbones last evening, and in the chat after dinner over the promotions Dickenson told me about that episode which occurred after I was bowled over by that shot and you saved my life, according to your noble custom. When Bob D. told me how I accused you of being a coward, I felt quite knocked over. Of course it is as Emden says—I was, in a way, mad as half-a-dozen hatters, and enough to make me, with a part of my something or another—I forget what the doctor called it, but he meant brain-pan—bent in on my thinking apparatus. You a coward! Why, I confess now that a petty feeling of jealousy often worried me, through every one thinking so much of you and the way in which you always came up smiling after no end of brave doings. A coward! My word! Why didn't you punch my head? There, I don't say forgive me, because I know you do one who is proud to call you his best and bravest friend. That last is what I told Bob Dickenson you were, and he looked quite proud. You will be glad to hear that my wound is quite healed up; and as to the lump on my skull, the absolute truth, honesty, and sincerity of every word in this letter must show you that there is no trouble as to my knowing what I say.—Yours always, my dear Lennox, Mark Roby. Captain Drew Lennox, V.C.